X

MOUNTAIN VENGEANCE

The excitement of the fight still churned within Maria as she reloaded her rifle and walked toward the prostrate body of Stephen Kruger.

The fear rose within her as she looked at him. Even sprawled lifeless on the ground, he seemed to emanate some malevolent power. The rage against him rose again. He had aroused the Blackfeet, and many good people had died in agony, including her own father. When she had been in his power, he had treated her like the lowest of animals, using her brutally for his own cruel pleasure.

Maria could hear his breathing; her bullet had only creased his scalp. She could kill him now, snuff out his life in an instant—but killing was not enough.

Her hand grasped her knife, drawing it slowly, relentlessly from the sheath . . .

The Mountain Breed

AARON FLETCHER

A Dell/Bryans Book

Published by
Dell Publishing Co., Inc.
1 Dag Hammarskjold Plaza
New York, New York 10017

Dell ® TM 681510, Dell Publishing Co., Inc.

ISBN: 0-440-07736-2

Printed in the United States of America

First printing—August 1979

Part One

THE MISSOURI CROSSING

1

It had rained all night and during most of the day, and the clothes draped over the rope behind the tent were hanging in soggy masses. The sky was still overcast, bulging black clouds hanging low and threatening more rain. The tent leaked, and the clothes Maria had on felt damp. There was nowhere to bathe, her hair was dirty, and she felt sticky, unwashed, and disheveled. She lifted the hem of her dress and walked back around the tent, picking her way around puddles. The soft ground was soaked, and it pulled at her shoes with a sucking sound as they sank into it. Her mother was kneeling by the fire in front of the tent, mixing dough in a pan. The wood was wet, and thick, acrid smoke swirled around the smoldering fire.

"They'll dry when they dry, Maria," Mercy said. "You could give me a hand and peel some potatoes

instead of just moping around and worrying about
a clean dress. Your pa will be back here directly,
and he'll want something to eat."

Maria averted her face from the smoke as she
knelt by the fire and picked up a pan from the
utensils, and she took it to the bags of provisions by
the tent. She opened the bag of potatoes and put
several in the pan, filled the pan with water from
a bucket, and went back to the fire and sat down
on a stone by it, arranging her skirt and trying to
keep it out of the mud.

"I want my own tent."

Color flooded into Mercy's face at the indirect
reference to the noises the night before. She glared
at Maria in embarrassed anger as she kneaded the
dough with hard, quick jabs of her fingers. "If you're
half as smart as you think you are, you'll bear in
mind what your pa told you, Maria. You can either
buckle down, keep your mouth shut, and do like
you ought to, or you'll get thrashed until you do."

Maria averted her face and fanned the smoke
away with her hand as it billowed toward her, and
she picked up a knife from the utensils. "I want
my own tent."

"You'll hush your mouth, or I'll get your pa to
do it for you! And you get that sulky look off your
face. Them women are coming over this way, and
I don't want them seeing you sitting there with a
marly lip, like the world has come to an end."

The tent and their piles of belongings were in the
edge of a cluster of scraggly trees, fifty yards from
the edge of a long, level plateau overlooking the
river. The muddy open expanse stretching back from
the edge of the plateau was scored deeply with
wagon tracks and littered with piles of animal dung.

A dozen large wagons were parked in a loose circle on the other side of the plateau, their oxen and mules in a rope-and-pole corral near them. Two women carrying buckets were crossing from the wagons, walking toward the tent. They were both large and heavy, in their late thirties or early forties, and they looked slovenly, their stringy hair pulled back and tied carelessly and their shapeless grey drill dresses wrinkled, stained and muddy. They talked and laughed as they splashed through puddles and walked through piles of animal dung. One of them was chewing tobacco, occasionally turning her head to one side to spit.

Mercy wiped the flour from her hands and stood as they approached, smiling brightly and nodding in greeting. "How do you do?"

The two women looked at Mercy, Maria, the tent and their belongings in intense curiosity, and the one chewing tobacco nodded. "How do. I'm Marsha Givens, and this is Rachel Otis. We was on our way to the spring, and we thought we'd stop over. . . ."

"We're mighty pleased you did. I'm Mercy DeVises, and this is my daughter Maria. I wish I had a drink of coffee to offer you, but we're just between makings right now."

"Oh, we've had our fill, and we've got to get on. . . ."

"Leastways you can sit by the fire and try to dry out a little. Is it always this damp around here this time of year?"

"Well, we can't stop, because I've got to get back. And I'd call this pretty dry myself, but it's probably pretty wet if you ain't got nothing but a tent. What do you say, Rachel?"

"I'd say it's pretty dry," Rachel said. "And I'd say you've got more smoke than fire there."

"That's right, but the wood being damp, it don't burn as good as it does when it's dry," Mercy said placidly, kneading the dough again.

Marsha laughed shortly, turning her head to one side and spitting a stream of tobacco juice. She rolled the tobacco in her mouth and wiped her lips with the back of her hand. "No, it don't, does it? Somebody said you all was going with the bunch gathering here for Broken Hand Fitzpatrick to pilot up the Platte and into the mountains. They said there was going to be another family with a woman along."

"That's right. And my man **did** mention that a Kruger family was due in any day, with the wife and mother amongst them. Are you all going to Santa Fe with your men?"

"If they ever get through getting ready. When we was talking about Fitzpatrick's bunch, somebody allowed that women couldn't be going on a pack train up the Platte, but I guess they was wrong."

"Wrong as wrong," Mercy said cheerfully. "But I expect you set them right, didn't you? I don't see that much difference between going up the Platte on a pack train or traveling to Santa Fe in a wagon, as far as being a woman goes."

"Oh, I don't know so much," Marsha said. "Going up the Platte on a pack train ain't like a trip across Kentucky or Tennessee, you know."

"Well, a body would wonder how Kentucky and Tennessee got as settled as what they are unless women went there with their men to have children to settle it, wouldn't they? And we'll abide. I come from settling stock myself. My pa was Frank Bryan from Bryan's Station in Kentucky, kin to Daniel Boone by marriage."

Rachel grunted and looked away, lifting her eyebrows skeptically. "The Boones must have the biggest family in the world. Hardly a day passes but what I meet up with somebody who's kin to them."

Mercy stopped kneading the dough and looked at Rachel frigidly. Then she shrugged as she reached for an iron skillet. "No doubt that a lot would like to claim what I own as a part of myself. But I know who my pa was, which is more than some can say, and my name was Bryan before I was married, the same as Daniel Boone's wife. And more than that, when my pa and ma died, Joseph Floyd adopted me, brought me with him to Missouri Territory, and raised me like I was his own. He was good friends with Mr. Fitzpatrick right up to the day he died. I expect Mr. Fitzpatrick won't lose any sleep over me and mine being along."

Marsha spat and wiped her mouth with the back of her hand. "I expect he won't. And I expect your man didn't have to make you come with him then, did he?"

Mercy shook her head, taking the lid off the skillet and forming the dough into a loaf. "I was ready when he was. The one who raised me longed to go on west with his dying breath, so I was raised with my face to the West. Maria, fetch me a plug of bacon."

Maria dropped the potato she was peeling back into the pan and went to the provisions at the side of the tent. She took a flitch of bacon from one of the bags, pulled the canvas covering back, and began cutting off a thick strip.

"That's a mighty pretty young'un," Marsha said.

"I wouldn't be surprised if you've had men wanting to crowd around her for a spell now."

"They've been crowding since she was fourteen, and she's sixteen," Mercy replied with satisfaction. "But she's young, and there's plenty of time for her to think about keeping company with men."

"Is she the onliest one you've got?" Rachel asked.

Maria glanced at her mother as she stepped back to the fire and handed her the strip of bacon. Mercy was sensitive on the subject of not having had more children, and her lips were in a straight line. She took the bacon and greased the skillet as Maria sat back down and reached into the pan for a potato.

"Yes, the Lord has seen fit to bless us with only one so far."

"Well, I've had six," Marsha said smugly. "I lost two of them when they was little, but I've raised four to a good size. And they're all boys, and able to help their pa." She spat again and looked at Rachel. "Do you think we'd better get the water and get on back, Rachel?"

"I expect we'd better," Rachel replied. "I've got to get something started to eat. I have two big boys myself, and them and their pa is going to want to eat when they get back to the wagons. But I don't mind cooking as much as I have to, because they look after me. They've got me the biggest pile of firewood over there you ever saw, and they trimmed off the wet wood so it won't smoke too much."

"Maybe if you'll cook them something really good to eat, they'll carry some water for you," the youngster Maria said quietly, looking down at the potato she was peeling.

The two women hesitated as they started to move

away from the fire, and Rachel smiled sourly as she looked at Maria. "Well, you can talk, can you? I thought the cat had got your tongue. And carrying water gives me a chance to stretch my legs and get away from the wagon, so I don't mind that. You know, you sure are a pretty girl, but you'll cost whoever marries you a pretty penny for victuals if you do everything like you peel potatoes. As thick as them peelings is, you'd be well off to cook them and throw out the potatoes."

"You can have them if you want to stop back by for them," Mercy said blandly, slicing the bacon into a frying pan. "My man don't count his pennies when he buys victuals."

"I hope he's able to keep it up," Marsha said. "My man allowed that he might go into trapping but for the fact that a body can have a mountain of furs worth a fortune one day, then not have two pennies to crack together the next. Indians can attack and steal all a body has, a boat can turn over and lose everything a body owns, or a lot of other things can happen."

"It is unsteady," Merry nodded pleasantly. "That's why my man is going to stay in it just until we have enough to put by something for our old age, along with enough to buy a few Santa Fe wagon trains or some other little something to keep us in victuals and such."

The two women looked at each other, trying to think of an appropriate response, then began moving away from the fire. "Well, we'll be talking to you again when we get a chance. . . ."

"I'll be looking forward to it. It was mighty nice of you all to stop by, and I'm glad to have met you."

They nodded and walked away, beginning to

talk quietly between themselves and looking back as they got away from the fire. Maria looked at them in disgust as she dropped a peeled potato into the pan and felt in the water for another one. "The old bitches."

"You watch your tongue!" Mercy snapped indignantly. "I don't know where you picked up talk like that, but it'll get you some lye soap in your mouth if your pa hears it. And start peeling them potatoes right unless you want the peelings for your supper. It's a sin to waste food, and you never seem to get a panful unless you peel a peck."

Maria sighed heavily, peeling the potatoes more carefully.

"And you might try to get a bright look on your face when your pa gets back here. He has enough on his mind without having to look at a long face when he's here. Most men who go off with fur companies leave their families behind. We're lucky he's the kind of man who thinks enough of his family to take them along."

"Just like he would a dog," Maria said, stirring the potatoes in the pan. She sat back and shook the water off her hand, looking out at the muddy plateau and sighing. "I wish he'd left me in St. Louis."

"What would a girl your age do by herself in St. Louis? I'll swear, I think I had more sense when I was ten than you have at sixteen, Maria. And you watch how you talk about your pa. Hand the potatoes here if you're through with them, and I'll cut them up in this grease. You can put on some coffee."

Maria handed the pan to her mother, picked up the coffeepot, and carried it to the tent. The coffee and coffee mill were in the last bag she looked in, as everything always seemed to be. She ground a handful of beans and poured them into the pot, filled the pot from a bucket, and carried it back to the fire. It was heavy and she had to use both hands to carry it, and the hem of her dress dragged in the mud. She put the pot on the edge of the fire and sat back down, sighing as she looked at the hem of her dress. Mercy piled more wood on the fire, and it hissed, popped, and made billowing clouds of smoke as it smoldered. The two women who had visited them were walking back from the spring below the edge of the plateau, laughing and talking as they splashed through the mud.

"Here comes your pa. Now you see if you can't brighten up some."

DeVises walked toward the tent from the edge of the plateau, carrying a large canvas bag on his shoulder. He was tall, his height the heritage that made Maria somewhat taller than her mother, and he carried the bag effortlessly, his heavy boots sinking deep into the mud as he walked with his determined, plodding pace and looked straight ahead from under the wide brim of his hat. Mercy stood and smiled cheerfully as he approahced.

"Did you get everything seen to, Pierre?"

He nodded as he passed the fire, putting the bag down by the provisions at the side of the tent before stepping back to it. "As much as I could. I got some extra beans, rice, and salt while I was over on the other side."

"Well, it's good to stock up while we can. Sit down right here where you'll be out of the smoke, Pierre. We've just put some coffee on, and I'll move it over here and get it to boiling so you can have a cup. And we'll have a bite to eat in a minute."

DeVises pushed his hat back and sat down on a

stone, glancing at the pans. His expression became stern as he looked at Maria. Maria looked back at him, her eyes the same dark blue as his and her gaze the same level stare as his. Mercy glanced at Maria and cleared her throat with a warning sound as she moved the coffeepot on the fire and stirred the potatoes in the pan. DeVises looked away with a scowl, taking out his pipe and tobacco.

"I have a line on all the horses we'll need."

"That's good, Pierre. You're getting everything seen to before the others get here, so we won't hold anything up, will we? A couple of women who travel back and forth with them men on them wagons over there came to pass the time of day a while ago, and they seem to be a right pair."

DeVises grunted, filling his pipe, and leaned forward to take a twig from the fire. "I met some of those who'll be going with us when I was on the other side of the river. They were getting straightened out to bring their horses and packs across."

"They've already bought their horses?"

"They brought them with them instead of coming on a boat." He lit his pipe with the twig and puffed on it as he tossed the twig into the fire. "Most of them seem to be all right, but that Kruger family we've been hearing about was among them, and I don't think much of them. I told the man he could send his packs and woman across on the ferry and I'd help him and his boys swim his horses across, like some of the others were going to do, and he took the view that I was trying to run his business." He shook his head, looking into the fire and puffing his pipe. "I think we'll be well off if we have to do with them as little as possible."

"That's a shame, Pierre, because I'd like to be

friends with the woman. If there's just going to be the two of us, it would be good to be friends. But if they're contrary, it's best to stay clear and stay away from trouble."

"They're contrary, all right." He looked at Maria, his scowl returning. "And he has a pair of twin boys a couple of years older than you. I want you to stay clear of them."

Maria looked at him stonily, then lifted her eyebrows archly and shrugged. "I'm not going to follow them around, if that's what you mean."

"You get that look off your face when you talk to me!" he snapped, frowning darkly. "And if you think I'm going to put up with trouble out of you from now on, you'd better think again. I know you didn't want to come along, but it's not up to you to say what you'll do. And if I'd had anywhere to send you or anyone to take you in, you'd better believe you wouldn't be here. But you're here, and if I can put up with you, then you can put up with this."

His loud, penetrating voice and angry frown sent a quiver of fear through her. She clenched her fists tightly, steeling herself, and lifted her chin and kept her eyes on his, "I want my own tent."

He started to reply irately. Then he closed his mouth, his frown becoming puzzled. Mercy ducked her head and stirred the potatoes, her face crimson. DeVises looked at her, blinking, and an expression of understanding spread across his face, along with a dark flush of defensive anger, He pointed his pipe at Maria, his eyes narrowed. "Now I've warned you," he said quietly. "I'm not going to tolerate any more trouble out of you."

"I want my own tent."

"Have a cup of coffee, Pierre," Mercy said quickly

as DeVises stiffened, glaring at Maria in rage. She snatched up a cup, poured coffee into it, and held it out to him. "Here you are. We're all hungry, tired, and wet, and we'll all feel better after we've had a bite to eat."

DeVises took the cup, his face taut with anger, and he drew in a deep breath and looked away. "You'd better get her in hand, Mercy. If I have to thrash her again, I'll take my belt to her and put stripes on her from the nape of her neck to her heels. And I'm not far from doing that right now, I'll tell you."

"I will, Pierre, I will," Mercy said placatingly, darting a furious glance at Maria. "I'll see to her, Pierre."

He grumbled in his throat, smoking his pipe with short, quick puffs. Mercy stirred the contents of the pan and rattled the lid on the skillet with unnecessary force, looking at Maria resentfully. Maria's mouth was dry and her hands were damp, quaking fear seething within her. She controlled herself, keeping her lips and chin from trembling, breathing with a slow, steady rhythm, and maintaining an expression of detached insouciance.

Horses' hoofs thudded, climbing the road from the edge of the river to the plateau. The horses came into sight. They were wet from the river. Two of the men leading several of them were soaked from swimming them over, their buckskins black with water and hanging heavily, and their hair and beards plastered down with water. The other two men were also in buckskins, and they were older men, with streaks of white in their hair and beards. All four men carried rifles, had knives and tomahawks in their belts, and wore the wide-brimmed, low-crown trapper's hats. Each man led three to five horses, one with a saddle and the others with pack-saddles loaded with large canvas bags.

The men nodded and spoke to DeVises and nodded politely to Mercy as they passed. DeVises nodded, puffing on his pipe, and Mercy smiled faintly and dropped her eyes. Then they looked at Maria. The youngest, a man of about twenty-five, grinned widely. One of the older men studied the young girl with an intent, thoughtful expression, almost as if he recognized her. Then he gave her a warm, friendly smile that brought an automatic smile of response to her lips. They passed, leading their horses on along the muddy plateau, then stopped in a cluster of trees and began making camp.

Mercy snapped her fingers and pointed at the tin plates, and Maria handed them to her. More horses scrambled up the steep road. A short, heavy-set, swarthy man of about DeVises' age led the first four, a woman of about the same age and within an inch of his height walking by him. The man had hard, stolid features and walked with a heavy, stamping tread, snapping and jerking the reins on the horses he was leading, and the woman looked timid and self-effacing. All four had saddles on them, one a sidesaddle. Two other men were leading long lines of pack horses along behind them.

The two in the rear were identical twins, about eighteen. They were extremely handsome, taller than the older man and with youthful, sturdy builds. They walked with long, relaxed, graceful strides. Their features were strong and regular, and they had blond hair and blue eyes. They looked precisely the same, yet they were easy for Maria to tell apart, simply by the way they looked at her. One gave her a bold, insolent stare that affronted and repelled her. The other smiled in open admiration of her, his winning, boyish expression kindling a warm glow within her.

Maria suddenly became acutely conscious of her disheveled, slouching appearance. She sat up straighter, lifting her hand to tuck stray wisps of hair in place. She let her eyes pass over the one boy who'd smiled at her to acknowledge his presence. Then she moderated her look and kept it aloof and nonchalant as she moved her eyes on past him.

The older man kept his eyes averted from the fire, and DeVises didn't look at him. The woman and Mercy glanced at each other and quickly looked away. Mercy rattled the plates, spooning food onto them, and she glanced quickly at the two younger men as they passed. "Them boys are like two peas in a pod," she said quietly.

"Everyone will be well off if they're no more trouble than two peas in a pod," DeVises muttered.

"I can tell the difference between them," Maria said flatly.

"You keep your eyes to yourself!" DeVises snapped, glaring at her.

Maria did not meet his gaze. On the edge of her vision, she could see her mother looking at her reproachfully. But she could feel the pleasant, congenial twin's eyes still on her as he looked back.

Mercy leaned over, handing out the plates. "Seeing as how we're going to be together for a good while, it might make sense for us to get along with everybody if there's any way of doing it," she said cautiously. "Maybe it would be good if I went over tomorrow to pass the time of day with the Kruger woman."

"You let her come to you," DeVises said firmly,

spooning food into his mouth. "I'll get along with anybody who wants to get along with me, but they have to show me that they want to get along with me. That pack has gone in the oppposite direction."

Mercy started to say something, then changed her mind and silently nodded, taking a bite from her plate. Maria kept her eyes downward, seething inside. Her parents never argued. Her mother always asked or suggested to her father what to do about virtually everything, then did as he said. It seemed to Maria that it was desirable to live in harmony. But it also seemed to her that there were far worse things than arguing. She glanced surreptitiously along the muddy plateau. The Krugers were setting up camp in a clump of trees, not far from the four men who had arrived previously. When she felt her father's glare on her once more, she bent morosely to her plate and pecked at a bite of food.

DeVises handed his plate to Mercy to refill. "If you're through eating," he told Maria, "you could fetch some water and wash the dishes to help your mother instead of sitting around like you're someone that everybody has to see to and wait on."

Abruptly Maria rose, went to the tent and gathered up the two empty buckets in one hand. She lifted the hem of her skirt as she walked toward the edge of the plateau, picking her way around puddles, the muddier spots and piles of animal dung. The steep road to and from the river was slick, muddy and churned up by wagon wheels and horses' hoofs. She walked through the sprouting weeds and briars at the side of it, working her way down to the spring halfway down the slope.

The broad belt of the Missouri River stretching between the bank at the foot of the slope and the

opposite shore was yellow, turgid, swollen in its
spring flood. Across the river was a settlement with
two short, muddy streets of log and clapboard buildings on the shorefront. A scattering of other building spread back up a tree-covered hill overlooking
the river, and there were large stock pens, barns
and warehouses up there. Grey chimney smoke hung
over the entire settlement and stretched out over the
river. People and animals moved back and forth.
Two large flatboats, a decked keel-boat with a low
cabin, and numerous rowboats, pirogues and canoes
were afloat just below the settlement.

At the foot of the slope on Maria's side was
Chouteau's Post. This was a large, sprawling building on a rock outcropping, with stock pens, a couple of cabins and smaller outbuildings alongside it.
A large, raft-like ferry, which plied from post to
settlement during the day, was now tied for the
night at the post's landing, its long sweeps stacked
along the sides.

To Maria, everything looked drab, dirty and
shabby. The differences between this place and her
former Haywood Street home in St. Louis were
shockingly extreme to the young girl. In St. Louis
she had friends, parties and day school. There had
always been plans for some exciting, enjoyable event
or occasion, then anticipation for another as soon
as one event had passed. Each day had been bright,
different and full. But her whole life had crumbled
within short, cataclysmic weeks. Her appalled disbelief over what her mother and father were con-
templating had changed to utter despair as arrangements were made. She'd felt numb by the time the
flatboat had brought them up the river.

In St. Louis, she'd seen her father only late at

night and on Sundays. He'd been hardly a person to her, only the authority consulted by her mother on matters such as new shoes, dresses, her schooling, and the like. Dimly, she had perceived his dissatisfaction with her because she wasn't a son. There had been a wall between them, gradually built thicker and higher by her resentment of his aloof detachment.

But since leaving St. Louis, he had become a very real person to her. And a very unpleasant one. The friction between them had been constant, unremitting. Her father considered it his right to order her life as he saw fit. Maria deeply resented having its most crucial aspects dependent upon his whim. He told her what to eat, what to wear, who her friends should and should not be. The situation had made her reevaluate some of her basic assumptions. Marriage had always been her distant goal, but marriage, she saw now, would probably mean exchanging her father's authority over her for that of another man. Studying Mercy under these new circumstances, it appeared to Maria that her mother's life had been drab and hopeless for years.

Several dirty Indians and a couple of bedraggled white men sitting by the trading post stared up the slope at her as she dipped the buckets full in the spring. There had been a lumber yard at the end of Hayward Street in St. Louis, and the men who worked there had always stared at her when she passed. Jacob Hodges, tall, handsome and barely twenty, had worked there. He had come to her house and met her in the back garden a couple of times while her parents had been gone, and she had met him a few times in a copse of trees near the foot of Hayward Street. His smile had stirred a pleasant glow within her, and his kisses had turned the glow into a seething warmth. Now, with anticipation, she thought of the smile of the pleasant Kruger twin. It was the single bright feeling she had in the dreary misery that life had become.

Maria turned, sighing, and began climbing back up the slope with the filled, heavy buckets.

The hem of her dress dragged in the mud. She gave up trying to find a dry path and walked straight toward the tent. Her father was cutting wood with a hatchet and piling it on the fire, first splitting it into thin pieces and putting the damper ones beside the fire to dry. The light was beginning to fade under the heavy overcast, and the fire blazed up brightly, casting a ruddy glow in the dusk.

A leathery man of about fifty, one of the four who had arrived earlier, was sitting by the fire talking with her father. Maria recognized him as the one who had shown interest in her. He had a wrinkled, weathered face and a white beard. His buckskins were neater and cleaner than the others', though his trapper's hat was dusty and stained with sweat. There was a quiet, unobtrusive air of authority about him, as if it had been born of hardship and experience. He looked at Maria with the same friendly, thoughtful smile as before, and she put one of the buckets by the tent and carried the other one to the fire, smiling at him. Whatever her father had been saying to the old man, his voice now faded as he saw the old man wasn't listening. DeVises glanced between the man and Maria, clearing his throat with an impatient sound.

"This is our girl, Maria."

The old man nodded, his smile widening and

making deep creases at the corners of his pale blue eyes. "Seth Harnett."

"I'm pleased to meet you, Mr. Harnett."

"And I'm pleased to meet you, Maria."

His eyes studied her face, his expression congenial but intent. Maria put the bucket down by the fire and began gathering up the dishes and dropping them into it.

"I was saying that it looks like Kruger has a lot of goods with him," DeVises said. "A lot more than most free traders have. He could stock a post with what he has."

Harnett looked at DeVises and nodded mildly. "Maybe that's what he's going to do, then. He's done some trading on the Missouri, I understand, and maybe he's worked hisself up a good stock."

"Or maybe he's hooked up with some company."

Harnett shrugged, taking his pipe and tobacco from his buckskin hunting bag. "Maybe so, in which case Fitzpatrick won't be doing hisself or his company any good by piloting him in. But he's paying Fitzpatrick to pilot him in, so maybe he don't care." He looked at Maria again, tamping tobacco into his pipe. "You sure do put me in mind of my little Sarah, Maria."

Maria looked at him, leaning over and pulling the pans and skillet toward her. "Who is Sarah?"

"She was my daughter."

"Do you have a family then, Mr. Harnett?" Mercy asked.

Harnett shook his head as he put his tobacco away and reached for a twig. "No, no'm. Not no more. Me and my brother Tom was bringing our families down from the falls of the Ohio to Memphis a few years back, and river pirates set upon us." He held the twig to his pipe, puffing on it, then tossed the twig into the fire. "Me and my brother's oldest boy was the onliest ones who got away."

"We're real sorry to hear that," Mercy said sympathetically.

Harnett nodded, exhaling smoke and looking into the fire. "I don't mind saying that it took me a while to get over it. But my getting over it was holp along by the fact that I got situated so I could hide my brother's boy in some brush and go back to clean out the nest."

Maria looked at Harnett as she dipped water into the dirty pans and skillet. There seemed to be vast understatement in the mild, quiet words, a spare and inadequate reference to a fury of vengeance and death. A wicked-looking tomahawk and a wide, long knife were tucked under his belt at the back, and a smaller knife was hanging in a buckskin sheath at his side. He was a friendly old man, and yet he wasn't. The pale blue eyes that twinkled when he smiled had a potential for cold wrath. Maria put the pans and skillet on the stones around the edge of the fire for the water in them to heat.

"Girls take some minding," DeVises said with a heavy sigh. "This one does anyway."

"Oh, mine did." Harnett chuckled. "She was a handful, and more. I had two boys older than her, and it took me, my wife and my two boys to keep track of her. When we lived up at Fort Recovery, she got riled one night and flung a shovel of hot coals out of the fireplace just out of pure cussedness, and we come within a cat's whisker of having our cabin burned down around us right in the middle of winter. And that's not the worst she ever did, not by a long shot. She was a regular sidewinder, my little Sarah was." He chuckled again, puffing his pipe and shaking his head. "I expect that was why she was the one I catered to most. Like one time when I had a hound bitch lay out in the woods and drop her litter, and they was curs when she brought them in. I was gathering them up to knock them on the head, and one of them reached out and bit me. So I kept that one."

"Well, that shows how different people can be," DeVises said impatiently. "I wouldn't have a dog that would bite me."

Harnett said mildly, "And I wouldn't have one that wouldn't."

DeVises jabbed at the fire with a stick, looking irritated by the turn the conversation had taken. Silence fell around the fire. It was growing darker, and the fire made a bright circle of light. Sparks leaped up as DeVises put another handful of wood on the fire. Distant sounds of laughter and conversation came from the other fires gleaming in the darkness, and the horses stirred in the rope corrals. Harnett looked at Maria reflectively, puffing on his pipe. The water in the pans began steaming, and Maria took them off the stones and began washing them out.

"Some say that I'm doing wrong in taking my womenfolk into the mountains," DeVises said. "But I don't think so."

Harnett looked at him, exhaling a puff of smoke, then looked into the fire and shrugged. "I was on a pack train out to the Powder about four years ago, and we had this little fellow named Jacques Thibideau along as a bush loper. He was a quiet little fellow, never having much to say, keeping to

hisself, and not much more than a boy. Mostly Indian, we figured. He wouldn't say where he was
from, but we allowed he was from New Orleans or
down there somewheres because he was cold all
the time and wore this big buffalo hide coat day
and night. Not very stout because he was little, but
he could move like a blue racer and carried more
than any other bush loper in the brigade, only he
did it a piece at a time. And meaner than a sidewinder caught out of his hole in a prairie fire. He
could trim a man's beard with his tomahawk from
thirty feet, and he could whack the hairs out of a
man's nose with his fighting knife without drawing
blood. Some of the fellows tried to fun him a little,
and it turned out to be fun on them when he backed
four of them up in a hollow with his knife and
tomahawk and knocked a hornet's nest down on
them. Anyways, we got up to Bennet's Fork on the
Powder where we was to meet the trapping brigade,
and there was a Jake Hensley amongst them. When
we met up with them, Jake looked at Jacques like
he was the dead come alive. And Jacques jerked
this pistol out of his coat and blew Jake's brains
out on the spot. Then it turned out that Jacques
Thibideau was Annette Thibideau, and Jake had
done her wrong down in Natchez. So she just
tracked him down and killed him."

"A woman?" DeVises marveled. "And you say
she was an Indian?"

Harnett shook his head. "We thought she was,
because we thought she was a man and she didn't
have no beard, of course. But she was white. And
once a body knowed she was a woman, there wasn't
no doubt about it, because she was right pretty. But
she didn't have no trouble out of nobody, because

she didn't shed her meanness with that buffalo hide coat. The last I heard of her, she was in a brigade up north of the Ohio, giving the Hudson's Bay Company fits."

"Well, if that woman could do that, it proves that a woman can get along in the mountains, especially if she has a cabin and everything. And we have a cabin waiting for us at Fort Henry."

Harnett pursed his lips, then shrugged. "Annette had a mighty powerful reason for going. Maybe all it proves is that a woman can abide the mountains when she has a good reason. Then again, maybe it proves that a body can do anything they set their mind to, be they man or woman."

He smiled at Maria, puffing his pipe. "I expect that everybody has got their mountains. Maybe for some they ain't made out of dirt and rock and covered with trees. Likeways, I figure everybody has got their road to their mountains, even if the road ain't the kind that's traveled by people, animals or wagons. If that's true, then it's up to a body to find their mountains and the road to them, and then to travel it, bearing in mind that every step taken is a step behind them."

His tone and expression seemed to invite comment from Maria, but she wasn't sure of his meaning and didn't know what to say. She smiled silently, stacking the dishes. DeVises looked at Harnett with a puzzled expression, then shrugged and looked at the fire.

"Yes, well . . . well, when do you think Fitzpatrick will be here?"

"Day after tomorrow, or the day after that, I expect. And the rest of the fellows going along should be in before then."

"The sooner it is, the better it'll be for me. All I have to do is get my horses and load them."

"I'm ready to get back to the mountains myself," Harnett replied, standing. "For right now, I'm ready to find my blanket. I enjoyed the fire and the company, and I'll see you folks tomorrow."

DeVises and Mercy murmured and nodded, and Harnett smiled at Maria as he walked away from the fire. Maria finished stacking the dishes, stepped away from the fire with the bucket of dirty water and threw it out, then returned to the fire and sat down, holding her hands out to the heat to dry them. DeVises jabbed at the fire with a stick, shaking his head.

"We'll meet a lot like him. Old men who've been in the mountains until they've gone simple and just sit around and talk a lot of foolishness."

"It made some sense to me," Maria said.

"It would, all things considered," DeVises said irritably. "And no one asked your opinion on anything. If you've finished the dishes, go on to bed."

Maria sat motionless and stared at him for a long second, and his face flushed with anger. She rose and walked toward the tent, and he muttered something to Mercy in a low, irate voice. Mercy replied in a placating tone.

The interior of the tent was dimly lighted by the glow of the fire outside. Maria went to her pallet and undressed. The hems of her skirt and petticoat were stiff and heavy with mud, and masses of mud were stuck to her shoes. She folded her clothes and got between the blankets. They were cold and clammy from the damp ground, and they smelled musty. She shivered, curling up tightly and wrapping her arms around herself. The voices of her mother and father were a soft murmur as they sat by the fire and talked.

And presently there would probably be the sounds she had heard the night before from their pallet on the other side of the tent.

Maria pondered. Harnett had said that anyone could do anything they wished if they wanted it enough. Right now, there was nothing she wanted more than her own tent. She wanted privacy, that's what she wanted; she didn't want her father hovering over her. But how could she get it? Further requests would only anger her father, as they had before. He didn't spend money for things he didn't consider necessary. She lay in the dark, thinking. She thought of what was likely to happen in the tent just a few minutes from now. She thought of her parents' own desire for privacy. Then she giggled. An obvious solution had occurred to her.

The sounds of laughter and conversation from the fire outside died away. The murmur of her parents' voices became softer. The firelight coming through the opening in the front of the tent faded. Her parents came inside, moving stealthily. They quietly undressed and got into bed. Then there was silence. The noises had started almost immediately the night before, but long minutes passed as Maria listened and her parents were still silent. It began to appear as if her plan would go awry.

It did not. There came a surreptitious movement, a soft, barely audible whisper in her father's deep voice, and a reply from her mother.

Maria yawned, stretched, and turned over, sighing loudly.

There was silence again.

Several minutes passed and then there was another quiet movement and a breath of a whisper.

Maria cleared her throat.

The tent suddenly stilled again. The minutes stretched out until Maria began to doze off.

A slight noise from the other side of the tent brought Maria wide awake again, listening closely. There was an exchange of whispers, and a rustle of the blankets stirring.

Maria drew in a deep breath and sneezed.

There came a somewhat louder whisper from her mother in a whimpering tone. Her father made a muffled sound of disgust in his throat, and the blankets stirred as he turned over. A few minutes later, he was snoring.

Maria smiled to herself in satisfaction. She relaxed and settled herself to go to sleep. She'd be given her own tent now. She knew that for sure.

She just didn't know then what it would cost her.

2

The river came into sight again, a gleam of yellow water through the trees on the left side of the narrow, muddy wagon road. Barry's uncle turned and looked back at him, pointing ahead. Barry grinned and nodded. He stood in his stirrups, turned and looked at the long train of heavily loaded pack horses behind his own mount. The trees opened out ahead, and the road curved and went down a slope to the river. Barry sat back down in his saddle. The horses slowed as they started down the slope, taking short, careful steps.

Scattered log cabins with barns, then a cluster of larger clapboard shacks came into Barry's view. It was a little disappointing. He wasn't sure what he had expected to see, but the place looked much like many other river settlements, a couple of muddy streets of shops and stores, with dwellings, stock pens, storage buildings and other ramshackle structures spreading out from them. It looked too dull and prosaic to be the Missouri crossing, the gateway to the prairies, mountains, and adventure.

Something else gnawed at Barry. For him, the trip was coming to an end. His uncle, Thomas Fitzpatrick, would join the party he was taking to the mountains and travel on, to trap, hunt and explore. Barry would return to his father's stockyard in Columbia, to the daily grind of monotonous work. The trip had been enjoyable, with ample opportunity to talk with his uncle and listen to his stories about the distant mountains, but the satisfaction he had anticipated hadn't been realized. The trip had only stimulated his desire to keep traveling. He didn't have the freedom to go on, though, only a vague commitment from his father that he might be able to the next year.

The horses, moving downhill, neared the river bank. Barry saw moored boats of various sides, then a ferry, which was moving slowly across the yellowish water much the same as ferries did in other places. But as they neared the settlement, Barry detected an unusual bustle here, a flurry of vital activity that quickened his curiosity.

For one thing, the men moving about among the buildings looked generally different from the men further back east. Many more of them wore buckskins, as his uncle did, and looked weathered, with unruly beards and hair, and an aspect of having ventured afar in solitude. He had seen a few buckskinned men before, aside from his uncle; sometimes passing through Columbia, one would stop at his father's place to trade for or buy a horse. But Columbia was largely a town of tradesmen, farmers and merchants. To see so many in buckskins was evidence of a borderline of sorts.

Three men standing and talking in front of a barn several yards off the trail waved and shouted at Fitzpatrick, who waved back. Barry grinned proudly. Just about everybody along the wagon roads from Columbia had either known his uncle or known of him. Almost always, they were eager to talk to him and ask him about the mountains, trapping, the fur trade, Indians, other things. Barry had loved every minute of it. Youths had looked at him enviously and girls had taken particular notice of him, which had been even more gratifying.

Even now it was happening. A pretty, red-cheeked girl of sixteen or so who was digging a lettuce patch in the corner of a garden just off the trail looked up as Fitzpatrick passed. They exchanged polite nods, and then the girl turned her head and looked at Barry. Barry grinned at her. She flushed and began digging again, a smile playing around her lips.

The road widened as it passed through the concentration of clapboard buildings. Fitzpatrick was headed for the narrow path at its end that led to the ferry dock, but the last building was a tavern and there a familiar figure stopped him. The man was sitting in the mud in front of the tavern, his knees pulled up and a bottle between his feet. His eyes were closed until he heard the horses approach. He opened them then, saw the train's leader, and a bleary grin spread across his face.

"Broken Hand Fitzpatrick!" he exclaimed in a slurred voice. "By God, if it ain't old Broken Hand!"

"You still drinking the country dry, Henry?" Fitzpatrick chuckled. "I thought by now your squaw would have your scalp for your boozing."

"Every time she tries it, I get her'n instead," the man laughed. "I did it last night. But I don't take it away from her. I let her keep it for when I'll need it again."

Fitzpatrick laughed and shook his head, riding on past the man. The man looked at Barry and nodded gravely, then closed his eyes and dropped his head back against the building with a thump. They went on down the narrow trail into the mud of the river bank. Three men in buckskins were standing at the landing, watching the ferry moving slowly across the river toward them. They turned and waved as Fitzpatrick approached.

"By God, here's Tom. How are you, Tom?"

"I'll do, Jake. Amos, Sam, how are you?"

"We're a lot better now that you're here and we can get away from the taverns. It looks like you got some good horses there, Tom."

"They'll do," Fitzpatrick said, reining up and dismounting. "My brother picked me out a good bunch and held them for me."

"How'd you do on goods? It looks like you got plenty."

"I did, and the amount I saved on buying them in St. Louis made the trip worth it." He turned to Barry as he reined up and dismounted. "Barry, this is Jake Ludlow, Amos Porter and Sam Innes. Fellows, this is my brother's boy Barry. He came along to give me a hand with the horses."

The men nodded, shaking hands with Barry. Fitzpatrick had mentioned the names before as among those who were employees of the Rocky Mountain Fur Company, in which he was a partner. Ludlow was a tall, thin man of forty or so, with lean, hawkish features above his grey beard. The other two were younger, Porter a little shorter and heavier than Barry, and Innes a short, brawny man with powerful arms and wide chest and shoulders.

"Are you going up the Platte with us, son?" Ludlow asked.

Barry shook his head regretfully. "No, I guess not."

"He'll be going back from here," Fitzpatrick explained. "My brother's a stockman in Columbia, and he wants Barry to stay around and help out for a while. But he'll probably be coming out next year. Has everybody got here?"

"Bridger's going to meet us at Trail Junction," Ludlow said. "Everybody else is here. Vail, Ashe and Johnson are up on the hill, along with the bush lopers we recruited. A few free trappers and traders are here, old Seth Harnett, Price Hughs and a couple more, and they'll be traveling with us, I expect." He hesitated, then chuckled. "And the men who have women with them are here, Kruger and DeVises. How did DeVises go about getting you to hire him?"

"Like anybody else," Fitzpatrick replied, shrugging. "He should be a good man. He was an agent in St. Louis, so he should know furs, and he trapped along the Mississippi and north of the Ohio when he was younger. As far as his wife is concerned, Mercy DeVises was raised by Joe Floyd, and she won't be any trouble on the trip. And she'll be staying in a cabin at Fort Henry, so she'll be all right. On Kruger's wife, that's another thing again. He's a free trader, so once we get to the Snake, he's on his own."

"Well, Kruger has a pair of twins who are about the size and age of Barry here, and three men shouldn't have no trouble in looking after one woman. DeVises ain't got no boys, but I'd bet he'll have plenty of help because that girl of his'n is about as pretty a girl as I ever saw. Matter of fact, I'll bet you'll have your hands full getting shot of Barry here and running him back to his pa when he gets a good look at her."

The men laughed. Barry flushed and smiled self-consciously. Fitzpatrick chuckled as he nodded. "I know, I've seen her and she's a pretty girl, all right. Well, let's get set to load these bags and saddles on the ferry. Amos, you and Sam can take the horses up a piece and swim them across."

"Are they broke to swimming rivers?" Innes asked.

Fitzpatrick laughed and shrugged. "I don't know, Sam. But if they're not, I guess they'll be on their way to being broke to it directly, won't they?"

Innes groaned ruefully, and Porter laughed good-naturedly as he began helping Barry untie the ropes on the horses' packsaddles. Waves lapped against the bank as the ferry approached. It was long and wide, large enough to hold the largest of wagons, with ten long sweeps attached to the low gunwales. The men pulling on the sweeps strained, fighting the current as they neared the bank, and heavy timbers in the ferry squeaked and groaned as the waves washing the landing became higher. The end of the ferry scraped against the rocks that had been laid to stabilize the muddy bank, and a man jumped off it to tie a thick rope around a short, stout pole that had been driven into the mud. Four oxen came off the ferry, followed by a man with a team of horses and another leading a balky, nervous mule pulling a small, homemade wagon. Several others got off too. One looked at the pack trains and walked toward Fitzpatrick, waving.

"I see you made it all right, Tom. And it appears you got plenty of goods."

"How do, Pierre. Yes, this ought to see us through the winter, maybe a bit longer. How are Mercy and the girl?"

"They're all set to go. Mercy's no trouble, and the girl does as she's told. The only thing I have left to do is get my horses."

"Well, there's plenty about, from the looks of the stock pens up there. This is my brother's boy, Barry. Barry, this is Pierre DeVises."

DeVises' manner was abrupt and impatient as he shook Barry's hand. He turned back to Fitzpatrick and began talking to him about how many horses he would need. Meanwhile, Fitzpatrick's pack horses were being unloaded onto the ferry, and Barry went off to help, struggling through the mud with large canvas bags of trade goods and supplies. Fitzpatrick talked to DeVises quite a while. When the latter had left, Barry's uncle rejoined him, and, once the unloaded horses had been led away, they and a few other passengers started across the river.

Barry was once more struck by the special atmosphere of the place. The jerrybuilt ferry itself, as it scraped off the landing and swung into the roiling current. The mountain-men passengers, several of whom were boisterously drunk. The ferry operator, who had to argue and haggle loudly with some of them before they grumbled and paid their fares. Barry sat down with Fitzpatrick and Jake Ludlow, who were chuckling as they watched the arguments. To them, Barry supposed, this was a routine crossing; they must have made such hundreds of times. But he hadn't, and he glowed with the freshness of frontier colors, sights and sounds.

Once underway, Ludlow rummaged in his buckskin hunting bag, took out a chaw of tobacco and bit a good hunk before getting on to what he had to say to Fitzpatrick. "Do you know Kruger pretty good, Tom?" he asked.

"No, all I know is what I've heard and what he told me. Why?"

Ludlow spat tobacco juice over the side and shrugged. "He has a lot of goods to be a free trader. About the same as you've got here, matter of fact."

Fitzpatrick lifted his eyebrows. He had a large mound of goods piled on the ferry. "That is a lot for a free trader. Well, maybe he's been doing pretty good and has worked hisself up a good stock. He's been trading up along the Missouri, I understand."

"If it was that good, why didn't he stay there? I can't help but wonder if you mightn't be taking somebody working for another company to the Snake with you."

Fitzpatrick pondered that. "He didn't say anything about that when he talked to me about going along," he said. "Course he wouldn't, if he was."

"Not unless he was simple, and he don't strike me as that. I've been giving it some thought, Tom. The American Fur Company don't send in anything but rendezvous pack trains as far as you're going. So I just put myself in the place of a lone trader for them and figured what I'd do to get to the

Snake. And I come up with just what he's doing. It's a cheap way to get in, ain't it, getting piloted by somebody like you taking others in rather than having to hire bush lopers to form a brigade? The bush lopers would be a waste, because two or three men can set up a trading post once they got there. I ain't trying to run your business and I know I'm just a worker for the company, Tom, but I'm giving you my thinking on the matter anyways."

"You're not just a worker, Jake. You're one of the best men in the company, and I'm always glad to hear your views. Tell me more. You really think Kruger might be in with the American Fur Company?"

Ludlow leaned forward and spat more tobacco juice on the deck. "I think he has a lot of goods to be a free trader, and I think you ought to think about that," he said stubbornly.

"Well, now," Fitzpatrick replied, chuckling. "Tell you the truth, Jake, I did think about it some when he first talked to me. Trouble is, if he is with another company and I didn't take him in, he'd just find another way of getting there. A more expensive way for him, maybe, but then I wouldn't get anything out of it at all. If he is with a company, which we don't know, I'd just rather it was the Missouri Fur Company. I don't like the way that American Fur Company goes about things. They bought one post on the Missouri, and then before a body could turn around, they'd covered the whole damn river as thick as hair on a grizzly and run near everybody else off."

"They sure did. Raised the prices, broke everybody, then lowered them again. And it ain't unknown for them to get Indians riled up against a body when nothing else works. They're as bad as the Hudson's Bay Company for that."

Fitzpatrick nodded slowly. "Well, the Snake ain't the Missouri," he said grimly. "They could boat their goods up the Missouri from St. Louis and have things pretty much their way, but it's a little different in the mountains. I 'spect Kruger'd have a peck of trouble working for another company up there. Anyway, I'll talk some more to him and see what he says, if he'll say anything."

Ludlow nodded, leaning forward to spit again, and Fitzpatrick folded his arms and leaned back comfortably against the canvas bag behind him. Barry glanced at them and looked away. Many of the implications of the conversation had been lost on him, but he did know, because it was common knowledge, that competition between the various companies in the fur trade was intense. He knew that the American Fur Company, owned by John Jacob Astor and supported with virtually unlimited capital from his financial empire in the East, had monopolized the fur trade east of the Mississippi and was beginning to take over much of it west of the river. It was the hows and ways of it that escaped him, because that wasn't written up too much in the papers.

Barry stood up, leaning against the bags and looking up the river. It looked even larger as the ferry moved farther out into it. Swollen in its spring flood, its current had to be fought hard by the men heaving on the sweeps. Here and there it boiled with turbulence around snags and sawyers. The horses left behind were out of sight behind a tree-covered point of the bank. Then, as the ferry changed course slightly, they came into Barry's view again.

"When do you think you'll be heading back, Barry?"

Barry looked at his uncle and shrugged unhappily. "Oh, whenever you don't need me anymore. Maybe in a day or two?"

Fitzpatrick hesitated. "You can see us off then. I don't expect your pa will be too put out with me because of another couple of days, do you?"

Barry grinned and shook his head. "No, I don't expect so."

Ludlow glanced up at Barry, then spoke to Fitzpatrick. "He was probably a good help to you in getting here, wasn't he? That would be a bunch of horses for a man to try to handle by hisself."

"He was a lot of help," Fitzpatrick admitted. "He knows stock, and he's a good worker."

Barry flushed with pleasure. Looking back at the horses, he saw Ludlow's co-workers, Innes and Porter, begin to hustle them over, whipping and forcing them into the water far upstream. The horses swam out in two large clusters. The current caught them and swept them rapidly downstream, so that, wide-eyed and frantic, they soon passed fifty feet behind the ferry, swimming their way to a jut of bank close to the ferry landing on the far shore. They weren't unattended. Innes and Porter had hold of their tails, this one and that one, all the way.

The ferry landed at Chouteau's Post. Getting off, Barry saw the place as a mess of cabins and stock pens, populated on first view only by several loitering Indians who watched the docking listlessly from the main cabin's sagging porch. Their drooping, rarely blinking eyelids made Barry's neck prickle, though they seemed friendly enough. The trader Chouteau's hired hands, he figured, assuming more confidence than he felt. He helped unload his uncle's goods, then waited with Fitzpatrick for the horses. They came soon enough, in his estimation, a couple being ridden bareback by Innes and Porter, their hair and beards stringy and their buckskins hanging wetly against them. The other horses trotted briskly behind.

"Did you go by way of St. Louis?" Fitzpatrick laughed as they approached. "Those horses'll be worn out before we even start."

"I figured we were going to see St. Louis before I got my feet on the ground again," Innes replied, laughing. He winced and limped as he dismounted. "I picked me a bad one to pull me over. That son of a bitch kicked me and almost broke my leg."

"You had hold of the wrong end," Porter said. "You ought to know better than to hold onto a horse's tail if it can still touch the bottom with its feet."

"I had hold of the wrong horse, not the wrong end," Innes retorted. "He was biting on one end and kicking on the other. There wasn't any right end."

"Well, you can still walk, so you'll do," Fitzpatrick laughed. "Let's get these saddles and bags on just solid enough to get to the top of the hill. I want to sort out everything and reload it before we start out west."

The men did as ordered. Barry put a packsaddle on a horse. He was starting to pick up a canvas bag to put on it when a flash of color up the slope caught his eye. A man and woman were walking down towards a spring some distance up from the river bank. They were too far away to see them clearly, but the woman was slender and young and wore a bright blue dress. A girl, really. The man was a weather-roughened sort in buckskins and had a white beard. Barry picked up the bag, lifted it onto the packsaddle and began tying it on, still looking up the slope.

"Seen her, have you?" Porter chuckled, picking up a bag. "Well, you ain't really had yourself a good look. When you get a little closer, be sure and hold your hand under your chin so you can catch your eyes when they fall out."

Barry laughed as he lifted another bag onto the packsaddle. He glanced up the slope again. "That's the girl Jake was talking about?"

Porter nodded, jerking at a rope to secure a pack. "Maria DeVises. She's as pretty as you'd want to see. But she can be as contrary as hell."

Barry kept working. "If that was her pa across the river, who is that up there with her?" he asked casually.

"It'll be old Seth Harnett," Porter said, gathering the ends of a girth and tugging on them. "Seth lost his whole family a few years ago, and he had a girl who looked like Maria. Or at least so he says. So he sort of took up with her." He grunted as he tightened the girth's ends. "I expect the Kruger boys, they's twins, would like to hang around her, but Pierre don't like the Krugers and he'd just run them off. So it's too bad you ain't going along, Barry, because you'd have a clear shot at her."

Barry grinned. He went to pick up another bag, then stepped back to the horse with it and looked briefly up the slope again. Maria DeVises may have looked slender, but she sure wasn't having any trouble carrying a full bucket of water back up from the spring to wherever she was going.

He found out exactly where a short time later when Fitzpatrick led Ludlow, Innes, Porter and himself, along with the packed horses, up the hill to a camp clearing on a broad plateau. Several covered wagons stood in a circle off to the side, and there were numerous campsites in thin, scattered clumps of trees elsewhere on the plateau. He saw Maria DeVises at one of these campsites, standing by a fire with a woman who was obviously her mother. There were two tents at the site, one fairly large, the other small. Fitzpatrick angled toward the two women, and Barry followed him.

Maria, he saw now, was not merely attractive; she was breathtakingly beautiful. To Barry, she looked more like her father than her mother. She had DeVises' facial structure, the same wide brow and wide cheekbones, and the thick, long hair piled up on her head was light brown like his, whereas her mother's hair was red. There was even something of her father's manner about her. She gazed at the men and approaching horses with blue eyes that were direct, level, even a bit hard. She was tall for a girl, taller than her mother certainly. The long sleeves and bodice of her dress outlined a full-breasted, narrow-waisted figure that made Barry swallow nervously, it was so lovely.

Barry smiled at her as they approached. He had an impulse to say, "Hello again," for he had already seen her from the ferry landing and had perhaps fallen in love with her even then. But he said nothing, and she gave him, he thought, a neutral glance.

Fitzpatrick nodded at both women. "Mercy, Maria. It's good to see you again, Mercy."

"It's mighty good to see you too, Mr. Fitzpatrick. Pierre is over on the other side of the river, but he ought to be back directly. . . ."

"I met him over there as he was getting off the ferry. How are you, Maria?"

"I'm very well, thank you. How are you, Mr. Fitzpatrick?"

"I'll do, I expect. This is my nephew Barry. Barry, this is Mrs. DeVises, and her daughter Maria."

Mercy smiled and gave Barry a polite greeting too. To him her look, voice and few words came with an impact close to a physical blow. Her voice went with the rest of her, a clear, ringing, contralto. He managed to stammer a greeting in reply.

"Well, we'll get down here and find a place to camp," Fitzpatrick decided. "If there's anything I can do to help you, Mercy, just let me know."

"We're mighty obliged, Mr. Fitzpatrick, we sure are."

Fitzpatrick led his batch of horses away from the fire, discussing something with Ludlow. Porter and Innes followed, joining in the talk. Though Barry tugged his own horses and went along close behind, he had no idea of what plans they were making. He'd barely heard a word after Maria had said, "It's good to meet you" to him. He felt numb, lightheaded and breathless. He'd made one observation at the DeVises' campsite and it was dominating his concerns. He'd noticed a couple of large tree limbs and an axe near the fire, but the stack of split firewood had been small. He'd see how quickly he could get his horses unloaded and hobbled. Then he'd get back to the DeVises' fire and cut some wood for them.

One other thing was on his mind, this one troublesome. It wasn't as if he just would like to go on to Fort Henry now. He *had* to go. He had to think of some way to persuade his uncle to let him.

3

The hundreds of times Barry had seen his mother peeling potatoes had left him with no particular impression of potato-peeling as an art. He'd always figured it as a mundane chore. But Maria DeVises' way of peeling potatoes was definitely an art. It was interesting, how she did it. Her long, graceful fingers were sure and economical but not sparing, exerting all the necessary effort but not wasting a motion. She held the potatoes and knife firmly but not tightly. Other women held the potato and used the knife to pare away the peeling, but her approach was novel in that she held the knife stationary and spun the potato against the blade.

The axehead brushed the side of Barry's boot as he chopped the piece of wood. He stopped looking at Maria from the corners of his eyes and concentrated on the limb as he lifted the axe again.

"Laws, you sure do come close to your foot with that axe, Barry," Maria's mother, Mercy, said. "You be careful there."

"Yes, ma'm. I was just trying to get through this knot."

"Well, we can burn that knot like it is, but you can't grow no more toes. You say your pa is a stock dealer?"

"Yes, ma'm. The main business is in Columbia, and he has a yard in St. Louis that my oldest brother manages for him. It's on Fairfax Road."

"Fairfax Road? Well, St. Louis is a mighty big place, and I'm not sure whether or not I . . . do you know where that is, Maria?"

Barry froze, holding the axe poised and looking at Maria. She was exquisite, even as she dropped a potato into the pan and took out another one to shake the water off it. Her hands were small, feminine, but also looked strong. The water gleamed on her skin. She brushed back a stray wisp of brown hair with her wrist and lifted her long lashes to glance at Barry and her mother before answering.

"Yes. That's where we went to see that man about the stove that time. A man named Wilkerson, I believe."

"Oh, is that where it is? Laws, that's been years ago, Maria, long before you started day school. You wasn't hardly as big as nothing. You sure do have a mind like a steel trap, and I have a head like a sieve when it comes to remembering things. Yes, I believe his name was Wilkerson, Wilkinson, Wilson, something like that. A crippled man with a wart on his nose, wasn't he? And he had just lost his oldest girl to the king's evil, hadn't he? Yes, I remember it now. That was a good stove, but your pa sure had his hands full carting it home. So that's Fairfax Road. Well, I've been there a few times, and I've probably passed right by your brother's place and not known it, Barry. Has he been there long?"

"About ten years, I believe," Barry said, happy for most any sort of conversation involving Maria. "He started out with horses, and now he has horses, cattle, hogs and sheep."

"Then he's doing right good, ain't he? And there's a need for more like him in St. Louis, because a body can't hardly buy a piece of pork or beef worth the price."

"My pa says that's because of the butchers," Barry offered. "He says that he sells a hog to a butcher for ten dollars, and the butcher gets forty out of it when it's cut up."

"Well, I can believe that, because I know how they are. There was this one where I used to deal all the time, and I finally had to tell him that if I bought his thumb one more time I was going to take it home with me and cook it for my cat. Are you going into business with your pa then, Barry?"

"No, ma'm. I'm going to be a fur trapper."

"Is that right? Well, the fur business is a good one if a body goes at it right, or else my man wouldn't be in it. Your uncle is well set up in it, so that gives you a little start over most." She pointed her chin towards a distant fire. "You just don't want to get mixed up with anything like that pack over there. That's the roughest bunch of men I've ever seen."

Barry looked. "Oh, those are bush lopers, ma'am. Some of them take watching all right. From what everyone says, a lot of them are wanted by the law."

"Yes, that's what my man said. Now why would anybody want to hire people like that? A body wouldn't be able to trust them with anything."

"They're cheap, because they don't get paid much. They're usually hired just for the season or trip, and they don't do anything or handle anything so that they have to be trusted. They just carry things, look after stock, chop timber, and such."

"Be that as it may, I don't like being around them. But they say there's a place in creation for everybody and everything, don't they? Did you say you was going on to Fort Henry with us?"

"It's not settled yet. I still have to talk to my uncle again about it."

Mercy nodded and looked back down at the pan she was kneading dough in. Barry turned the last piece of wood to split it, glancing at Maria to see if his reply had caused any reaction. It hadn't. While talking, he had tried to think of things to say that would interest her, and it appeared that he had failed. He split the piece of wood, then knelt and began stacking.

"Some of this is pretty wet, so I'll put it over on this side to dry out. The dry pieces will be right here."

"All right, I'll use it from that side, Barry. Laws, it didn't take you no time at all to chop up all that wood, did it? And we sure are obliged for your trouble."

"I'm glad to be able to help. Is there anything else I can do for you?"

"I can't think of what it might be, Barry, but we're much obliged all the same."

"Nothing at all? You don't need any water or anything?"

Mercy smiled and shook her head. "No, Maria and Mr. Harnett filled the buckets just a little while ago, and we've got plenty. All we have at hand is just fixing supper and doing a little tad of washing."

"I could help with the washing."

Maria lifted her eyes and dropped them as she took another potato from the pan. There was a suggestion of amusement in the line of her lips. Mercy laughed cheerfully. "Help with the washing? No, you couldn't do that, Barry. But it's been a big help having all that wood cut up, and you've fixed us up with enough to last for mighty near all the time that we'll be here."

Barry looked at them, unsure of whether or not he had committed some gaffe. Then he grinned and nodded, dusting his hands together as he stood up. "Well, if you need anything, just let me know."

"We sure will, Barry, and we're mighty obliged."

"I'll see you again directly then."

"All right, we'll see you directly, Barry."

"I'll see you again directly, Maria."

Maria lifted her eyes and looked at him. That was all.

Barry, nodding, grinning, and walking from the fire with his heart pounding, had some more figuring to do. About romance, and things. It wasn't as if girls hadn't remained speechless in his company before, leastways when their mothers were present. But usually they'd been speechless with embarrassment, which was accepted as normal for a young woman in the presence of a young man who might be eyeing her romantically. Maria just hadn't been embarrassed at all. She had simply been silent behind a wall of imperturbable composure.

It was impossible to judge her reaction to him.

Maybe she was aloof with everyone—who could say? The fact was her remote, detached manner made her even more fascinating to him. It was a challenge. So he hadn't found out all about her by asking her the dozens of questions he wanted to— what of it? Key pieces of information had fallen into place anyway. Maria's diction and grammar was like that of a schoolmistress; well, her mother had explained that by letting it drop she'd attended day school. Then, too, she had lived in St. Louis most of her life, which explained her generally cosmopolitan air.

Other things about Maria had become clear to Barry. Her mother gave her tasks to do, but she wasn't as dictatorial toward her daughter as many mothers were. Maria wasn't broken, not by a long shot; she had plenty of spirit. She also had a stubborn will and maybe an explosive temper; you could tell that by the lines of her mouth and chin. All in all, Barry felt, she was perfect. And while he was unsure of the impression he had made, he was as satisfied as he could be with the way he had presented himself.

The sunset seemed especially beautiful as he walked across the muddy field. There was a soft, ruddy light across the bottoms of the clouds. Birds chirped as they flew about finding roosts for the night. They sounded cheerful, and so did the breeze, whispering through the spring air and stirring up green, growing things. It gnawed at Barry that he had still to convince his uncle to take him on to the Snake River, but the task failed to depress his buoyant spirits.

Fitzpatrick was still at the Kruger fire, talking to the short, heavy-set Mr. Kruger himself. The twins were there too. Barry, introduced to them by his uncle, had decided he didn't like either one. Not that he was sure of his feelings, not really. One had been amiable enough, but the other had struck him as a cold fish. Since he couldn't tell them apart by their looks, he'd concluded that the only self-respecting means of dealing with them and avoiding a rebuff was to assume either of them was the disagreeable one. Further—and much more importantly—they were about eighteen, and although Porter had said DeVises would keep them away from Maria, they both had blond good looks that she might find attractive. Barry felt stabs of jealousy. He passed the Kruger fire and nodded at them both. Coolly.

Barry went on to the fire Innes and Porter had built. They had a large camp kettle on it giving out an appetizing odor. Ludlow and Seth Harnett were also there, looking companionable. So Barry plunked himself down on the ground next to them.

"Here is the beau," Porter said teasingly. "Are we going to have us a wedding before we take off up the Platte, Barry?"

Barry flushed, then shrugged. "All I did was go cut some wood for somebody."

"Did you hear that, Sam?" Porter chortled, kicking Innes' foot. "Did you hear what he said? He just went to cut some wood for somebody. I guess the reason he cleaned the mud off'n his boots was so he could steady the wood better with his foot to cut it. And I guess the reason he slicked his hair back was so it wouldn't fall over his eyes and blind him."

Innes grinned widely. "Did you take her some flowers, Barry?"

"Flowers? Why would I do that? And where would I get any flowers?"

"Hell, a beau ain't supposed to go see his girl without flowers," Innes laughed. "You could have pulled her some weeds or something."

"Leave him be," Harnett said, adding wryly. "This pair would be over there theirselves if they wasn't so ugly that dogs run from them, Barry. She sure is a pretty girl, ain't she? She's the spitting image of my little Sarah when she was alive."

Barry sighed heavily and looked into the fire. "She's the prettiest girl I've ever seen, no doubt about that."

"Well, tell us what you all talked about, Barry," Porter said. "We've been sitting here and waiting for you to get back and tell us."

"Oh, she's not a great talker. . . ."

"What'd you do, just go over there, cut some wood, then come on back?" Innes said slyly.

"Well, they didn't need anything else. They had plenty of water and everything, and . . . they had some washing to do and I offered to help them do that, but—"

"You did what?" Porter shouted. "Did you hear that, Sam? Did you hear what he just said? He wanted to help them with their washing. . . ."

"What's wrong with that?" Barry said defensively. "I don't see any reason why that's so—"

"You don't see nothing wrong with that?" Porter crowed. "Why didn't you just come right out and tell her that you wanted a look at her drawers? What do you think she was going to wash? Her shoes or something? God damn, Sam, we'd better tell this boy some things!"

Barry looked at him, appalled. "But she didn't

... I didn't think. . . ."

"Stop pestering him!" Harnett barked. "God damn it, leave the boy be!" He looked at Barry, shaking his head. "Don't pay no attention to this pair, Barry. She wouldn't want you helping with the washing because it would look funny for a man to be helping with washing. And that's it. May be funny to some people, but I don't see anything wrong with washing myself."

"Well, I sure ain't never done no woman's washing for them," Porter retorted.

"You never even done your own," Harnett shot back. "Anybody who gets downwind of you can tell that, by God. Is that meat done? I'm getting so hungry that my stomach thinks my throat's slit."

Porter picked up a large spoon and moved closer to the fire, still chuckling as he stirred the kettle. "It looks like it's at least boiled to death and won't snap back, Seth. We'll have a taste of it as soon as Tom gets back."

"Here he comes now," Ludlow said. "And he don't look any too happy to me."

Barry turned and saw Fitzpatrick walking along the edge of the muddy field with his long, loose stride, his craggy features set in hard lines of dissatisfaction. Porter rattled tin plates and spoons as he began ladling on chunks of boiled beef and potatoes. When Fitzpatrick got there Ludlow moved over to make room for him to sit.

"What did he say, Tom?"

"Nothing," Fitzpatrick said flatly. "He said that someone was backing him, and that it wasn't any of my business who it was. Which is right enough, I suppose."

"It's your business if it's another company," Ludlow said. "A man can't be expected to slit his own throat."

"Maybe it's my business, and maybe it's not, Jake. I made a bargain that I'd pilot him to the Snake, and I'll stand by my bargain. But I told him not to look to me or anyone else in the company for any help he might need if it turns out he's with another company." He leaned over and took the plate that Porter held out to him. "We'll just have to wait and see what happens."

"I can't think of what kind of help he might need," Ludlow said. "From the looks of his outfit, he's got everything."

Fitzpatrick said, "A lot can happen to a man in the mountains. He can get sick, his cabin can burn down, or anything else. . . ."

They continued talking about it in quiet tones as Porter passed out the rest of the plates. Barry began musing while eating. Before, in the flush of meeting Maria, convincing Fitzpatrick that he had to go on to Fort Henry had seemed simple enough. But his uncle and these men had business on their minds, not his longings. He figured he was in a tough spot—warm in one way but out in the cold in another. The only thing he could say was that he wanted to go to be near Maria. It was unlikely that Fitzpatrick would be persuaded by that.

Daylight faded as they ate. The firelight brightened, highlighting men's lined, weathered faces. Spoons rattled against tin plates. Fitzpatrick and Ludlow talked on about the trip, speculating now on the grazing conditions they'd find for the horses along the Platte. Porter told Innes about a whore he had found in St. Louis. Harnett ate and stared into the fire, lost in his thoughts. Barry just worried.

Fitzpatrick put his plate down, drained his coffee cup and looked toward the other fires, sighing comfortably and patting his stomach. "That tasted mighty good, Amos. Well, Pierre should be back with his horses by now. Think I'll step over there and talk to him for a few minutes."

Barry put his plate down and stood up. "I think I'll look around for some more wood."

"Barry's going to stack wood so high around that girl's fire she won't be able to get to it to put wood on it," Porter laughed.

Barry forced a smile as he stepped around the fire. He was gathering his courage to talk to his uncle. Fitzpatrick waited for him. They walked out of the shadow of the trees and into bright moonlight. "She sure is a pretty girl, Barry," his uncle said gently, as they walked.

"Yes, she's . . . ah, I wanted to talk to you. . . ."

Fitzpatrick looked at him, glanced back at the fire and walked a few more paces away from it, then stopped. "All right."

"Well, I wanted to . . . I want to . . . ah, I need to go on to the Snake River with you."

Fitzpatrick was silent for a long moment. Then he slowly nodded. "I might have looked for it, I guess. You're really took with her, Barry? That much?"

"Well, it's just that . . . yes."

Fitzpatrick said gravely. "There's nothing wrong with that, Barry. And there's a lot about Maria to be took with, for the right sort it would take to get along with her. But this is the wrong way to go about it."

"What do you mean?"

"I know Mercy DeVises and I know Pierre pretty

good, and I know what they'd think about a seven-teen-year-old without two pennies to crack together being after their girl. And the girl wouldn't favor it herself, regardless of how much she was took with a boy, unless she's a lot more of a fool than I think she is. A girl and a boy being took with each other is fine, but that makes mighty thin soup in a kettle. There's got to be more to it than that."

"I could work and get money and . . . whatever I had to do, I'd do it."

"How, Barry? You don't know the first thing about trapping or trading, and you don't have no outfit to do either, even if you did know. You couldn't even feed yourself between here and the Snake."

"I could join up as a bush loper."

"You could, and now and then a bush loper turns out to be a pretty good trapper. But that's after he's been a bush loper, and he does something else to work up the money for his outfit. A man couldn't buy a set of traps on the wages a bush loper gets in a year, never mind all the other things he needs."

"Well . . . I have to do something. . . ."

"I know you do, Barry. And I know that when a man is took with a woman, he's ready for things to happen right then. Come hell or high water, everything has got to stand still and the sun can't rise again until he gets her churched. Or at least gets her bedded. A man who's took with a woman is like a bull buffalo with a nettle stuck in his balls, charging this way and that and rooting up everything in his path. But a woman has got more sense, Barry. A hell of a lot more sense. And that Maria has got more sense than most, or I'll miss my guess. So you're wasting time running in the direction you're heading. And if you want me to tell you what you ought to do, then I will."

"What's that?"

"What you intended to do to start with. Your pa will probably turn you loose next year, and he's going to fix you up with an outfit when he does. Then you'll be in a position to do something. You'll be a little older and more able to handle yourself, and you'll be able to offer a woman something better than starving to death in a cabin in the mountains. Not that Maria would take you up on that anyway, or I'd be fooled."

Fitzpatrick's voice was sympathetic and understanding, and his words had the clear, weighty impact of reason. Everything he said was logical, and at one level in his mind, Barry was forced to agree. But another and a more imperative part of him rejected everything Fitzpatrick said. There had to be a way, because it would be impossible to go in one direction while she went in another. But he couldn't think of a way. Tears of angry frustration stung in his eyes. He looked away, swallowing and blinking.

"And there's something else, Barry. I talked to your pa and got him to let you come along with me. Now your pa is my brother, and while we don't see eye to eye on everything, we're still family. I'd hate to be in the position of borrowing his boy for a while and then never sending him back. I promised your pa that you'd be back."

It was a consideration that hadn't occurred to him. And it was far more important than other considerations. His conscience would twinge for a time if he sent his parents a letter to tell them what he was doing and traveled on, but he couldn't put his uncle in the position of betraying a trust. Barry lifted his hands and dropped them in a helpless gesture, nodding.

Fitzpatrick put his hand on Barry's shoulder. "I know what I'm going to say is no help to you, Barry. I can remember that when I was seventeen, it didn't set right in my craw for somebody to try to tell me that he knew more than I did about something. But I think that in time, you'll see that there was no way at all of getting what you want in the direction you was heading. In the direction I've pointed you, things can go wrong and keep you from getting what you want, but at least there's a chance. I believe you'll see that in time."

Barry nodded, turning away. Fitzpatrick made a sound, as though he were going to say something else, then he turned and walked away. Barry shoved his hands into his pockets and walked slowly along the long, muddy expanse of the plateau, his shoulders slumped.

Large fires burned inside the circle of wagons, and the sounds of laughter and conversation carried out from them. Beyond the wagons, the plateau was covered with large clumps of dried grass, with fresh, tender new grass sprouting up from the center of the dead, dessicated tufts. The breeze rustled the grass softly. The plateau came to an abrupt end, and a gentle slope fell away from its edge, leading down into a shallow valley. The beginning of a narrow, overgrown wagon trail, cut into the plateau, was visible on the slope until it disappeared into the darkness of the valley. The pale, blanched moonlight shone brightly down on the rolling hills that stretched to the limits of vision to the west.

Barry walked the trail to the top of the slope. The lonely, mournful cry of a night bird came from the valley. A dark shadow passed over the grass below. It was an owl, stalking for prey on silent wings. The shrill, agonized scream of a nearby rabbit caught by a predator reached him, as did wolves baying further off. Barry stood silently, gazing over the valley towards the distant hills. The breeze was chilly, and clouds passed across the moon.

"Barry?"

Barry turned. Fitzpatrick had come up behind him and was standing a few feet away. Barry waited for him to speak, which he did after some hesitation.

"I've just been talking to Abner Yancey, the head trader in that bunch of wagons there. They're pulling out day after tomorrow, the same time we are. We figured that we would travel together to Trail Junction, about forty miles west of here, and then we'd have us a little shindy before we split up. We've got a fiddler along, old Gabe Jenkins, so it should be pretty good. I thought you might like to travel that far with us. It'll mean a few more days before you get back to Columbia, but I don't think your pa would be too put out with me."

Barry looked at Fitzpatrick, his feelings beginning to soar. It wasn't much, forty miles, but it was sure as hell more than nothing. And the more he thought about the forty miles, the longer and happier they seemed. He didn't speak, just broke into a wide smile.

Fitzpatrick chuckled and put his hand on his nephew's shoulder. "Let's go see if there's any of that coffee left."

Barry stood there and grinned. Fitzpatrick chuckled again, slapped his shoulder, and they walked across the plateau toward the fire.

4

The bush lopers at the front of the column of pack trains began whooping and shouting, and Barry stood in his stirrups and stretched, trying to see ahead. The dim wagon trail wound in serpentine fashion between the rolling hummocks of the prairie, and all he could see was the Kruger pack trains disappearing around the next bend. He sat back down in his saddle, looking at Maria. "It sounds like we're here. It's Trail Junction. I'd better ride up and see if my uncle needs me."

Maria's face was concealed from the side by the wide brim of her sunbonnet, but she did at least turn her head and give him a slight smile. Barry nudged his horse to one side of the trail and rode past Maria's parents. He'd been helping the DeVises set up camp every night, usually spending at least a few minutes with them by their fire, and he had ridden beside Maria more often than not while moving on west. He had to concede he hadn't made much progress with her, notwithstanding a few warm and amusing conversations they'd had together. Her mother had been cordial towards him, her father at least tolerant, but it had become increasingly obvious that Maria either had no romantic inclinations toward him or, as his uncle had suggested, just wasn't interested enough in a youthful suitor of few prospects.

Barry had lain awake at night, meticulously analyzing the situation, and he had concluded that it was the latter. Maria could be blunt. If she hadn't cared anything about him, she would have been very direct in telling him to stay away. So he had a chance. He'd be leaving for home soon. The separation would be painful for him. She might meet someone else in his absence. But it was something he had to risk. He was determined that when he came back the next year, he would have more going for him. And then he would stay.

As Barry rode past the whole line of pack trains. he saw that the rolling swells of the grassy prairie had opened out into a shallow valley with a grove of elm trees on one side. A tiny, ramshackle trading post was set in the grove. The bush lopers riding with Fitzpatrick's pack trains were starting to unload goods. Some of the free trappers and traders were already milling about the post, and Fitzpatrick was talking with a man in front of it. He introduced the man as Barry rode up.

"Barry, meet Jim Bridger. Jim, this is my nephew I was telling you about."

Barry dismounted and led his horse over. Jim Bridger was very famous; most everybody in the east knew of his exploits as a guide and a scout in the mountains. He was also a partner in the Rocky Mountain Fur Company. Bridger was older than Fitzpatrick, tall and heavy, with powerful arms and shoulders. His buckskins were fringed and heavily decorated with beads and dyed porcupine quills, and his hat was dusty, sweat-stained and weathered. He had dark, aquiline features and penetrating blue eyes, and there was an aura of authority about him. Barry nodded, shaking hands with him.

"I'm pleased to meet you."

"I'm pleased to meet you, Barry. Too bad you're not going on to the Snake with us."

Bridger may have looked forbidding in his get-up, but his manner was open and congenial, and Barry liked him on sight. "Yes, but I'll be back next year. Count on it," he said.

Bridger smiled. "Well, the mountains will still be there. You can count on that too. Tom, I'll get on in here and see the trader about settling the bill for feeding my horses."

"I'll go in with you." Fitzpatrick glanced at the DeVises pack train as it approached and smiled. "We'll be spending the night here, Barry. I imagine you have work to do, don't you?"

Barry grinned and nodded, tugging on his reins and turning his horse away. As the two men chuckled and went into the trading post, he rode back towards the DeVises. Daydreaming about what it would be like to be married to Maria had occupied him frequently for the past few days. He couldn't seem to turn it off, even now. He was up to the point where he was speculating about his family's reactions to Maria. His mother was a domineering woman. When his two older brothers had been married, she had immediately set about establishing firm control over their wives. Barry suspected that was why his oldest brother had gone off to St. Louis to manage the stockyard there. Well, his mother would find her match in Maria, because she was anything but submissive.

Still, that same quality of independence, or maybe rebelliousness, was bringing Maria into frequent conflict with her father. That was the rub, Barry thought. That's what was giving him problems.

There was an atmosphere of tension in the De-Vises camp when Barry joined it. Mercy was fluttering about anxiously, DeVises' face wore an angry scowl, and Maria was quieter than usual, her cheeks tinged with color. They'd been arguing again. Barry was always uncomfortable around them when they were arguing, because he felt like an intruder whom DeVises might order away at any given moment. Although it made him feel disloyal to Maria, Barry also couldn't help but consider how unusual it was for a daughter to openly defy her father. He particularly regretted that a dispute had arisen between them now to blight the last hours he would have with her for a long time.

Whatever the issue the DeVises were thrashing out now, Barry could see the atmosphere was particularly hot and discordant, so, despite Mercy's forced cheerfulness towards him, he decided to stay out of their way as much as possible and simply do the chores he'd taken on for himself. He set up Maria's small tent, took DeVises' horses to hobble them, carried water up from the creek, chopped wood, and the like. Then, since the tension in the air showed no indication of relaxing, he left for the fire Porter and Innes had built.

The wagons had arrived to form a circle in the valley. The noise, as the sun set, was bedlam-like, beds creaking and rattling, wheels rumbling and jolting heavily over ruts, drivers whooping and cracking their whips. Dogs raced around barking madly. Several of the bush lopers had found drinking companions among the wagon drivers, and whisky was being swigged amidst whoops and shouts, while women shook their heads and set about cooking. Somehow, necessary things got done. Despite all signs of disorder, teams were unhooked, fires were built and, as darkness fell, people sat around in a wide semicircle of yellow pools in the bright moonlight.

Barry ate and drank with Innes and Porter, for the most part wondering about the quiet that had fallen around both the DeVises and Kruger campfires. He couldn't see the shadowy figures too well. Were the Kruger twins socializing with Maria? He dwelt somewhat miserably on that possibility. Then his uncle showed up with jovial orders to some of the men that bonfires be built. They were soon blazing. Nearby, Gabe Jenkins, a wizened old trapper with snowy hair and beard, dug among his belongings, took out his fiddle and capered toward them, sawing his bow back and forth. People got up to dance. That was Barry's signal. He got up and trotted hastily back toward the DeVises campfire.

Maria had changed into the blue dress she had been wearing the first time he had seen her. Her thick tresses, piled up on top of her head, caught the firelight in shimmering glints. Barry, slightly befuddled by the whiskey he'd had and struck almost speechless by her dazzling beauty, managed to say, "Would you dance this one with me, Maria?"

"Of course, Barry, I'd be happy to." She smiled at him, like a queen.

It wasn't until they began dancing that Barry remembered that he knew little about dancing. He'd rarely tried it, even at the church sociables back home. But Maria seemed to be a part of him, moving as he moved with no hesitation or awkwardness. The men gathered around the bonfires, clapped their hands in time with music he never seemed to have heard before. He heard it now. It was the first time he had touched Maria. Her small hand was warm and silky in his. He could feel the lithe movements of her slender body through his hand on her waist. The sweet, alluring scent of her hair and body filled his nostrils.

Then Seth Harnett tapped Barry's shoulder and cut in on him, catching Maria's hand and spinning her away. Barry was only briefly upset. The pleasure of watching Maria was almost as intense as dancing with her had been. She spun and leaped lightly in Seth's arms, her skirt swirling. Barry backed up into the circle of other onlookers, clapping his hands, his eyes riveted on her. Bridger soon stepped in and took her from Harnett, and Seth began clapping his hands as he walked toward Barry, smiling widely. Barry grinned and nodded happily.

Then his pleasure abruptly turned sour. After several more sets, with both him and some of the older men, Maria began dancing with one of the Kruger twins. The dance she did with him was different from the others she'd done. The movements were sedate and graceful, rather than boisterously energetic. And this dance called for a good deal more intimacy. Maria performed it expertly, and

she appeared to be enjoying it. Jealousy tore at
Barry. Angrily, he turned his head away and, as
he did so, happened to glimpse DeVises on the far
side of the bonfire. Barry blinked. DeVises was glaring at Maria in rage. Barry suddenly knew, without
needing to be told, that it was the Kruger boy who
had caused the argument between them. DeVises
had ordered Maria not to dance with the Krugers,
and she had refused to obey him.

The flurry between father and daughter lasted
only long enough for Barry to discern it. Harnett
cut in and began dancing with Maria again, and
the Kruger boy ambled away. Barry couldn't tell
which twin had danced with Maria, but it didn't
matter to him. He walked out purposefully and
danced with another woman. The woman was heavy-
set and powerfully built, and she spun him around
until he was dizzy as she whooped and shrieked
deafeningly. When he'd finished the dance, he
looked at Maria and felt miserable. She didn't even
appear to notice that he had danced with someone
else. Barry finally moved away from the dancers
into the bonfires' shadows. As he was musing about
what to do next, there came an uproar from among
the wagons. A fight had started there. The music
stopped, and Fitzpatrick, Bridger, and others ran
to stop it. They returned, dragging and cursing at
a couple of bush lopers who had pulled knives on
some of the wagon drivers.

This ugly incident cast a chill over the dancing,
which soon ceased as people began moving away
from the bonfires and Gabe Jenkins quit fiddling.

Barry caught up with Maria as she walked back
toward her tent. Her mother and father were up

ahead of her, and he stood with her alone in the moonlight. In her presence, he'd all but forgotten his jealousy. Only tender feelings were his.

"I'll sure be looking forward to seeing you again, Maria," he said. "I'll be looking forward to that more than anything else in my life."

Maria looked up at him, the moonlight shining softly in her eyes. Then she looked away. She appeared to be pondering what to say. Suddenly, she turned back to him, stood on tiptoe and kissed him on the cheek. "Good night, Barry." She moved hurriedly away.

Barry stood there a few moments. His cheek burned, and his shoulder tingled where she had touched him while kissing him. He turned and stumbled through the grass toward the fire, trying to assimilate her unexpected show of affection. He grinned widely to himself in the darkness and began skipping.

Porter and Innes were already wrapped in their blankets, and the fire was burning low. Barry found his blanket, put a couple of pieces of wood on the fire, then took off his boots and wrapped the blanket around him. Fitzpatrick come toward the fire as he was lying down, taking a purse out of his hunting bag.

"Here, I'll give you this tonight in case it slips my mind in the morning, Barry. It'll see you home."

Barry looked at the coin, then up at Fitzpatrick in surprise. It was a double eagle. "But you don't have to pay me."

"You earned it. You might need extra supplies on the way back, and you'll need money for crossing the ferry and such."

"But this is too much."

"Give it here, and I'll take it," Innes said sleepily. "Then maybe both of you will be quiet so a body can get some sleep."

Fitzpatrick chuckled, turning away from the fire. "I'll see you in the morning, Barry."

Barry nodded, looking at the coin again. It was far more money than he had ever had at one time. Fitzpatrick walked to Jim Bridger's fire several yards away and sat down for a pipe-smoking chat. Barry put the coin carefully in his pocket, then pulled his blanket around himself and lay down. The whiskey burned in his stomach, and he felt like he was rotating when he closed his eyes. He opened his eyes again, looking up at the stars and thinking about Maria. His eyelids became heavy, and he dozed off.

He woke abruptly, unsure of what had awakened him but feeling an imperative need for immediate response. The fires were out, the moon had set, and he could see only dark, shapeless shadows around him. Porter and Innes were murmuring and stirring in their sleep. That was all. Then Barry heard it again. Maria was screaming.

He tore at his blanket, threw it aside, sprang up and ran. Stubbled grass jabbed at his feet. He ran through the hot ashes of one of the bonfires. As he neared Maria's tent, he saw a man coming out of it, straightening up. He could tell from the man's blond hair that it was one of the Kruger twins. He kept running. As the Kruger boy left the tent, he looked backward over his shoulder and suddenly broke into a run. Barry charged into him and slammed him to the ground, grasping at a leg. A boot thudded into his side, knocking the breath from him, and his hands went weak. The man got

up and raced away. Lying there, Barry heard De-
Vises struggling and cursing. There was a sound of
tearing cloth, then DeVises cursed louder in rage
as he floundered to the ground.

"What is it," Fitzpatrick shouted, running toward
the tent. "What is it?"

"It was one of them God damned Kruger sons of
bitches," DeVises bellowed. "I'm going to get my
God damned rifle and go kill the whoreson's whelp!"

"No, you're not! You stay right where you are!
Jim?"

"Right behind you," Bridger replied from the
darkness.

"Go get Kruger and his boys over here. Is that
you, Isaac? Get this fire built up so we'll have some
light and can see what we're doing. You stay right
where you are, Pierre, and we'll settle this right,
not with rifles. Is that you over there, Barry? What
did you see?"

"I could tell that it was one of the Kruger twins,
but I couldn't tell which one it was."

"Nobody can tell the difference between the sons
of bitches," DeVises snarled. "But it was one of
them. You can be God damned sure of that, because I had my hands on the son of a bitch and I
got a look at him." He called into the tent, "Are
you all right, Maria?"

"Yes."

"This is what comes from my giving you your
own tent! Did he . . . ? Did he . . . ?"

"No."

More men gathered and DeVises cursed angrily
under his breath. Mercy went into Maria's tent.
Barry could hear them as they murmured softly.
Shadowy figures broke wood and stirred the ashes

of the fire in front of the tents until a small flame licked up, highlighting the faces of Porter and Harnett as they bent over the coals, blowing on them and coaxing the fire to life. By the time it was bright enough to see clearly, Bridger had returned, bringing Kruger.

"God damn you to hell." DeVises thundered, shaking his fist and stepping toward Kruger. "I'll kill you and your whole God damned pack, you God damned—"

"Let me handle this, Pierre," Fitzpatrick said, pushing in front of DeVises. "Now you just be quiet and let me take care of this." He looked at Kruger. "Where are your boys?"

Kruger looked from DeVises to Fitzpatrick, his expression perplexed and wary, his fists knotted, his thick, heavy body poised to fight. He jerked his chin over his shoulder. "Here they are. Now what's going on here?"

"One of them got into Maria's tent and tried to rape her, that's what's going on!"

Kruger sneered at DeVises, started to say something, then closed his mouth and folded his arms, looking away in disgust. The twins stepped out of the darkness. Their clothing was rumpled, both looking as though they had been asleep, and they both looked around with puzzled expressions. Fitzpatrick beckoned them closer, looking at them stonily.

"All right, now. It appears one of you two got into Maria's tent and tried to rape her. Now I'm going to figure that both of you are going to deny it and save a lot of arguing back and forth, because I don't expect the one who did it to own up to it. So I'm just going to tell you both one more time what I told everybody when we had our meeting. The main rule of the trail is that when somebody does something that would get them put into jail in a town, it gets them put out of the party on the trail. If I had any way of telling which one of you did this, I'd put that one out of the party now. But I don't know, so I'm going to have to let this go with a warning. If anything like this happens again, the whole family gets put out, with the exception of the woman, and she can go on with the party if she wants to. Do you understand that, Kruger?"

Kruger looked at Fitzpatrick with a sardonic expression and silently nodded.

"You'd better, and you'd better keep your boys in hand. Do you two understand what I meant?"

The twins nodded, looking defensively angry.

"All right, enough said. The next time I'll do what I said I would instead of talking. Now let's everybody get back to sleep. We have a long way to go tomorrow."

They turned away. Then Kruger turned back, looking at Fitzpatrick. "There's something you could do now, if you've a mind to be fair about this. You could stop that girl from displaying herself like she does."

Barry stiffened with anger, taking a step forward. DeVises uttered a growl of rage and rushed toward Kruger. Men stepped forward to seize him, but Fitzpatrick barked an order, waving them away as Kruger lifted his fists to meet DeVises' charge.

DeVises swung at Kruger's head. The thick, heavy-set Kruger ducked the blow and sprang forward, driving his head into DeVises' stomach. DeVises bounced back, the breath knocked out of him and staggering. Kruger closed in, driving his fists into DeVises' stomach. DeVises took quick steps backwards, evading Kruger's fists until he'd recovered his balance. Then he drove forward again, swinging at Kruger's head. Kruger dodged the blows again, throwing himself forward and driving his head solidly once more into DeVises stomach. DeVises' face twisted with pain. He stumbled backwards, his arms windmilling, and he fell to the ground.

A sneer of triumph spread over Kruger's face. He leaped forward and kicked at DeVises' body. DeVises rolled on the ground, partially deflecting the kick. Kruger gathered himself and kicked again, but this time DeVises' heel shot up into Kruger's crotch in a quick, hard jab. The blow lifted Kruger's feet from the ground, and he screamed in agony, clutching at his crotch as he fell backwards, his knees beginning to collapse. DeVises bounced up from the ground and closed in on him, swinging at his face. Kruger lowered himself, still holding his crotch, and tried to get under the blows so as to bull with his head yet again. DeVises took a quick step backwards, gripping Kruger's hair and brought his knee up into Kruger's face. There was a sickening crack. Kruger's features went slack as his head jerked up from the force of the blow. He took a wavering step backwards, blood streaming from his nose and mouth. Then he collapsed.

DeVises kicked, and his toe slammed into Kruger's crotch with a meaty thud. Kruger screamed again, writhing on the ground. DeVises gathered himself to kick again, and would have done so had not Fitzpatrick snapped his fingers and motioned for a couple of men to pull him away.

"All right, you two get your pa back over to your fire. And everybody else get back to your blankets. It's over and done with, and we have a long way to go tomorrow."

The Kruger twins lifted Kruger by his arms. Kruger's wife stepped into the edge of the light, looking at him fearfully as his sons began pulling him away, his toes dragging along the ground.

DeVises clutched his stomach as he staggered weakly to the fire and sagged to a sitting position. Blood ran from a cut eyebrow and his face was taut with pain. The men began moving away, murmuring among themselves. Fitzpatrick motioned to Barry, and Barry nodded and walked back toward his own fire.

The silence resumed. Barry lay in his blanket, looking toward the DeVises' fire. For a long time, DeVises sat there, humped over. Then Mercy came out of Maria's tent and said something to him, and he started pushing himself painfully to his feet. She took his arm to help him, and he jerked away from her. She went into their tent, and he followed her in. Barry pulled his blanket tighter around him, looking up at the stars. Rage seethed within him as he thought of one of the Kruger twins touching Maria, seizing her, trying to rape her. Then a different aspect of the situation occurred to him. A firm wedge of enmity had been driven between the Krugers and the DeVises. If he lost Maria to anyone, it wouldn't be to a Kruger. And they were the only truly eligible men in the party. He mused about it as his eyelids became heavy and he dozed off again.

Motion and noises awakened Barry before dawn. The fire was blazing up. Porter and Innes were hurriedly rolling up their blankets and gathering up their belongings, their hair tousled and their faces pouchy with sleep as they coughed and shivered in the chill. Men were stirring around the other fires and shouting at each other, and horses were stamping and whinnying. They were preparing to move on.

Barry sat up with his mouth dry, his stomach queasy, and a headache throbbing in his temples from the whisky he'd drunk the night before. He pulled on his boots, rolled up his blanket, and walked toward the DeVises' fire, straightening his clothes and running his fingers through his hair.

DeVises' eyes were swollen and he walked stiffly. He was in ill humor. He had already caught his horses, and Maria and her mother were cooking and making coffee at the fire. Barry helped DeVises take down the tents and roll them. He helped load the horses. Then Maria went to the creek for water, and Barry followed her. At the creek, he took the bucket from her, dipped it full, and looked down at her in the dim light as they walked back toward the fire. Her silent, withdrawn manner was a warning to make no reference to the night before.

"I'll be looking forward to seeing you again, Maria."

"And I'll be glad to see you again, Barry."

He wished there was more that he could say to her. He wished he could go with her. They returned to the fire, and Barry said goodbye to DeVises and Mercy. DeVises nodded, and Mercy smiled in her anxiously cheerful way, wishing him good luck.

The sky brightened, and the wagons began moving out, men shouting, whips cracking, wheels rumbling and dogs barking. Barry caught his horse, led it to the fire and tied his belongings behind the saddle. Porter and Innes were wolfing down cold boiled meat and drinking coffee. Barry took a cup. The last of the wagons trundled out of the valley, with Fitzpatrick and Bridger shouting at the bush lopers to speed them up. Porter and Innes finished eating and prepared to leave too. They shook hands with Barry, slapped him on the shoulder and wished him good luck. Fitzpatrick walked over to say goodbye to him, and so did Harnett, Bridger, Ludlow, and others he had come to know and like.

The sun was rising as Barry watched all the pack trains and wagons disappear between the folds of the rolling hills. The valley was suddenly empty and quiet, the grass trampled. Circles of dead ashes were scattered about. The trader stood in front of the small, shabby trading post, yawning and scratching himself as he looked up at the sky. Barry mounted his horse and rode to the top of the hill overlooking the valley. The pack trains wound between the grassy hills, disappearing and coming into view again, becoming smaller in the distance. The front of the column went through a cleft in the hills and passed out of sight for the last time.

As the end of the pack trains came into sight, Barry waved. There was a flicker of a blue-clad arm in the distance. Maria was waving. Barry waved his arm frantically until she was out of sight. He dropped his arm and sat motionless for a moment, his shoulders slumped. Then he turned his horse back down the hill and toward the trail to the river.

Part Two

THE ROAD TO THE MOUNTAINS

5

"Here's a good patch, Maria," Harnett said. "We ought to be able to fill the bag right here."

Maria reined up, kicked her foot out of the stirrup, and slid down from the horse. Riding sidewards on a standard saddle with a shortened stirrup was uncomfortable and made her left leg numb, and she stamped her foot to restore the circulation. Her father had said he had been unable to find sidesaddles when he had bought the horses, but Maria suspected he hadn't searched too hard, being more concerned with the potential value of the saddles he did buy in the event he wanted to sell them when they reached Fort Henry.

She untied the canvas bag from behind the saddle, shook it open and began picking up the buffalo chips. Harnett hummed softly under his breath as he gathered handfuls and tossed them into the bag. He was always cheerful around her, and he had been helpful. He had helped her at the river crossings and at the crossings of the innumerable streams, seeing that she and her things got across safely, and he had helped her when the spring duststorms and thunderstorms sweeping the prairies had crossed the path of the pack trains.

During the early part of the journey, he had spent at least a few minutes with her every day, just as he had before they'd left the Missouri. He had showed her how to dig into the bank of a river to get clear, filtered water, showed her how to check the water to see if it had to be boiled before drinking it, showed her how to shape a trench into the wind to build the best fire with buffalo chips. He had taught her many things. But of far more value to her than his practical advice, he had seemed to sense when she needed him to help her through a darker moment. A bond of friendship had formed between them, based on Maria's resemblance to his long-dead daughter and on her need for a mentor. Their friendship had leaped the chasm between their ages and had become strong and firm.

As they crossed the sandy approach to the Platte, Seth had started spending even more time with her. Sometimes riding with her throughout the day, he had pointed out different plants and told her about their medicinal qualities, or he had showed her where to find bright, pretty stones in places where the wind had eddied and scoured dirt and sand away from rock outcroppings. About such matters, DeVises had grumbled darkly. He didn't want Maria's mind filled with pretty stones and other foolishness. But he hadn't interfered. Harnett was well-respected among the trappers and traders, not a man to alienate.

Three days before, after they had crossed the wide, shallow South Platte and started traveling along the North Platte, Harnett had simply gone off with Maria. After perfunctorily asking DeVises' permission as a matter of form, he'd left his pack horses in another free trapper's train and taken her on wide sweeps out into the prairie. His ostensible purpose was to collect buffalo chips, but as these were scattered all along the river in the travelers' path, Maria herself wasn't sure of what Seth had in mind. He pointed out and talked to her about the various forms of wildlife, how they were caught and killed. He was educating her still more, and she enjoyed it. But since hunting animals wasn't ordinarily women's work, she wondered what his motivation for teaching her about them was.

She loved being out in the prairie. It stretched out all around them in long grassy swales, broken only by occasional gullies that had been dug by runoffs from rock out-croppings during drenching downpours. The vastness of the prairie was awesome. It stretched for endless miles into the distance. The sun beaming brightly down on it and the breeze washing through it kept the deep grasses constantly changing color as they swayed and flattened. The shifting patterns fascinated Maria. She saw the prairie as beautiful. Though it made her feel diminutive and insignificant in her enormous surroundings, she also had a deeply satisfying sense of timelessness, her very insignificance being a source of pleasure.

"You don't mind bothering with buffalo chips now, do you?" Seth was saying.

Maria smiled and shrugged. "I certainly did at first, but now I suppose I sort of overlook what they are. Until I pick up one that's a little too fresh, that is."

Harnett chuckled, shaking his head. "No, you've got used to it, Maria. That's one thing I've noticed about you—you get used to things and make do with what's around you. A lot of people I know would be better off if they was more like you in that, and most of them have a bunch of years on you and ain't learned yet. There, that's about a bagful, ain't it? Let me have it, and I'll tie it up and put it on the saddle for you."

Maria gave him the bag and rawhide thong, and he began shaking the bag to settle the buffalo chips in it as he wadded the top to tie it. She stepped to her horse's head and stroked its nose as she looked off across the prairie.

"A body can catch their breath out here, can't they? There's room to breathe, and more."

"I like it. It makes me feel good and small."

His smile faded and he looked at her thoughtfully. Then he nodded and grunted as he lifted the bag to tie it behind her saddle. "You look at things a little sideways instead of straight on, don't you? The prairie can make folks feel satisfied that way, but they have to look from it to theirself instead of from theirself to it, and not many look at it that way. Not many can."

"Why aren't there any trees?"

He shook his head. "Mostly what I know is what I've seen, and I don't know much about how it got that way. But I'd say it's because of the prairie fires that come along a little later in the year. The reason I think that is is because there's plenty of birches, willows and whatnot on the islands in the rivers, where the fire can't reach. The fires are started sometimes by lightning, and sometimes they're started by campfires the Indians build."

"I haven't seen any Indians since we saw those Kanza Indians a long way back."

"Then you ain't been looking. You look right over there and tell me what you see."

In the far distance, there was a tiny line of black dots against the silvery green of the grass. "Will they bother us?" Maria said.

"No, the Indians around here are too busy bothering each other to bother with us. Them's Pawnee, without a doubt, and they're hunting buffalo, not wearing war paint. When you see an Indian wearing war paint, you'll know the difference. And when you see one with his face painted black, he's really one to stay clear of. He's out to settle something with somebody and do them some real dirt."

"Are there buffalo over there, then?"

"Maybe so, maybe not. Like I told you, you never know where the buffalo will be. They'll be climbing over the top of a body for weeks at a time, then you won't see a one for weeks at a time."

"The bacon we brought with us won't last much longer."

"Nobody's will, and beyond running out of bacon, I've had a hankering for a good kettle of buffalo for a while now. But buffalo's not the only meat to be found. See if you can show me some antelope."

Maria slowly scanned the prairie, lifting her hand to shade her eyes as she turned her head and the sun shone under the brim of her sunbonnet. Her eyes stopped on a shadowy, moving patch of light brown in the distance, and she pointed to it.

"That's right, and there's another bunch right over there. And another one there. Sooner or later, you'll get to where you can spot them right off, Maria. It's more sort of feeling where they're at instead of looking until you see some."

"How do you get close enough to them to shoot them?"

"There's ways, and there's ways. The only thing as skittish as an antelope is another antelope, but there's ways. But before a body can shoot an antelope or anything else, they've got to be able to shoot. Can you?"

"Shoot a rifle?" she laughed. "Why would I want to be able to shoot a rifle?"

"Well, to kill something to eat, and there's other things. I've known a lot of men who was married and lived in Indian country, and all of them showed their women how to load a rifle so they'd have somebody reloading for them if they was attacked. But a lot of them didn't learn their women how to shoot. I guess they figured if they got shot it would be all right for the woman to just stand there and keep on loading a rifle while the Indians was scalping her. Now what kind of sense does that make?"

"Do you think we might have trouble with the Indians in the mountains?"

"I ain't saying we will, but it happens. But beyond Indian troubles, I don't see no reason why a woman shouldn't be able to shift for herself. A lot can. I've known some women who could make a lot of men hide their face when it comes to shooting a rifle. And my girl Sarah could shoot her little rifle as good as any man. What's more, she could look after herself as good as any man who was as little as her. Of course, you don't find a lot of men that little."

"Do you want to show me how to shoot a rifle, then?"

Harnett said, gathering up the horses' reins, "That's what I had in mind, Maria. Come on."

He led the horses a few yards away and hobbled them, took a square of white cloth from the bag behind his saddle and went to a rock outcropping a hundred feet away. He spread the cloth on a rock facing and walked back to Maria. "Now this rifle is too heavy for you to stand up and shoot it from your shoulder, Maria, and there's nothing around here for you to prop it on, so you're going to have to lay down to shoot it."

Maria nodded, trampling the grass to make a spot for herself. "I hope everything I ever want to shoot will wait until I have a chance to lie down and get ready to shoot, then."

Harnett smiled and shook his head, folding his legs and sitting down on the ground. "I have a little short-barreled buffalo rifle in my packs that you might be able to shoulder. We'll try you out with it. But for right now. we'll just get you used to the idea of shooting a rifle. Prop your left arm on your elbow and put the barrel right in your hand—that's right. Now put the bead in that crack as you look down the barrel and line up both of them on the rag. I'll cock it for you. You just take your time and squeeze the trigger back any time you're ready. . . ."

Earlier on the trail, buffalo had been plentiful and men had brought in one every day or two. But during the past few weeks, none had been sighted and the party had been subsisting on the supplies in their packs. The idea of being able to shoot and bring in food appealed to Maria. But beyond that, just learning to shoot thrilled her. It seemed to her that if she got it right, it would be a sort of cornerstone of a foundation of being able to do things for herself. She lined up the sights on the cloth and pulled the trigger. The hammer snapped, the pan flashed and the rifle cracked.

"No, the pan flashing made you jump, and you pulled it off the target, Maria. Now it does that to everybody at first, and you're going to have to get used to it so it don't bother you. I'll just prime the pan and cock it, and you take a bead and everything just like the rifle was going to shoot. We'll do that a few times and see if you can get used to it that way."

He pulled his powder horn around, primed the pan with a pinch of gunpowder and closed the lid, then pulled the hammer back. Maria took aim on the target again, steeling herself from flinching, and pulled the trigger. The hammer snapped down and the pan flashed. Harnett nodded, priming the pan and re-cocking the rifle. Again, Maria squeezed the trigger.

"Tarnation, Maria, I think you're holding it steady as a rock now. I figured we'd be at this a week, because it took me longer than that to break one of my boys from jumping from the pan flashing. Stand up now and I'll show you how to load. First you blow down the barrel to make sure the touchhole by the pan is clear, like this. Then you take the powder horn, fill this little measure and pour it in. . . ."

Maria watched him as he reloaded the rifle and

explained each step. Then she stretched out on the ground, shouldered the rifle and took careful aim at the cloth target. An insistent determination to keep from flinching possessed her, and she steeled herself as she pulled the trigger. The hammer snapped down and the pan flashed.

"By God!" Harnett chortled gleefully. "You just killed that rag deader than hell, Maria! I'll be durned if I don't think you're going to be a natural hand with a rifle. All right, you load it this time."

Maria smiled and nodded, climbing to her feet and taking the powder horn and shot bag from him. "I don't want to use up all of your powder and shot. I know they're expensive."

"I've got plenty. I'm having more fun than if I was shooting from the middle of a herd of buffalo. The side of that bonnet gets in your way when you're aiming, don't it?"

"I could take it off."

"No, then the sun would be in your eyes all the time. What you need is a hat."

"A hat?" she laughed. "Wouldn't I look good wearing a man's hat!"

"You could do worse. It would shade your face, and you could still see to the sides. That bonnet is like a pair of blinders on a mule. You have to turn your head all the way around to see anything. Now the last thing you do after you load is make sure your flint is tight in the hammer, Maria. A body would be in a hell of a shape with buffalo or Indians all around, and them scratching around on the ground trying to find their hammer flint, wouldn't they? Push the ramrod good and hard to settle the ball, Maria. That's right. . . ."

Maria slid the ramrod back into the thimbles,

primed the pan and closed the lid. Then she lay down again, cocking the rifle. She was more confident and sure of herself now. The rifle had an almost familiar feel to it. She propped the barrel across her left hand and shouldered it. She pulled the trigger back, holding the rifle steady as the hammer snapped and the pan flashed. The rifle cracked, smoke billowing from the end of the barrel.

"You hit it again!" Harnett shouted in delight, patting her shoulder. "Well, that settles it, Maria. You take to a rifle like you were born to it. That's a pretty easy target and you're going to have to learn how to pull a fine bead and squeeze that trigger instead of jerking it for when the target ain't so easy, and you're going to have to learn how to compensate for shooting uphill and downhill, how to draw your windage for when you've got a stiff wind, and how to elevate for long shots. But all that'll come. Go get the rag while I reload the rifle, and we'll head on back."

Maria handed him the rifle and tramped over to the target, her skirt dragging through the deep grass. Shards had been chipped from the rock and there were two holes in the cloth. She picked the cloth up and walked back toward the horses, looking at the holes. "You say it's really hard to shoot an antelope?"

"Mighty hard, but I know some tricks I learned from the Indians. I was thinking about trying you out with that little buffalo rifle sometime later. Now I think I'll bring it along tomorrow and see how you do. After you've got used to it, we'll think about an antelope. In the meantime, if you're tired of bacon, I'll find a river island with some willows on it when we get back. We'll cut some willow branches and make us some prairie chicken traps."

"Prairie chicken traps?"

"That's right, little willow branch cages with a hole that they can get in but can't get back out. We'll bait them with bread, ride a good ways out in front in the morning and set them out, then pick them up in the afternoon. Prairie chickens is easy to trap, and they make some of the best eating you've ever had. But for now, what direction do we head in to meet the others?"

Maria looked to the north, thinking, then pointed.

"No, you're a little to the east, Maria. You've got to remember that they're heading almost due west while we've come a good way south. Just keep how fast you're going and which way you're heading in the back of your mind all the time, and you'll always know where you're at. Think about it without thinking about it, the way I do. Come on. I'll help you onto your horse."

Maria pulled her reins over her horse's head. Harnett lifted her onto it and mounted his own horse. They cantered to the north, the long, gentle swales of the prairie stretching out ahead of them in monotonous regularity, and the grass took on a golden tinge as the sun inclined to the west. The river, wide and shallow, came into sight as they crossed the tops of the swales, then the lines of small, black dots which were the pack trains traveling along its low bank. The river was a greyish brown under the sun. It appeared to be higher than they were as they rode toward it.

"Why does the river always look as though it's uphill from us?" Maria called over the sound of the horses' hoofs.

"It always looks like a body is going uphill on the prairie when they've got something a good ways ahead to fasten their eyes on," Harnett called back. "A body's eyes can play tricks on them. That can be bad on west a ways. You can see a mountain twenty miles away and think it's two. There's been people starve or die of thirst because they thought they could reach somewheres in an hour, and it was more like a two-day trip. The way to get around that is to turn your back, bend over and look at it between your legs. Then if it's twenty miles away, it'll look twenty miles away. I don't know why that is, but it works every time."

Maria nodded, looking back to the front. The terrain here was more broken, marked with gullies and washes where rainfall had dug channels to the river. The swales were flattened out, the grass more lush from the moisture and the richer topsoil that had been washed down into it. Harnett's uncanny sense of time, direction and distance had brought them back to the pack trains just before sunset, as they were stopping for the night. Seth smiled and nodded as he turned toward the front of the column, and Maria waved goodby as she nudged her horse toward her father's pack train in the rear.

DeVises was unloading the horses, and Mercy was sorting through the bag of cooking utensils and provisions. As Maria reined up and slid down, De-Vises glanced at her stonily. Mercy forced a wanly cheerful smile.

"Looks like you got a lot of chips there, Maria," her mother said. "That'll last right through the night and then some, won't it?"

"She could have filled fifty bags along the river,"

DeVises said sourly. "We've been riding through tons of buffalo chips all day."

Maria barely glanced at her father. She undid the bag behind her saddle, let it fall to the ground and dragged it toward her mother. "Mr. Harnett said we'll see if we can catch some prairie chickens tomorrow.

"Prairie chickens?" Mercy said, perking up. "That would be mighty good, Maria, because we've been using up our bacon real fast."

Maria nodded. She started to tell her mother about shooting the rifle, then hesitated. It wasn't an ordinary activity for a woman. It would probably displease her father, and it probably wouldn't please her mother. She went back to her horse and silently began unsaddling it.

Late, after hobbling the horse and helping her mother start a fire with handfuls of dried grass, Maria took a spade, bucket and tin cup and walked along the river, looking for a gravel bed. The river was mostly liquid mud, only inches deep in many places. Maria found a gravel deposit close to a bank a short distance from the campsite. She hopped down and began digging in it. The gravel became damp a few inches down, then wet. At eighteen inches, water began seeping into the hole. Maria put the shovel aside and knelt by the hole, letting the water settle. Then she began dipping it out with the cup and pouring it into the bucket.

Intent on her work, it took her a while to realize someone was watching her. She turned her head quickly then and saw, above her on the bank, Curtis Kruger. Maria flushed. She knew it was Curtis rather than Stephen because he was smiling with amiable interest in what she was doing, something that the arrogant, self-absorbed Stephen never did.

One look at his blonde good looks and Maria lowered her head. She began digging again, absently, her heart pounding. She wasn't supposed to speak to either of the Kruger twins. But her heart was torn and troubled by the problem facing her.

Even after weeks, the night of the attack was still a raw terror in her mind. She'd suddenly awakened in the dark, with powerful arms crushing her, a lean, hard body holding her down and a large hand pressed tightly over her mouth. The memory of her panic and wild, frantic struggle was very strong, as was the memory of her humiliation the next day when everyone had stared at her, knowing what had happened.

The fact was that Maria did not know for sure which Kruger twin had tried to rape her. It had been too dark for her to see the man and neither had confessed.

She felt in her heart that it must have been Stephen. There had been a strong smell of whiskey on the man holding her, and Curtis didn't seem to drink that much. Also, there was nothing in Curtis' congenial bearing to suggest that he would rape a woman even if he was drunk.

Maria had even further feelings on the matter, more positive feelings she was helpless to deny. She was drawn to Curtis. From the first time she had seen him, she'd felt a subtle inner tug toward him. She had liked many young men at first sight, and there had been a few she had liked exceptionally well. Barry Fitzpatrick, for example, had stirred a deep affection in her, even if it had contained strong motherly overtones because of his boyishness.

But Curtis was unique in her experience. She felt differently about him. They had danced once and exchanged a few words, no more. But each time she had passed him in the camp and he had smiled at her, she'd felt they were communicating at some deep level.

When she had finished filling her bucket and looked up at the bank, Curtis was gone. She looked further down the river bank and saw him gathering driftwood for his family. She missed him.

And yet she didn't know for absolutely sure, for neither had confessed, which of the Kruger twins had tried to rape her.

6

Maria lay in the deep grass with the rifle to her shoulder, watching the approaching antelope through the thin screen of grass in front of her. There were eight of them, cautiously moving forward. A nervous tremor raced through her, and she forced herself to relax and breathe with a slow, deep rhythm.

"Just take your time," Harnett murmured. "You've got all the time in the world. Now put your left hand about a foot in front of your face and lift your thumb so you can size your target."

Maria did as she was told. When she slid her hand towards the front of the barrel and lifted her thumb, the nearest antelope appeared to be about two thirds the size of her thumbnail.

"Just wait'll he's as big as your thumbnail, and he'll be in range. You'll get to where you'll be able to look at something and tell right off if it's in range, but that'll take a while and you can use your thumb until then. Half your thumb for a buffalo, and your thumbnail for an antelope. And give it plenty of elevation, because that's a long shot for that rifle."

Maria's rifle was short and stubby compared to Seth's. While it was almost as heavy as his, its point of balance was nearer the stock and she could hold it on target while standing. And while it had a shorter range than Seth's rifle, it was even deadlier, since it fired huge balls, only sixteen of them to a pound of lead.

Her thumb trembled as she stared past it at the antelope, and she stiffened it, holding it still. Two hundred feet away, in the shallow valley below their perch, Harnett had planted a tall, thin willow branch with long strips of cloth tied near the top. The cloth fluttered in the breeze. The antelope were approaching it, their ears cocked forward and their bodies poised to bolt away with each step they took.

"Curiosity killed the cat," Harnett chuckled, "and it'll kill an antelope too. Give them something funny to look at, and they'll walk right up to it as long as it don't look like it'll bite them."

"Which one are you going to shoot?" Maria whispered.

"Don't you worry about me, Maria, I'll get me one. You just pick out whichever one you want and cut loose at him. I'll shoot one that you don't."

Her thumb trembled again. She couldn't make it stop. She licked her lips and swallowed. With the top of the nearest antelope's ears on the tip of her thumbnail, the base of her nail was about where the antelope's feet would be in the deep grass. She swallowed again. "I'm going to shoot now."

"All right, go ahead."

The antelope looked very tiny compared to the bead on the end of the barrel. She centered the bead, placed it on the antelope's chest, then lifted it just above the antelope's head. The antelope took another step, quivering with excitement as it looked at the strips of cloth streaming in the breeze. Maria drew in a deep breath, released half of it and tightened her right hand, gently squeezing the trigger back. The hammer snapped down and the pan flashed. She froze. The rifle boomed, leaping back against her shoulder. Harnett's rifle fired with a sharp crack. Boiling clouds of gunpowder smoke swirled in the deep grass in front of her. She leaped up, looking. Her antelope was down. Another one was going down, its mouth open and its tongue thrusting out in its frantic struggles to stay on its feet as its rear quarters sagged and its legs folded. It fell, thrashing in the grass. The others disappeared, scampering wildly away with long, bounding leaps.

"I got it!" Maria squealed with glee, starting to run forward. "I got it!"

"You hold on!" Harnett laughed, holding her arm. "You reload that rifle before you go anywhere. The first thing you do when you shoot is reload, and you do that before you move out of your tracks."

Maria nodded, blowing down the barrel of the rifle and pulling the powder horn and shot bag hanging over her shoulder around to the front. "I was afraid I was going to miss it."

"I wasn't. It was a long shot, but I wasn't afraid you'd miss."

Maria hesitated and looked at him as she started to fill the powder measure. He smiled, his eyes twinkling. Maria smiled and nodded, filling the measure and pouring it into the barrel.

They reloaded their rifles and walked across the valley. The willow pole was swaying and the strips of fluttering cloth were making slapping noises against it. Maria looked at the two antelope sprawled in awkward, grotesque positions, their eyes glazed and large spots of moist crimson on their brown fur.

"They're pretty, aren't they?" she said.

Harnett looked at her musingly as he put his rifle down and took out his skinning knife. "They're pretty animals. Most animals are. I'm glad you see that. Most people can kill without ever having a thought or feeling for what they've killed, but I believe that takes something away from what was killed. It makes it as though it wasn't ever alive to start with. A body kills because they have to, but even so I believe they ought to own to theirself that they've killed something that was alive."

Maria looked at him, taking in his meaning, then searched the horizon for the other antelope. "They won't be back, will they?"

He shook his head, kneeling by the antelope she had shot and turning it onto its back to slit it open. "No, not here. But we still have plenty of time to move on to the west a piece and try for another one or two. You go get the horses while I'm doing this, and we'll load them up and move on over. No, wait a minute. . . ."

Maria, who was turning away, turned back. Har-

nett rose from her antelope, his right hand coated
in its blood, and reached out to touch her face with
it. She backed away. "What are you doing?"

"You've been blooded," he said. He held her
firmly by the shoulder and painted streaks of blood
on her cheeks as she flinched. "You've killed for
the first time, and you've been blooded."

The thick blood was sticky on her cheeks, drying
as the breeze brushed her face. It had a hot, meaty
odor. Staring at Harnett, she touched it and looked
at her fingertips. At first, she was repelled, even
nauseated. Then, after a moment or two, she saw
the blood as the symbol Seth intended her to see
it as—a kind of badge of honor. She took that in
too. Then she turned away to get the horses.

They rode along for several miles, Harnett scanning the horizon. Presently, he reined back to a
walk, pointing. Maria, also slowing, saw spots of
brown in the hazy distance. They rode down into
the next valley, Harnett dismounted and they once
more staked out for a hunt.

The sun was hot on Maria's back as she lay in
the grass. The dried blood on her cheeks itched and
insects rustled on her dress. Harnett came back from
putting up the willow pole and lay down beside her,
feeling in his hunting bag for a plug of tobacco.
He started to offer Maria a chaw, then grinned and
put the plug back in his pouch. The strong, acrid
odor of the tobacco wafted to Maria's nostrils as
he chewed and spat.

They waited. Looking at the strips of cloth fluttering on the pole, Maria began musing about the
new situation she was helping to create. It was com-

plicated. For weeks, hunters had been returning to
the pack trains empty-handed, as no buffalo had
been roaming within the range they could ride in
a day. Now, she and Harnett had been catching and
sharing with the others between eight and a dozen
prairie chickens a day. Even though they had hardly
more than flavored the kettles when spread among
the large group, most everybody had been thankful
for them. The one or two chickens Maria had kept
daily for her own family had made substantial meals
for them when cooked with rice or beans; they'd
also been a welcome change from the salt bacon.
The trouble was that her part in catching them had
been widely commented upon, and her father dis-
liked her calling attention to herself. He had resented her bringing in the food, even though he ate
it. She still hadn't mentioned that Harnett had been
teaching her to shoot a rifle. Her father would surely
be even more displeased over the antelope, which
would fill the kettles in the entire group for a day
or two.

Maria was angry, both with her father and herself. They were both acting like fools. She just didn't
know how to change things.

Harnett touched her shoulder. Maria turned her
head slightly, looking. The antelope had approached
from the side, but she'd been too busy with her
thoughts to see them. Quickly recovering, she lifted
and shouldered the rifle, then pulled the hammer
back. Harnett spat and shifted in the grass, shoul-
dering his own gun. The antelope were moving cautiously toward the pole. Crossing from right to left,
they presented a larger target than before. Maria
slid her left hand back along the rifle, lifted her
thumb and looked at a large buck. It was already

within range. She took aim, then slowly squeezed the trigger.

The rifle boomed and kicked. Maria sprang to her feet and looked over the cloud of gunpowder smoke as Harnett's rifle cracked. The antelope she had shot was down, knocked sidewards by the impact of the heavy rifle ball. Another one staggered and fell, kicking. The others darted away with long bounds, zigzagging from side to side. Maria began reloading as Harnett stood up, and he nodded with satisfaction as he pulled his powder horn and shot pouch around.

"I expect we've got enough to last everybody for a while now, ain't we?"

"There should be plenty. If they're this easy to kill, why haven't you been bringing in some before now?"

Harnett spat to one side and shrugged. "I'd as lief eat bacon as antelope myself. You got to remember that I'm a free trapper, Maria. I'll share a kettle with some of the men now and then and I'll ride in the same direction they're going, but it ain't as though I'm traveling with them. I travel by myself." He reloaded and they started to walk. Harnett hesitated, looking at her. "Maybe, for a change, I am traveling with somebody now."

"I certainly hope so."

They reached the antelope, and Harnett took out his skinning knife as he studied them. "That was a good shot, Maria, right in the chest."

"I was hoping it wouldn't take another step just as I shot. I should help you with the skinning, you know."

"It won't take me but a minute, and you'd probably get blood on your dress."

"It has everything else on it now," she laughed, looking down at herself. "Look at the stains. That's because I get my feet tangled in my hem in this deep grass."

"My little Sarah used to complain about her dress getting in the way. I let her run a trapline with me when we was living up at Fort Recovery, and durned if she didn't take to wearing buckskins. When her ma saw her, I thought she was going to skin me out and make whet leather out of my hide."

Maria laughed. She'd like to wear buckskins herself. Her dress kept tripping her, holding her back. For the first time since she'd left St. Louis, life seemed bearable to her. It was the expanse of the prairie and Harnett's teachings and good humor that had made it so.

Maria's hope that they could rejoin the others with a minimum of notice was shattered when, as they rode at sunset down the last slope toward the pack trains, Harnett let out a piercing victory whoop. Men making camp for the night saw him lift his rifle and shake it. They waited, grinning expectantly, until the two riders arrived. Then, when they saw the antelope carcasses, they set up a whooping and hollering of their own.

Fitzpatrick himself came over. "Did you finally get some meat, then?" he laughed. "Looks like you got plenty once you got started, Seth."

"No, there's plenty for everybody, but I can't claim it all. Maria here shot two of them."

Maria blushed as several of the men gave her a round of applause. A few didn't, just stared silently at her blood-stained cheeks. Fitzpatrick chuckled.

"She sure did, from the looks of her. All right, some of you men get them carcasses skinned out, and we'll divide them up. I'll see you right on your powder and lead, Seth."

"You'll see me right on them hides, too."

"Rocky Mountain Fur Company don't buy no hides still on the animal, Seth." Porter laughed. "You'd better get to skinning them yourself."

"Then you'd better get you out some bacon for your supper."

The two kept bantering as men untied and took the antelopes off the horses. Maria felt acutely self-conscious as she sat her horse and held the rifle. Men all around her kept looking up at her, as if they didn't know quite what to make of her. She hardly felt human; maybe she was part-animal. Her father stood a few feet away, looking so bleak she found it difficult to look into his eyes. Her mother stood by him, lifting herself on her toes and craning her neck to see over the men in front of her. She had an absent, bemused smile on her face.

"Laws, did you shoot some of them deers, Maria?"

"Antelopes."

"Is that right? And you shot some of them? Laws, what are you doing shooting a gun? Whose gun have you got there?"

DeVises abruptly turned and walked away. Mercy hesitated, then hurried after him.

Harnett had been watching the DeVises intently.

"I'll make sure you and your folks get a hind quarter, Maria," he said quietly.

"Thank you. Here, don't forget your rifle."

"It's been getting a little rusty. You go ahead and keep it oiled up for me."

Maria smiled and nodded. As Harnett rode up toward his own position in the column of pack trains, Maria turned her horse toward her father's. DeVises had his back turned as Maria reined up near him. He was making a show of unloading his horses. Maria dismounted, put the rifle, powder horn and shot bag down, and began making a show of untying the bag of buffalo chips from behind her saddle. She had gathered the chips, after all; that was more or less woman's work. Her father glanced around at her, briefly, then went back to jerking at the rope on a packsaddle.

The evening proceeded in like silence. Maria did her regular chores. which included getting water from the river. She had an instant's exhilaration when she saw Curtis Kruger also walking toward the river, but by then she felt herself so much under her father's watchful eye that she avoided him scrupulously. Her spirits sank lower and lower. Returning with the bucket, she put it down by the fire, then began sorting out her things. The sudden, fierce winds that could arise on the prairie had made it impossible to put up her tent for weeks, so she was using it as a ground sheet. She laid her blankets out on it, then put the rifle, powder horn and shot pouch close by.

Only when she had her own few things in order did she return to the family fire. DeVises sat there, apparently listening to Mercy rattle utensils and make coffee. Maria felt a futile rage boiling inside her. It was no use. Nothing was any use. She and her parents ate heated rice and beans left over from the morning meal and the day before.

Mercy put on a kettle of water to boil. Maria didn't even ask what for. She felt as if she were walking on eggs, that all would break if she took a step in any direction.

They were sitting that way when footsteps approached. Maria turned and her spirits rose. Harnett was coming toward the fire with an antelope quarter, the hoof and tufts of hair around the ankle still on it. He carried a new trapper's hat in his other hand.

"How do, Pierre. Mercy. Here's your hind quarter, Mercy."

"Laws, look at all that meat. We'll be eating on that for a good while. We're much obliged, Mr. Harnett."

"Well, your girl there shot it. Maria, Tom has a stack of these hats in his trade goods. I got one from him for your share of the hides."

Maria took the hat. Aware of her father's instant disdain and her mother's nervous reaction to it, she turned the hat over in her hands, examining it.

"Those hides couldn't be worth all that much," she said then. "A hat like this costs a lot of money."

"That's true, but I expect Tom might be thinking you'll let him have the next few without charging him. How are your horses doing, Pierre?"

"Fair to middling. They could use a day of rest and feeding up, but they'll do."

"Everybody's could use a rest, and I believe Tom might be aiming to stop for a day or so when we reach the Laramie or thereabouts. . . ."

Harnett and DeVises continued talking. Excitedly, Maria rose and slipped away to her tent. Searching through her belongings. she found a ribbon, with which after removing her bonnet, she tied her hair back. Then she put the trapper's hat on. It was large but comfortable. And her vision to the sides was unrestricted. Proudly, almost uncaring. she came back to the fire wearing it. Harnett and DeVises were still talking. Mercy glanced up at her, then looked back down. Apparently, she had anticipated the antelope meat. She was cutting pieces from it and dropping them into the kettle she'd boiled. Harnett looked at Maria and smiled as he rose.

"Well, I'll get on back. I'll see you all in the morning."

DeVises nodded and murmured, and Maria smiled at him as she sat down by the fire. To no avail. He didn't like her hat; she hadn't thought he would. Looking nervously from one to the other, Mercy kept putting meat in the kettle.

"I'll just boil up plenty while I'm at it so it won't get a chance to spoil," she explained hastily. "It looks good, though I believe it's a little tougher than buffalo meat."

DeVises grunted and shrugged. "When we come across buffalo, I've no doubt we'll have plenty," he said sourly. "We have another man in the family now to do the hunting, don't we?"

Maria's smile faded. Tears of resentment welled toward her eyes. He didn't have to *like* her new hat, but why couldn't he accept it and her as she was—someone who had found something in this God-forsaken country to love and enjoy? For the moment, she was too angry to reflect on what he had said. Then she did, and her resentment faded too. After all, he hadn't forbidden her to go with Harnett, had he? And apparently he wasn't going to.

* * *

Harnett was waiting for her on top of a grassy knoll just after dawn. Earlier, the pack trains had moved on, leaving a lonely, deserted feeling hanging over the river bank. Maria, after making sure none of the DeVises belongings had been left behind, rode up to join him. She held her rifle in one hand now, and she'd given up her sunbonnet for the brimless trapper's hat, which afforded her far better side vision.

Harnett turned his horse south as she approached. They rode at a slow canter into the rising sun. Soon the sun warmed the night chill.

"Are we going to hunt more antelope today?"

Harnett shook his head. "Tomorrow or the next day will be plenty of time. We might even run onto some buffalo by then."

They rode through swales until the horses began to pant heavily. Harnett reined to a walk and glanced sideways at her. He said quietly, "Your pa's put out with you, isn't he?"

"Yes. He doesn't think it's right for a woman to go hunting and do things like that."

Harnett shrugged. "Well, maybe it ain't right. Then again, while I ain't one to go up against a girl's pa, maybe it is. All my life I've run onto people who never had a doubt in their mind as to what was right and wrong, and all my life I've been tore in first one direction and another as to what was right and wrong. And I figure that for the most part, them who thinks they know what's right and wrong really don't know enough to know that they don't know, if that makes sense. The onliest one who ever had me believing that he did know was a preacher over in Maysville, Kentucky. You know, I was to where I'd take that man's word for anything. But if you'll excuse me for saying so, I just lost all of my faith in that man when they locked him up because of what they caught him doing to a mule. And it wasn't even a mare mule."

Maria flushed furiously, laughing. "Seth!"

He chuckled. "Well, after that I just don't have no faith in anybody who always knows what's right and wrong. Where would you make the pack trains at now?"

Maria lifted her arm without hesitation and pointed. "There."

"That's about what I'd say too. But if we started back now, they'd still be moving along the river, wouldn't they? So what direction would we take to come over the last rise and ride down into the middle of them?"

"That way."

"You do know where you're at, don't you? Well, I just thought we'd do some looking around today, Maria. And by ourselves instead of with each other."

"By ourselves?"

"That's right. Are you scared to be by yourself out here?"

"No."

"All right, you can head over that way then, and I'll go this way. Start on back to the pack trains well before sunset, and I'll meet you on the way. A girl who shouldn't be hunting sure shouldn't be off in the prairie by herself, should she? So I'll cut you off on the way back, and we'll ride the last piece together. Now when you stop to fill your bag with buffalo chips, put down a stake and tether your horse so he won't run off. If you're thrown, follow him. He'll head for the pack trains, and I'll follow his trail backwards to find you. If he steps into a prairie dog hole or something and hurts hisself, stay with him. I'll circle around and pick up his trail and follow it to you. All right?"

"All right."

Harnett turned his horse, kicking it with his heels, and rode away. He crossed the valley below the rise, went over the next rise, and disappeared into the next valley. Then he came into sight again on the following rise, becoming small in the distance. He became smaller, a black, moving dot coming into sight and disappearing, then faded into the prairie.

It was the first time in Maria's life that she had been totally alone, without another human being within summoning distance. Solitude closed in with a sudden, crushing impact. Then, as she looked about the vast prairie, her feelings of being over-powered by loneliness diminished. The sun beamed down. The breeze brushed her face and stirred the brim of her hat. She breathed deeply of the green, gold, sweet-smelling grass.

For the first time in her life, she was at her own devices. Seth, who had guided her this far, was gone. The only limitation on her freedom was their planned rendezvous at sunset.

But being free also meant she had no one to advise and protect her. Maria looked down at her blunt, heavy rifle. She lifted the pan lid to check the priming and snapped it closed. The rifle was a solid, substantial weight across her thighs. She lifted her reins and nudged her horse with her heel, urging it to a slow canter. She surveyed the prairie with satisfaction as she rode along.

7

Along about noon, as Maria was peering for game, she saw a distant rider moving along a line west of her and going almost straight south. She thought at first it was an Indian. Then, when he suddenly veered toward her from about a mile off, she saw it was a Kruger twin. Stephen or Curtis? She stiffened and gathered her reins, ready to gallop off if it should be the former.

But it was Curtis who drew up, reining his panting horse back.

"Hello."

"Hello."

His smile reflected pleasure over finding her, but he was also a little diffident and unsure. He glanced around curiously. "Where is Mr. Harnett?"

"Off over that way somewhere."

"Do you mean you're out here by yourself?"

"Well, if I meet the bogey man, I'll just shoot him."

He looked startled, then tossed his head back and laughed heartily. He was particularly handsome, now that he was darkly sun-tanned. The tan set off his white teeth and blonde hair dramatically. He sat his horse with a relaxed ease. "I wouldn't doubt it. You shot the first meat we'd had for weeks, didn't you?"

"Such as it was. It was pretty tough, I guess. Did you have to boil yours long?"

He nodded and said, "It tasted good to me." His eyes moved over her face. Then he pushed his hat back. "Well, I managed to get loose from my pa today, and I thought I'd see if I could get a buffalo."

"You're upwind from them. That dust over there is from a scattered herd, but you'll have to circle around and come up to them from downwind."

"Are you going to hunt one?"

"No, I don't think so. I'm just riding around. There's a lot of meat in camp right now."

He nodded. "Yes, I just wanted to get away for a while myself more than anything else. I made a bargain with my pa to help him get the pack trains to the Snake River. He holds me to chores most of the time. But every now and then I can get away."

"Aren't you going to stay with him when you get to the Snake?"

"No, no chance of that. I'm going to work for myself as a free trapper. I trapped some on the Missouri, and I brought traps and things along."

Maria suspected from his tone that Curtis and his father didn't get along. But then, why should they? Curtis was totally different from either his father or his brother. She had wondered what sort of person he would be to talk with. He was even more pleasant than she had anticipated. They rode along together for a while. He knew, it turned out, quite a bit about guns from having hunted small game back east, and he was openly admiring of Harnett for having taught her what she knew. He was sensitive to the prairie too, maybe not so much as she was since he was looking forward with hungry eagerness to the mountains ahead. But he enjoyed the grass; she could tell that from his deep, soulful breathing of it. And he liked being with her too. At one point his admiring look at her was so frank that she blushed and looked away.

"It's strange, but I feel as though we've known each other for a long time," Curtis said, smiling. "We've never really met properly, have we? I hate it that things started off as they did. About what happened. . . ."

"You weren't the one, were you?"

"No. It wasn't me."

Maria swallowed. Her heart stopped pounding. Then she frowned. "I knew in my heart it wasn't. But I've been wanting to talk with you about it. I've wanted to ask you why you let your brother get away with what he did."

The smile that had formed on his face disappeared as she finished. He looked contrite and shamefaced and cleared his throat uncomfortably. "Well, he didn't exactly get away with it, you know. I had it out with him, and so did pa. And . . . well, even though we don't get along, he is my brother. . . ."

"But why did you let everyone keep thinking it might have been you?"

"Telling that he had done it would be doing something to myself, not to him."

It wasn't the reply Maria had expected. He wasn't merely protesting a family loyalty as if he had no choice in the matter. He apparently had clearly formulated principles, a code of personal conduct. He knew he was innocent. He knew himself. That was enough for him. Maria was suddenly struck by his maturity, even though Curtis was only a couple of years or so older than she.

"In any event, I'm very sorry it happened, and if there's any way I can make up for it, I'll be more than glad to do so."

Maria shrugged and nodded. "Needless to say, I'm also sorry it happened. But it wasn't your fault, so let's forget it, Curtis."

"That's good of you to say that. I couldn't blame you if you held a grudge against me because of what Stephen did and my pa said, as your pa does. I just wish that somehow our families could have got off to a better start, and . . . well, what's done is done. Would you like to get down and rest for a few minutes?"

At the moment, Maria wished for nothing more than that. She kicked her foot out of the stirrup and let Curtis help her down by the waist, which he did effortlessly. They hobbled their horses and walked a few feet away from them. They were just two people now, lost on an expanse of prairie. And yet not lost.

"Had you always been interested in hunting and things like that?" Curtis asked.

She laughed and shook her head. "My goodness, no. Only since Mr. Harnett showed me so much about it."

"Everyone says he's the best trapper and hunter we have with us."

Maria nodded, proud of her friendship with Seth. "I'm sure it would take years to learn what he knows."

They kept walking until Curtis found a patch of shorter swales for them to sit down in. She pulled her skirt around her and sat next to him, putting her rifle at her feet. "Are you going to Fort Henry. then?" she asked curiously.

Curtis shook his head. "We'll split off from the party before that. Stephen and I will help pa set up a trading post, then I'll go my way and Stephen will go his. He intends to go into trading too, but I don't believe he'll do it with pa."

"You don't believe?" Maria smiled. "You all don't tell each other much about what you're doing, do you?"

He grinned and put a stem of grass in his mouth. "No, all three of us go our own way. When we were on the Missouri, I trapped and Stephen and pa traded, and none of us worked together. Stephen was doing his trading with Hudson's Bay Company, and pa was with the Missouri Fur Company."

"Some of the men think your pa might be with the American Fur Company now."

Curtis shrugged, chewing the stem of grass. "I don't know. All I know is someone must be backing him or he wouldn't have so many goods. He wasn't doing good enough on the Missouri to have the money to buy all that. What are you going to do when you reach Fort Henry?"

Maria sighed and shook her head morosely. "I don't know. Just sit in a cabin, I suppose."

Curtis said hopefully, "Maybe I could come and see you. . . . No, I guess not. I guess your pa would shoot me if he was there, and he'd track me down and shoot me if I came when he wasn't there, wouldn't he?"

"I suppose he would," Maria said, shrugging again. "When he gets his mind made up on something, he doesn't change it. And he has a bad temper. He'd have a fit if he knew I was sitting here talking to you."

Curtis smiled wryly. "Well, I wouldn't want to get you into trouble with him, Maria. But that's the only thing that would keep me away. I'm not saying that I could whip your pa, but I will say that he couldn't do anything to stop me from seeing you if you said that's what you wanted."

His voice was quiet and determined, and Maria felt a flush rising in her cheeks. She could tell Curtis meant it. His words were simple and heart-felt.

But the situation wasn't that simple. It was decidedly dangerous. She had seen what her maddened father had done to Mr. Kruger, all but kicked him to death. If she encouraged Curtis, what might he not do to *him?* In an isolated mountain cabin, there might be nobody around to stop him. She looked away, searching for some comment or question to change the subject.

"What's it like to have a twin?"

Curtis shrugged. It was almost as though he had expected the subject to change. "People get us mixed up a lot, of course, until they get to know us. Other than that, I don't think it's all that different from just having a brother of about the same age. You've never had any brothers or sisters, have you? Have you ever wished you had?"

"No, not really. Perhaps I did when I was small, because there weren't many of my age where we lived. But then I started to school, and after that I went to day school. It's always bothered ma a lot, though, because mother's always been a little ashamed of not having more than one. . . ."

As she talked on, it suddenly occurred to her that she was rambling, even babbling which was unlike her. And she was freely touching on private family matters and other things that she had never discussed with even her closest friends. But she was totally relaxed and at ease with Curtis, having a firm conviction that no indiscretion on her part would lead to his embarrassing her in any way. Few young men she had known had enjoyed listening. They'd preferred to talk. Curtis wanted to listen more than talk, though talk he did too—about his childhood, some of the friends he'd admired, his ambitions. He wanted to do well enough as a lone trapper, he told her, to be able to hire a trapping brigade. Then he hoped to expand and get his own supply brigade together to bring goods in and take his furs out of the mountains. It was just a dream for now, he knew that. But he felt if he worked hard, he'd have a chance at realizing it.

Time fled. Maybe it was about three o'clock when Curtis glanced up at the sun, sighed heavily and put his hat on. "Well, it's getting on along, Maria. . . ."

Maria nodded and they both rose and started walking. "It's been truly wonderful, Curtis," she said. "I'm sorry it has to end."

He smiled. "It was a real lucky day for me, Maria, meeting you on the prairie like that. Pa has those horses overloaded and it takes all three of us to look after them most of the time. But whenever

I can get away again, I'll sure have a look around
for you. And if it's all right with you, I'll be coming
by Fort Henry now and then."

Maria stopped, midway to their horses.

"I don't want trouble between you and my pa,
Curtis."

"I don't either, Maria, but like I said, it would
take more—"

"I heard what you said, Curtis," she interrupted
him in a firm tone. "And I don't want any trouble
between you and my pa. I want you to promise that
you won't do or say anything to cause it."

"Well, how can I . . . does that mean that I
can't come and see you? Not ever?"

She hesitated, her lips gradually relaxing into a
smile. "Well, Fort Henry is a trading post, isn't it?
And if I happen to be there when you happen to
come by needing something, no one would think
anything of your saying hello. I imagine I could set
off from there to pick berries, and you could—"

He smiled and nodded. "All right, Maria. But I
don't see why I can't just talk to your pa and tell
him that—"

"You can't, because you're going to promise me
that you won't."

"You do have a mind of your own, don't you?
Very well, I promise."

His smile was amused and thoughtful as he looked
down at her. Then his smile faded. Maria swayed
toward him. He took her in his arms, bending over
her. Their lips touched, and he pulled her closer,
lifting her as he covered her lips with his. She
breathed in the fresh, masculine scent of his body
and the taste of his mouth was in hers. A golden,
tingling warmth built up within her, becoming fiery

and demanding. She thrust herself against him, opening her lips wider. He kissed her passionately, crushing her to him.

He put her down, breathing heavily. Her trapper's hat had fallen off, and he picked it up and handed it to her. She put it on, feeling dizzy and numb from the breathless, urgent forces pounding within her. They walked to the horses, unspeaking. Curtis untied the hobbles on both, then put the thongs through the ring on the side of her saddle and handed her her reins. She tossed the reins over the horse's head and mounted while Curtis was getting up on his own saddle.

"If I can get away again, Maria, then I'll . . . well, we'll see what happens."

"Yes, all right."

"Goodbye, Maria."

"Goodbye, Curtis."

Maria watched him canter away northward until his figure disappeared. Then she rode toward her rendezvous with Harnett.

She didn't tell Seth about her day with Curtis Kruger as they rode slowly back to the pack trains. Maybe he knew anyway. Her lips still burned redly from the torrid kiss and her eyes were wet and shining.

Days passed, and Maria's only contacts with Curtis were surreptitious—looks and fleeting smiles when they passed each other at campsites. As the trains moved on west, she continued to ride out with Harnett, on a hunt now for young calf buffalo among some scattered herds which had separated from a massive herd several miles south of the river.

She'd search the prairie for Curtis on those days but did not see him. He was busy helping his father. Or could not find her on the vast prairie if he was occasionally riding out. She did not know, knew only that she missed him.

She had a feeling of priceless opportunity slipping by, of herself powerless to do anything but watch it fade. The grass grew sparser as they traveled west, the buffalo more scarce. Harnett told her the country would change radically soon, They'd be passing bluffs and chimney rock as they approached the Laramie crossing. The high flat plains would end and the broken country leading into the mountains would begin. He didn't think it wise to let her ride alone when they reached the rocks, he said, because of the increased dangers and the greater likelihood of her becoming lost.

So soon she would have no chance of meeting Curtis alone. At night as she tried to sleep, the memory of his kiss and of the blissful few hours they had spent together gnawed at her torturously.

Almost two weeks had passed and her hopes of a tryst with Curtis had begun to dim. That morning she saw a rider to the north. It was early, Harnett had ridden away to the southwest a short time before, and Maria, sitting her horse, struggled vainly to keep her excitement down, fearful she would be plunged into despair. The rider was distant and could be any man from the pack trains out on a hunt. Yet this rider was moving slowly, as though searching for something harder to find than a band of buffalo.

The distant figure disappeared and reappeared, moving across the swales on a line that would take him east of her. Then he swerved toward her. Maria watched with bated breath, straining her eyes to distinguish characteristics. Shimmering heat waves rising from the prairie distorted her vision, and the yearning throbbing within her made her wary of seeing things that weren't there. Then she became ecstatic. It was him. Pride and self-respect dictated some measure of reserve, but she couldn't contain herself. She shouted with delight, drummed her heel against her horse and waved wildly as she rode toward him in a pounding run.

Then she pulled up, leaning back against the reins and bringing her horse to a sliding stop. The head and wide, strong shoulders were the same, but instead of being held back and straight, they were hunched forward in a kind of bullying pugnaciousness. The man's hat brim was pulled low. It was Stephen. She was crushed with disappointment.

She watched Stephen continue to ride toward her, chilled now with apprehension. This was the man who had tried to rape her. Her mouth became dry, her hands damp. He reined up a few yards from her and surveyed her with callous, boldly insolent eyes. She felt naked. A sardonic smile spread across his face.

"I wondered why Curtis has been in such a heat to get away. Now I see. But I got away instead. I expect I'll do, won't I?"

Maria, turning crimson, jerked her horse around, thumping her heel against its side. "You'd better stay away from me if you don't want my pa to kill you!"

His horse leaped forward as he jabbed it with his heels. He wheeled around in front of her horse and jerked it to a stop, snapping the reins back so that it arched its neck, opened its mouth and stamped, trying to ease the hard pressure of the bit. "You don't know the difference," he jeered. "You thought I was him, didn't you? Well, just pretend that I am."

"I said for you to stay away from me!" Maria shouted, her voice trembling with anger and fear. She backed her horse away from his. "My pa will kill you!"

"No, he won't." He chuckled scornfully, shaking his head. "Because he won't know anything about it. When the time comes for you to tell him, you won't want to."

"You're crazy!" she stormed. "Do you think you can do anything you want and get away with it?"

"No. But I know what you'll do better than you do." He laughed derisively as he nudged his horse, keeping it in front of hers. He moved his rifle to his other hand and reached for her arm. "Now get off that horse!"

Panic gripped Maria. She fumbled at the hammer on her rifle as she pulled away from him and tried to swing her horse around. Her hands were damp with sweat and trembling. The hammer slid from her fingers as he swerved his horse closer to hers again. Suddenly, the rifle thundered, belching a thick cloud of smoke, almost flying from her hands as it recoiled. His horse's flailing front hoofs, only dimly visible through the smoke, reared up as it screamed in fright. Her own horse reared and she felt herself sliding from the saddle. She snatched at the saddle horn and threw her weight forward over its neck, clutching the rifle to her. Her horse settled and shot forward. The saddle bounced wildly under her, slamming into her thighs and buttocks as she struggled to pull herself upright. The horse fought the bit as she pulled back on the reins. Then she regained her balance and got control of it, putting her weight back on the reins until the horse slowed, tossed its head once and began cantering away with a hard, nervous gait.

Some distance off, Maria turned and saw that Stephen had been thrown to the ground during the melee. His horse was a hundred yards from him and galloping toward the north. He had climbed to his feet and was shaking his head dazedly. She saw him take an abortive running step toward his horse, then turn to gaze at her. She had stopped her horse to look at him. An expression of amused disdain crossed his face as he saw her still there. Then he laughed out loud.

Maria flushed and spurred her horse on southward. A maelstrom of fury, disappointment and mortification seethed within her. She'd escaped being raped again, yes, but her frustration was as great as her relief. There was something Stephen had said that was true; she *wouldn't* tell her father. Or anyone else. The tears came in a sudden, hot flood. She wept brokenly as she rode along. Then she sank into a dull, leaden depression. It had been worse than the night in the tent. There Stephen had seemed only a disembodied, threatening force, inciting no feeling in her but the desperate need to resist. Now, though he hadn't touched her, he had defiled her. She felt hollow, lonely and lost. Somehow, he had cast a blight even over the happy moments she had spent with Curtis and over her expectations of seeing him again. He had made her joy with Curtis a cause for shame.

Further on, she stopped to rest her horse and reload her rifle. As she watched the horse munch mouthfuls of grass, a new and grim determination grew within her. She took a harder look at herself. She wouldn't speak of the rape attempt because she couldn't afford to become a target of gossip, not here in the wilderness where people were so few. It was unjust—terribly unjust—to let Stephen go free and unpunished. But the world, this world, this society, was as it was. She wanted revenge against Stephen but not at the price of exposing herself as a fallen woman. Even if her father killed Stephen, that's what he and the others would call her, a fallen woman.

Maybe, if need be, she could handle Stephen herself.

She would have to be careful because he was dangerous. Absently, she cocked her rifle, her eyes fixed on the prairie's waving grasses. Then she realized what she was feeling and doing and a cold shudder ran through her. Kill Stephen? The idea of killing anyone horrified her. In the confusion that had unhorsed him, her gun had gone off by accident.

She could not make the notion of killing Stephen real in her mind. There was a shadow between the idea and the reality.

But—for self-protection—she could keep the rifle constantly with her from now on, couldn't she?

She rendezvoused with Harnett late that afternoon. By then she had a firm resolve about her and, as she rode up to the rise on which he was waiting, he scrutinized her closely.

"Did you see anything today?"

Maria shook her head. "Just a lot of prairie. How about you?"

He shrugged and shook his head, then frowned slightly. "Are you all right?"

Maria forced a bright smile, sitting up on her saddle. "I'm just a little tired. You didn't see any buffalo up that way?"

"I seen some dust off to the south. We should be able to find them when we want them for a while yet. And it won't be long until we'll be able to find us a deer. I'll show you how you can get right up to one close enough to salt its tail."

Maria nodded. They rode at a slow walk for a while, Maria absorbed in her thoughts. Then she said quietly, "You never have told me why you've gone to all this trouble to teach me things, Seth. You've told me many things, but somehow . . ." After her encounter with Stephen, feelings of trust were weak within her, and she looked at Seth wonderingly.

"It ain't often that a body has got just one reason for doing something, Maria." Harnett smiled fondly. "You do put me in mind of my Sarah but I expect it's more than that, since Sarah's dead. You're young and growing. Like I'm growing, being with you. I like to see you learning things and stretching your wings. I'm learning, watching you. Hunting's what I know, and maybe shifting for myself. Maybe you'll never really have to shift for yourself, if'n you marry some good man who does all your shifting for you. But you never can tell what you'll need to know. It sort of depends on what you want to do."

Maria mused as they rode, then looked back at him. "I'll tell you what I want to do. I want to be able to do as I like and go wherever I feel like, not do and go as somebody else tells me. My ma has been at my pa's beck and call most of her life, and I don't want to be like that."

Harnett shrugged. "Mebbe so. But when somebody puts the victuals in your mouth and the clothes on your back, Maria, seems to me they got a right to tell you what to do."

"That could be, but a lot of people do as they like. You do."

"I ain't always done as I liked. I learned to. And I ain't saying it can't be done, only that it ain't easy. First you find your mountain, then you climb it. Maybe you're close to finding yours. Maybe you even found it."

"How do you mean?"

"I told you a long time ago that the mountains for some ain't made out of dirt and rocks and trees, Maria. A lot of people have climbed mighty high mountains without stepping off the boardwalks in a town. But finding where they're at is more than half of the problem.

"Here you want to do what you like. That's your mountain. Well, part of the climb, maybe just the foothills, is finding the money to put your own victuals in your mouth and clothes on your back. Now, that ain't easy. It ain't easy for me, and a woman on her own is in an even chancier shape, Maria. She ain't big and she ain't strong like a man. But then a porcupine ain't big and strong like a grizzly, and I ain't never heard of a grizzly giving one any trouble. A little woman can whittle a big man right down. If that's what she wants to do, she can find a way to do it."

Maria cast a quick look down at her rifle, then sighed heavily. "I think my big problem is going to be finding money, Seth."

"It might be. So stick with that for now. There ain't a lot of ways a woman's got of getting money. Could be as tough as Eli Bodine found it. Is it all right if I tell you about Eli? I admire him."

"Yes, please tell me about him."

"There was this mountain trapper, old Eli Bodine, and him and a bunch was headed in to the post to trade their furs. It was on down into spring and the Bighorn River was flooded, and they was worried about how they was going to cross it. Except for old Eli. He hadn't had a taste of tobacco or whiskey in a year, and he was damn sure he was going to cross one way or t'other. Well, they struck the Bighorn just below Pilchard's Gulch, and it was a raging froth, yea wide, yea deep and white water and rocks everywhere. Old Eli just built hisself a bullboat and commenced. The others just stayed to see where he was going to wash up so's they could bury him. So there old Eli went, with a crowd of vultures watching him. He had mebbe ten boatloads of furs. The first time he crossed, his boat got near tore to pieces. So he fixed it and come back for another load. Back and forth he went, tearing his boat to pieces, fixing it up, tearing it, fixing it, like that, until he had all his durned furs across. Then he went on to the trading post. The rest of the bunch stayed on the other side, gawking at him. That spot on the Bighorn where he went over, they call it Bodine's Crossing now."

Maria smiled as he finished. She'd liked the story. Then she fell to musing. "Beaver pelts are worth a lot of money, aren't they?" she said.

"Soft gold," Harnett said, nodding. "That's about all I trap for."

"Would you show me how to catch beaver?"

Harnett hesitated. "There's more to it than that, Maria. Trapping's a way of life, not just a thing somebody does. There ain't no beaver around Fort Henry, for one thing. They like to be where people ain't. You got to want to go after them."

She pondered for a moment. "Would you take me out trapping with you?"

Harnett rolled the tobacco in his mouth, leaned over and spat. "You've got time to give it more thought, Maria. Take the time. If you got to stumbling around lost while I was in the midst of my trapping, I probably wouldn't see my way clear to looking for you until I got done. That's one thing. Then, you know what your pa would think about your going off."

"He'd have a fit."

"He rightly would."

"He would be put out at you too, wouldn't he?"

"I ain't worried about that," Harnett said.

Maria wet her lips. "If I went, if I crossed over like that, it would be sort of like Bodine's Crossing, wouldn't it?"

Harnett laughed. "It shorely would."

"Well, I'll think about it. And maybe when I get to it, I'll just bust right on across."

He looked at her, his eyes twinkling. "If you do, I'll be waiting on the other side, Maria." He glanced up at the sky, nudging his horse with his heels. "It's getting late, and we'd better get on in."

Part Three

THE MOUNTAINS

8

Maria put the hatchet down, turned the bench back over onto its legs, and rocked it back and forth. The legs were firm and even, and Maria picked up the hatchet and stood up. "That should take care of it."

Mercy looked over her shoulder from the washstand, a pleased smile on her face. "Oh, yes, I can see from here that it's setting more even, Maria. It's awful to try to eat when the bench is trying to dump you on the floor, ain't it? Would you see if you could do something about my stool? Your pa said he would look at it, but it looks like he ain't going to have time. . . ."

Maria crossed the cabin to the fireplace, ducking her head as she walked under the bunches of onions, clusters of herbs and strings of dried fruit hanging from the low beams in the ceiling. She knelt by the

135

hearth, turned the stool over and examined it. "I'll cut some wedges and drive them in around the legs. That should tighten it up."

"I'd sure be obliged, Maria. I've been afraid to sit on it. You might chop me another stick or two of wood while you're out there at the block."

Maria nodded as she went out. Outside, she caused a stir. The cabin was one of four spaced several yards apart in a line facing the trading post across a bare, dusty stretch of trampled dirt. Sheds, storage buildings and a low barn extended from the end cabin to the trading post, making an open-ended rectangle of buildings. Four half-breed children playing in front of a cabin looked at her with frank curiosity, as did an Indian squaw mending clothes on a bench. Men shoeing horses in the open-fronted blacksmith shop craned their heads around at her. Maria put the stool down and went to the chopping block. She selected a log from a nearby pile and set to work hatcheting some wedge-size slivers from it.

Maria had just about gotten used to being stared at. The Indians who hung around the fort had never seen a white woman, and many of its white employees hadn't seen one for months or years. For Maria, the fort had been a pleasant surprise, not at all a place of miserable isolation, such as she had anticipated. She liked the old, solid buildings, and, at some point, Harnett's obsession with the wilderness had been at least partially communicated to her. She'd learned to feel at home on the prairie; now she was still appreciating the beauty and grandeur of the towering, craggy mountains. St. Louis was gone, if not forgotten; at least, she no longer yearned for her old life there.

Not that her enjoyment of the trek through the

mountains had been unmixed. Each day's journey had brought her closer to a separation from Curtis. She hadn't been close to him again, not since that one time on the prairie, but at least she had known he was nearby, working with his father's pack trains.

But then, finally, the day of parting had wrenchingly come. It had been marred by an explosive confrontation between Kruger, Fitzpatrick and several of the other Rocky Mountain Fur Company men. Sometime during the trip, Kruger had talked to the bush lopers and offered them higher wages than they were being paid by Fitzpatrick. He had lured away several which had enraged the company men. Maria had thought there was going to be a fight. But Kruger had ignored their angry curses and threats. With stolid indifference, he'd readied his pack trains and led the bush lopers away. Curtis had looked back to catch a last glimpse of Maria as they rode into the forest. She'd never forget the forlorn expression in his eyes nor the forlorn ache in her heart.

Now the breeze stirred Maria's hair and dress as she turned the stool over and pushed wood slivers into the holes around the legs. She shivered. The trading post was located in a place of rare beauty, a high mountain valley with wooded slopes and jagged peaks towering into the sky around it, but it was autumn and the peaks were snow-capped and the air had a frosty bite where she was.

The activity around the blacksmith shop was another indication of the advancing season. Trappers were shoeing their horses, ready to leave. When Maria had arrived three days before, a Rocky Mountain Fur Company brigade led by the famous trapper and guide Jedediah Smith had already left for the mountain streams. Now the free trappers were going, bagged up with their supplies and equipment. Only a few, including Seth Harnett, were being more leisurely about their departure. Seth would be at the fort a few more days yet, she hoped.

Maria hammered in the slivers of wood with the back of the hatchet, chopped up a piece of a thick branch for firewood and brought it and the stool back inside. Her mother had a Betty lamp lit on the table. The lamp and the fireplace filled the cabin with a cozy, cheerful glow, and it felt comfortably warm after the chilly breeze outside. Maria crossed the room to the fireplace, and her mother pulled a pan on the hearth out of the way as she knelt to put the things down.

"Just throw a couple of pieces of that wood on the fire and put the rest over there, Maria. Could you do anything with that stool?"

"Yes, I wedged in the legs, and it's all right now."

"Laws, you're getting as handy to have around as a man, ain't you, Maria?" Mercy peered through the cabin window at the gathering darkness. "Sakes, it's only four o'clock," she mused. "Don't it get dark early here?"

"The sun sets early with these high mountains all around, and it's getting late in the season. Winter isn't far away from the feel of air outside."

Her mother frowned as she stirred and salted a pan of mixed rice and beans on the hearth. "It'll probably snow a lot here. But we'll be really snug in this cabin, won't we? Ain't it a nice cabin?"

"Yes, it's a nice cabin."

"I just love this hearth with the nice big hob and everything, and that big washstand over there and the bowl somebody left for us. And you know, I was thinking about scratching out a garden patch out behind here in the spring, Maria. Somebody's been growing corn over by the stock pens behind the trading post, and I'll bet they done really good as rich as this soil is."

Maria nodded, rising and walking toward her room. "Yes, they probably did."

"I'll bet they did. Maria, are you feeling all right?"

"Yes, I'm all right, ma. Why?"

Mercy looked at Maria worriedly. "I don't know, it just seems like you've been happy one minute and mopesy the next ever since we got here. Are you worried about your pa being gone? If you are, you can set your mind at ease. All them men at the trading post will still be there if we need anything, and we'll be all right."

"No, I'm not worried, ma."

"All right, then, Maria. . . ."

Maria went to her room and sat down on her bunk with a heavy sigh.

She'd become indecisive again about going off with Harnett. Unexpectedly, she'd grown concerned about leaving her mother. True, her mother had made friends with the Indian squaws of men who worked in the trading post, and the men themselves would be available for assistance and advice. So she wouldn't be alone or helpless. Still, Maria felt guilty. She'd been observing her mother closely during the past days, perhaps more closely than ever before now that they were cooped up together in the small lean-to cabin. It touched her with a wrenching pathos that her mother should take such apparent pleasure in these few meager sticks of homemade furniture, her stool, her plans to make a garden. Her mother had little and it seemed to take little to satisfy her. But Maria saw herself as her mother's major concern, and if she left it would distress her greatly.

As a result of her talks with Harnett, Maria's attitude toward her father had also changed somewhat. Before, she had regarded him as a ruthless tyrant, with no fair basis for the authority he exerted over her. But Harnett saw her version of "fairness" as totally irrelevant to life, and that was beginning to make sense to her. Rights had to be carved out through painful effort rather than granted. Maria could acknowledge that her father did have some basis for his authority over her, since he fed and clothed her. That much she could see. But she was still terribly afraid of his rage should she attempt to leave and feed herself.

All in all, she was still finding it extremely difficult to leave home. Her mountain remained high and forbidding.

Maria sighed again, rose from her bunk and, bending over under the low ceiling, went back into the front room. "Is there anything I can do to help you?"

"No, I've about got it in hand here, Maria. I just hope that your pa will be here while everything's still hot and . . . oh, that's him coming there, ain't it? Well, he's just in time." She looked over her shoulder at the doorway. "Come on in and sit down at the table, Pierre. I was just getting ready to dish everything up."

Maria had noticed that her mother could recognize her and her father's footsteps even when they were buried in the sound of other people's footsteps or obscured by other noises. And she had noticed her mother's intense pleasure when everyone was ready to eat just at the time that the meal was freshly-cooked and hot. DeVises closed the door and hung his hat on a peg by it. He glanced around as he took off his coat. His eyes passed over Maria without hesitating, his expression neutral.

"You sure are getting things fixed up, Mercy."

"Well, this is a really nice cabin and I like fixing it up, and Maria sure has been a good help, Pierre. Go ahead and sit down. You sit down too, Maria. You won't have to go back after you eat, will you, Pierre?"

"No, we're about through now. Maria, you could give your mother a hand instead of watching her."

"No, I have everything ready now, Pierre. We'd just be in each other's way. You say everything's about done?"

"That's right, we'll be leaving in the morning."

Mercy carried two bowls to the table and walked back toward the fireplace as Maria and DeVises sat down at the table. "Laws, with all the people around here, I don't see how you men keep it straight in your mind as to who's going with who."

"It's easy enough. Fitzpatrick, Bridger and several others are partners in the company, and they lead the brigades. I'm in Fitzpatrick's brigade, along with several other trappers and a bunch of bush lopers. Jake Ludlow is an employee rather than a partner, but he's a good man and has been with the company for a while, so he leads a brigade and gets an extra share of the furs for doing it. I'm hoping I can do the same within a year or two."

"I hope you can too, Pierre. They were talking about another brigade that left before we got here. Who were they?"

"Well, they were Jed Smith's men, and he's also

a partner. Ben Clyman is still another partner who left with his brigade before we got here. They both came here straight from the rendezvous, like we will next year. We'll go out to the trapping grounds and come back in here for supplies in December or January, then we'll go back to the trapping grounds, finish off the season, and go to the rendezvous. One of the Sublette brothers, who are also partners in the company, will meet us there with pack trains of supplies and take the furs back to St. Louis."

"There's sure a bunch of partners, ain't they?" Mercy chuckled, putting another bowl on the table and taking the plates and spoons from a shelf. "And from what you said about that rendezvous before, it's not the kind of thing I'd like to be at."

DeVises laughed. "Well, you got to expect some cutting up, Mercy. It's a big company, with up to six trapping brigades out at times and a supply brigade to bring things in. And as far as the rendezvous goes, it's a big thing for a lot of the trappers and traders, as well as the Indians. Different tribes and just about all the free trappers and traders in the mountains meet there along with the company men. The American Fur Company also sends a pack train to try to get some of the business, but our company has been getting most of it so far."

"Well, as long as the company's doing good, that's good for us, I expect," Mercy said.

"It is. You won't be out here in the woods forever, Mercy. If things go right for us, we'll be set for the rest of our lives within the next four or five years."

Mercy took the coffeepot back to the hearth. She smiled and shrugged as she returned to the table and sat down. "Don't hold your breath until you

hear me complaining, Pierre. This cabin here and
knowing that we're prospering suits me just fine.
Here, get all you want of this pork. I fried plenty
of it, because it's starting to go off a little and we
need to get it eat up. Pass your pa the beans and
rice, Maria."

They passed the bowls around and filled their
plates, and DeVises took a bite from his plate and
looked at Mercy again, chewing. "The men at the
trading post will keep plenty of game meat in. And
if you need any corn, flour, salt, spices, anything
like that, just go over and get it. They'll keep a bill
on it. And as I said, if you need any help with anything, just let them know. Porter will be in charge
over there, and he's a good man."

"Laws, we'll be all right, Pierre," Mercy said.
"Don't you worry about us. You just worry about
all them Indians and the other things that you'll be
running into."

"Well, we probably won't even see any Indians,"
DeVises replied, taking another bite. He looked at
Maria.

"Mind your mother while I'm gone, hear?"

"She'll mind, Pierre," Mercy said. "We have
plenty to keep us busy. We have the Bible and our
books to read, and we have all new quilts to make
and everything. We have enough to keep four
women busy."

DeVises grunted, chewing and swallowing, and
took a drink of coffee. "Then you keep her busy,
because I don't want any trouble among the men
at the trading post over her displaying herself. Half
the young bucks in the brigade that's leaving decided they wanted to stay and work at the trading
post when they saw her."

"She's a pretty girl, Pierre," Mercy chuckled. "Of course boys are going to want to be around her. You might as well try to get the sun to rise in the west as to try to stop that. And you remember how that young Fitzpatrick boy was mooning around her."

DeVises smiled thinly and nodded as he took another bite. He looked at Maria thoughtfully. "Tom has mentioned that two or three times too. That boy comes from a good family and he's supposed to be coming out here next year. If he's set up right and does all right, we might be well off to make him welcome."

"There's plenty of time to think about things like that," Mercy said, shaking her head. "She's just a girl."

"Just a girl? You were a married woman at her age. I'd give a lot to have her half as settled as you were then instead of all the time into some foolishness with Seth Harnett."

"Laws, you don't remember, do you?" Mercy chortled. "I didn't have enough sense to crack a walnut when I was her age. Don't you remember that first kettle you bought me? The first time I had it on a fire, I burned a hole clean through the bottom of it. And Maria ain't short on sense, Pierre."

DeVises smiled slightly and shrugged. "You were a little addled, Mercy, but you had plenty of the kind of sense that a woman needs. And while Maria might have sense in some things, she needs to have more like you."

"Everybody's different, Pierre, and she'll more than do."

DeVises made a doubtful sound in his throat and shrugged again, and they became silent as they ate.

Mercy finished eating and went to the fireplace for the coffeepot to refill DeVises' cup, and Maria rose and began collecting up the plates.

"I'll do that, Maria," Mercy said. "Just leave them be."

"There's no reason why she shouldn't wash a plate now and then," DeVises said.

"Yes, but I'm still trying to get everything clean from the trip, and I'm using wood ash on them, Pierre. I'm used to it, but I don't want Maria to get her hands in it. You do something else, Maria, and I'll do that."

Maria nodded, putting the plates down, and she walked toward her room. She had been using wood ashes to polish pots, pans, and other metal utensils from the time she had been a small girl, but for some reason her mother had continued with the practice she had started on the trail of doing all the cooking and washing of dishes, declining Maria's help and giving implausible reasons for doing so. Maria wasn't sure but from learning from Harnett to keep her eyes and ears open a bit more, she saw her mother as having strong feelings of propriety. She'd reacted about the same the few times her father offered to help in the kitchen. Regardless of the many different reasons she'd given, she just didn't want him to do it.

Maria and her mother had washed all the clothes the day after they arrived, and torn seams had shown up on some of Maria's clothing. In her room she picked out a petticoat and two dresses so damaged and took them back to sew up. DeVises was sitting on his stool by the hearth, smoking his pipe, and Mercy was washing dishes at the washstand. Maria put the clothing on the table, opened her mother's sewing box and took out a needle and thread. She sat down and started, threading the needle.

"I forgot to do that stool for you, Mercy. I'll take a look at it directly."

"Oh, Maria fixed that, Pierre. She also fixed that bench, this shutter here, the latch on the door, and a lot of other things too."

The reply didn't please him. He looked at Maria, puffing on his pipe. "If you have the notion that you're going to do any hunting here, you can just get the notion out of your mind. You leave what should be done by a man to the men here, and you stay in this cabin."

Maria nodded silently, a cold feeling in the pit of her stomach. He was impossible. She was afraid to open her mouth. She was afraid of her own rage, afraid that she would scream here in this—this wilderness—this lonely place in which the person she was was being totally ignored. Her fingers trembled as she continued sewing, threading the needle, stitching up a seam, biting off the thread, and stitching another seam.

It is the mountain, she thought, *my mountain, nobody else's. I must learn to climb it.*

But she went numb with the effort. She finished repairing the petticoat and two dresses, took them into her room and put them away, then went to bed. DeVises and Mercy talked for a while longer by the fireplace, then they went to bed. The cabin was quiet and the breeze rustled outside, blowing through the cracks between the logs and making Maria's face and hands cold as she looked up at the low, slanted roof in the darkness. Her mind raced into a daydream. It would be cold in the mountains during the winter. It would be beautifully sharp and clear. But she might become ill. Harnett was an old man, and he might become ill or be injured. She lay sleepless for a long time, wrestling with herself. Then her thoughts became sluggish and the mists of sleep closed in.

Noises from the front room awakened her at dawn, though she did not feel awake, not truly. Her mother and father were talking quietly and moving around, her father sounding hurried and her mother tearful. Maria groggily pushed the blanket down, got up and dressed slowly. The front door opened and closed. Maria went into the front room, pulling her hair back and tying it. Her mother was kneeling in front of the hearth moving pans around, and her eyes were red and damp as she looked over her shoulder.

"Your pa said he'd be back in a little while to say goodbye. He didn't have time for me to warm this up, and he just ate a bite of it cold. I'll heat it up for you."

"I'm not hungry."

"Well, I'm not neither. I'll just leave it here where we can get a bite of it if we feel like it, and I'll fix a good supper."

"All right."

"And I'll heat up the coffee."

"All right."

The cabin was cold from the chill of the night, and Maria sat on a stool by the hearth. Mercy put the coffeepot on the hob by the fire, sniffling and wiping her eyes with the back of her hands, then went and sat at the table, pulling her shawl around her shoulders. Presently the coffee in the pot made a singing noise as it heated. Mercy went to a shelf and took down a cup, came to the fireplace and filled it with coffee, then put the cup on the hearth in front of Maria and returned to the table.

It was all like a dream to Maria, a continuation of the one she'd had while asleep. She sipped the coffee, and it was tasteless.

A muffled sound of activity around the trading post gradually became louder, as men bustled about shouting at each other and horses stamped, snorted and neighed. Maria's hands suddenly trembled on the coffee cup. She wondered if Harnett would be leaving today.

Rapid footsteps approached the door, and Mercy stood up. DeVises came in hurriedly, and Mercy moved toward him. They embraced and kissed, and DeVises moved back toward the door with her, his arm around her shoulders. "I'll see you in a few months, Mercy."

"Yes, be careful and . . . well, goodbye, Pierre."

"Goodbye, Mercy. Goodbye, Maria."

"Goodbye, pa."

He went back out, and Mercy stood in the doorway, sobbing quietly. Maria put the cup down and crossed the room to the doorway. Dawn was breaking, and the air had a frigid, penetrating touch. Men and horses were shadowy and indistinct in the flat, grey light as two of the brigades moved out with their long lines of pack horses. Mercy stepped outside, and Maria remained in the doorway. She saw the three Indian squaws who lived in the other cabins doing the same, standing in their doorways, their children around them, waving their men goodbye.

Bridger's brigade filed across the rectangle of packed dirt. Ludlow's brigade was going in the other direction, out from the rear of the trading post and across a field. The stock pens looked deserted, with only a few horses in them now. Fitzpatrick shouted orders, and a large cluster of horses in front of the trading post began forming a line. They clopped across the rectangle and out of the fort at a slow walk, Fitzpatrick first in line and DeVises right behind him. They waved, and Maria and Mercy waved back. The light in the valley brightened as they moved across it toward the creek. They grew smaller in the distance as they crossed the creek and went through the meadow on the other side. Then they were gone.

The sun peeked over the high mountains now flooding the valley with its full light. Mercy went back into the cabin. Maria started to go in, then hesitated. Her heart lifting, she saw Harnett among the men still in front of the trading post. He waved a cheery hello. Maria waved, then went into the cabin.

There were chores to be done, Maria supposed. Mercy began scrubbing the puncheon floor in the front room of the cabin, and Maria went back outside, nervously looking for something to do. A lot of the mud chinking had fallen from between the logs in the cabin, so she went to the creek for water and handfuls of long grass and laboriously began re-chinking them.

The sun warmed the air as it rose higher, and Maria worked her way around the cabin, going to the creek for more water, mixing mud and cutting up grass in it when she had to. At midday she went back inside. Mercy was still scrubbing the floor, her face pale and her eyes red. Maria felt nauseous. It seemed to her she had to be hungry for it was lunchtime. So she ate some of the food left over from the night before, then went back outside and finished filling the cracks.

She saw Porter come out of the trading post and help Harnett load up his pack horse. Suddenly, her head spun. So soon Seth was leaving, so soon? In her confusion, she clutched at her stomach—the high hot sun, the leftover food she had eaten, they were making her ill. But she knew better than that. She leaned on the door jamb but stood her ground as Harnett, seeing her, mounted his saddle horse and slowly rode over.

"How do, Maria."

"Hello, Seth."

"Well, I'm setting out. I'm always skittish that some of these fellows around here will follow me to my trapping ground, so I'll be camping for the night up on top of that hill there so I can watch my back trail."

"That's a good idea."

Seth spat, wiped his mouth with the back of his hand and nudged his horse with his heels. "Goodbye, Maria."

"Goodbye, Seth."

She watched him move away toward the meadow, the nausea churning in her stomach and her face in a cold sweat. When he was gone, she tried chopping wood but it was no use, she couldn't do it, all she could think of was the long distance she would have to go on foot to get to the hill before dark. She stuck the axe in the chopping block and walked into the cabin.

Her mother had a large stack of pots and pans on the washstand, and she was polishing them with wood-ashes. Maria went into her room. She had rehearsed this moment dozens of times in her mind, but never had she done it with fear tearing at her vitals. She quickly collected up a few underclothes and a blanket and pushed them into a canvas bag. She put on her hat, slipped the thongs of her powder horn and shot pouch over her shoulder, then picked up the bag and her rifle and went back into the front room.

"Maria, I know you didn't have much to eat today, so I'll fix you a really good . . ." Mercy's mouth dropped open. "What are you doing, Maria?"

"I'm going trapping, ma."

The pan Mercy was holding clattered to the floor and her face blanched. "You're going *what?* Why, Maria, you know what your pa would . . . you can't go out in no woods, Maria. Why, you could get . . . anything could happen. . . ."

"I'll be all right, ma. You'll just have to believe me about that. Goodbye, ma."

"No, you can't go!" Mercy shouted. Tears gathered in her eyes. "I'll go right over there and get some of them men, and they'll bring you back here so fast that—"

"They'll get killed trying," Maria said narrowly, "You send a man after me, ma, and you'll be sending him to his death. I can shoot this rifle good."

"Don't do this to me, Maria," Mercy pleaded. Her features twisted and she began weeping as she stumbled toward Maria and clutched at her. "You're my daughter, Maria, and I love you. God, don't do this to me. . . ."

"I'm going, ma," Maria said, jerking her arm away from her mother and walking toward the door. "I'll be back in a few months."

"No, Maria, no . . . don't do this to me. . . ."

Maria went out and walked rapidly toward the

end cabin as Marcy collapsed against the doorjamb, weeping hysterically and calling to her. An Indian squaw came out of the end cabin to look at her, puzzled, then quickly stepped aside. Maria strode on, her ears deaf to her mother's pleadings behind her. She followed the trampled path the horses had made through the meadow. Her heart pounded and she heard nothing. Only when she reached the foot of the hill did she stop and turn. The fort was silent. No men had been sent after her. But now, as her head and heart cleared of her dark storms of anger, she seemed to hear a distant whisper, the sound of her mother's weeping.

She turned. The horses had left a wide, deep trail through a soft forest that skirted the near side of the hill. She went through the forest, as through darkness, and then started climbing.

She felt now as if she was on a perilous journey alone. She was utterly lost. When she came back, if she came back at all, she would have to come back a changed person, someone who might bear the name Maria DeVises but would not be the same long-cowering child she had left behind. She did not know if she could do this. Still now in her mind her mother pleaded, "Come back, Maria, I *need* you," and her father threatened, "You shall suffer for this, Maria, you shall suffer." Their voices were growing stronger with each step up the hill she took.

Maria trudged on.

Harnett was sitting on a stone near his campfire. Maria had found him by following the scent of his woodsmoke. He was stirring a small kettle. Near him horses stamped and snorted.

"How do, Maria."

"Hello, Seth."

Maria put her rifle and bag down, took the powder horn and shot pouch off her shoulder and sat down on the stone next to him. She was soaked with sweat. She began shivering almost immediately as the sweat began drying in the cool mountain air. Harnett stood up and bent over the stack of bags, pulling a heavy buffalo skin from one of them.

"I have a blanket," Maria said.

"This'll be warmer. That's a good climb, and you have to watch getting het up and cooling down too fast. I see you tore your dress. I have a roll of buckskins you can use to make yourself something more fitten to wear. And another buffalo skin you can use to make a coat when it turns chilly."

Maria pulled the buffalo skin around her. It smelled pungent, musky, heavy with animal scent. Harnett gave her some coffee from the kettle, then a tin plate of jerky. Maria started to take a bite. Almost immediately her mother's voice came back and she saw her pleased face: "I'm fixin' something good for you for dinner, Maria, something real good."

The spoon rattled against her plate and she sobbed violently. She managed to put the plate down before burying her face in her hands.

Harnett watched her cry.

After a while, she picked up her head and said, sniffling, "I'm sorry, Seth, I—"

"That's all right, Maria. Take your time. That jerky's dried. It'll keep."

He smiled at her.

Maria nodded, sniffling and gulping. A minute or so later, she picked up her plate again.

9

"There's another one just on this side of that big rock over there. Now tell me how I know it's there."

"The ground is low and it would be soft and easy to dig in, and the tunnel would stay under water even if the level of the pond fell a little."

Harnett nodded. "That's right. Now like I told you, they have these tunnels dug all around their pond to run into if a wolverine, bear, or something like that starts rooting into their lodge trying to get at them. They're in and out of them tunnels all the time, and it's one of the best places to catch them. You can get to where you can stand and look at a pond and figure out where every tunnel in it is, if you'll just think like a beaver. It's important to be able to do that, because you won't be able to walk along and pick out the tunnels after the ponds freeze over and we get a foot of snow on the ground. You set this one, and I'll watch."

Maria's buckskins still felt strange on her. Her feet were almost bare on the ground with only the soles of her moccasins under them, and she felt bare too around her legs, with no petticoat and skirt brushing against them. She also felt immodest in buckskins, the breeches and leggings clinging to her thighs and calves and the shirt fitting tightly over her breasts, waist and hips. And they were chilly even under the buffalo skin coat, because some of the stitches she had taken with the awl and buckskin thongs had been hurriedly made and left small openings for the frigid air to seep in. She put her rifle down, selected a trap and one of the green willow stakes from the bag, and walked toward the water.

"If you can, always leave your gunpowder behind when you go anywhere near water."

Maria slipped the powder horn thong off her shoulder and put it down by her rifle, then stepped to the edge of the pond. A long piece of wire was attached to the trap through the ring where the chain was connected. Maria straightened out the wire, set the trip with her foot and lowered it into the shallow water near the tunnel opening. Harnett watched, nodding approvingly, and pointed to a rock a few feet away. Maria went to get the rock and knelt at the edge of the water again, straightening out the chain and reaching for the stake. It had a fork halfway along its length, and she put it through the ring on the end of the chain and drove it into the ground until the fork had the ring pinned firmly. She moved closer to the water and, leaning out over it, picked up the wire and wrapped the end of it around the rock. Then she lowered the rock into the water and carefully laid it on the edge of the deep water by the tunnel.

"Is the water there deep enough?" she asked.

"Plenty deep enough. The first little jerk he gives, he'll snatch that rock off there and it'll carry him to the bottom and drown him before he can twist his foot off. That's a good set, Maria. You go ahead and bait it, and I'll get you some dirt."

Maria took out her skinning knife as she stepped to a sapling a few feet away. She cut a small limb from it, trimmed it and cut off to a twelve-inch length. From her bag she took a small, earthenware bottle and unstoppered it. It gave off the penetrating, pungent odor of the castoreum glands of a beaver. Maria dipped the end of the stick into the bottle, re-stoppered it, then took the scented stick back to the water and planted it by the trap, with the scented end standing a few inches above the surface. Harnett carried a double handful of soft soil to her, and she took it and dribbled it slowly into the water, letting it settle onto the trap.

"That's to hide the trap, isn't it?"

"That, and to help take the human smell off it. When traps have been around people and horses for a while, it might take up to a day or two for the smell to wash off them. After that, human smell will be on them only for a little while when they're reset. But it don't take but a few hours to wash off."

"Isn't there any way to keep the human smell off them while resetting them?"

"If there is I don't know what it would be, because a body's got to touch them to reset them. How many traps do we have left?"

"Three."

"All right, I've got a lot more ways of setting traps to show you, but only enough traps to show you one more. So I'll show you that one, and I'll show you the others when we start moving traps around. Let's walk on down to the dam."

Maria picked up her powder horn, rifle, and the bag of traps, and followed him on along the pond. "Why didn't we put out some traps in these places along here where they've been climbing in and out of the ponds? I've seen them all along the banks."

"Because anybody can do that, and that's what most do. But they don't catch many beavers, because beavers is mighty skittish when they're climbing out of the water. Put your stuff down here, get one of these rocks, and follow me out here."

Maria put her rifle and powder horn down by his as he picked up two rocks. She picked up a rock of her own and followed him out onto the dam, taking careful steps and planting her feet firmly in the tangled mass of interwoven limbs and branches. Harnett stopped a few yards from the bank, looking down into the water. Then he knelt at the edge of the dam and reached down into it, feeling. He nodded, smiling in satisfaction.

"Reach down in here and feel this. You see how them limbs right there make a little platform? Now hand me a trap."

Maria took a trap from the bag and handed it to him. He set it and placed it on the ledge under the water.

"Aren't you going to bait it?"

"I sure am, but not the way you think. Come on."

A few yards farther along, he found another ledge under a few inches of water and set another trap, then set the third one on a ledge near the other end of the dam. After that, he picked out a large underwater limb, gripped it firmly and planted his feet, then heaved up. The limb cracked and loosened. Smaller branches slipped out of place, and water began gurgling through to the surface. As they walked back across the top of the dam, he loosened other limbs and started leaks near the other two traps. He smiled and nodded with satisfaction as they reached the bank.

"Now that's the best bait you can have. When they come out there and start fixing them leaks, then three of them are going to get a foot in a trap and we'll have us three pelts."

"You said they aren't prime yet, didn't you?"

"That's right, but they're in winter hair and they'll be good ones. Come on, let's get back to the cabin. It's getting late, and I'm hungry. I expect you are too, ain't you?"

Maria nodded, picking up her rifle and powder horn. They had been out setting traps since early morning, with Harnett slowly and carefully explaining the different ways one could choose to set a trap in any given place. Maria was weary and cold as well as hungry. Harnett turned and walked back along the edge of the pond, Maria following him. The smooth surface of the pond was broken by three large, dome-shaped beaver lodges spaced along its length, and there were numerous pointed stumps among the aspens, birches, and poplars bordering the pond and extending up the gentle slopes of the valley.

At the upper end of the pond, the creek gurgled over stones for a distance of a hundred yards. Then there was another beaver dam. Harnett slowed, walking more cautiously through the trees as he approached this dam. He craned his neck and looked around a tree, then looked back at Maria and pointed. She stepped up beside him. There were two lodges in the pond, and the brown, chubby shapes of several beavers on top of them stood out sharply against the bleached, greyish wood. Rippling wakes spread back from other beavers swimming about. Maria smiled and nodded. Harnett began walking forward again, skirting around a clutter of sticks and limbs. There was a loud crack of a flat tail slapping the surface of the water, then two more. The airing beavers scrambled into their lodges, and those swimming about dived, leaving small ripples that spread across the pond's surface. The ripples and all sounds faded as Harnett and Maria walked along.

The trees had shed, and the ground was carpeted with a thick bed of leaves. Harnett moved through them with little more than a quiet rustle, and Maria imitated his pace, lifting her feet high and stepping straight down into the leaves instead of dragging her feet through them. He was completely at home in the mountains, constantly monitoring small signs to see what kind of animals had passed that way and when, ceaselessly alert to all the sounds around him. He was as much a part of his surroundings as the bears, deer, and other animals. During the trip in from Fort Henry, he had told her many things; here he could show her those things as well. At the mountain divide he had selected, near the north fork of the Snake River, he was giving her a constant, wide-ranging flow of information on survival, hunting, animal habits, Indian sign. It had been difficult for her to absorb it all, but he was slow, methodical and thorough in his explanations, and his patience was unlimited.

The valley narrowed as they walked to Harnett's cabin. The last pond was barely thirty feet wide but almost a hundred feet long, with four lodges along its center. Above it, the valley flattened out into a small, marshy plateau, where springs flowed together to form the headwaters of the creek. The winter-dried grass on the plateau was thick and deep, brushing against the horses' bellies as they cropped it, and a tall, craggy face of limestone ran along the bottom of a bulge in the mountain overlooking the plateau.

Their cabin, a small structure of logs and sod, was built between the side of the limestone facing and a cluster of trees, on a horizontal outcropping of limestone that served as its foundation and floor.

Maria went straight to the cabin while Harnett tended to the horses outside. The doorway was covered with a stiff, heavy buckskin, which she had to toss back onto the roof to get inside. She hung her rifle, powder horn, and shot pouch on pegs over her bunk, took her tomahawk and long knife from the back of her belt and put them on a shelf at the end of her bunk, then went to the small fireplace in the center of the rear wall and stirred the ashes to uncover the hot coals. She pulled slivers and bits of bark from sticks and dropped them on the coals, blew on them until they burst into flame, then piled sticks onto the fire and held her hands in front of it, warming them.

"That one horse keeps on figuring out how to loosen his hobbles," Harnett said as he came in. "I'm going to break him of it, even if I have to tie his feet together. I'll go get some water."

"All right, I'll start supper cooking."

Harnett gathered up the buckets and carried them out, and Maria followed him out and went around to the side of the cabin. Several skinned rabbits and a quartered deer were hanging in a close-by tree, suspended out of reach of small predators and covered with canvas bags to protect them from birds. Maria took down a rabbit and cut a piece from a quarter of the deer with her skinning knife. She took them into the cabin and began cutting them up into the kettle. Harnett came back in, puffing as he carried the full buckets.

"It's getting cold out there, Maria. I wouldn't be surprised to see snow in the next day or two."

"I wouldn't either. I almost froze today."

"Well, I'll catch some wolverines in the next couple of days so we can make us some boots," he said. He rummaged through the bags of supplies along the front wall of the cabin and got out a bag of flour, which he carried to the fireplace, sitting down then and pulling a pan to him. "And when you make yourself some buckskins with the seams a little tighter, that'll help a lot."

"You can bet that I'm not going to be long doing that."

Harnett chuckled and nodded, pouring flour into the pan. Maria poured water into the kettle and put it on the fire, built up the fire around it, then went to the bags of supplies and took several potatoes and an onion from one. The bags filled the entire front wall of the cabin. It had become obvious to her that Harnett had planned on her joining him from the start. He had brought additional supplies of food staples, gunpowder and lead, many new traps, an extra tomahawk and extra knives. Many of the foodstuffs were of types considered luxuries by most trappers and traders. He had even brought along bags of beads for her to decorate her buckskins.

Maria sat down in front of the fireplace again and began peeling the potatoes. "Do you think we might have some beavers tomorrow?"

"Oh, we might have two or three, but I don't look for many until the traps have been in the water for a while. We'll get our share before we leave here, don't you worry about that."

"I'll need a lot just to pay you back for all the things you brought for me and for my half of all the supplies."

He smiled and shook his head as he kneaded the dough in the pan. "You don't owe me nothing, Maria. All I want to do is what I'm doing. I've still got money left over, and I'll take beaver pelts out of here that'll bring me a bunch more. You don't owe me nothing."

"But that isn't right, Seth."

"I don't know anything about that, Maria. I just know that you don't owe me a cent."

The kettle began steaming, and Maria leaned over and gathered up the bottles of salt, pepper, and sage from beside the fireplace. She opened the bottles and seasoned the stew, then put the bottles back and began peeling another potato. "Are there a lot of places this good for trapping?"

"There's good trapping all through these mountains, but this is an especially good place. And there's more of them around, but you have to have the right nose to smell them out. That's what I'm talking about when I keep telling you that you've got to have the feel of the mountains. Another good thing about this place is that it's high, and Indians like to winter lower down. It wouldn't make a lot of difference, because this is Shoshone country and they're pretty friendly, but a body can always run into a feisty one or two."

"How far have you ever gone to trap?"

"Farther than far, all the way up to Canada and beyond. And all over Blackfoot country. I went up there one year with old Rufus Hany, and we took his wife along because she's a Blackfoot. But I sort of got my feet on the ground up there and got the lay of the land, and I went by myself after that. I ain't never been one for going with somebody all the time. I've done most of my trapping by myself, even in Blackfoot country."

"Have the Blackfeet always been unfriendly?"

"They have to us. They're a mean bunch. Every now and then you'll see one of them who has got mad at the world and painted his face black. And that's one who's sure out to do misery to somebody. They do all their trading with the Hudson's Bay Company, and they don't want to know nobody else. And they sure don't want nobody else in their territory."

"The Hudson's Bay Company doesn't worry much about staying in their own country, do they?"

"They sure don't," Harnett chuckled, pulling the iron skillet toward him. He put the dough in the skillet, put the lid on it, and leaned forward to set it on the fire. "I've seen their brigades all the way down the Missouri to Council Bluffs. But them and the Blackfeet both couldn't keep me out of Blackfoot territory. I've sure carried me a lot of furs out of there."

Maria smiled. The kettle was boiling briskly now,

and she began cutting up the potatoes and onion and dropping the pieces into it. Harnett put the flour away, filled the coffeepot and put it on the fire, then settled himself in front of the fire, shredding pieces from a plug of tobacco and filling his pipe.

Darkness was falling outside as they ate later. Harnett told Maria a ghost story, the tale of a trapper who had killed a wolverine, then had been haunted by the wolverine's mate for the rest of his life; it followed him about, springing and robbing his traps. He had an inexhaustible accumulation of such stories—short, fable-like animal yarns with the ring of some human truth about them. He had tales of hunters and trappers in improbable situations as well. Maria liked the way Seth spun his stories; they were amusing or they were scary, but they all made her think.

They washed the dishes, and Maria worked the buckskin over the straking board as Harnett smoked his pipe and told her still another story—this one about the windigo, a giant demon in human form that stalked the mountain forests and fed on rotten wood, swamp moss, stump mushrooms and human flesh. He laughed as he told it, which did Maria's heart some good. For some reason, as he was beginning to describe the demon, she was thinking chillingly of her father. Only when Seth grinned did she grin. Then it was all right.

They went to sleep early, as most trappers did in the mountains. Harnett simply pulled a buffalo skin over himself on the floor. The wind moaned around the corners of the cabin. Maria built up the fire until it was roaring. Then she went to her bunk and huddled under her blanket and buffalo skin robe, peering over the edge of the covers at the buckskin over the door as it swayed in the wind.

At dawn, a low, grey overcast covered the sky and a stiff wind blew from the north. Harnett's cheeks were red from the cold when he came back in from checking the horses. They ate, then started walking along the creek, checking the traps. The icy wind blew the loose leaves in rustling swirls around them. Maria huddled in her coat and shivered. She was disappointed when she did not find beavers in the first few traps. Her disappointment mounted as they went past one pond after another, Harnett examining the sets from a cautious distance and shaking his head.

At the fifth pond, Harnett grinned widely over his shoulder at Maria as he stepped to the edge of the water and carefully pulled in the taut trap chain. The limp body of a large beaver hung from the trap by a forefoot. Harnett pulled it out onto the bank, gathered in the wire and the large rock on the end of it, then bent over the beaver and ruffled the damp fur with his fingers. He nodded with satisfaction.

"That's a good pelt, Maria. It ain't what I call prime, but it's what a lot of people do, and it's a good, heavy one. Cut us a bait stick and let's get this trap reset."

The cold was forgotten as Maria cut a branch from a sapling and scented it. She kept glancing at the beaver, the first she'd seen actually trapped. When the trap had been reset, Harnett motioned to her and she gathered the beaver under her arm and followed him, looking at it and feeling the fur.

The sets on the next two ponds were undisturbed, as were the sets along the side of the eighth pond. But the dam Harnett had ripped up had been repaired. Maria stood at the end of the dam and waited as Harnett walked out onto it. He looked down in the water at the first trap and walked on, then knelt at the second and pulled up another large beaver, lifting it to show her. There was another beaver in the third trap too. After resetting the traps and loosening the limbs to make leaks in the dam again, he brought the two catches back.

"These are both good ones too, Maria. This one here is so close to prime that it don't make any difference. And seeing as how the upper four ponds are set with my traps and these down here are set with yours, these here beavers are yours."

"Oh, no, Seth, I couldn't do that. . . ."

"It's the onliest way to do it. When the snow gets deep and we spread traps over to the other creeks, we'll have to split up to run them, because we won't be able to cover them all together. So we'll just split them now. These four down here are yours, and the upper four are mine."

Maria started to shake her head again, then hesitated. "How much are those pelts worth?"

"It's hard to say, but skinned out right and without grease burns, I'd say about fifteen dollars."

Maria looked at the beavers again. It was almost unbelievable. Fifteen dollars was more than a week's wages for a man in St. Louis. She looked up at Harnett and grinned widely. He chuckled.

Further on, Harnett pointed out willow branches

for Maria to cut down and bring along. They walked back up the creek, then sat in front of the cabin, where he showed her how to skin the beaver out and make drying hoops out of the willow branches. He stretched the pelts on the hoops, scraped them lightly with his knife to test them, then handed them to her.

"Now those are ready to hang up and dry, Maria. We'll scrape them good in a day or two to get all the fat off them." He turned back to the carcasses and began cutting off the tails. "And here we've got some mighty good eating—just like pork."

"They look just like big, flat snakes."

"You wait'll you taste them. This beaver fat is good for putting on your hands and face when it gets cold too. And right here. . . ." He sliced down through one of the beaver carcasses with his knife and cut out two large glands in front of the rectum. "This is the castoreum, and it's good for headache, earache, colic and a lot of other things, so they say. I don't know about that. But I do know it's good for making trap bait, so you can just collect them up until you have enough to boil and fill a bottle. Put them out on a rock to dry, and hang your pelts over there in one of the trees where the wind can hit them."

Maria nodded, gathering up the soft, flabby castoreum glands and the three pelts, and she carried them around to the side of the cabin. She spread the glands out on a stone, then carefully hung the three pelts on a tree limb. They swung and bobbed stiffly in the wind. She pulled a bit of fatty tissue from one of them, smoothed the hair down on all of them, then turned and walked back around the cabin, smiling happily.

The clouds hung lower during the afternoon and

the wind became gusty. It whipped particles of fine, dry snow against the side of the cabin. Harnett took two large traps from one of the bags, carried them down to the first two ponds and set them on the banks where the beavers had been climbing in and out. He baited them with castoreum, the scent of one of the wolverine's favorite foods. The next morning, snow had drifted into wind-sheltered spots and a thin skim of ice was beginning to form around the edges of the ponds. There were two beavers in traps along the ponds, and two wolverines in the large traps. When they returned to the cabin, Harnett showed Maria how to hone her skinning knife to a razor edge, and she began gingerly skinning the beavers as Harnett skinned the wolverines and went to collect tanbark to tan the skins so boots could be made from them.

The wind stopped. The snow began coming down in large, soft flakes, quickly covering the ground with a deep layer. Harnett caught two more wolverines and began making boots for himself and Maria. Maria worked on another set of buckskins for herself, cutting each piece carefully and leaving long overlaps at the seams to make fringes down the outside of the sleeves, breeches and leggings. Three or four beavers were in the traps along the ponds each day, and almost all of them were in full winter prime condition, the fur dense, soft and silky.

The grass on the plateau in front of the cabin became sparse, and Harnett and Maria moved the horses to the next valley to the north, three miles away around a bulge in the mountain. There were seven ponds along the creek, all heavily populated with beaver, and Harnett moved several of his traps to this valley. Ice continued forming and thickening on the ponds, cracking up during occasional heavy winds during the day and freezing over again during the still nights. It continued snowing. Harnett finished the fur boots and began making snowshoes from thick willow branches and rawhide thongs. Maria finished her buckskins, all the seams laced with small, tight stitches, long fringes down the outside seams and around the wide collar and the bottom of the shirt, and heavy patterns of beading on the front of the shirt and the tops of the moccasins. In the new buckskins, thick wolverine boots over her moccasins and leggings and her heavy buffalo skin coat, she was comfortably warm except for her hands and face, and she coated them with beaver fat, as Harnett did.

The ponds froze over completely and the ice became thick enough to bear their weight. Harnett showed Maria how to crack holes in it to set traps near the escape tunnels, and how to set traps in deeper water that were baited with fresh birch and alder limbs. The catch along the creek where the cabin was located diminished as the beavers became more wary of the traps, and Maria moved part of her traps to a creek to the south. A winter storm swept through and left a heavy snowfall, and Maria learned how to walk on snowshoes, the muscles in her legs becoming painfully stiff and sore until she became accustomed to them.

The temperature plummeted. It became difficult to crack the ice with the back of a tomahawk. Dipping her hands into the frigid water to reset traps was painful, so Maria made herself a pair of gloves out of the thin, pliant belly pieces of a buckskin, sewing the pieces together with tiny stitches. The buckskin absorbed the water, and she put beaver fat, deer fat and gun oil on the gloves in an attempt to waterproof them. Nothing worked satisfactorily. She also tried waterproofing them with castoreum oil, squeezing the thick liquid from the glands of recently killed beaver. The combination of things made the gloves more or less waterproof, but the odor of the castoreum was disagreeable, particularly in the cabin, which was already cluttered with smelly pelts in various stages of drying and being scraped. She left the gloves outside, stuck in a hole in the deep snow on the cabin roof.

Then she found some of the beavers she was taking from her traps stiff, indicating they had been caught hours before, shortly after she had checked and reset the traps. After thinking about it for a time, she concluded this might be because she was handling the traps with the castoreum-scented gloves and leaving no trace of human scent that would have to dissipate before beavers would approach. So she soaked her gloves liberally with castoreum oil and began putting in long, hard days from daylight until dusk to check some of her traps twice daily. And in a few of her traps on ponds with larger beaver lodges and beaver populations, she began catching two beavers each day.

Harnett had his traps checked and was back at the cabin well before dusk each day, skinning beavers, scraping pelts and occasionally going out to hunt a deer or set rabbit snares. He showed a quiet, intense pleasure over the ease with which Maria had rapidly absorbed what he had taught her. He was even more gratified by the determined way she threw herself into the work. He was pleased when she caught as many beavers as he did. Then he grew puzzled and thoughtful when she began spending

more time each day in running her trapline and con-
sistently brought in one or two beavers more than
he did.

One day she brought in six beavers, four from
her first check around the trapline and two from a
second. Harnett sat on his bunk and scraped on a
pelt as she came in the door with the heavy bag,
eyeing it speculatively as she slipped off her coat
and fur boots and warmed her hands at the fireplace.

"Looks like you got a good catch there today,
Maria."

Maria grinned, blowing on her hands and rubbing
them together as she held them out to the fire again.
"Six."

He lifted his eyebrows. "Six? And five yesterday?
And the same the day before that, wasn't it? While
I've been getting me three or four a day. Them must
be mighty good ponds on that creek south of here,
and spreading traps thin must be working good for
you."

"They're not spread all that thin. I've been getting two beavers a day in some traps."

"Two a day?" he said in astonishment. "How have
you been doing that?"

Maria grinned again, walking to the doorway. She
stepped outside, pulled her scented gloves out of the
hole in the snow on the roof and came back in.
"Here's how. These gloves don't leave any human
smell on the traps."

He looked, sniffed and was silent for a moment.
Then he burst into admiring laughter. "Well, I'll be
durned! Talk about somebody learning a dog how to
bark, that beats it all! What made you think of that,
Maria?"

"I tried to make the gloves waterproof because I

was losing all the skin off my hands. It just worked out that the castoreum I used helped me catch more beavers." She explained in detail what she had noticed and what she had done.

"By God, if anybody's ever thought of that before, I've never heard of it. But now that I've heard of it, I don't know what I didn't think of it myself. It looks like I'm going to have to make me some gloves, don't it?"

"There's plenty of buckskin left. I'll help you." She went outside to put the gloves back into the snow on the roof, then came back in and knelt by the bag, pulling the beavers out of it. "It's getting colder out."

"It'll get colder yet," he said, rising from his bunk and stepping to the fireplace. "I'll put on some coffee and see what we've got for supper. We don't have but one or two potatoes left, and we're getting sort of short on coffee. I got all the potatoes they had at the post when I was buying supplies, but they didn't have many."

Maria looked at him as she stepped to a shelf in the corner and took down the whetstone. "Having me here has cut you short, hasn't it?"

"No. I usually make me a trip in during the season. Or I've been doing it since they moved the post into Fort Henry, I should say. There was a good while when a body had to go clean back to the Missouri to find one. But about everybody goes in during the season now if they can. It gives the beavers a chance to forget they had neighbors and the trapping is better when they get back."

Maria sat down by the beavers, spat on the whetstone, and began honing her skinning knife. "When do you usually go in?"

"About Christmas." He put the coffeepot on the fire. "You know, there's a place up north of Cooper's Canyon where I trapped three years ago, and it was a good bit better than this here. I call it Lost Valley, but I don't know what others call it and I ain't never heard nobody talking about it. There ain't many who can find it, because the way into the valley is up by a waterfall in a blind canyon. And there's another place about like this west of Cooper's Canyon called Eagle Ridge. It's been a long time since I've been there, and I'd sort of like to take a look at it. Would you like to try over that way?"

Maria shrugged as she pulled one of the beavers to her and turned it over. "It's all right with me, Seth."

"Well, there's two or three ways we could do it. Do you want to hold onto all your furs and take them to the rendezvous to trade? You might be able to get a better price for them there than you would at Fort Henry."

Maria carefully sliced the skin open on the beaver, her tongue in the side of her mouth, and she shook her head. "I don't want anything to do with the rendezvous. What I want to do is get my own outfit just as soon as I have enough pelts. It isn't right for me to use your horses and everything."

Harnett nodded. "I can see why you'd want your own, Maria. The way you're trapping, you'll have enough pelts to buy an outfit well before Christmas. I tried to learn my brother's boy how to trap, and you've learned more in a day than I could pound into that boy's head in a season. But there ain't many with the natural woods sense you have, Maria, or with reasons pushing them like you have. Anyways, if you have your own outfit, there's a couple

of things we could do. We could go up to Eagle
Ridge together and see what it's like and then go
over to Lost Valley, or we could split up before we
get to Eagle Ridge. You could go on over to Lost
Valley and I could meet you there. I don't think
Eagle Ridge will be anywheres near as good as Lost
Valley, but I want to check it anyway. And you
wouldn't have no trouble finding Lost Valley."

"That sounds all right to me."

"That's what we'll do, then. We'll go to Fort
Henry along about Christmas and mosey up toward
Eagle Ridge from there."

Maria finished skinning a beaver and hesitated
as she reached for another one. Her father had said
that he might be back at Fort Henry in December
or January. It was likely that his brigade would
want to come in to spend the holiday at the post,
so she would see him. Even if he wasn't there she
would have to face her mother. Maria rarely spoke
to Harnett about her parents. But they were ghosts
in her head who still haunted her balefully some
nights.

She didn't have to go to Fort Henry. She could
remain at the cabin and continue trapping, and let
Harnett go in by himself to trade the furs and pick
up supplies. But everyone had undoubtedly long
since figured out that she was with him, and it would
amount to subjecting him to anger directed at her.
Harnett would do it if she asked him, but it wouldn't
be fair. And the confrontation was inevitable. The
sooner it came, the sooner it would be done with.
Maria nodded.

"All right, Seth."

10

The tree trunks were stark, black columns on each side, and branches sagged limply and hung low from the weight of the snow and ice piled on them. The heavily-laden horses, gaunt and weary, struggled through the deep snow as lower branches brushed against and showered the snow on them. The sharp odor of woodsmoke was stronger in the cold, still air and the trees thinned out ahead, but all Maria could see on the other side of them was an unbroken sheet of whiteness.

Harnett sat up in the saddle and straightened his hat as he rode out of the trees. The pack horses followed him, plumes of condensation coming from their nostrils as they pushed through the last deep drifts. Maria leaned to one side then the other to dodge the last low-hanging branches. Then she too was in the clearing, nodding as Harnett pointed.

Fort Henry looked tiny and lost in the expanse of snow-covering the valley. Smoke rose lazily from the chimneys. The snow in the open rectangle in the center of the buildings was trampled and dirty, and the stock pens behind the trading post were dark squares where the snow had been packed down into the dirt by the corraled horses. Several crude huts and lean-tos were in the field by the stock pens, cooking fires smoking in front of some of them, and several men were moving about the post and other buildings. At least one of the brigades was in.

As they rode up to the Fort, the man and the girl and their pack-laden horses were quickly noticed. Men ran into the blacksmith shop, brought out others to look, point and set up a whooping and hollering of a greeting. Maria was swallowing nervously as she and Harnett pushed their way through the snow across the meadow and approached the rear of the cabins. Harnett, guiding his horse wide of the end cabin as he neared it, lifted his rifle skyward and fired it as his own friendly greeting, and the crack sounded thin and soft in the still air. A cabin door opened and an Indian woman looked out. The whooping and shouting among the men died away as they moved and craned their necks to peer at Maria. Looking at her parents' cabin, Maria was numb with apprehension.

The door of that cabin also opened shortly after the rifle shot. Mercy looked out, blinking as she saw Harnett. Then her eyes moved to Maria and she began shrieking ecstatically. She ran towards her, holding her arms out.

"Maria! Maria! Pierre, it's Maria! Maria's home!"

Maria dismounted and stepped toward her mother, then stumbled back awkwardly from her clutching embrace. She smiled, patting Mercy's back. "Hello, ma."

"Oh, how are you, honey? I've been so worried. . . ." She stepped back, looking Maria up and down. "You are all right, honey. Laws, I've been worried out of my mind. . . ."

"Yes, I'm all right, ma. Are you?"

"Yes, but I ain't been out in no woods," Mercy said, hugging Maria again and patting her face. "Oh, Maria, I've been so worried. . . ."

Maria started to reply, then closed her mouth and looked at the cabin's doorway, her smile fading. Her father was standing there, glaring at her. Quaking fear raced through her; her knees felt like water. The men approaching Harnett stopped, looking at DeVises. Mercy made a soft, equivocating sound, then remained quiet. DeVises' boots squeaked in the snow as he took a couple of steps towards her. He planted his fists on his hips, gazing slowly at Harnett, then moving his eyes to the buckskin-clad Maria on her horse.

"So you decided to come back, did you?"

Maria swallowed dryly and lifted her chin. "Hello, pa."

"Don't you hello me! And you can forget about calling me pa. I did everything I could for you, and then the first time I turned my back, you did something like this. You're not worth bothering with." He looked at Harnett again and said narrowly, "I don't see how you can look me in the face after what you did."

"It ain't all that hard."

"It's not his fault," Maria said. "He just happened to—"

"You shut up!" DeVises stormed at her. "When I

want to hear anything out of you, I'll tell you! As far as I'm concerned, it would do me just fine if I never heard anything out of you or about you again!" He started to say something else, then closed his mouth and turned back toward the cabin with a motion of dismissal. The door slammed behind him.

Mercy hesitated, looking at the cabin. Then her lips set in a determined line. "You come on in, Maria," she said quietly, "I've got hot coffee on, and there's plenty left over from dinner."

Harnett smiled and nodded as Maria turned and looked at him uncertainly. "I'll take the pelts on into the post and see to the horses."

"Well . . . maybe I'll be over there directly, then. . . ."

He nodded again, taking the reins, and turned his horse toward the trading post. The men crowded forward again, talking, laughing and gathering around him. Mercy held Maria's arm, leading her toward the cabin.

"Laws, have you growed some more that fast, Maria? You look another inch taller somehow . . . well, come on in and sit down, and maybe you can tell your pa and me all about it. . . ."

They went in. Maria leaned her rifle against the wall inside the door and hung her powder horn and shot pouch on a peg. DeVises, sitting on a stool by the hearth, glanced at her once and looked back at the fire. Mercy closed the door and bustled toward the fireplace as Maria slipped off her fur boots, dropped them and pulled at the thongs on her coat.

"Well, it's sure cold out there, but you're dressed for it, ain't you, Maria? Them boots look warm, and that's a nice, heavy coat."

Maria nodded. "Yes, they're good and warm."

"You look like an Indian," DeVises sneered, still looking at the fire. "And not a squaw, either. You should be ashamed of yourself to go around like that."

"Well, I don't know so much, Pierre," Mercy said doubtfully, filling a cup from the coffeepot. "What she's got on ain't so. . . ." Her voice faded as she looked again but grew stronger again as she continued. "Well, them beads look mighty pretty, don't they? Did you sew them on, Maria? I guess you did, didn't you? Go ahead and sit down at the table, Maria."

Appetizing odors of cooked onions, sage, pepper and boiled beef came from the kettle and pans on the hob. Maria hung her hat on a peg, put her tomahawk and long knife on a shelf by the door and walked toward the table.

Mercy beamed. "Laws, it's good to see you're safe and sound, Maria. You look a little thin, but I've never seen anybody more healthy-looking. You're as brown as a nut and your eyes just shine. But what did you do to your hair, honey?"

"It got in the way, and I cut part of it off."

"But you had such pretty hair and you always enjoyed fussing with it so much that I would have thought . . . well, it's done, ain't it? And I don't really see the harm." She brought over a plate filled with beef, vegetables and a piece of bread. "Did you get any furs?"

"Yes."

"Well, that's good. Here, eat this up and I'll get you some more when you're ready." She smiled down at Maria, patting her shoulder, then walked back toward the fireplace.

"What kind of furs did you get?" DeVises grunted skeptically.

"Beaver."

"Where did you get the traps?"

Maria took a bite from the plate and looked at him, chewing. "Seth loaned me some of his."

"Seth?" DeVises stormed angrily. "Is that what you call him? A man older than I am, and you call him by his first name? By God, I'm going to straighten out a lot of things with you and—"

"Now let's let her eat her supper, Pierre," Mercy said, smiling entreatingly. "It's been a while since we've seen her, so let's—"

"Well, whose fault is that?" he barked irately. "But you won't have to worry about her being gone again, I'll tell you that. I'm going to deal with the cause of the trouble. I'll have a word with Harnett, then deal with her. You won't have to worry about her wearing any such garb as that any more, you won't have to worry about her hair being cut off again, and you won't have to—"

"It don't have to be dealt with right this minute, Pierre," Mercy said, her smile taut. "There'll be a proper time to see to everything properly. She's eating her supper now."

DeVises subsided, grumbling in his throat and looking into the fire. As Mercy hovered nearby, nodding encouragement, Maria looked down at her plate, the food tasteless in her mouth and her hunger changing into an empty, nauseated feeling. The sense of freedom she'd had while trapping was gone. The bright feeling of accomplishment over her catch of beaver pelts became tarnished by the old, familiar and terrible feeling of being stifled, hemmed in, thwarted. She took a drink of coffee, then another bite from the plate. Stubborn anger boiled within her, and she chewed slowly, thinking. He couldn't stay and keep watch over her for the rest of her life; she wouldn't permit it.

Voices approached outside, and there was a knock at the door. Mercy crossed the room and opened it, and Fitzpatrick stepped in, followed by Harnett. They took off their hats, nodding to Mercy, and Fitzpatrick looked at DeVises.

"Pierre, we need to talk to Maria about her pelts and explain what's going on over at Ebbot's Creek."

DeVises looked at him in surprise, then smiled sourly and grunted. "There she is. But does she have enough to go to so much trouble over?"

"She has a few." Fitzpatrick chuckled dryly. "She brought in over two packs."

"Over two packs?" DeVises stared at Fitzpatrick in amazement. "Do you mean that she . . . ?"

"That's what I mean," Fitzpatrick said, nodding. He spoke to Maria. "Maria, Seth didn't want to speak for you on your pelts. I feel bounden to tell you like I did him that Kruger has set up over on Ebbot's Creek, about twenty miles from here, and he's supposed to be paying more than we are. Some say he's paying up to three dollars a pound. Now we'd like to have your pelts, but we can't pay that."

Maria looked at him, taking a drink from her cup and swallowing. Before, Fitzpatrick had treated her with the kindly condescension of an adult toward a very young girl. His manner had changed. He might be talking to any trapper. She looked at Harnett's wide smile of satisfaction. During the trip back to Fort Henry, he had shown a bland, sometimes infuriating unconcern about her apprehension over meeting her father. Suddenly she understood why.

Among trappers, success was the primary measure of a person's worth and she had brought in a sizeable catch. She had abruptly moved into a different category in Harnett's and just about everyone else's eyes. Including her father's. He was looking at her with defensive, querulous perplexity.

"What are you doing, Seth?" Maria said.

"I'm trading here, Maria. They're paying two dollars a pound, which is fair, and they're my friends."

Maria nodded, looking back at Fitzpatrick. "What are you getting for your horses?"

"We have some good ones that we'll let go for sixty-five dollars a head, Maria. Seth mentioned that you wanted to put together an outfit, and you'll get that and have plenty left over."

"I'll trade here, then."

"Well, we appreciate that, Maria." Fitzpatrick said, turning and moving back toward the door. "I'll have the men weigh your furs in and make up your tally, and you can come over and pick out your horses, traps and supplies whenever you're ready."

"Thank you, Mr. Fitzpatrick."

"It's no trouble, Maria. We're much obliged for your trade."

Mercy looked blankly from Maria to the three men as they moved toward the door. Then she collected herself and smiled weakly. "Would you all care for a cup of coffee?"

"No, we need to get back over, but we're obliged all the same," Fitzpatrick said. "Good day, Mercy. Good day, Pierre."

When they were gone, the room was silent except for the crackling of the fire and the sound of Maria's spoon against the tin plate. Maria glowed. Her father was looking glumly into the fire, his brows still drawn in thought. He hadn't challenged her on anything she had discussed with Fitzpatrick. She cleaned off her plate and sat back on the bench, sucking her teeth and drinking her coffee.

"You put that away right handy, didn't you, Maria? Would you like another little bit of it before you have your pie?"

"I believe I will, ma. That's really good."

"Well, I'm glad you like it," Mercy said, gathering up the plate and cup and walking back toward the fireplace. "There's plenty of it, and you need to feed up a little, honey."

DeVises cleared his throat loudly, as he turned on Maria. "Where did you and Harnett go to get so many pelts?"

"West of here."

"Whereabouts west of here?"

"A good way west of here. Why is Kruger paying so much for pelts? He can't be making much money."

"He's not making any!" DeVises snorted in disgust. "He's losing. He's in with the American Fur Company, and that's the way they do business. They'll raise the prices and run everyone else out, then lower the prices again. They did it all up and down the Missouri."

"Are his sons working with him?"

DeVises looked at her, frowning darkly. "Why do you ask?"

"I just wondered."

"Well, I wonder how you can bring yourself to even speak of them, considering what one of them tried to do to you. Now I'll tell you something, Maria. You might think you've got to where I can't get a handful of you, but I'll give you good cause to change your mind if you ever mess with that pack. I should have killed them all off a long time ago, and it's not too late to do that yet."

His tone was loud and harsh, but somehow it did not produce the quaking fear in her that it had before. Maria felt a mild caution, but nothing more. She took a bite and chewed of the new helping of food Mercy brought her, looking at DeVises with a nonchalant smile. "I just wanted to know whether or not to keep my rifle cocked if I rode by there."

DeVises grunted, looking back at the fire. "You'd be better off to stay away from there. Anyway, the boys are gone. One of them went up north to do some trading. The other one's trapping. Somebody said they had seen him up around Cooper's Canyon."

Maria stopped chewing. So Curtis was really trapping, as he said he would. And at Cooper's Canyon. That's pretty much where Harnett said he'd meet her after they'd split up for a while, just north of Cooper's Canyon. She'd have to go there in any event.

Maria glanced at her father and nodded disinterestedly. She took a drink of coffee and another bite from her plate. A warm glow stirred within her.

11

Maria woke and lifted the edge of the buffalo skin robe from her face. The frigid cold tingled on her skin and burned in her nose and lungs as she breathed. The darkness was impenetrable, but there was a feel of early morning. Harnett's snoring was a rhythmic, rasping noise, muffled by the blanket over his face. One of the horses shifted its hoofs and snorted quietly a few yards away. The silence was steely, not softened by the whisper of snow flakes. It had stopped snowing during the night. The warmth of the blanket and buffalo skin robe was luxuriously comfortable, inviting the thought of dozing for a few minutes longer, but Maria gathered her will and pushed them aside. She knelt under the low roof of the lean-to and pulled on her coat and hat, shivering.

Harnett stopped snoring with a snort, yawned,

then groaned in the darkness. "By God, it's turned colder, ain't it? I can tell from the way my lumbago is twinging."

"It's cold all right."

"It sure is, but I've seen it colder. I've seen it so cold that trees didn't split, they flew all to pieces like they was full of gunpowder. Why, I've seen it so cold. . . ."

Harnett talked on in a sleepy, yawning voice as Maria crawled to the front of the lean-to and felt in the darkness for the stones around the fire. He told about a winter on the Musselshell so cold it had been impossible to cook because the top of a stew in a kettle froze while the bottom boiled. A winter in the Tetons so cold he had fled and returned the following August to find ice still in the coffeepot he had left behind. Maria raked the ashes off the hot coals with a stock, then dropped splinters on the coals and blew on them until the fire started up again.

"That's pretty cold," she admitted. "It didn't get very cold in St. Louis, but it used to get hot. I can remember a lot of times during the summer when my mother used the roof for a cooking stove."

"That's mighty hot."

"Yes, but I'll cool that roof off a little if you'll let that coffeepot thaw out in about March or April."

Harnett wheezed with laughter, pushing his blanket down and reaching for his coat and hat. "Durned if you ain't turning into a real mountain liar, Maria. You're getting like the best of them. . . . You know, that batch of bacon we got from the post is real tasty, ain't it?"

Maria smiled and nodded at the hint. She took a square of bacon out of the canvas bag of supplies by the fire, pulled the frying pan closer and began cutting thin slices into it. Coughing and groaning, Harnett squirmed into his coat and went out, shivering, to see about the horses.

Dawn was breaking as they loaded the horses for the trail. The horses, a bit gaunt from sparse grazing and crusted with ice, wouldn't have any prizes in a show, but they looked mighty good to Maria. She had a proprietary feeling toward them, the same sort of appreciation and sense of responsibility she felt toward her traps, packsaddles and the like. She owned property now. Caring for her horses, making sure her equipment was in working order, she felt herself growing. She was a good deal less concerned about appearances than she had been, for one thing, and she was a good deal less troubled by what other people—any other people—might think of her.

She followed Harnett's horses out of the cabin clearing. The trail wound variously through clumps of poplar, maple, oak and other deciduous trees, with a few pines and cedars among them. The horses picked their way around the deeper drifts, moving along with a slow, plodding pace, and Maria snuggled down into her coat, sinking into a musing reverie. Then Harnett angled the horses upward. As they climbed higher and higher, pines, cedars and spruce alone faced them; then these trees too thinned out as the horses approached a rocky bluff, then began to skirt a path on a limestone cliff. Maria stirred, sat up in her saddle and lifted her reins. There was a hundred-foot drop below the horses. Their hoofs knocked rocks into the chasm below as they felt for firm footing in the snow drifted along the ledge. Then Maria could relax again as, leaving the cliff-side path, the horses pushed through the drifts in a snow-clogged gully and entered thickets of pines, cedars, and spruce again.

They'd ridden for the better part of three hours, through awesome scenery the likes of which Maria had never dreamed she would see. Suddenly they broke into an open plain and had a panoramic view of more mountains and valleys in the misty distance —snow-covered ridges with a black haze of winter trees looking stark and bleak in the flat, dim light. Harnett reined his horse up.

"That's Eagle Ridge there, Maria. Now you follow this ridgeline on straight to the north, and it'll slope down to Cooper's Canyon about five miles from here. Just as you start up the canyon, there'll be a valley off on the right side, and you go up that. At the head of the valley, there'll be a waterfall, and it'll look like that's as far as you're going to get. But there's a way up on the right side of it, and you can find it if you'll look around. But there'll be a lot of ice around there and it's steep, so you'll have to lead your horses up one at a time. When you get up to the top, just follow that creek that makes the waterfall, and it'll lead you straight to Lost Valley."

"All right. How long is Cooper's Canyon?"

"Oh, it runs a long way, but you don't have to worry about that. You'll find that valley when you're not much more than in the canyon. There's trappers and Indians in Cooper's Canyon pretty often, so you don't want to spend any more time than you have to in moving. You won't find no other trappers or Indians in Lost Valley, though. You'll see why when you get there."

"All right."

He looked at the jagged mountain again, scratching his beard and thinking. "The trapping below Eagle Ridge might not be too good," he said then, "but I'd still like to check it because it's been a while since I've been over there. I could ride on up to Lost Valley with you, help you get settled there and then come on back. Or you could ride over to Eagle Ridge with me. . . ."

"What for?" Maria chuckled. "I can find the valley, Seth. And I want to catch some beavers, not look at ridges."

He looked at her musingly, then nudged his horse. "Well, it won't take me but five or six days to get over there and back to Lost Valley. If there's been a burn or something in Lost Valley and it ain't too good there, we'll just turn around and go home."

"I'll see you in a few days, then."

Harnett nodded and waved as his horses moved away. Maria nudged her horse. It started to follow Harnett's horses, then turned along the ridgeline as she reined it around. Harnett looked back and waved for the last time.

The sun was concealed behind the thick overcast, giving no hint of the time of day, but Maria had been riding for several hours more and was beginning to feel tired and hungry. She had sticks of jerky in her hunting bag, but the bacon had made her thirsty and the jerky would make her even thirstier. She'd reached the edge of the burn. Her horses slowed in the deeper drifts among the trees. The snow on low branches looked tempting, but she resisted slaking her thirst with it, knowing that eating snow could lower her body temperature dangerously.

Daylight was beginning to fade when she reached the bottom of the canyon. The canyon wall on the other side of the frozen river was dimly visible through the snow and the shadowy darkness of winter foliage. Maria turned towards it, angling across the river, and the foliage became more distinct. The mouth of the first valley Harnett had told her about came into sight and she passed it, angling back across the river. Another small valley where a creek flowed into the river came into sight on the left, and that was the one she turned into.

It was steep, there were large humps where snow-covered boulders littered the creekbed and, in spots, the wind had scoured the snow off the frozen creek's surface. The horses took slow, careful steps. Crossing the patches of bare ice, Maria saw a pond with a beaver dam in it and headed that way. There was a single large beaver lodge in the pond. There was no track or other indication that anyone had been trapping here or anywhere else along the creek. The valley leveled and widened on the pond's far side, and the trees opened out into a clearing. Maria crossed the clearing and rode into more trees, then reined up by a massive tree which had fallen across two boulders, making a kind of natural shelter from the wind. There she dismounted, unloaded her horses and began making a fire.

Darkness fell. The heat of the fire warmed the shelter as Maria melted snow for coffee and put up a kettle of beans and jerky. She stared into the fire and pondered as she waited for the food to cook. If what her father had said was correct, Curtis Kruger was somewhere in the canyon. But Harnett had said that the canyon was not only long, which would make it difficult to find him, but that it might be teeming with Indians, which made Maria apprehensive about starting a prolonged search for him. The fire burned down as she thought and ate, and she unrolled her blankets and buffalo skin robe and went to bed. She'd decided to look for Curtis a little while longer.

It was still snowing the next morning; the fall had piled up and turned her shelter into a kind of white-walled cave. Maria knocked the snow away, built up the fire and ate, then mounted her saddle horse and moved on, following the general directions Harnett had given her but checking beaver ponds for signs of a trapper. By midday, she had checked eight creeklines along the river without luck. She turned back and returned to her camp, where she tended to her hobbled pack horses, then sat in front of the fire and stared into it morosely as darkness fell, her shoulders slumped with disappointment. She'd allowed herself a half day's search in each direction, no more; she didn't have time to move her camp about. The next day, if her search proved fruitless, she would give up and move on to the spot Harnett had picked out for them.

Next morning, she set out again. It had stopped snowing during the night. Visibility was good. She approached the river furtively along the creek, painfully aware that she could be seen by hostile Indians for a long distance along the wide canyon. She reined up at the mouth of the creek and looked in both directions for several minutes. The only sign of movement was a wolverine loping through the snow far downriver to her left. She turned that way for want of a clearer choice and began riding along the river bank, staying close to its bordering trees.

Of the creeks she passed leading off from the river,

she noticed one that seemed to have irregularities in
the snow along its bank. She reined up by it, examined what turned out to be hoofprints and drew certain tentative conclusions. Three or four horses had
come this way, almost certainly before the last snowfall since new drifts had all but covered the prints.
Maria hesitated in indecision. Then she checked the
priming in the pan on her rifle and turned her horse
up the creek. It was a wide creek with low, heavily-
forested banks. When she saw more hoofprints, now
in the center of the creek, she tracked them, maintaining her hidden position in the trees, and reining
to a slow walk. A hundred yards further on, she
saw a large beaver dam in a pond. The prints went
in the pond's direction and so did Maria.

Four traps had been set along the sides of the
pond. Maria sat on her horse and looked at them
for several minutes. They were baited but unsprung.
Footprints nearby indicated they had been checked
not long before. She followed the footprints. Soon
she found depressions in the snow where beavers
had been laid out. One of the little hollows had
been freshly made.

Drawing in her breath, Maria lifted her reins and
began riding forward at a slow walk again. There
were more beaver ponds at intervals of a quarter of
a mile along the creek. As she rode on, the distinct
odor of woodsmoke reached her and then she detected the warm, barnyard odor of horses. Her horse
suddenly cocked its ears. Her blood racing now,
Maria very quietly dismounted and led her horse
towards the odor, her hands on its nostrils ready to
pinch them to keep it from neighing. The creek narrowed. She glimpsed tall limestone bluffs through

the thick trees ahead. Then she heard horses pawing at the snow.

Maria moved forward and stood behind a thick clump of underbrush. Past it, some fifty yards off, she saw three horses hobbled in a clearing at the base of the bluff. There was no cabin or lean-to in view, but when she looked at the bluff, she saw a cave in it. The woodsmoke was coming from there, in thin grey spirals almost invisible against the grey limestone. She watched, unsure of her next move. She could not tell from the horses, which were unsaddled, whether their owner was a white man or an Indian.

Suddenly a man wearing a wide-brimmed hat came out of the cave. He tossed the carcass of a beaver away, then bent over to wash his hands in the snow. Still Maria watched, as the man gathered up an armload of wood from beside the cave entrance, bent over and went back inside.

Maria's eyes glowed and her heart pounded. She'd caught only a glimpse of the man's features under his wide hatbrim, but there was no mistaking his tall, strong build and the lithe grace of his movements. She leaped onto her horse and raced across the clearing towards the cave.

The three hobbled horses, lifting their heads and neighing shrilly, brought Curtis Kruger out of the cave with his rifle at the ready. His wary frown changed into stunned shock as he saw the young girl galloping towards him. Then, a wide smile of delight spreading across his face, he dropped his rifle and ran forward. Maria slid down from her horse. Once more Curtis looked at her, this time closely, still with that amazed and joyful look on his face. Then he took a step forward, and she was in his arms.

"Maria . . . Maria . . ."

Maria clung to him, pressing herself against him and lifting her face as he kissed her again and again. She forgot the winter cold. Eyes closed, she felt herself in some kind of warm paradise without borders of time or space. He stopped kissing her momentarily and, smiling tenderly, put a finger on her eyelids so as to open them and look deeply into her eyes. She shook her head impatiently as passion kept seizing her. Instead, she tightened her arm around his neck and pulled his lips back down to hers, biting at them. A tremor raced through him and, following her lead, he crushed her to him savagely and ground his mouth down hard on hers.

His face was flushed when he finally let her go. He looked down at her searchingly for a long moment, touching her face with the tips of his fingers. Then he slowly shook his head. "Maria, I can't believe that it's really . . . how in God's name did you get here?"

Maria smiled shakily. She was still trembling from the kiss. "Someone said you were trapping around here, I was passing this way, so I decided to . . . aren't I shameless? Tracking you down like a deer. . . ."

"No!" he said emphatically. He pulled her to him again and bent over her, moving his lips over her cheek. "You could never do anything wrong, Maria. I heard at my pa's trading post that you'd left home. Everyone figured you were with Seth Harnett, but I had no idea that you were anywhere near here. If I had, I would have been there so fast that . . . anyway, you're not shameless." He moved his lips to hers and kissed her again, gently. "I haven't thought of anything except that afternoon we spent on the prairie, Maria."

"Neither have I, Curtis."

"I was afraid you'd find someone else."

"How could I?"

"Because you're the most beautiful woman in the world, and every man must be after you." He murmured against her throat, then straightened up and looked about him. He was disturbed by what he saw. He said hesitantly, "I'm short on the amenities here, as you can see. But I do have some coffee on and a million things to ask you. Would you like to go inside?"

Maria nodded. He turned to her horse and began unfastening the saddle girth for her.

"Where is Seth Harnett, then?"

"He's over at Eagle Ridge. I'm supposed to meet him at a place north of here in three or four days."

Curtis looked at her, then nodded as he lifted the saddle and blanket from the horse. Maria pulled off its bridle and slapped its rump, so that it turned and ambled toward Curtis's three. Then she walked with Curtis toward the cave.

"I feel like I should say that Harnett shouldn't have let you go off by yourself. But I'm glad he did."

Maria smiled. She recovered the rifle Curtis had dropped near the cave entrance, and they went inside. The rock ceiling was high and dank, the cave shallow and dark. But a fire burned in a grate near the entrance, cheering it, and Curtis had arranged things in a home-like fashion. His supplies and pack-saddles were stacked neatly along one wall and his cooking utensils were in an orderly pile by the grate. It was almost hot by the fire, despite the icy wind just outside. Maria leaned his rifle and hers against the wall and took off her hat, coat and boots. She was aware, as she sat down and he got tin cups for coffee, of his eyes almost constantly upon her.

"What did your pa think about your going off trapping?"

Maria, undoing her hair and pulling it back to retie it, shrugged. "About what you'd think. But I made a pretty good catch during the early part of the season, and he didn't try to stop me from coming out again."

Curtis nodded, poured the coffee and gave her a cup. "You're even more beautiful in buckskins than you are in a dress."

"They're a little immodest, I'm afraid. But I'd have a hard time trying to run a trapline in a dress."

"They're not immodest. They suit you fine, Maria." Sitting by her, he sipped his coffee slowly and said, "Funny. Of all the things I had to say to you and ask you, somehow I can't think of . . . Stephen found you on the prairie that afternoon, didn't he?"

"Yes. My rifle went off, and his horse threw him."

"I wish you'd shot him. He and I had it out when he got back. He made certain insinuations to me, all but told me what he had tried to do. He seemed proud of himself, didn't seem to mind that you had . . . well, rebuffed him."

"Where is he now?"

"North of Three Forks, trading with the Blackfeet for the Hudson's Bay Company. And causing trouble as well, from what I hear. Some free trappers were coming back from the Missouri headwaters when they were attacked by a party of Blackfeet. Stephen was with the attacking party, they said.

Two of the trappers were killed and another one lost all his horses, pelts, everything."

"They say your pa is with the American Fur Company."

"That's right, he is. And he's taken most of the Indian trade along the Snake River. He hired a couple of free traders to work for him, and he's already sent one of them back to recruit some bush lopers and bring in a pack train of goods."

"The man might not make it. That's a hard trip in winter."

"It'll be worth it to him if he does, though. My pa pays a lot. And he'll keep on doing it until he runs everyone else out. Then he'll pay what he wants to, or I'll miss my guess. I don't like the way he does business and I'm not very welcome at Fort Henry, so I'm saving my pelts until the rendezvous next summer."

There was a note of resignation in his voice as he talked about his brother and father, a tone of grim acceptance of his fate as a member of a family totally unlike him. But whatever forces had made him different from them had also made him a man who could stand alone, who could go his own way without support and assistance. The independence and self-assurance in the lines of his firm chin and mouth struck a responsive chord within Maria.

Looking at him as he grew silent, Maria felt nervous and tense. She could see that Curtis did too. His kisses had only stimulated her desire. She felt half-naked with her heavy outer clothing removed, but it wasn't enough just to have his eyes on her buckskin-clad legs. Her hand trembled as she took a sip of coffee and put the cup down. He reached out and took her hand.

"This is like a dream for me, Maria. A dream come true."

"It is for me as well, Curtis. . . ."

He lifted her hand to his lips, then pulled her toward him. Maria quickly slid her arms around his neck as he lifted her onto his lap. His arms closed around her as his lips found hers. His slow, gentle kiss suddenly built in intensity and she found herself gasping with the hard and exquisite pleasure of it. His hand trembled as he cupped her breast and began caressing it slowly. The buckskin, where he touched it, felt silky against her skin and her nipples hardened. She moaned and began gnawing at his mouth as her own hands traveled greedily over his body. She felt the hardness between his legs and gasped again, holding onto it, not willing to let it go. He groaned with pleasure and held her hand there even as, with his other hand, he touched and felt the moistness between her thighs, then fumbled to unfasten the thong at her waist.

Maria slipped from his lap to a blanket near the fire, lifting her hips as she lay there so as to help him get her pants off. His breath was warm against her upturned face. He'd all but torn his own clothing off when she'd freed him for a moment, and he was bronze and godlike now above her in the firelight. It was the first time Maria had seen a man's penis; she was wide-eyed with excitement at its length and rigidity and she gasped again as she touched and fondled it.

They could not wait too much longer, either one of them. Tenderly, angrily, his needs playing havoc with his emotions, Curtis lowered himself to her belly and plunged into her. She felt a slight twinge of pain, but it was all right, it was all right. When thoroughly wet and on fire from her sensations, she wound her legs around his waist and began pulling and thrusting her hips up to meet his pumpings, her eyes fixed on his eyes and glazing rapidly.

She felt lifted out of herself. The numbing ecstasy mounted higher and higher, then peaked. She whimpered, then lurched suddenly and violently, flooded with orgasmic juices, her own or Curtis's she hardly knew. But he had come too; that she could tell, and it gladdened her wildly, to a point she could not measure.

She lay quietly with Curtis still in her for several moments. She began to sob when he withdrew from her. He sat by her side and kissed away her tears.

"I love you, Maria."

"And I love you, Curtis."

"I won't let you go again, Maria. You're mine. Let's go get married, and then we can go see your pa and tell him that—"

"No. You made me a promise, Curtis."

"But we can't just leave it like this, Maria. I can't live not knowing if I'm ever going to see you again."

"And I couldn't live if I was the cause of trouble between you and my pa that got one of you killed. Maybe I'll think of some way to bring pa around to seeing things our way. But to up and get married would be wrong and dangerous. . . . Besides," she smiled, "there's no preacher between here and the Missouri."

"We could go to St. Louis. You didn't want to leave there to begin with, did you?"

"No, but I've changed my mind. I've found something here that I want and need, Curtis, and I don't want to leave it."

He moved his lips over her forehead. "But when will we be able to meet again?"

"At the rendezvous."

"You're going to the rendezvous?"

She looked up at him, sliding her arms around his neck. "I hadn't intended to," she said, pulling his lips down to hers again. "But if you're going to be there, then I'll be there. . . ."

Part Four

RENDEZVOUS

12

"Rider coming there," Sublette said quietly.

Barry glanced at Sublette's bearded face as he straightened up in his saddle, then squinted into the bright glare of the setting sun. Several days before, during a brief, running attack by a party of Blackfeet, several of the spare horses had been lost, and Barry shifted his rifle, ready to shoulder it. The tiny cloud of dust was almost lost in the glare of the sun, but he could make out small, moving figures under it, one larger than the other.

"Two riders," Sublette said.

"It looks like a rider with a spare horse to me," Barry said.

"If it is, you've got sharp eyes," Sublette replied, then turned and looked back at the pack trains. "Rider coming!"

The bush lopers stirred, craning their necks and

looking ahead. Sublette turned back around, resting his rifle across his arm and looking ahead. After a moment he glanced at Barry and nodded. "I believe you're right, Barry. That looks like a rider and an extra horse."

"He's sure burning up the grass. I wonder what he's running from?"

"It might be to. That could be one of our men coming out to hurry us up."

Barry nodded. All during the trek from the banks of the Missouri, up the Platte and across the Laramie, Sublette had driven everyone mercilessly, cursing at the bush lopers, abandoning lame horses that would slow the pack trains down, making each day a grueling struggle from before dawn until after sunset. Indians and free trappers and traders were gathering at Pierre's Hole for the rendezvous. They were coming from every corner of the West, from Taos and Santa Fe, the Gila and the Colorado, the Yellowstone and the Bighorn, the Great Basin and the Sierra Nevada. And they would trade with either the Rocky Mountain Fur Company or the American Fur Company, whichever arrived first.

The rider disappeared into a dry wash rimmed with low, scrubby trees, the first hints of the thick forests covering the foothills in the distance, then came into sight again. Barry leaned forward in his saddle, looking closer. "It's my uncle!"

"By God, you're right!" Sublette exclaimed. "It's old Tom!"

Fitzpatrick waved his rifle and whooped as he approached at a run. He reined up and slowed as he neared the pack trains, the horse he was riding and his spare horse streaked with sweat and panting heavily. He wheeled his horse around by Barry's and leaned over to slap his shoulder. "By God, it's good to see you out here again, Barry. How's the family?"

"They're all fine, and it's good to be here."

"Bill, you've been bringing them right along, ain't you?"

"We ain't been dallying around. You got any idea where the others are?"

"Nobody's heard from them, so it's anybody's guess. But I do know that we have a mighty big bunch of Indians and free trappers and traders collecting up at Pierre's Hole, all of them with a lot of furs to trade. Have you had any trouble along the way?"

"We had a little set-to with some Blackfeet, but it didn't amount to much. Nobody was shot and we didn't get none of them. They got a couple of our horses."

"That wasn't near as bad as what some have suffered. Blackfeet've been raising hell all over the place for the past few months."

"Is that right? You might have thought of that before you come all the way out here by yourself, Tom. You going to ride in with us?"

"No, I'll stay with you as far as the Sweetwater, then I'll ride on in ahead and let everybody know you're coming. I'll be all right. I travel mostly at night and keep my eyes open when there's hostiles about. When are you going to make camp for the night?"

"I'm about ready to most any time now."

"There's a good place about two miles ahead, in a gulch. There's water, good grass for the horses and some wood scattered around."

"That'll do good," Sublette said, kicking his horse

with his heels. He looked back at the bush lopers. "Let's get them moving! We're camping just up ahead!"

The bush lopers shouted in relief and began bellowing at the pack horses, urging them to a canter. Fitzpatrick guided his horse away from Barry's, and Barry kicked his horse with his heels, keeping up with Sublette. Dust swirled up. The heavy drumming of hoofs eliminated conversation. Barry contained his seething impatience over the fact that he hadn't had a chance to ask about the one who had haunted his thoughts for the past year, Maria DeVises.

The horses cantered through the dry wash, then moved more rapidly toward a ravine that stretched across the valley. They scented water. Sublette lifted his arm and signaled the bush lopers to slow down. The first horses slid down the ravine's steep bank and rushed toward a spring, and the pack horses stumbled and slid after them, the bush lopers cursing and trying to control them.

The ravine soon seethed with activity as the bush lopers began unloading the horses. Barry unsaddled and began collecting dried, sun-bleached wood that had been washed from the nearby foothills and deposited along the sides of the ravine during downpours. Fitzpatrick and Sublette saw to their horses. They were opening a bag of supplies and cooking utensils and discussing the rendezvous when Barry returned to the campsite with an armload of wood. Fitzpatrick broke off and looked at him as he began arranging stones in a circle to build a fire.

"You say the family's all right, Barry?"

"Everyone's fine, and they send their best. Have you seen the DeVises lately?"

Fitzpatrick chuckled. "I saw Maria last Christmas. You'd better brace yourself for a surprise."

Barry straightened up, frowning. "A surprise? She's not married, is she?"

"No, she's not married," Fitzpatrick laughed. "Where in the hell would she find a preacher? No, she's a free trapper now, Barry."

Barry was bewildered. "Maria? You mean she's a . . . you mean she's trapping pelts?"

"Who's this?" Sublette asked.

"Pierre DeVises' girl, Maria," Fitzpatrick said. "It all started when I was taking that bunch of people and supplies in last summer. One of the people along was old Seth Harnett, and Maria reminded him of his girl who was killed or something. While we was traveling along, old Seth spent a lot of time with her, riding out into the prairie with her and helping her collect buffalo chips and first one thing then another. Then he taught her to shoot a rifle. I'll be damned if she didn't get to where she was bringing in as much or more meat than any man in the party."

"Maria?" Barry said in astonishment.

"Maria," Fitzpatrick replied firmly. "Barry, instead of just looking at them pretty eyes, you want to take a look at what's in them. If I go to get into a tussle with a man and he has eyes like that, then I think again about how mad I am at him and how much I need to tussle with him. She's got as steady a look about her as anybody I ever saw. I noticed that the first time I saw her. She knows what she wants, and she'll go to it like a martin to its gourd, come hell or high water."

"Well, what about her trapping?" Sublette mused. "She sounds like another Annette Thibideau."

Fitzpatrick laughed. "You ain't far off, except that she might learn Annette Thibideau how to go about it, from what Seth says. When we got to Fort Henry we split up and left, and Pierre was in my brigade. We stayed out a while and made a pretty good catch, and we come back in just before Christmas to thaw out and get some more supplies. And Maria was gone, left the very day we did. Everybody figured she was with old Seth, and Pierre was like a bobcat with its foot in a hornet's nest, going to choke her and Seth both to death when he laid eyes on them. Well, about three days after we got in, damned if Seth and Maria didn't come moseying in too." He slapped his thigh. "And I'll be damned if Maria hadn't caught over two packs of beaver pelts."

"Over two packs?" Sublette said skeptically. "Some girl just went out and caught over two packs of beaver pelts in half a season? Was it her or Seth running the traps? And did he have any pelts?"

"He had about the same hisself, and it was her running the traps," Fitzpatrick replied. "Of course, she had the best trapper in the mountains learning her, but Seth said she had more natural woods sense than anybody he had ever seen, along with a mind like a snapping turtle. And I can believe it. You will too when you see her. She wears buckskins more fancied up with beads and doo-dads than Jim Bridger ever thought of wearing, and she carries her a tomahawk and fighting knife. What's more, Seth says she can use them. He says it didn't take her a week to learn how to fling a tomahawk good enough to trim a gnat's whiskers from thirty feet. Anyway, I went over to Pierre's cabin to talk to her about her pelts right after her and Seth got in, and she was sitting at the table and eating her supper as big as you please, her and Pierre both looking like they was fixing to jump at each other's throats. Damnedest thing I ever seen."

Sublette laughed and shook his head. "Well, I guess he had to let her go back out then, if she caught over two packs. Wish we had a few trappers like that ourselves."

"Nothing else he could do," Fitzpatrick pointed out. "When somebody catches pelts like that, then they're a trapper, be they a man or a woman." His smile faded, and he said grimly, "We can use her pelts, God knows. That son of a bitch Kruger has just about cut us out of the trade on the Snake."

"Is that the bastard who's with the American Fur Company?"

Fitzpatrick nodded morosely. "And I'm the one who took him to the Snake. I keep telling myself that he would have got there one way or the other even if I hadn't took him, and I keep having a harder time convincing myself of it. He's been paying the Indians half again as much as we can for pelts, the same trick they pulled on the Missouri."

"Well, you wasn't to know what he was up to Tom, from what I heard."

"Like I said, I keep having a harder time convincing myself, Bill. You know, that's the damnedest family I ever saw. He's got a pair of twins about the age of Barry here, or maybe a little older, and one of them is up north of Three Forks and working for the Hudson's Bay Company. And I sure have a suspicion that it's him who's causing all this trouble with the Blackfeet. The Hudson's Bay Company would like nothing better than to run everybody else out and have the whole territory, and that might be what he's up to. But the other boy is as good a man as you'd ever want to meet. He's a free trapper, and he won't deal with his pa or give the time of day to his brother."

"I don't have much use for any of them myself," Barry said, piling slivers from a stick in the circle of stones. He pulled the canvas bag around and took the flint, steel and tinderbox from it. "You never know which one of those damned twins you're looking at."

Fitzpatrick laughed and slapped Barry's shoulder. "Well, you might have something against them that I don't, Barry. They're set up good with their yellow hair and all, the kind that a woman wouldn't find it hard to look at, but see, I ain't worried about no woman who might be looking at them."

Barry shrugged, knocking the flint and steel together over the tinderbox. "I just don't like to wonder who I'm talking to, that's all."

"Or who might be talking to them, or I'll miss my guess," Fitzpatrick said teasingly, climbing to his feet. "Well, I'll go get us some water so we can get some coffee on. I've been traveling light, and it's been a few days since I've had any."

"I'll see what we've got to eat here," Sublette said. "Tomorrow's going to be another hard day, and I'm ready for a bite and my blanket."

Fitzpatrick picked up a bucket and walked toward the spring, and Sublette rummaged through the bag for the flitch of bacon. Barry put the flint to the tinderbox and lit the fire, feeding it with wood until it blazed. It was still difficult for him to believe what his uncle had told him about Maria. All during the endless months of the autumn, winter, and spring, a vision of a beautiful young woman in a sunbonnet and calico dress had sustained him.

It was almost impossible to imagine her in buckskins, a trapper. But the constant worry that had gnawed at him was that she would find someone else, and that she apparently hadn't. The fire began burning hotly and he sat back with a satisfied sigh.

The sun set and darkness fell as they cooked and ate. Later, Barry drifted off into a comfortable sleep, hearing the nearby Fitzpatrick and Sublette discuss the choices of trails from South Pass to Pierre's Hole. Then the men rolled in their blankets, the fire died down, and Barry, asleep, dreamed of Pierre's Hole and Maria.

Next morning, they left the plains behind them, entered the foothills and began the long climb to South Pass. The first few sparse and spindly trees thickened into deep forests. Water became plentiful. The trail led upwards through folds and clefts in the hills and Sublette then began to drive the bush lopers and horses even harder. They struggled along the rocky, brushy trail and across streams and creeks. Canvas bags burst open. Loads shifted and fell from packsaddles. More horses went lame. Barry, sore and weary each night from hurriedly repacking loads and catching up with the pack trains, was nevertheless captivated by the primitive, untouched beauty of the wilderness. And he was caught up in the spirit of competition that motivated Sublette and Fitzpatrick, moving them relentlessly to reach the rendezvous before the American Fur Company did.

The trail wound deeper into the mountains. Along gullies and streams, the trees were dense now—oaks, poplars, birches and elms abounded. Then, higher up, as they neared the Sweetwater River, came thickets of pine, cedar and spruce. Barry, like

Maria before him, found the mountains incredibly beautiful and a supreme challenge. He worried about the Sweetwater crossing. But when they got there, during a late afternoon, they found the river had subsided from its spring flood, and the crossing was relatively easy, with no horses injured or loads spilled. They made camp on the wide, rocky west bank. Fitzpatrick was to leave them here. He was up early the next morning, looking through all the horses to pick out two of the best for his fast ride ahead toward Pierre's Hole. When he had them, he came over to Barry, who, for breakfast, was heating the leftover food and coffee from the night before.

"I'll see you at Pierre's Hole, Barry."

"I'll be looking forward to it. Be careful of those Indians."

"I'll keep my eyes open. When you get there, we can talk about what you're going to do."

"All right. Do you think Maria will be there? I had a dream that she would be."

Fitzpatrick said gravely, "As like as not, I expect. I'm taking a brigade out after the rendezvous, and that would be a handy way for you to get your hand into trapping."

"I'm obliged, but I was thinking about going with a free trapper if I could find one who'd take me along. Do you think that Seth Harnett would?"

"No, Seth wouldn't, Barry. He's trapped a season with first one then another, but he's mostly a loner. Maria's the only one I've known him to have a lot to do with. You know, if you're took with the mountains, Jim Bridger has got an idea to take a brigade all the way over to Alta California. Jed Smith was over that way a couple or three years ago, and it's good trapping and a lot to see. There's mountains there that touch the sky, and beaver so thick you have to kick them out of the way to set a trap."

"Well, I was thinking more about staying pretty close to the Snake."

Fitzpatrick nodded. It was pre-dawn and the stars were still out. He looked up at them, fingering his beard. Then he looked back at Barry and sighed. "I hope you ain't got something in your craw that'll choke you if it won't go up or down, Barry."

"What do you mean?"

"About Maria. She's got trapping on her mind, Barry, not marrying. A man can get took so hard on something that he loses hold on hisself if he can't have it, and I'd hate to think you're took like that. You've got a lot ahead of you here, Barry. You can learn to trap, do some trading if it suits you, or go with Bridger and see places white men have never seen before. And a lot of other things besides. I want you to think on that, Barry."

Barry said slowly, "I will."

"I'll see you at Pierre's Hole."

"Yes, in a few days. Be careful."

Fitzpatrick waved, mounting his horse, and his horses' hoofs clattered against the stones as he rode away.

Barry watched him go for a while, musing. Then he gathered up his horse's reins and led it toward the cluster of horses the bush lopers were loading and forming into pack trains.

13

There was a movement at the top of the sloping meadow. A half-dozen Indians suddenly charged out of the trees, leaning over their horses' necks as they shrieked piercingly and brandished lances, bows and rifles. Another dozen shot out of the trees behind them; then more ran out in scattered twos and threes.

Barry's stab of alarm faded as Sublette whooped with delight, standing in his stirrups and looking back at the bush lopers.

"The other company ain't here yet, or these Injuns wouldn't be acting that way! Get them horses to moving! Let's go! Let's go!"

The bush lopers began shouting and whipping the weary horses into yet another maximum effort. Barry cantered his horse over to Sublette's. The Indians thundered down on them, circling the pack trains and howling wildly.

"God damned pesky savages!" Sublette muttered. "Nuisances, all of them."

He looked back, storming angrily at the bush lopers to get a move on. Then he whipped his horse, as if fleeing the welcoming Indians. Barry kicked his horse into a run to follow. Their two mounts and the pack horses behind them weaved from side to side in fright from the uproar around them. More Indians came out of the trees, some on horses and others on foot. While they crowded around the goods-laden pack trains, Barry, galloping ahead, leaned low to dodge some low branches, then swept down into a wide valley.

What he saw astonished him. The valley's level floor was crossed by streams lined with shimmering green cottonwood groves. The snow-capped peaks of the Tetons towered above its east wall, as if just recently etched against the blue sky. Everything was clear and sparkling in the mountain air. The Indians had arrived in force. Clusters of brightly-decorated tepees were scattered along creeklines, with streamers dancing in the breeze at the tips of their lodge poles. Lean-tos, piles of belongings and smoking fires lined other creeks, where scores of Indians without women and children were camped. Barry saw the trappers and free traders encamped as well, in lean-tos much like the Indians but with more familiar cookfire equipment in front. Hundreds of horses were roped in corrals or hobbled in herds on the meadows between the creeks. Some were being raced by groups of Indians from different tribes, on a trampled space between clusters of lodges, the hubbub sending scores of onlookers scurrying about.

An outbreak of whooping and shouting came from the valley as the pack trains behind Barry came into view. Rifles went off, and the horse-racing stopped as crowds of Indians surged past him for a glimpse of the goods.

Standing in his stirrups as he rode, Barry peered through the milling throng, searching for faces he recognized. He saw Ludlow, Porter, Innes, Bridger, DeVises and a few others he knew, but Maria and Harnett weren't among them. Nor was Fitzpatrick. At one side of the main cluster of men, he saw Curtis Kruger standing silently, his arms folded.

Barry reined up and waited for Sublette, who soon came up with the pack trains. Most of the Indians began leaving, racing toward their camps for the furs they had to trade for the merchandise they'd seen. Through them pushed Bridger, who finally got close enough to Sublette to shout a greeting.

"You made it, Bill! Bunch them right over here, and let's get them unloaded and get set up!"

"Swing them around this way!" Sublette shouted back at the bush lopers, motioning. "Get a move on, and let's get them unloaded!" He looked back at Bridger. "Where's the American Fur boys?"

"Nobody knows. They could be coming across the ridge within the next five minutes. We've got plenty of help here, so let's get at it. Jake, get your men over here to help unload. Pierre, get your men to put out some blankets for a trading line. Amos, get these fires along here built up to make some mountain liquor."

The men set off on the run. Sublette looked around as he dismounted. "Where's Tom?"

Bridger shook his head. "We ain't seen hide nor hair of him since he left here to come and meet you. You didn't see him?"

"Yes, but he left us at the Sweetwater to come on in and tell you all that we were on our way."

"Well, we ain't seen him since he left. . . ." He smiled and extended his hand as Barry dismounted. "It's good to see you again, Barry. And mighty good to have you out here."

"It's good to see you again. You say my uncle didn't get back?"

"Oh, don't worry about old Broken Hand," Bridger chuckled. "He's run into a little piece of trouble somewhere, but he'll be along directly. Don't you worry about him." He turned back to Sublette. "Bill, me and you and Jake can do the dickering for the furs, if that suits you."

"It suits me."

"Let's go on down here and get ready, then. Sam, get the bags of trading sticks and bring them down here! And get us some bush lopers to bundle the furs! Jake, come on down here and give me and Bill a hand with the dickering!"

Bridger and Sublette walked away. Barry led his horse to one side of the frenzied activity, nodding and waving to men he recognized. The bush lopers and men from a trapping brigade, having unloaded the pack horses, were piling the bags at the end of the cluster of lean-tos Bridger had had built. DeVises and a crew of a half dozen men were unfolding and spreading blankets in a line a few yards from the creek. Porter was bringing buckets of water in preparation for a whisky still. All looked so busy at the moment that Barry somehow felt out of place.

"It's good to see you again," a man said quietly.

Barry turned. It was Curtis Kruger, looking at him with a neutral expression but with something of a frank, congenial air about him. Barry hesitated. He felt an urged to be friendly towards the blond youth in spite of himself. "It's good to see you again," he said. "Have you been here long?"

"I got in day before yesterday."

"I don't guess all the free trappers and traders are in yet, are they?"

"Well, I don't know all of them, but I know a couple who aren't, and I've heard the other men mention some more who aren't. Tincey Appleby and Shoat Tyler aren't here, and neither is Charlie Jackson. Seth Harnett and Maria DeVises haven't shown up, and Red Frobisher hasn't either. There are some others, and some of them might not come, of course. Or they might be having trouble with the Blackfeet."

Kruger's tone hadn't changed when he said Maria's name. Her name had been nonchalantly tucked in among the rest, apparently not occurring to him before any of the others. Barry felt perceptibly warmer toward him. "I guess there's still plenty of time for them to get here yet, though, isn't there?"

"Oh, yes. None of the free trappers and traders do business with the pack trains until the Indians are taken care of. We get a different price for our furs, and no one wants the Indians finding out."

"Where did you go this past season?"

"Cooper's Canyon, south and west of here. It was better than where I used to trap along the Missouri, though not as good as some of the places other people went, judging from the amount of furs they brought in. Will you be going with Tom this coming season?"

"I'm not sure yet. I hope he's here to take a brigade out. He left us at the Sweetwater and came on ahead, and there's no sign of him."

"I wouldn't worry about it. He's been in and out of a lot of tight places. He's probably run into something and has holed up for a while."

Barry nodded unsurely, looking away. He glanced over the clusters of lodges and encampments along the creeks. "There's sure a lot of different tribes of Indians here. Have they been having any trouble with each other?"

"Nothing their chiefs couldn't settle. It shows that people can get along with each other when they want to, doesn't it?"

His voice seemed to carry an undertone of meaning beyond what he was saying about Indians. But his mild, amiable smile remained unchanged. Barry hesitated, gathering the reins on his horse. "Maybe so. Well, I think I'll unsaddle my horse and settle down."

"A lot of the others have been stacking their saddles and things over there on the other side of the lean-tos."

"That looks like as good a place as any. I'll be talking to you again directly, then."

Curtis nodded as Barry turned his horse and led it away. He unsaddled his horse and left his belongings by the lean-tos as Curtis had suggested, then led his horse to the corral and roped it. By then, most of Bridger's ordered preparations had been made and trading with the Indians had begun. DeVises and men helping him were sorting through the bags of trade goods and carrying some of the goods to the line of blankets on the ground, and Porter and other men were taking out demijohns of whiskey and carrying them around to the front of the lean-tos. Bridger, Sublette, and Ludlow were spread out several yards from the end of the blankets, greeting the Indians who were swarming back across the creek with their furs. Barry walked toward Bridger's group.

The three men were examining some furs and bartering with the Indians who'd brought them in a mixture of sign language and broken English and French. The Indians were trading for counters: smooth hickory sticks with rings cut into them. They had hides and furs of different kinds, but all the skins were valued in relation to the standard of exchange, a prime winter beaver pelt, which the rings on the counters represented. When a transaction with an Indian was completed, the purchased furs were baled and thrown into a pile by company workers.

All of the white men were working feverishly to acquire the furs before the American Fur Company pack trains arrived, so the bartering place was a seething, noisy mass of activity. Pushing among the Indians was common, with those near the white men shoving each other to be next. Angry shouts and blows were exchanged in the middle of the crowd when someone was pushed too hard, and there were further arguments between the Indians and traders over the value of the furs. Sometimes these arguments became heated. When one group of Indians didn't get a trade they felt entitled to, Barry saw them snatch up their furs and stalk away, muttering and glaring belligerently.

Some of the Indians who had exchanged their furs for counters were moving along the line of blankets and looking at the goods DeVises and his men had arranged in tempting displays. They peered and squinted at rifles, powder horns, shot pouches, tomahawks, axes, and axe heads. The next blanket might have cannisters of gunpowder, rifle flints, bar lead, bullet molds, and rod iron for making arrow and lance points. Further along were bolts of cloth, ribbons, packages of needles, awls, stacks of hand mirrors. Still other blankets were covered with stacks of kettles in various sizes, piles of hats, shirts and blankets, pots of ocher, vermillion, and other colors of face paints.

It seemed to Barry there were more goods here than in many a small Missouri town. There were mounds of twists and plugs of tobacco, a large assortment of foodstuffs and spices, a wide variety of bright decorative trinkets. He walked along the blankets, just looking at things. DeVises glanced at him and nodded, cordially enough. Barry, grateful for that, smiled and nodded back. DeVises was bartering over a rifle with two Indians who looked to Barry like father and son, one with grey hair and a kind of stand-offish dignity, the other a rebellious youth who didn't seem to care for DeVises at all. He showed it by sneering at every rifle DeVises showed him, which had DeVises blinking in rage. Barry shrugged. So be it. That was DeVises all right; the diplomatic touch was something he lacked.

Porter was stirring a kettle on a fire in front of a lean-to a few yards away. A line of Indians holding new kettles and tin cups were waiting patiently for his kettle to get done. Barry walked Porter's way. He was greeted like the missed friend he was.

"It's good to see you again, Barry."

"It's good to see you, Amos. How did you do last winter?"

"Oh, I spent most of the time in the trading post and drew wages. So you've come out to join us, have you?"

Barry nodded, looking at the kettle on the fire. The steam from it had a rank, strong odor, and it was filled with a thick, dark liquid. "That's the whiskey?"

Porter nodded. "The fixings for some of the best mountain liquor you'll ever taste." He had a keg nearby, which he put some boiling water into. "My own recipe. Two handfuls of Spanish peppers, a pound twist of tobacco and about a handful of wormwood, all ground up. And I put in a pound of Jamaica ginger, a quart of molasses, and a gallon of whiskey." He dumped the ginger into the keg, then stirred it with a wooden paddle and poured in the molasses. He grinned at Barry. "Some say that a couple of rattlesnake heads give mountain liquor a little more spunk, but I don't use them. With my mountain liquor, I'll guarantee that you wouldn't be able to tell the difference if a whole rattlesnake jumped out of the cup and down your throat." He poured in a demijohn of whiskey and stirred the keg. "You want to try her out, Barry?"

"No, I'm not thirsty right now, thanks."

Porter laughed uproariously. "This ain't to cure thirst, Barry, this is to make it. Hell, I'll try her myself. Let me see that cup, chief. Just give me your cup a minute."

An Indian in the front of the line handed Porter a tin cup as he snapped his fingers and reached for it. Porter dipped it into the keg and half filled it. The Indians nodded, chuckled and smiled as Porter lifted the cup toward them, then watched raptly as he tilted his head back and drank the liquid rapidly.

A flush spread over Porter's face. He lowered the cup and handed it back to the Indian as he wheezed, coughed and stamped his feet.

"By God, that's mountain liquor! I'd like to see anybody make a better batch! All right, chief, just step right up. No, give me your trading stick first, then I'll fill your kettle. That's right. . . ."

Most of the Indians were in twos and threes, sharing a kettle, and one in front of the line handed Porter a counter. Porter took out a knife and cut a deep notch into the counter's end ring, handed it back, then took the gallon kettle from the Indian and lowered it into the keg. He lifted it back out, the dark liquid dripping from it, and the Indian and two others carrying cups walked toward the creek with it. Porter motioned to the next Indians in line, and one of them handed over a counter.

Several Indians were already sitting on the creek's far bank, downing cups of Porter's mountain liquor, and two of Porter's men were making more of it at fires on along the front of the lean-tos, where long lines of Indians waited for it. Barry watched all this in amusement, but also with a sense that it might be a bit dangerous to ply Indians with whisky, whether it was romanticized as "mountain liquor" or anything else. Still, the whisky-fur trade seemed to be satisfying both parties to it and no Indian was really acting rambunctious, so all in all he figured that it was all right. When Porter's helpers began shredding tobacco to put in a new batch of the brew, something he had seen before, he moved on.

He had a hankering to get back to DeVises sooner or later so as to learn from him what he could about Maria. But DeVises remained busy with the Indian trade for the rest of the day, so Barry kept wandering and observing. As the hours passed, he saw incidents that genuinely disturbed him.

There were shrieking battles between Indians and their squaws, for one thing. The squaws wanted blankets. More and more, the braves wanted mountain liquor. Scuffles broke out. As some squaws tried to snatch the priceless counters from their men, the men shouted and cuffed them. The squaws kicked and scratched back. Some were hurled roughly to the ground for their efforts. Onlookers, both Indians and white traders, pointed and laughed, which sent the infuriated braves back for more whisky.

Elsewhere, several Indians who had been disappointed by the traders' offers and had refused to take them, stood around in twos and threes, frowning and muttering. They were apparently too proud to dicker further. After a while, they began to drift towards the creek to drink, wrestle and have rifle-shooting matches with the Indians already there. By then, several of the squaws who had fought with their men to no avail, had given up and joined them in drinking sprees along the creek. Squaws and braves laughed aimlessly, rolled around and wrestled drunkenly, then staggered back to the kegs to trade for more when their kettles were empty.

Barry still couldn't decide whether what he was perceiving was merely boisterous play or something portentous of further displays of rage. If the latter, he felt there wasn't much he could do about it. Bridger was far wiser than he in Indian matters, and Bridger was in charge.

The Indians began drifting back to their lodges and encampments as the sun set. Smoke from their cooking fires made a filmy haze over the valley. Many lay along the creek in sodden sleep, while others kept racing horses wildly about. Occasional rifle shots rang out. The first trading day having ended, the traders gathered up their goods and blankets and put them into the lean-tos, under guards posted by Sublette and Bridger.

Darkness fell, and Barry joined Bridger, Sublette, DeVises and several others at their company fire. The men were in expansive good humor. They had collected an enormous amount of furs and they had gotten a good head start on the American Fur Company. They laughed and slapped each other's backs as they ate and drank cups of mountain liquor.

But Barry was weary. Saying little during dinner, he left soon afterwards, got his saddle and belongings from where he had left them and walked to an opening between two lean-tos, where he'd decided to bed down. On the way, he noticed Curtis Kruger sitting by a fire and eating by himself. He wanted to talk to Kruger, who looked lonely, but the situation in his mind was complicated. Several comments Barry had overheard at dinner indicated that Curtis was being avoided because of the general disfavor in which his father and brother were held. Also, Curtis had made little effort to make friends, it was pointed out. DeVises, for one, had made several acrimonious remarks about all the Krugers, which was the final rub, as far as Barry was concerned. He didn't want to do anything to alienate DeVises, not with Maria in the balance. Feeling cowardly and aggravated at himself for not going to talk to Curtis, Barry passed him by with a slight nod.

He lay on his bedroll, looking at the stars, then, as the night developed, at the activity teeming all about him in the valley.

Many of the bush lopers and trappers were drunk and crowding into shelters with Indian squaws, arguing loudly over who was next.

A large fire burned on the far side of the creek. Indians shuffled around it in a wild, drunken dance. Others lay sprawled in the edges of the firelight.

An Indian chased a young squaw from one of the encampments, snatching at her as she shrieked and tried to evade him. He caught her near the creek. They were silhouetted by the fire there as they struggled. The Indian pulled at the girl's meager dress with clumsy determination, while onlooking white traders shouted ribald encouragement. The woman struggled harder. The Indian pushed her down to the ground, and she screamed shrilly as her limbs flailed. A white man suddenly splashed through the creek, stumbling from drunkenness and laughter. He and a couple of Indians from the fire moved toward the couple and knelt by them. They seized the girl's legs and held them apart. Her screams became louder as the Indian on top of her fumbled with her and his hips began moving.

Barry rolled in his blanket and pillowed his head on his saddle, but the noisy confusion around him and his racing thoughts kept him awake. He worried about what might have happened to Fitzpatrick and he wondered if Maria would come to the rendezvous.

14

"Ain't you going over there and learn them fellows how to shoot a rifle, Barry?" Bridger chuckled through a mouthful of bacon and beans.

Barry shrugged and smiled, taking another bite from his plate. "I might go take a shot directly, but I'm not that good."

It was early the next morning. Trading had already begun and there was a rifle match taking place in the meadow beyond the Indians' encampment. Nearer by at the creek, a few Indians were sleeping in their vomit.

Sublette looked at a face-painted subchief barking at several Indians already in line for mountain liquor. He chewed rapidly, his beard twitching, and he took another large bite. "That chief sure don't like to see them getting drunk, does he?"

Innes grunted morosely, chewing with an expression of distaste. He put his plate down and picked up his coffee cup, sighing and rubbing his forehead. "I sure wish I'd had me some kind of chief or somebody to wean me of it before I got my hide so full last night."

"Maybe you just got hold of a dirty cup, Sam," Sublette chuckled cheerfully. "Somebody might have had some water or something like that in it."

"I got hold of me a bellyful of brimstone, is what I got," Innes muttered, taking a sip of coffee. "I'd have to feel a lot better than I do right now just to die."

The men chuckled, and Bridger looked at Barry again. "Are you going with Tom this coming season?"

"We talked about it. but I'm not sure yet."

"Well, after the rendezvous, I'm going to be taking my brigade to Fort Henry to shoe our horses and get everything set. Then we'll be leaving for Alta California. I wouldn't mind having another good man along, so you can think about—"

He broke off and turned as some bartering between Ludlow and an Indian suddenly turned into a heated argument. The two were bellowing at each other at the top of their lungs. Barry put his plate down and rose along with the others around the fire. Sublette looked at DeVises and motioned. DeVises and another man behind the blankets stepped toward the lean-tos and picked up rifles. The Indian arguing with Ludlow leaped back, jerked out his tomahawk and lifted it threateningly, his face twisted with rage.

There was a frozen silence and lack of motion for an instant. Then Sublette and Bridger walked toward Ludlow and the Indian with long, rapid steps. Barry glanced at Innes uncertainly. Innes was just watching, sucking his teeth and moving his tongue around in his mouth absently, his eyes narrow and his hangover apparently forgotten. Sublette stepped in front of Ludlow, pushing him back with his shoulder, and Bridger started talking to the Indian. The Indian took another step backwards, glaring at Bridger and shaking his tomahawk menacingly.

A single loud, piercing syllable suddenly rang out in a commanding tone, and everyone's attention shifted to the subchief who'd been haranguing those on the mountain liquor line. The subchief gazed stonily at the tomahawk-wielding Indian, his lips thin and his features lean and craggy under his stripes of ocher and vermillion. The Indian stared back at him, his expression becoming sullen and resentful. Again the subchief spoke, this time in a quiet, steely voice. The Indian lowered the tomahawk and pushed it under the back of his belt. The subchief then walked toward him with a slow, dignified pace, the carapace of bear teeth and whitened bone on his scarred chest rattling softly. A single feather hung motionless from his scalplock.

When he reached Sublette, the subchief stopped and motioned him aside with an imperious gesture. Sublette stepped away. The subchief looked down at the furs on the ground, moved them with his toe, then held out his hand to Ludlow for the counter he had been offering in the trade. Ludlow handed it over. The subchief scrutinized both the counter and the furs again, then looked at Ludlow and lifted a finger. Bridger nodded to Ludlow, who then reached into the bag of counters at his feet and substituted one for the counter the subchief was holding. The subchief stonily gave this new counter to the disputatious Indian. The latter hesitated, then took it and stalked angrily away.

The argument had ended as quickly as it had begun. The subchief turned and walked back toward the liquor line and the traders suddenly relaxed. All came back to the breakfast fire except for De-Vises and Ludlow, who remained at the blankets and started trading, now amicably enough, with several chuckling Indians who'd seen the near-fight.

"Pierre, give the chief there some tobacco!" Bridger called out from the fire.

DeVises leaned over his blanket, got some cured twists from his pile and tried to do just that. But the subchief, now at the liquor line, merely glanced at DeVises and the tobacco and shook his head disdainfully. DeVises looked at Bridger and shrugged, and Bridger shrugged back. The subchief was obviously intent on other matters. As an Indian turned away from the keg with a brimming kettle of mountain liquor, he snarled angrily, took a quick step forward and slapped it out of his hands. The dark liquid gushed out on the ground. Its purchaser looked at it in dismay, but under the subchief's baleful gaze said nothing.

Watching from the fire, Innes shook his head.

"That fracas with Ludlow looked a little troublesome there for just a minute," he said as he picked up his coffee cup.

"It could have been," Bridger said nonchalantly. "You remember that fracas Ben Clyman had last year. I'm just glad that chief was here so we didn't have to take care of it ourselves."

"He ain't exactly helping our mountain liquor

trade," Sublette remarked, watching the subchief renew his haranguing of others in the line.

Bridger laughed. "He ain't hurting it that much, either. About half of them ain't in his tribe, and he can't tell them what to do. And the ones that are in his tribe will still be around when he gets tired and leaves."

"Do you have a lot of trouble with them when you're trading?" Barry asked Bridger. He'd been studying both the conflicts and the traders' nonchalance, trying to make more sense out of them than he had.

Bridger shook his head, picking up his plate and taking a bite. "Not a lot. Some of them get feisty, just like white men do, but we can take care of it when we have to. The only time trouble is really bad is before we get the furs took up. Right, Bill?"

"That's right. I don't like anything holding up the trading, but we've got most of the furs now. They hold back a few to stretch their trading out some, but we've got enough. I wouldn't care if the American Fur Company trains came over the hill right now."

"Well, it ain't the American Fur Company pack trains," Innes said, stretching and looking at the distant meadow. "But look who's coming. I'll be goldarned!"

Barry craned his neck and looked. Abruptly, he stopped chewing. It was Maria. She was alone, riding a white paint.

Barry leaped to his feet and peered at her disbelievingly. He had been told about her, yes, but seeing her, taking her in as she approached, was something else again.

Her buckskins had been made of hides broken and softened until they were a pale buff. Brilliant beading ran down the front of her shirt, on her moccasins, and on the bands holding up her leggings. Long fringes hung from the shirt's yoke, from the seams of her sleeves, from her breeches and leggings. Even the short, heavy rifle resting across her arm had been decorated in the wilderness with wilderness things; tufts of fur and feathers dangled on short thongs from the end of the barrel, the ramrod thimbles, the forearm. Her hair was shorter, barely down to her shoulders, and it was tied back. Her hat was tilted forward, the brim partly shadowing her face. As she sat the charcoal-spotted white paint, her back as ramrod-straight as an Indian's, she was, to Barry, even more beautiful than ever.

"Here comes your girl, Pierre," Bridger called.

DeVises stepped away from the blankets, craning his neck, then came over to the fire to see out at his daughter better. Barry glanced at him nervously, wondering what his reaction would be. In that glance he also saw, past DeVises, Curtis Kruger, who was just leaving his lean-to with his rifle, headed for the rifle matches. He saw Kruger look once at Maria then walk on, apparently uncaringly, towards the distant firing of guns.

Barry looked back at Maria and saw now that she wasn't alone after all. From behind her over the hill came Seth Harnett, leading four pack horses, each heavily loaded with what seemed like a small mountain of furs. They came down the meadow and past the rope corral at a slow, casual walk, with an attitude of having covered vast distances at a deliberate, patient pace.

When they were close enough, Barry saw that

both were bronzed by the sun and looked somehow alike in other ways. The year had taken the traces of girlishness from Maria's features; she was a beautiful blue-eyed woman now. But more than that, her mouth and chin were set in the same grim, determined lines as the man she rode with.

They drew up to the fire.

"It's good to see you again, Seth, Maria," Bridger said heartily. "It took you a while to get here, didn't it?"

"How do, Jim, Bill, Sam," Harnett said, dismounting. "Why, Barry. It's good to see you again, boy, and you too, Pierre. We took our time getting here because there's a Blackfoot behind every tree and rock in the Rockies."

"It looks like you did all right, though," Sublette said. "That's a bunch of furs there."

"We did all right," Harnett replied. Nodding and smiling, he stepped forward and shook hands with the men.

Maria still sat on her horse, she and her father looking at each other. "Hello, pa."

"Hello, Maria. Did you see some Blackfeet, then?"

She nodded, dismounting and extending her hand. "We saw a few, but they didn't see us." They shook hands, and she smiled at Barry, holding out her hand. "It's good to see you again, Barry."

Her hand was small, warm and firm, and her smile was as dazzling as her brightly-decorated buckskins. "It's sure good to see you again, Maria."

She stepped past him, shaking hands with the others. "Hello, Jim, Sam."

"It's mighty good to see you, Maria," Bridger said. "This here is Bill Sublette, Milt's brother."

"I'm pleased to meet you."

"I'm pleased to meet you, Maria. Broken Hand was telling me a lot about you."

"I'm glad to see what he told you wasn't so bad that you wouldn't come on in."

"No, no," Sublette laughed. "Broken Hand's mighty taken with you, Maria, and he didn't have nothing but good to say."

"Well, I won't lie about him either, then."

The men laughed uproariously. Bridger almost slapped Maria on the shoulder, but dropped his hand without touching her. "Tom got held up somewhere between the Sweetwater and here," he said. "He rode out to meet Bill here and then left him at the Sweetwater to come on in, but we ain't seen hide nor hair of him."

Harnett grunted, frowning thoughtfully and stroking his beard, then shrugged. "Well, Tom knows what he's about. . . ."

"Oh, I've no doubt he'll be in directly," Bridger said confidently. "He's just got held up. Would you all like to sit down and have a bite? There's plenty of bacon and beans left in the pan here."

"We had a bite this morning, and I'd like to see to these furs and our horses and settle in," Harnett said. "What do you say, Maria?"

"That's all right with me. Where do you want the furs?"

"Let's just unload them right over here by the huts," Bridger said, pointing. "Me and Bill will make up your tally, and you can take whatever you want in goods and we'll settle with you in gold."

Harnett nodded, turning his horses toward the end of the lean-tos, and the men walked with him, talking to him about his trip in. As Maria turned to follow him, she asked her father about her mother, and he walked beside her, replying. Barry followed, his eyes drawn irresistibly to Maria's slender figure outlined by her buckskins.

She fascinated him now with her more completely developed personality. Her manner was serenely poised and confident. She was quiet and reserved but neither haughty nor arrogant. She was affable enough with the men, for example, talking with them easily in her quiet, ringing voice and even bantering with them, but somehow she managed to keep a distance between herself and them, friendly but not familiar. The buckskins, rifle, and the tomahawk and long fighting knife in the back of her belt were very much a part of her, but she was utterly, totally feminine, with a feline grace in her every movement. She radiated her female nature. To be a woman and a trapper was unusual, but she made it seem commonplace.

The bundles of furs made large stacks on the ground, and Barry helped Maria with hers, peeling the canvas back out of the way and pulling the knots in the ropes loose. Bridger and Sublette knelt and glanced through the furs, nodding with satisfaction. Then Bridger stood back up, dusting his hands together and looking at Harnett. "I'd say they're all prime pelts, Seth."

"I'd say if you can find anything else, it crawled in by itself. You go ahead and take the tally, and me and Maria will settle in."

"All right. Anything we can do to help you?"

"No, we do it all the time," Harnett replied, reaching for his horse's reins. "We'll see you again directly."

He and Maria led their horses around to the rear

of the lean-tos. DeVises walked back toward the blankets to trade some more. Barry hesitated until he'd gone, then followed Maria, taking long steps and catching up with her.

"Could I cut you some poles for a hut or something, Maria?"

She glanced up at him and smiled. "Yes, thank you, Barry. Where are we going to make the huts, Seth?"

"Oh, over there, I guess," he replied, gesturing toward the end of the lean-tos. "I'll meet you down at the creek, Barry."

"Right, Seth." Barry went and got an axe. Down by the creek, he started looking for straight, thick willows. There was a dense stand a short distance up the water, and he was cutting them down and dragging them out onto the bank when Harnett, having roped his horses in the corral, finally approached with his own axe. He looked at the willows Barry had cut down and scratched his head.

"We ain't going to build no cabins, Barry. Just enough for frames will do, because we use them canvases."

"All right, I'll pick out the straightest ones." He groped for what he wanted to say. "Maria must be a good trapper, from all the furs she had."

Harnett nodded, sliding down the bank to a fallen tree. He began chopping limbs off it. "There's things that experience will teach her, but trapping's in her nature and she's better than most right now."

"Are you all going back out to your trapping grounds from here?"

"No, Maria's wanting to see her ma and our horses need to be shod, so we'll be going by Fort Henry before we go back out."

Barry nodded, turning a willow trunk with his foot and trimming it with quick strokes of the axe. The reply answered a vitally important question in his mind. Whatever else he did, he would be going to Fort Henry immediately after the rendezvous.

Harnett chopped several large limbs off the dead tree for firewood as Barry trimmed several of the willow trunks. Together, they dragged the wood back. Maria gave Barry a handful of rawhide thongs and continued sorting through her canvas bags, with Harnett now helping her. Barry watched her from the corners of his eyes and listened to their conversation as he tied the ends of the poles together. He remained absorbingly interested in the way she had changed. She seemed to have new sources of energy. And she was self-sufficient; she needed no one. Her extra clothing and other things were bundled and tied neatly; and the traps in her canvas bags were well-oiled and had the chains and wires wrapped neatly around them. It was evident that Harnett hadn't tended to her traps; she'd done it herself. She had bags of beads and a number of raccoon and fox tails, clearly things of her own choosing, and her love of decoration extended to almost everything—her hunting bag, tomahawk and fighting knife were all decorated with such beads or furs. She made Barry wonder about himself. He wasn't satisfied with his seeming inability to choose and act firmly, though he liked himself well enough for the most part. He wondered whether something of the decisiveness Maria had found in herself might not rub off on him.

But it would take time, even years, before he could come up to her knowledge—even of trapping alone. He'd have to work hard, learn more. But he would do it.

So thinking, Barry put up the lean-tos, gathered stones for the campfire, then left before his presence could become a nuisance. As he walked past the other lean-tos, it occurred to him that Maria's was close to Curtis Kruger's, something that had happened by chance but that was still bothersome.

The American Fur Company pack trains arrived that afternoon, the long lines of horses plodding wearily along and the bush lopers looking dejected, knowing they were late. They went to a creek farther down the valley and put out their fresh merchandise. The horse races and rifle matches on the meadow began breaking up as crowds of Indians collected to see it. Bridger and Sublette went too, partly to see the goods, partly to gloat about how late they were.

But the trade for merchandise actually picked up for both companies once the American had arrived. Porter began doing a booming business in mountain liquor again, despite competition from the rival company's own whisky trade. The revelry in both quarters became more unrestrained again as the sun set. For some reason, Barry was tempted to drink with the traders, to have one wild time of drinking and dancing and singing and to wake up with the rest, sharing their headaches, sharing the grim challenge of the new working day. But, barring the taking of a polite sip of mountain liquor pressed on him at dinner, he did not drink with them. He had memories of a night's drinking a year before. It had left him befuddled when he'd tried to dance with

Maria. He didn't want to get befuddled now. He wanted to see things as clearly as possible.

As he settled himself for the night, pillowing his head on his saddle, it suddenly occurred to him that though he had seen Curtis Kruger come back from the rifle matches, he hadn't seen him since nightfall. Against his will, the image of Maria's lean-to, so close to Curtis's, burned in his mind. Impatiently, he shrugged the image out of his mind. Curtis didn't have a lot to do with the other men; just because he hadn't seen him didn't mean he hadn't gone off somewhere by himself. Why did he have to be with Maria? Why? Bush lopers around a nearby fire were having a loud argument over who had the longest penis. Barry pulled his blanket tighter around himself, trying to blot out all the noises around him from his mind, and he slowly drifted off to sleep.

Sometime during the night, his shoulder was shaken roughly and he snapped awake, sitting up. Seth Harnett was kneeling by him, both shaking him and looking toward the front of the lean-tos. "He's here, Bill!" he shouted. Then he looked down at Barry as he stood up. "Tom has come in, son. He's at the fire down at the end of the huts."

Barry shielded his eyes from the light of the torch, pushing his blanket aside and climbing to his feet. "Is he all right?"

"I've seen him in a hell of a lot better shape, but he's alive. Come on."

Barry hesitated, then snatched up his hat and pulled it on as he followed Seth.

15

The firelight gleamed on the bearded faces of the men crouched around Fitzpatrick as he ate ravenously, shoveling beans and meat into his mouth with a large spoon and washing it down with gulps of coffee. His face was drawn and emaciated, his buckskins were in tatters, and his feet were wrapped in large swaths of dirty cloth.

"They had you treed twice, then?" Sublette asked.

Fitzpatrick nodded, choking, then took a drink of coffee and swallowed. "The sons of bitches is everywhere. They spotted me as I was coming up the Green, and we went hell for leather for twenty miles, until my horse gave out. I hid out in some rocks for two days while they was sniffing all around me and looking for me. I got away on the second night, slipped past them in the dark." He took another large bite and chewed rapidly. "Then I come on up the valley on foot, and I'll be God damned if I didn't run smack into another bunch. I got away from them finally, then I lost my rifle and everything else crossing the river."

"Well, you got away, Tom," Bridger said. "Not many could have done that."

"I might near didn't. And look at me. With my feet like this, I ain't going to be worth nothing for months."

"Hell, you'll be salting a buck's tail within a month," Bridger chuckled. "I've seen you in worse shape from drinking a kettle of mountain liquor."

The men stirred and chuckled, but Fitzpatrick shook his head glumly. "I wish you was sitting here in my hide and hurting while I was sitting over there in yours and grinning, and you'd change your mind mighty fast. Give me some more beans."

"Two bunches was all you saw?" Harnett asked, passing him the kettle.

Fitzpatrick sucked his teeth and shook his head, dipping beans onto his plate. "I saw more like ten bunches, but two saw me. Like I said, they're everywhere."

The men were silently thoughtful as Fitzpatrick refilled his plate and began eating again. Harnett leaned over, picked up Fitzpatrick's cup, refilled it and put it back beside him. "Well, me and Maria saw a God's plenty of them getting here. It's easy for me to tell you what you should have done, Tom, but I opine you might have had your mind set too hard on getting here fast and not hard enough on just getting here."

Fitzpatrick stopped chewing, looking at him, then nodded and shrugged as he began chewing again. "You're right. A man shouldn't run smack into Indians if he has his mind on what he's doing. Not unless they know he's coming and set up an ambush, maybe, and that's not what happened."

"Well, it turned out all right," Bridger said. "You're safe, and you'll be sound enough when you've had a chance to feed up and heal up."

Fitzpatrick grunted and nodded. "It might be a while, though. Have you thought about how we're going to go about breaking up here?"

"We've talked about it," Bridger replied. "Some of the bush lopers in the trapping brigades want to go back to St. Louis and some of Bill's want to stay, so we're going to swap them over. And we don't want for all of us to wind up at Fort Henry at the same time, with everybody waiting around to get horses shod and whatnot, so we thought we'd leave a brigade at a time. I can go last, because it's going to take me a while to get set for my trip to Alta California. We don't have much left over in the way of trade goods to take to the post at Fort Henry, so I thought I'd talk to Drips about buying his, because Bill got in so far ahead of him that Drips ain't traded much. If he'll sell them, then Ludlow ought to be the one to take them to the fort, because the horses in his brigade have been shod lately and they're in better shape. Going by that, you ought to pull out first. But maybe we ought to give you a while to rest and heal up, so we can think about another way of—"

"No, that sounds good to me," Fitzpatrick said, putting his plate down with a sigh and sitting back, rubbing his stomach. "Pierre can take the brigade to the fort, and I'll take things easy and mosey along with you. And if I ain't in good enough shape to take the brigade out when I get there, then Pierre can take it out and I'll stay at the fort. He's been commanding the brigade about half the time, and it's about time he was getting paid for it."

"Well, there's three partners here, so we can decide it," Bridger said. "What do you think about Pierre leading a brigade, Bill?"

"If Tom thinks he can do it, it's fine with me," Sublette said. "How does it set with you, Pierre?"

DeVises beamed and nodded with satisfaction. "I can't think of anything that would set better."

The men around the fire laughed at his emphatic tone, and Fitzpatrick rubbed his stomach again, belching. "Well, it would set good with me if somebody would find me a blanket. I'm going to coil up right here by this fire and get me some sleep."

"I'll get you one," DeVises said, rising. "We have plenty of them in the goods."

Ludlow got up and walked with DeVises toward the lean-tos, talking with him and congratulating him on his possible promotion to brigade leader. Some of the other men began leaving the fire as the conversation with Fitzpatrick died away. Barry, having seen his uncle was all right, got up and left too. He started to lie back down at his camping spot. Then, on an impulse, he walked out from between the lean-tos and looked toward Maria's. The moon was behind a cloud. The meadow was in darkness. There was a movement somewhere out there that could have been a hobbled horse moving quietly. Or it could have been Harnett going off to his lean-to. Barry returned to his blanket and lay down, pulling the blanket around him and settling himself.

In the morning, after breakfast, he visited Maria. Smoke hung over the valley in the early light, men sat around fires and groaned as they drank coffee and nursed hangovers, and Indians were sprawled in drunken sleep all along the creek. At breakfast, Fitzpatrick had been in a more cheerful mood than the night before, but he was thin from the days in the mountains on foot and without food, and he hobbled about on his bandaged feet with a stick for a cane.

Barry found Maria sitting with Harnett by their fire. They were discussing what Fitzpatrick and Bridger had talked about the night before.

"How are you planning to get back to Fort Henry, Seth?" Barry asked.

"Guess we'll leave with the first brigade," Harnett answered, shrugging. "That all right with you, Maria?"

Maria reflected. "Suits me. We already have the gold for our furs. We could leave now."

"Mebbe so. A little company won't hurt, though. Could be more Blackfeet out there than even you could handle."

Maria's eyes twinkled. "I'll acknowledge that," she said, grinning.

Barry immediately decided that he would be leaving with the first brigade too.

While they were talking, Curtis Kruger left his nearby lean-to and started toward the creek. He had his rifle. Across the creek, in the meadow, new shooting matches were about to begin.

Barry hesitated. He did not like himself at all at this point, but he said anyway, "Isn't that one of the Kruger twins, Maria?"

Maria's eyes flickered over the distant walking figure. "So it is," she said casually. "Curtis, I believe."

She took out a pair of new moccasins she had traded for and began beading them. She did not look up from her work.

"Goodby, Barry," she said.

"We'll see you soon again, son," Harnett said cheerily.

Barry stared at Maria, puzzled. Then he stared out at Curtis, equally puzzled.

"Yes, I'll be around," he said tonelessly as he stood. "Goodby, Maria."

He walked off. He did not know why, there was no reason for it, but jealousy throbbed in him anew.

There was a feeling of an ending. When Barry returned to the other lean-tos, some of the free trappers and traders were preparing to leave. Long lines of Indians were queued up for mountain liquor and consuming the brew frantically while it was available. Some of the tribes had already left, drunkenly or otherwise.

Almost immediately, Barry received a bitter disappointment. The leaders of the American Fur Company pack trains had sold their trade goods to Bridger to keep from having to transport them back to St. Louis or make a wide detour through Blackfoot-infested mountains. Fitzpatrick wanted Barry to leave with Bridger's second brigade as an extra rifle to protect these goods, instead of leaving with the first. It meant that he couldn't go with Maria after all, but there was no graceful way to refuse his uncle. Barry accepted the news as cheerfully as possible.

The American Fur Company encampment, which bustled with activity as darkness fell that day, left early the next morning, the long lines of horses filing out of the valley, most of them with empty packsaddles. More of the free trappers and traders left. Tepees were folded and more Indians left. As the valley was depopulated, the peaks of the surrounding Tetons took on a frosty saliency against the empty blue sky. Sharp and clear as they were, they did not exhilarate Barry as they had when he'd first ridden into the valley. As he helped DeVises and his first brigade move out, he had a sense of desolation from them. They towered over him and made him feel small. Something was indeed ending for him, something more than the rendezvous. He could not quite put his finger on what it was. He did not want to. And yet, he knew. He had seen Curtis and Maria and he knew.

DeVises had aroused his men well before dawn, and they began moving out at daybreak, DeVises riding across the creek and the pack trains falling into line behind him. All the pack trains straightened out and fell into line. Then Harnett and Maria rode past as Barry stood by the fire and watched. Barry waved and they waved, but it almost seemed to him that Maria was looking past him and along the line of lean-tos. The sun rose as the pack trains crossed the valley, and Barry watched them until Maria was out of sight. As he turned and sat down at the big fire, he noticed Curtis sitting by his own fire in front of his lean-to, looking dejected as he prodded at the wood with a stick.

Later, Barry went through his belongings and got everything ready to load up the next morning. He went to the corral and checked on his horse, then walked back toward the lean-tos. In addition to DeVises' brigade, Sublette and his men had left, on their return trip to St. Louis, and the valley was taking on an almost deserted appearance. Many of the lean-tos were empty. The frames Barry had assembled for Maria and Harnett looked naked and spindly in the trampled meadow, and litter was scattered about. Curtis hadn't moved, he was still staring into his fire.

Bridger and Fitzpatrick were still there, though. Fitzpatrick, with the bandages off his feet and smearing a thick coating of tallow on his soles, beckoned Barry over to their fire.

"There's some fresh coffee here, Barry. Sit down and have a cup. You'll see her again in a few days."

Barry sat down, reaching for a cup and the coffeepot. "How are your feet feeling now?"

"Oh, they're a lot better. And I've made these moccasins to go over the bandages, so I can get around a lot better now."

"I told you that you'd be good as new within a month," Bridger said.

Fitzpatrick grunted doubtfully, putting the top back on the tallow pot and picking up a bandage. "Well, we'll wait a month and see . . . How'd she take leaving you, Barry?"

Barry thought and shrugged. "With disheartening aplomb," he said sourly.

Fitzpatrick grinned. "You have a mighty colorful way of speaking, Barry, and it's right to the point. I believe you have something of the poet in you."

"I do? I thought *you* did." Barry looked at his colorful mountain-man uncle in some perplexity.

"Shucks, I just talk natural, the way I see things. When you do the same, talk the way you see things, maybe we're both a couple of poets. All right?"

Barry, though pleased, said slowly, "Well, I don't

know about that. About me being a poet, that is. Guess I'll just have to think more about what I am. Sometimes, I just don't know."

Bridger broke in on Barry's musings. He was looking idly at some Indians who were moving out with pack trains, women, children and dogs. "They've got a good way to go," Bridger said. "Seems like they brought their whole tribe over from far off."

Fitzpatrick glanced at the Indians and nodded. "That's the Pawnees from Cheyenne River, ain't they?"

"I believe so."

Fitzpatrick tied the moccasins, then leaned forward, refilled his coffee cup and sat back with a contented sigh. They were silent, Bridger staring into the fire and drinking his coffee, and Barry watching the Pawnees absently as they moved slowly toward the head of the valley. He was still wondering if he would ever see things clearly and know for absolutely sure how he felt about them. An Indian at the mountain liquor keg objected loudly over getting short measure in his kettle, Porter poured more into it, and the Indian turned away with a smugly satisfied expression. Barry looked back at the Pawnees, wondering how much they'd had to drink.

"This coffee sure is good," Fitzpatrick said musingly. "While I was out there eating grass and berries and wearing the bottom off my feet, all I could think of was coffee. Not victuals, just coffee."

"A man gets that way," Bridger replied. "I've gone a hundred miles in the dead of winter to get a chew of tobacco."

Fitzpatrick grunted and nodded. They became

silent again, looking into the fire. Barry watched two Indians on the creek bank as they argued and wrestled drunkenly over the dregs of mountain liquor in a kettle, then spilled it as the kettle slipped from their hands. One of them sat down and held his head in his hands, and the other one tried to get his head into the kettle to lick it.

The Pawnees became small in the distance, individual figures fading into a mottled mass. Barry drained his cup and put it down, then folded his arms and sat back, looking into the fire. Ludlow's voice rose in an angry roar behind the lean-tos as he cursed at bush lopers over something to do with packsaddles. Fitzpatrick and Bridger listened, chuckling. Barry yawned, looking at the Pawnees again. They were nearing the trees at the head of the valley.

Suddenly, a moving ripple spread through the Pawnees. They began spreading apart, the warriors in front forming a line and the women, children, and animals fleeing back into the valley. Barry frowned and looked closer, puzzled. Then he saw the puffs of smoke in the trees ahead of the Pawnees. A muffled popping noise carried across the distance.

Fitzpatrick dropped his cup and sprang to his feet, looking. "God damn, somebody's shooting at them! Barry, go get me a horse! Ludlow, get around here! Form a guard for the horses and goods! Amos, form a company and get them mounted! Sam, get around here. . . ."

Barry ran for a horse. Orders continued ringing out behind him as Fitzpatrick snatched up two bridles from a pile of saddles and more bridles from the end of the lean-tos, bellowing as he went along at a limping run. The sleeply, indolent atmosphere around the lean-tos had dissolved into a bedlam, men shouting and darting about to gather up weapons. Barry swerved in between the two lean-tos where he had left his belongings, picked up his rifle, powder horn and shot pouch, and ran toward the rope corral.

Other men were running toward the corral, Curtis Kruger ahead of everyone else as he raced along with long strides, his rifle in one hand and a bridle in the other. Curtis untied the rope gate and dropped it, then plunged into the horses with the other men on his heels. The horses began rearing and snorting with fright and excitement. Barry shouldered his way in and seized one by an ear, digging in his heels and throwing his weight against the horse as he pushed a bridle onto its head. The horse tried to rear. Curtis started to lead his horse out, then stopped to help Barry. Barry nodded his thanks. While Curtis held the terrified horse, he pushed the bit into its mouth and jerked the bridle onto its head. Then he gathered the reins and helped Curtis pull both horses toward the gate. Once there, he left the one horse, which he'd gotten for Fitzpatrick, momentarily in Curtis's care, pushing back into the crowded corral to get one for himself.

The Indian encampments still in the valley were a melee of frantic activity when the two young men got back to Fitzpatrick. Drunk Indians were staggering about, others were running for their horses, women were collecting their children, and dogs were barking and scurrying about. Swearing, Fitzpatrick swung into the saddle and led the other mounted men, including Barry and Curtis, at a gallop across the meadow, passing the panic-stricken and fleeing Indians as if they were not there. The Pawnee warriors had fallen back from the trees in a scattered line and were exchanging shots at long distance with the attackers in the trees. Several dead and wounded horses were sprawled on the ground near the trees. Three Pawnees lay dead.

Fitzpatrick craned his neck around to look over the riders behind him. Bridger had acted efficiently. He'd taken a contingent around to the left side of the valley and was coming in to flank the attackers. Some braves from the encampments, Pawnees themselves, were strung back across the valley, whipping their horses and trying to catch up with Fitzpatrick. Fitzpatrick lifted his rifle, pulling his horse back to a canter and shouting at the top of his voice.

"Hold up! Hold up! Amos, take twenty men and circle around to the right! Take your time and let the Indians catch up and go in on the left with Bridger!"

Porter wheeled his horse to the right, shouting at men and waving his rifle, and part of the men rode away behind him. Barry pulled his horse back to a trot, checking the priming in his rifle. He snapped the pan lid closed and pulled the hammer back. The Pawnees under attack were moving slowly back to join the approaching riders, shouting imprecations at their enemies concealed in the trees. The reek of gunpowder smoke hung in the air, and the screams of the wounded horses on the ground in front of the trees were loud and shrill over the shouts of the Indians.

"Blackfeet," Fitzpatrick muttered to Barry, reining his horse back to a walk. "I knew it when I heard the first shot."

"Let's go in there and get them, Tom!" someone shouted.

"You wait your God damned hurry!" Fitzpatrick replied angrily. "We're here to do some killing, not to get killed!"

The retreating Pawnees came up. One of them shouted to Fitzpatrick and motioned toward the trees. From the guttural sound he made, he was demanding an immediate attack. Fitzpatrick shook his head, and pointed to Porter and his men, then at Bridger and his flanking group. The Pawnees were furious, their faces contorted with rage under their stripes of paint. Fitzpatrick, adamant, merely waited, ignoring their storms of anger, their continuing wavings of their weapons towards the trees. More men were still riding up from the corral. The angry Pawnees turned from the unswerving Fitzpatrick and began shouting at the Blackfeet, daring them to come out of the trees. Barry's horse was stamping heavily and bobbing its head nervously from the uproar on all sides. He tightened his reins and patted its neck, calming it. Curtis was beside him. Curtis had lost his hat, and his blond hair gleamed in the bright sunshine. He smiled slightly as his eyes met Barry's.

Barry said gruffly, "Thanks for the help with the horse. Better keep your head down when we ride in."

Curtis laughed good-naturedly, pushing his hair back from his forehead. "I will. No point in making any better target than I have to, is there?"

"Guess not." Barry smiled. He felt a sudden warm flush of camaraderie toward Curtis in their shared danger.

A Blackfoot suddenly burst out of the trees, leaning low over the neck of his horse and shrieking wildly. The attack took Barry by surprise, and rifles were firing and arrows were hissing through the air by the time he lifted his rifle. The Blackfoot's horse screamed and floundered to the ground, and he leaped up and ran on foot, still shrieking wildly as he lifted his rifle to fire. His face was painted black; it looked strangely blank, as though he had no features. Barry centered the face in his sights and squeezed the trigger. The Blackfoot fired at the same time, and a man a few feet from Barry uttered a muffled cry and gripped his wounded shoulder as he sagged toward the ground. But the Blackfoot was a dead man. He spun to the ground, someone else's arrow in his stomach but nothing on his face save the red blob Barry's bullet had made.

Still another Pawnee-taunted Blackfoot raced from the trees, wielding a rifle and a tomahawk. Another arrow thudded into the Blackfoot's stomach, and one went into his chest. He threw the tomahawk as he went down, and it skidded across the ground. The muscles in his shoulders knotted as he pushed himself up again, pulling out a knife and cocking his arm to throw it. An arrow smacked into his chest, and spots of red showed in the black paint on his face as a distant rifle fired. His body jerked convulsively as he collapsed. Pawnees raced forward, whooping, and began scalping and mutilating the body with their knives and tomahawks.

Fitzpatrick cantered over to the man who'd been shot in the shoulder. He was getting to his feet, clutching it.

"Did he get you bad, Joe?" Fitzpatrick shouted.

"No, it didn't hit no bone! I'll be all right!"

Fitzpatrick grunted, glancing at Barry as he reloaded his rifle. "I hope we don't have any more in there with their faces painted black."

"What does it mean?"

"Somebody's done something to them or something's happened to give them such a hate in their craw that they've joined the spirit world and ain't even human no more. I can believe it, because they'll do things that would make a panther seem like a house cat. You saw how hard that last one was to kill."

Barry nodded, reloading his rifle. Fitzpatrick looked back across the valley as he slid the ramrod back into the thimbles. The Indians coming to help were still somewhat scattered, but most of them were in a bunch heading toward the left side where Bridger waited, the hoofbeats of their horses a pounding rumble. Porter and his men had disappeared into the trees on the right. Fitzpatrick waved his rifle, shouting.

"All right, spread out! Spread out, wait for me to give the word, then go in shooting!"

The men turned their horses, kicking them, and the group spread apart, the Pawnees shouting and whooping impatiently. Bridger and the first bunch of Indians from the encampments disappeared into the trees and then the rest of the Indians poured in, whooping and waving their weapons. Rifles began firing in the right side of the trees as Porter closed in. Then they began firing on the left. Fitzpatrick uttered a shrill war whoop, kicking his horse and waving his rifle, and Barry drove his heels into his horse's sides, leaning low over its neck.

The thunder of hoofbeats pounded at Barry's ears as he clung to the horse's back, and puffs of gunpowder smoke blossomed in the trees ahead. A Pawnee in front of him threw his arms up, sliding off his horse, and Barry jerked his horse to one side and rode around him. Then the trees were in front of him, and he guided his horse toward an opening in the foliage. Horses crashed through underbrush and leaves on each side of him. He could see movements through the trees ahead of him as the Blackfeet fled. He pounded his heels against his horse's sides, then aimed down the barrel of his rifle at a fleeting form and pulled the trigger. The smoke blinded him for an instant; he could not tell if he'd hit the Blackfoot. Other rifles fired around him.

The underbrush thickened, and Barry's horse leaped, pushing through it. Thick limbs tore at Barry, pulling him sidewards, and an Indian was suddenly in front of him with a lifted tomahawk. He swung his rifle, striking the Indian across the body with the barrel, and the impact almost jerked the rifle from his hands. His horse stumbled, going down, and Barry leaped clear. The breath was knocked from his lungs as he slammed heavily into the ground, and he scrambled to get his feet under him, pushing himself upright against a tree.

The Blackfoot was climbing to his feet, a thick stream of blood flowing from his nostrils and running down over his lips and chin. He looked at Barry, lifting his tomahawk. Barry steadied himself and gripped his rifle by the barrel, then moved away from the tree and toward the Indian. A rifle fired with a penetrating crack, and the Indian staggered and fell. Barry turned. Curtis was sitting on his horse a few yards away, lowering his rifle. He smiled, waving Barry toward his horse, and Barry grinned and nodded as he ran, tugging at his ramrod to reload.

The whoops, rifle shots and sounds of horses tearing through the underbrush spread out and grew fainter. Fitzpatrick's bellow came out loud and clear as he recalled everyone to the meadow, and other men shouted and relayed the order. As Barry and Curtis rode back through the trees, white men and Indians were scalping the dead Blackfeet, dragging them behind their horses on ropes, disemboweling them and hanging their entrails on tree limbs. It was a ghastly sight. Barry looked at it cold and hard.

A number of the men had collected at the edge of the trees around Fitzpatrick, laughing and talking, and Fitzpatrick beckoned Barry as he and Curtis rode out. "Did you get you any, Barry?"

"No, don't think so, but Curtis got one who was about to get me. Most of them got away, didn't they?"

"Oh, yes, they could see what was coming. But we showed them that we know how to break a dog from sucking eggs, and that's the main thing. You got you one, Curtis?"

"Barry had him treed. Did we lose anyone?"

"We had a few who got nicked, but as far as I know, we didn't have anyone get it bad. As soon as I get everyone out here, we'll see who's hurt and. . . ." His voice faded as he glanced around and looked across the valley. A rider was coming from the lean-tos at a pounding run, lashing his horse. "Is that Ludlow? What's he in such a hurry about, I wonder?"

The men became silent, glancing at each other and looking at Ludlow as he leaned over his horse's neck and whipped it with the reins, racing toward them. The patter of hoofs became louder, the horse's heavy breathing became audible, and he leaned back on the reins, bringing his horse to a sliding stop.

"Blackfeet attacked Pierre's brigade! There's been a bunch killed, the horses are scattered all to hell and gone. . . ."

Ludlow continued, but his words were lost behind Barry in the drumming of his horse's hoofs as he lashed his reins down on its shoulders, heading back across the valley. Hoofbeats pounded behind him, then caught up. Curtis rode beside Barry, his blond hair waving in the wind as he leaned low over his horse and whipped it.

16

DeVises' features were frozen into lines that could have been rage, or could have been the final agonies of his death. His skull gleamed redly in the sunshine where his scalp had been ripped off. Eight more bodies were laid out on the grass in a row. Two others had been scalped. The tools the bush lopers were using to dig graves made damp, thudding noises in the soil. Several dead Blackfeet were scattered about, sprawled in the grass. A tomahawk was standing in one Blackfoot's chest, the blade buried deep in the bones over the heart. The breeze moving through the clearing stirred a decorative tuft of fur and feathers hanging from its handle.

A somber, funereal atmosphere hung over the clearing, which seemed quiet despite the motion and activity. Riders moved through the trees and collected scattered pack horses, and bush lopers unloaded those that hadn't thrown their loads and penned them in a rope corral. Other bush lopers searched for loose canvas bags, repaired torn ones, sorted out their contents. Their usual noisy banter was missing, and the riders combing the trees were also grimly silent as they rode in and out of the clearing to bring horses in. Several men worked over the five wounded on the ground. One of the wounded moaned softly with every breath. Another one groaned loudly in protest as Bridger probed for a rifle ball with his skinning knife.

Fitzpatrick, Ludlow, Curtis, Porter, and others knelt around Harnett, talking to him, and Barry walked back toward them. Curtis glanced up at him as he approached and moved over to make room for him, his pale and taut face reflecting the sick despair and frustrated rage that Barry felt. Fitzpatrick glanced at Barry as he sat down, then looked back at Harnett. Blood had run down the side of Harnett's face from the deep gash on his temple, drying and cracking on his cheek and matting in his white beard. His eyes were dazed, and he slumped loosely back against the large rock behind him, looking numbly down at the ground as he talked quietly.

". . . then one of them got my horse, and I went into that tree. That's the last I remember until you all got here."

"And you opine there was twenty or thirty of them," Fitzpatrick said.

Harnett nodded, motioning toward the demijohn of whiskey. Ludlow handed it to him, and he lifted it and took a drink, his hands shaking. He swallowed and cleared his throat as he lowered the jug, then nodded again. "About that."

"And you think it was the Hudson's Bay Company that sent them."

"I know it was. They had a British flag with them, and every one of them had a rifle, not a one in the bunch with a bow and arrows. And that's what we've been thinking all along, ain't it?"

Fitzpatrick grunted and looked away. "Well, it looks like we know it now."

"They must have been in a hell's fire big hurry, Seth," Ludlow said. "They didn't take but three scalps, they didn't kill the wounded, they didn't carry off their dead, and it looks like they didn't get but a few of the pack horses. That ain't like Blackfeet."

"They knew we had help not far off, and they wanted to get away before we could get untangled and pin them down. They hit, and then they run. Like I said, I shot one and got into it with that other one with my knife and tomahawk. By the time I got him killed and got back on my horse, they was already past the end of the clearing down there with what pack horses they could grab—and with Maria. I started out after them, along with Johnson and Wilson over there, and I had just got into the trees when one of them got my horse."

"And you figure it was an ambush, all set up and waiting," Fitzpatrick said.

Harnett nodded. "They knew we was coming, and they was waiting. Still, I was feeling a little edgy because it sounded pretty quiet, and Maria had just said something about hearing a jay. Going by that, they hadn't been waiting too long, or the birds would have settled again."

Fitzpatrick nodded, looking down at the ground and frowning. The jug gurgled as Harnett lifted it and took another drink. Bridger walked toward the group, wiping his skinning knife on a handful of grass and sliding it back into the sheath, and Fitzpatrick looked up at him.

"How is he doing?"

"I got the ball out, but I don't hold much hope for him. Or for Seymour either. The other three should be all right if they don't fester." He shrugged and shook his head gloomily, crossing his legs and sitting down in the circle around Harnett. "How are you feeling, Seth?"

"I'll catch my breath in a minute. And then I'll need one of your horses."

"No, you can't go off half-cocked, Seth," Bridger said. "There's nothing you can do by yourself. We're going to have to figure out what we're going to do."

"He won't be by himself," Barry said.

"No, he won't," Curtis said.

"Everybody hold their God damned horses," Fitzpatrick said firmly. "We've had enough killed to hold us for a while, and we don't need any more."

"I ain't going to sit here and do nothing," Harnett said, his pale blue eyes becoming sharp and clear with anger. "I'm going after Maria, and I'm going to get me some God damned scalps while I'm at it."

"I didn't say we're going to do nothing," Fitzpatrick said. "Like Jim said, we're going to have to figure out what we're going to do and go at it the right way. Now we can go at this in a big way or we can go at it in a little way, but whichever it is, it ought to be the smart way. To my way of thinking, this is a job for a party of no more than twelve. We're a fur company, not an army."

"The Pawnees and Shoshones back in the valley

would be glad to go along," Ludlow said. "So would the Bannocks, Flatheads, and plenty of others."

"They would if we could provision them," Bridger said. "But we don't have the rifles, gunpowder and lead, horses, nor everything else we'd need. Like Tom said, we're in business to trade furs, not make war. And the only way to go into hostile country is with an army or a small party, nothing in-between. So it's a small party, like Tom says. Now we've got to decide if we're going to do anything except go after the girl."

There was a long moment of strained, frozen silence. The futility of sending a party after Maria was the implication behind Bridger's words, raw and glaring even though it was unspoken. Her fate was uncertain, but there was a high probability that she would be raped and tortured to death before a rescue party could find her. Barry looked at Curtis. Curtis glanced at him, then looked down at the ground, muscles moving in the sides of his face as he snapped off blades of grass and shredded them into bits.

"I think our quarrel is with the Hudson's Bay Company more than the Blackfeet," Fitzpatrick said. "We ought to go after the girl, and when that's done, we ought to try to find out where the Blackfeet are being stirred up from. And then give them a taste of what they've been feeding us, if we can do it without getting ourselves all killed off."

"I think you're right," Bridger said. "And seeing how your feet are, I think I ought to lead the party."

"My feet'll do for this," Fitzpatrick said. "And I'll crawl on my God damned hands and knees, if need be. Beyond that, it makes more sense for me to go. As soon as the men we sent out to check on Bill get back, you could take everybody on over to the fort and set about getting ready to send them out and to take your brigade to Alta California. That would take a while with everybody there at one time, but you wouldn't have to worry about a party that big being attacked on the way there. I'll be back in two or three weeks, and we can go on from there."

Bridger mused, thinking about it, then shrugged and nodded. "I can't think of anything better, Tom."

"Maria's horse has a bent cleat on one of its shoes," Harnett said, gathering himself to stand. "If they keep her on that horse, I can track them to the gates of hell."

"All right. I'll pick out the men and we'll get started while the trail's hot," Fitzpatrick said, standing and helping Harnett to his feet. "We'll carry jerky and corn so we can travel fast and make cold camps."

"I'm going along," Barry said.

"I am too," Curtis said.

Fitzpatrick looked at Barry and nodded, then he looked at Curtis, his brows drawing in a reserved, thoughtful frown. "I've got nothing against you, Curtis, but I figure if we find where the trouble with the Blackfeet is coming from, we're going to find your brother right in the middle of it."

"That's the way I figure it as well," Curtis said quietly. "And if that's what we find and I get a bead on him, he'll never cause any more trouble for anyone."

The men were silent, glancing between Fitzpatrick and Curtis. Then Fitzpatrick nodded and turned away. "All right. Jake, get the bush lopers to find the corn, jerky and gunpowder among the bags there. I'll round up the men and pick the rest of the party."

The group broke up, and Barry went to where he had tethered his horse in the edge of the trees. The horse was exhausted from the hard run to the scene of the ambush, its head hanging wearily. He led it to the corral, picked out a fresh horse and led it to the pile of saddles and other equipment by the canvas bags. Harnett was saddling a horse, his lips pale and drawn with grief and pain, and his eyes shining with fury. Curtis had a cannister of gunpowder and was refilling his powder horn, and he motioned for Barry's powder horn to refill it for him.

The clearing became crowded as the men came back out of the trees. They gathered around Fitzpatrick, all of them clamoring to go. The bush lopers were handing out bags with corn and jerky and stacking blankets, and Barry tied two of the bags and a blanket behind his saddle. Other men Fitzpatrick picked out hurriedly prepared to leave. The party formed into columns behind him and Harnett and rode toward the end of the clearing. Other men shouted and waved as they rode back into the trees to search for more horses, Ludlow went back to the pile of bags, Bridger returned to the wounded, and the bush lopers continued digging the graves.

The trail was broad and clear, a wide path churned in the forest mast by the hoofs of running horses. The columns rode along at a swift canter for a time, following it easily as it curved back along the slope of the mountain and paralleled the bottom of the valley below. Then Harnett and Fitzpatrick slowed as sunset approached and the trail became less distinct under the dense canopy of trees. When it led out onto a wide stretch of rocky meadows and sparser stands of trees, the party stopped. It was too dark to see. Then the moon rose, its pale light illuminating the meadow. They started out again, following the trail across the meadows, entering denser trees, waiting at one point while Harnett and Fitzpatrick searched on foot for the trail on the grove's far side. Then the trail led into thick forest again, and they stopped for the night.

The cold mountain air and the chill of the damp ground penetrated the thin blanket, the gnawing anguish and uncertainty about Maria churned in Barry's mind, and he lay sleepless for those few hours.

At dawn's first light, Harnett moved around in the trees and looked at the trail for Blackfeet sign. They started out again, chewing mouthfuls of jerky and corn. They cantered along the trail again for several miles, then slowed once more. Here it was evident that the Blackfeet had slowed to a walk. The trail branched where two or three riders had turned off to the sides as decoys. Brush had been dragged at the rear of the main party to blur the trail. They went ahead and picked up the main trail again. Harnett dismounted occasionally and gingerly raked the mast aside to look for the characteristic hoofprints of Maria's horse in the soft earth. When he found them, they continued at a slow walk. There were further signs of turnoffs. The main trail diminished to the hoofprints of a dozen horses or less, and it curved and led down the side of the mountain. The gurgling of the wide creek in the valley below became more audible as they approached it. They stopped there, watered the horses and dismounted to drink and refill their water bottles. Harnett rode across the creek, then returned, shaking his head. The Blackfeet had gone either up or down it.

Fitzpatrick and Harnett rode out into the creek, looking at the stones and gravel under the shallow water and conferring. Then they returned and the party began traveling up the creek, Harnett leading five men on one side and Fitzpatrick five on the other. The horses stumbled and floundered over the slippery rocks under the rushing water, and the damp air became chilly after the sun went behind the towering mountains to the west of the valley. They moved slowly along, Harnett and Fitzpatrick looking at the creek banks, and there were frequent halts at small streams and dry washes to let those two ride up them to examine them.

During late afternoon, Harnett found stones that looked suspiciously unnatural in the bed of a shallow stream that joined the creek. He moved them and found horseshoe marks on other mud-encrusted stones under them. The Blackfeet had left the creek and gone up the stream towards the mountains. They had concealed their trail for a distance of a hundred yards. Harnett and Fitzpatrick found it again, and the party began moving up a rocky slope until the trail reached a series of precipitous bluffs overlooking the creek far below. Darkness fell, and Barry spent the night on a cold, windy ledge above a sheer drop of a hundred feet, his horse tethered to a rock. At first light, they traveled on.

Throughout the early hours of that morning, they kept running into backtrails and cleverly made false trails that ended at the banks of creeks. Harnett patiently unraveled them, always looking for the hoofprints of Maria's pinto. They followed the true trail as it led north, through the deep valleys and across the spiny ridges south of the headwaters of the rivers that joined at Three Forks. The trail then turned northeast, then north again toward the headwaters of the Musselshell, and now it was clear and easy to follow, with no more attempts to conceal it. But Harnett and Fitzpatrick still led the party along slowly and carefully, for they were deep into Blackfoot territory.

The supplies of jerky and corn began diminishing, and the men picked berries and pulled roots along the way to supplement them. Occasionally Harnett smelled woodsmoke or detected some other indication of potential danger, and there were delays and detours. There were also delays because the horses were becoming thin and weak, so that they had to stop and let them graze.

As the days passed, the clear weather began breaking and afternoon thunderheads built up over the mountains to the west, threatening rains that could wash away all signs of the trail at some creek crossing or other place where it could be easily lost. Then one storm did come. Flashes of lightning crackled and crashing peals of thunder rolled through the valley they were traveling along. A drenching downpour pelted down. They waited until the rain diminished, then traveled on. It took Harnett hours to find the trail across creeks and flooded meadows at the head of the valley. But find it he did. Just before dark they reached a slope where the rainfall had been lighter and the trail was more distinct.

It was raining again at first light as they followed

the trail across an open slope covered with shale and a few wind-blasted weeds that had taken root in the thin topsoil. The gullies on the slope were muddy torrents from runoff, and Harnett and Fitzpatrick lost the trail several times more before picking it up again. Gradually they worked their way down into the valley at the foot of the slope. A creek there had flooded out of its banks, inundating the valley floor. There seemed no way to find the trail on the valley's other side.

They moved up out of the flooded area and camped, and it rained all night. Harnett and Fitzpatrick went out again at dawn to look for the trail, leaving the men in a wet, discouraged huddle. Fitzpatrick returned at midday, morosely shook his head as the men looked at him, then sat down by Barry and took a small handful of corn from his hunting bag and began eating it. A few minutes later, Harnett became visible as he approached through the rain. His horse was plodding slowly along at a walk, its pace a clear message that he hadn't found the trail either. He tied his horse to a tree and walked over to Fitzpatrick and sat down, taking a small piece of jerky from his hunting bag.

"Nothing?" Fitzpatrick asked.

Harnett shook his head, trickles of water running from the brim of his hat. "Not a sign."

"Perhaps you could find it when it stops raining and dries out a little," Curtis said.

"That could be," Harnett replied. "It's hard to see anything in the rain. The ground's so wet now that a man is liable to tramp all over a trail and ruin it before he sees it."

"We don't have rations enough to wait very long,

Seth," Fitzpatrick said. "Directly we're going to have to start looking for something to eat instead of that trail."

Harnett sucked his teeth reflectively. "All right, Tom, I'll tell you something I've been rolling over in my mind. I was all through here a few years back and got to know the lay of the land pretty good. There's an old Hudson's Bay Company fort not far from here. Fort Merrill is the name of it, and it was deserted and had been for some time the last time I saw it. And for the past three or four days, the trail we've been following has been heading toward that old fort as straight as an arrow. I've been thinking that Fort Merrill might not be deserted any more."

Fitzpatrick crunched a kernel of corn between his teeth, musing. "You think that's where they've gone, then?"

"It's where they've been headed. And even if they ain't there, it could be that the Hudson's Bay Company has set up in Fort Merrill again, because it's a good place. If they have, they'll have victuals, and I opine we're due something for the misery they've caused us. We could raise a little hell over there, then come back over here to see if the ground's dried out enough to find the trail. Course, there's plenty of good places between here and there to set up ambushes if anybody wanted to follow us."

Fitzpatrick nodded. "We'd be followed, because there's always an Indian village by Hudson's Bay Company forts. How far away is it?"

"A little over a day."

Fitzpatrick tossed the rest of the corn in his

mouth and dusted his hands together as he rose. "We'll have a look at it, Seth. Let's go, boys."

Harnett chuckled grimly and nodded as he pushed himself to his feet and walked back toward his horse.

The rain diminished to a drizzle as the men rode slowly up the east side of the valley and crossed a high saddle into the next valley. Near sunset, the sky cleared. Darkness fell and they camped, starting out again at first light. Harnett now led them through a winding maze of ravines and across a series of sharp ridges. That afternoon, they descended into another valley and cautiously approached a creek. It was a deep, swift creek with high banks, and a dim trail ran through the trees a few yards from its bank. Harnett led them into the forest and they traveled slowly along for a few miles, a faint odor of woodsmoke in the air gradually becoming stronger. Near sunset, Harnett left them. When he returned he motioned for them to tie their horses and follow him.

Barry crept through the trees with the others, crawling into underbrush as the forest ended. At its rim he cautiously moved a low branch to one side and looked. There was Fort Merrill, in the clearing. The trading post was a large structure of several rooms, with new shingles, shutters and doors, and a few new logs around the doors and windows. But the roof was sagging, most of its logs rotting from age. About a hundred feet behind the fort's two cabins, stock pens, barns and storage buildings was a cluster of some twenty Indian lodges.

Smoke rose from fires in front of the lodges and

from the chimneys in the cabins and trading post. Horses munched fodder in the pens. A few Indians, mostly women and children, moved around the lodges and across the open space between them and the post. The fort was moderately well defended. There was a wall of fifteen-foot-high palisades on the near side facing Barry. It had a wide, strong gate on it, though the gate was now open. The other sides and rear were palisaded too. Even though those palisades were sagging and propped up with poles in places, Barry could see the fort would be difficult to storm. But they paid little heed to this. His eyes were fixed on a horse in one of the pens. He moved over and pulled at Fitzpatrick's shoulder, pointing.

"That's Maria's horse, the one she rode out from Pierre's Hole."

Fitzpatrick lifted his head higher and looked, a grim smile of satisfaction spreading over his face. He nudged Harnett and pointed.

"I see it," Harnett said softly. "And I see that most of the braves in that village are gone, out causing somebody else some misery, no doubt. There ain't but four or five over there."

"And there'll be only another three or four men in the trading post and the cabins," Fitzpatrick said. "It won't be like falling off a log, but I figure we can do it."

Harnett nodded. "The rear palisades are the weakest. I know. There's a gulch behind them. We got to cross the creek to get to it, but that's the way we ought to go. I sure wouldn't want to run across this clearing to the gate right now, there just ain't no telling for sure what's in there."

Fitzpatrick nodded, moving backwards. "That's

what we'll do, then. Let's go on back to the creek and find a place to cross, and we'll get set to go in at first light."

The men moved back out of the underbrush, and Barry took a last look at the pinto as he picked up his rifle and slid backwards. For the first time since the day of the ambush, he felt some hope about Maria's fate. The fort was an outpost of civilization in the wilderness. Undoubtedly white men came here, employees of the Hudson's Bay Company. Maria's horse being here rather than in a Blackfoot camp made him feel there was less likelihood of her having been raped, abused, tortured, killed. He was convinced she was alive; every fiber in his being told him she was.

As they retreated through the forest and walked quietly along a deep creek they had passed before, they approached a ditch that runoff had channeled to its waters. Up the ditch was a stand of trees with some broken limbs lying on the ground. On Fitzpatrick's orders, Barry and five other men went up and got the limbs, then floated them down the ditch to the creek bank. They made a small raft for their rifles, powder and other things that had to be kept dry. Then they swam the creek with their horses, pushing the raft ahead of them.

Darkness fell as they moved through the trees on the far side and began circling around to the fort's rear side. Soon they stopped for the night. After tying his horse, Barry sat down against a tree and huddled in his still-damp clothes. He ate the last of his corn and jerky. It tasted sour. The other men coughed softly and made quiet sounds as they settled down. But Barry was still hungry and he was cold and he was having thoughts that didn't sit too well with him, so he couldn't rest as comfortably as they. He was thinking that his uncle and Seth Harnett were being perhaps a bit too confident about the ease with which they expected to take the fort. It was nothing he could put his finger on, just a feeling. He didn't see how almost all the Blackfeet braves would go someplace far away and leave their women and children unattended. It's nothing he would do. I mean, he thought confusedly, I wouldn't leave Maria, not for an instant, if she were mine. But then, he thought, I'm not an Indian. I'm a—a . . . Weariness overtook him before he could finish the thought. He leaned back against the tree and dozed.

A hand shook his shoulder, and Barry looked up into Harnett's bearded face in the grey half light before dawn. Harnett moved on, shaking other men, and there were murmurs and yawns as they stirred. Barry stood up and stretched, then picked up his rifle and felt in his shot pouch for the worm screw to draw the charge from his rifle and replace it so he would have fresh powder in it. It was time to move on to the attack. Gone now, in his nervousness, in his exhilaration at the prospect of rescuing Maria, were the doubts he had had. The forest was quiet. The other men were serenely loading their rifles. He shrugged and finished loading his. He was sure once again that Fitzpatrick and Harnett knew best. Some of Barry's quicksilver thoughts must have shown on his face. He looked up and saw Curtis Kruger winking at him. Barry flushed, but was grinning by the time the blond youth walked over. "Let's give 'em hell, huh, Barry?" he said. "You bet," Barry said. He laughed. "Look, you, don't forget to keep your head down."

The sky brightened. Fitzpatrick murmured a quiet order and the men sneaked through the trees, rustling branches as little as possible, headed toward the deep dry wash behind the fort. Now and then dry fallen leaves crackled under their feet. Barry kept swallowing. His mouth felt dry, and his heart pounded with tension and excitement. He glanced at Curtis next to him and saw that Curtis too was nervous; he kept wetting his lips as he peered ahead through the soft green forest light. Barry looked quickly ahead again, checking the hammer on his rifle.

Suddenly, an Indian stepped from behind a tree a few yards in front of them and gazed at them in stunned shock. It was at that instant, while the quickly reacting Barry was raising his rifle to shoot, that Harnett saw the Blackfoot too. With one hand Seth pushed Barry's rifle down; his other shoulder and arm moved with blinding speed. The tomahawk he threw tumbled through the air, its head gleaming dully. The Indian tried a short leap to one side, but the tomahawk slammed into the center of his chest with a wet, meaty thud. He uttered a hoarse, gagging scream, stumbling backwards and lifting his arms. His rifle fired into the air with a splitting crack, shattering the stillness of the forest. Harnett raced forward, cursing viciously, and snatched the tomahawk back out of the Indian's chest. The Indian lurched up off the ground and flopped back, gasping. Harnett drove the tomahawk into his skull, killing him, then jerked it out and shoved it back in his belt.

"Goddamn it, they know we're here now!" he swore. "Let's go get them! Let's go!"

Barry raced through the trees beside Curtis, heedless now of the noise they were making. The trees opened out. There was the dry wash to cross. Harnett was already sliding down in a shower of rocks and gravel. The light was still too dim to see the other side clearly, but Barry could hear in the distance the shouts of orders being given inside the fort. He held his rifle to him, protecting it with his body, and stepped off the edge of the wash. It was deep. Sharp rocks and gravel bit into him as he slid down the steep wall. Larger rocks, loosened by the men behind him, rained down on him. He tumbled sidewards, rolled to the bottom, leaped up and ran toward the other side.

The fort's rear palisades loomed before him, across a fifty-yard clearing. As Harnett had said, this wall was weak, with gaps in the logs providing footholds and armholds. Also there was a gulch behind it that might have provided cover. But it was too late for caution now. Harnett and ten other men were already scrambling up the wall. Barry raced across the clearing. Curtis was beside him. He had lost his hat again, and his blond head was bright in the early light. Barry held his rifle to him, leaped for a handhold on the wall, and began pulling himself up. Gravel dribbled down from above. He looked up the fifteen-foot height. For a startled instant, he thought Curtis had somehow already climbed the wall. Then he realized he was looking at Stephen Kruger.

Crouched on a tower just inside the wall, Curtis's twin was lifting a huge boulder, much like those in the wash. He was straining with the effort. Barry started to leap out of the way. Then he saw that Stephen was looking to one side of him, his lips pulled back in a sneering smile. The boulder came down heavily as Stephen stood for an instant, lifted it high over his head and flung it with almost demonic strength. By then, Barry had slid back down to the ground and was pointing his rifle upward. As he squeezed the trigger, he heard the boulder's thud, then a muffled groan of pain. Dust from his shot and a log fragment kicked off the top of the wall, and Stephen disappeared. Barry got back to his feet. Men were running up around him and climbing the wall. He looked to one side and saw Curtis sprawled limply on the ground, his blond hair matted with dark red blood. The boulder now rested partially on his chest. Barry sprang to him. Blood was coming from his mouth and nostrils. His eyelids fluttered and his lips moved weakly. Barry knelt by him and held the bloody head on his lap. "You'll be all right," he chattered. "You didn't keep your head down, you damn fool. Curtis!" But Curtis was gone, and Barry knew it. His eyelids fluttered once more and then he was motionless. Barry hesitated, then, choking back a sob, ran back to the wall to climb it.

Rocks rolled down as he clawed his way up. It became evident the defenders had collected an armament of them from the wash, lacking guns and arrows in force. But some of Fitzaptrick's men were already at the top, straddling the wall and firing rifles down inside. Shielding his face as best as he could with his forearms, heedless of the rocks hitting his body, Barry went up and over. Then, clutching a pointed palisade at the top and hanging from it, briefly, he dropped nine feet or so to the ground.

Inside, Harnett was screaming frantically at the top of his voice for Maria. The few defenders on the walls had either been killed or had fled. Though sporadic rifle fire was coming from the cabins and Indian lodges, the wide gate in the front palisades was open and mounted, fleeing Indians were already galloping into the forest beyond.

A rifle ball from a lodge hissed past Barry, and he ran for the cover of the trading post, tugging at his ramrod to reload. Then he saw Harnett come out of the trading post, his arms around Maria. She was hysterical. She was clutching Harnett and weeping wildly, her hair in strings, her face bruised blue, her buckskins in tattered rags. Barry felt sick. He gave up his cover and started to run towards her.

"Barry!" Fitzpatrick screamed at him from his own nearby cover. "My God damned leg's been hit! Get over to the lodges, shoot the buggers out and set fire to them! Whittaker, you and Crawford go with him! Locker, you and Cole get some fire out of the fireplace in the post and get it on the roof of that cabin! Kill the sons of bitches as they come out! Smith, round up the horses there before they all get away. . . ."

Fitzpatrick continued bellowing orders. Barry hesitated, looking at Maria. Then he turned and sprinted toward the lodges, the other two men running ahead of him. A shot came from inside one lodge. Crawford knelt, aimed and fired into the dark opening. There was quiet for a moment and Crawford reloaded. Then an Indian stumbled out of the lodge, clutching his chest but with his tomahawk raised. Crawford shot him in the stomach.

Barry ran in among the lodges while the other men kept firing. In front of one he found a large pan of hot coals by a cooking fire. He shoveled some of the coals into that lodge, more into the next. Smoke billowed up. He was about to fling the remainder of the coals into a third lodge when out of the second stumbled a very old and tottering Indian man, tugged along by his squaw. The old Indian was coughing and sputtering. Barry hesitated, swearing to himself. He went over and helped the two move further into the clearing. Then he returned to the third lodge and set it ablaze.

Lodges all around him were bursting into flame now as the other two men set fire to them. Barry ran alongside the rest of the lodges, checking them out, his rifle at the ready. He reached the end of the line and looked back. He didn't see a single Indian left alive from any of them. Crawford had tomahawked the old Indian and the squaw.

Barry trotted back to the trading post.

Harnett and Maria were gone.

The roof of a cabin from which some return fire had been coming was enveloped in flames. One of its occupants, a white man, was sprawled on the ground coughing, and a Fitzpatrick man was waiting either for more to show themselves or for the cabin to burn down. Fitzpatrick was still shouting orders. Men were carrying bags of Hudson's Bay Company supplies out of the trading post. Others were putting packsaddles on several of the left-behind horses, preparing to make off with them.

"Barry, take some of these extra saddle horses and ride back down to where ours are. Better go back across the dry wash and take them down to the creek on the other side. That'll save us some time. I'll send some men after you after a bit. Here, take this and gnaw on it on the way." He reached into a bag and handed Barry a large piece of jerky.

"Where's Maria?" Barry said.

"Now, don't you go worrying about Maria, son. She's all right. Seth's with her and she's going to be just fine. You might run into her along the way, don't know. I kind of hope you don't."

"Is she far from here?" Barry said steadily.

"I don't rightly know that either. It's been the better part of an hour since Seth left with her. Doesn't matter, though, because they'll catch up with us later. Now you head on out like I said."

Barry nodded. He took a half-dozen horses and rode out the front gate, leaving the burning wreckage of the fort behind him. As he circled to the rear and headed for the dry wash, he heard a single rifle shot go off in the fort. He figured one last stubborn defender or another had been killed. Already numbed by the carnage, he rode on, unblinking, seeing for a while only his haunted vision of the brutally beaten Maria.

The smoke and roar of the flames faded behind him. Leaves rustled loudly under the horses hoofs, as Barry, alone now and determined to get his job done, rode up to the dry wash and peered along it for the safest spot to descend. After a few minutes he found a slope relatively free of rocks and boulders and carefully led the horses down. It was only then, seeing the boulders, that he wondered what had happened to Curtis's body. Passing the fort's rear palisades, he hadn't seen it.

The floor of the dry wash was deep, sandy and soft, and the horses' hoofs thudded dully as they cantered along it. Barry couldn't see over the far wall for a while. He turned and drifted south looking for a safe ascent. When he found a soft slope with hoofprints already on it, he figured it had to be safe enough for his horses too, so he slowly led them up it.

At the top, he found himself bordering a part of the forest that had a glade just inside its perimeter. He was turning to follow the forest's rim when he sensed movements, then heard indistinct voices coming from the glade. He reached quickly for his rifle.

But the voices were soft, unthreatening, speaking English. Besides, their owners must have seen him and his horses. They were oblivious to him.

Barry nudged his horse and went through some underbrush to get a view of the glade. Then he stopped and stared. Tears began welling in his eyes.

Curtis's body was lying in the glade. Maria had washed the blood from his head and was pillowing it in her arms. She was looking down at Curtis's face and crying softly. Harnett stood just behind her bent back, leaning on a shovel. Beyond them, Barry saw an open grave.

As Barry sat his horse and quietly stared, Harnett lifted his head and their eyes met. Neither spoke. Barry bit the inside of his lip until it hurt. Then he dug a knuckle into his teeth until that hurt. But he didn't speak and, after a while, Harnett nodded at him.

Harnett looked down at Maria then, clearing his throat.

"It's time, Maria. Best we get on."

"All right, Seth, all right."

Maria bent lower and kissed Curtis on the lips. She sat up, pushed his hair back from his forehead, then eased his head off her lap and stood up. Her eyes, to Barry, looked blank; she didn't see him. She turned toward the grave, giving a tug to the thong holding up her torn buckskins, then strode to it purposefully while Harnett lifted the body. Barry watched them bury it. There was no ceremony, no words spoken. Just some simple thing. When the body was in the grave, Maria picked a wildflower from the ground and threw it in after it. Harnett shoveled in the dirt.

Only then did Maria look up and see Barry. At least, he thought she saw him. He wasn't sure. There was a cold fury in her blue eyes, with a kind of unnatural light dancing in them. Her hair was wetly plastered over her bruised cheekbones and there was blood on her lips from having kissed Curtis's.

"Hello, Barry, it's good to see you again," she said pleasantly.

It struck Barry that at that moment she was insane.

Part Five

THE MOUNTAIN BREED

17

"He raped me every day, if that's what you're asking. Sometimes more than once a day. He just tore my clothes off me, pushed me down on the floor and did it. Right then and there, whenever he felt like it."

Mercy looked at Maria in appalled consternation, her face crimson. She opened and closed her mouth, trying to say something. Then she turned back to the fireplace. "Well, that wasn't what I meant, Maria," she stammered. "Laws, I wasn't asking. . . ."

Maria sewed impatiently at the buckskin shirt spread on the table in front of her. She was beading it, digging her bead-looped needle harder than necessary through the softened hide. "What were you asking me, then?"

"You're my daughter, Maria, and I just wanted

to know if you wasn't treated too . . . well, I was beside myself worrying about you, and your pa being killed and all made these past weeks a burden for me. . . ."

Maria stopped her fingers from trembling as she threaded another bead. The terror was still fresh in her mind. She had a particular, recurring vision of Stephen's wolfish sneer as he stripped her clothes off and forced her down on the pallet in the dingy room in the trading post. While asleep, a fold in her blanket pressing against her shoulder could bring her awake in panic, thinking it was his touch, that his hard fingers would be tearing at her, then clawing her thighs apart again. A sound behind her could stab fear into her even in daytime in familiar surroundings. Stephen had taken pleasure in her weeping; it had seemed to spur him on to even greater acts of violence. Now her hands were damp, and the beads clung to her palm.

"It wasn't easy for me," she said.

"Laws, I wasn't saying it was, Maria. God knows a man like that would do his worst. . . ."

"Raping me wasn't the worst thing he did to me."

"Maria, I do wish you wouldn't use that word. It sounds plumb awful, just like what it means. . . ." Her voice faded as she stopped stirring the pan at the fireplace and looked over her shoulder again. "It wasn't? What in the world could be worse than that, Maria?"

Maria took another stitch through the buckskin. She remembered Stephen running back from the palisades and shouting gleefully to Phillips, as she listened from her hiding place, that he had just killed his brother. She slipped another bead onto the needle. "It doesn't make any difference."

"No, that's right, Maria," her mother said, stirring her pan. "Just put it right out of your mind and forget it. I'm just glad that they found you and got you away from him."

"I am too. I'm glad I found that nail I had. For two or three days before they got there, I'd been working one of the floorboards loose with that nail, thinking about getting under the floor and digging my way out after dark. When they started attacking, I took the board up and hid there. He was searching the place for me while Seth was still getting up to the trading post. If I hadn't had a place to hide, he'd still have me."

"You always have been a smart one, Maria," Mercy said. "Just give you a minute to think about something, and you'll figure it through. And you've always had the sand in your craw to do what you figured out too, even if you had a little too much to suit your pa, God bless his soul."

"It wouldn't have been too much to suit if I'd been a boy."

"But you wasn't, was you? Anyway, just put the whole thing out of your mind and forget it, Maria. Others have done that, you know. A lot of people would look upon a girl who that happened to as ruined, but it sure ain't changed the way that young Fitzpatrick boy looks at you, I'll tell you that. He don't think you're ruined. He's made it clear as glass that he'd marry you in a minute."

"I'm not going to get married."

"Not going to get married?" Mercy chortled in amusement. "Laws, the things you come out with, Maria. Of course you're going to get married. Every woman gets married if she gets a chance. But you're still upset, and anybody could see how you would be. And what happened to you ain't the same as when a woman is married to a man. He don't just grab her and. . . ." Her cheeks flushed as her voice faded, and she looked back at the pan and stirred it furiously, clearing her throat with embarrassment. "Well, a man shows respect for his wife, that's what I'm saying."

"I'm not going to get married."

"All right, Maria," her mother said patiently. "You're still upset, and that's no time to think about anything. And it's especially no time to think about what I think you're thinking. Are you making more of them buckskin things to go out trapping again?"

Maria hesitated, then nodded. "Yes."

"And take a chance on something bad happening to you again? Whatever for, Maria? Now I want you to know that I ain't been looking through your things they brought back here for me to keep and I ain't been asking anybody about your business, but I know you could buy and sell me ten times over. And I'm as good off as any woman needs to be, what with all your pa left me and with Mr. Fitzpatrick telling me I could just stay right here in this cabin."

"And with Jake Ludlow shaving and washing his face before he comes over to see if you need any water or firewood," Maria laughed.

Mercy flushed hotly, and a defensive smile tugged at her lips. "Well . . . but anyway, Maria, how much money do you want?"

"How much is there in the world?"

"How much is there . . . ? Laws. Now if I'd had the money to bring to a marriage that you have, me and your pa would have done real good, you know. With what you have, Maria, you can go to St. Louis. I know that men who are doing good for theirselves would take notice of you. On the other hand, if you go back out in the woods again, you're taking a chance on the same thing happening to you."

Maria turned her head slowly and looked at her mother. "I'm going," she said flatly.

Mercy's features tensed. She dropped her eyes as she stood up from the hearth and walked toward the washstand. "I'm not trying to tell you that you can't go, Maria," she said plaintively. "I sure wish you wouldn't look at me like that. I'll swear, you've got to where you can look a hole right through a body. Your pa used to have a solid look about him when he was riled about something, God bless his soul, but you've got to where you can look at a body in a way that makes the worst look he ever had seem like a grin. Them eyes of yours can get just like swords. . . ."

"I'm going."

"All right, Maria, all right," Mercy said in a placating tone. "Laws, I ain't trying to tell you what to do or how to . . . anyway, you've got as thin as a rail. I'm going to feed you up while I have a chance. I've got that pork roast on there for supper, and I bet you'll tuck into that."

Maria smiled and nodded, looking back down at the shirt. "It smells really good."

"It's coming along. And we'll have plenty of fresh vegetables, onions, and potatoes, of course. You know, talking about money, I should do all right on that garden patch of mine, because the men from the trading post have offered to buy me out of every vegetable I have left over. I ought to have plenty to spare, if I can just keep the rabbits and possums out of them."

"They sure taste good," Maria said, knotting the thread and snapping it off. She stood, picking up the shirt and looking at it as she shook it out, then folded it over her arm and walked toward her room. "Do you need any water?"

"Well, I guess I could use an extra bucket to get ready to wash the dishes after a while. My, you sure have got that looking pretty with all the beads and foofarows you've put on it. That struck me the first time I saw you in buckskins. Your pa didn't like you in them, but I thought you looked just as bright and pretty as a peacock."

Maria smiled at her as she went into her bedroom. The tiny room was crowded, the bags of traps, packsaddles, and her other belongings that the men had brought to her mother piled against the walls and stacked on the floor. After her moccasins, the shoes Maria had on felt heavy and clumsy on her feet and her dress and petticoat felt bundlesome and constraining. The new moccasins, leggings and breeches she had made during the four days she had been home were folded on the end of the bed, and she put the shirt on them and went back out.

She took two empty buckets from under the washstand and carried them towards the creek. Only one of the brigades had left Fort Henry. Many men were still at the fort, their lean-tos filling the field behind the trading post. Several were in the blacksmith shop shoeing horses, and more were buying up supplies at the trading post. There had been a subtle change in the way many of them looked at Maria. Before, they had looked at her in curiosity and admiration, some libidinously, but always at a respectful distance. Now they knew a man had seen her naked, touched her, done as he wished with her. That knowledge was reflected in the leering hints of smiles they gave her as she passed. She had an impulse to shrink away, to run and cower, sometimes just to hide her face behind a hand raised to her mouth. It was an impulse she chose not to give into. She lifted her chin, straightened her back and looked men squarely in the eye as she toted her buckets on.

As she had expected, Barry caught up with her on the path. He trotted up beside her and smiled as he reached for the buckets. "Here, I'll take those, Maria."

"Thank you, Barry."

"It's no trouble. I would have been checking at your cabin to see if you needed wood and water, but I didn't want to pester you. And Jake Ludlow seems to be looking after it pretty good. . . ."

"He is, isn't he?" Maria laughed. "He likes me. I don't know what he'll do when it's time for his brigade to leave."

Barry laughed and nodded. He started to say something, then thought better of it and grew silent. At the creek, he stepped out on a stone and dipped the buckets into a deep pool. "Well, Jim Bridger has got his brigade about ready to leave. He's been asking me if I want to go along with him to Alta California.

"Like I said, I didn't want to pester you right away, Maria, but I sure have been wanting to talk to you."

She didn't answer. They started walking back to

the cabins. "Ma has asked you over to supper, Barry."

"It's not your ma I want to talk to, Maria, it's you."

Maria frowned. It had been coming for some time and she'd had ample forewarning and time to think about it, but she still didn't know how to deal with it. She felt a deep affection for Barry, but it didn't compare with the poignant ecstasy she'd shared with Curtis. And Barry was still very much a boy. She felt an eternity older than him. "What do you want to talk about, Barry?"

He hesitated, then plunged in. "Maria, I've been wanting to come out here all my life. But if I hadn't wanted to, I would have still come, knowing that you were here. Now that's how I've felt about you, Maria. On the other hand, I know now how you felt about Curtis. And I liked him myself, although I probably wouldn't have if I'd known how you felt about him. Anyway, I know it takes time for a woman to get over things, so I'm thinking about going with Jim. But if I thought there was any chance that you feel about me like I do you, then I wouldn't go. What I'm saying is that I'd like you to marry me. And if you could feel about me like I do you, then whether it's a week from now or a year from now is up to you."

He'd blurted it all out and he stood there, blinking.

"Barry, there's no one whose affection means more to me than yours. I'm flattered that you think so highly of me. But I don't intend to marry."

He looked at her with a puzzled expression, then smiled slightly and shook his head. "Well, I'm not one to try to tell you what you want to do or don't want to do. But you're mighty young to have a set of mind on something like marrying that'll last you all your life. A lot has happened lately, and things will look different to you after a while. Maria, I know I don't have much to offer a woman right now, but I intend to work hard and get set up to where—"

"That has nothing to do with it, Barry. But on that subject, I believe I might possibly go into trading before too long. I'd like nothing better than to have you stay and go into business with me."

"No, I don't think so," he said stubbornly. "To tell you the truth, if I'm not going to stay here with you and because of you, then I'd just as soon go with Jim. I sort of have a hankering to go and see what's out there, and I want to learn to trap. Also, he's talking about finding a new good way through the mountains, and I'd like to be along for that."

"Yes, I can see how you'd want to do that, Barry. In a way I envy you."

He hesitated. "I'll be gone a year or more. That'll give you time to think about things. . . ."

"I'll be looking forward to seeing you again, Barry. But I wouldn't want you to think that you have some sort of commitment from me."

"No, I'm not asking you to say yes or no," he said. "I just wanted you to know how I felt, and I wanted to leave things as they were until . . . and I want you to know that anything that might have happened these past weeks makes no difference to me, Maria."

The comment was blurted out, and Maria breathed a soft sigh, keeping her features neutral. It would have been far better for Barry to have left what was on his mind unsaid and tacitly under-

stood. His saying it was further evidence that he
was still very much a boy. Curtis wouldn't have said
he loved her despite Stephen. He would have simply proven it in a thousand ways. Barry surely had
expected either a commitment or a warmer reaction from her, because the disappointment was plain
on his face. They were approaching the cabin, and
Maria stopped.

"Very well, Barry. And thank you for carrying
the water for me."

"It wasn't any trouble," he said, putting the buckets down in front of the step. "It'll be another day
or two before we're all straightened out and ready
to leave. I hope I'll be talking to you again before
then."

"I should certainly hope so," Maria laughed
lightly. "If you leave without saying goodbye, you'd
better not come back this way. Come to supper tomorrow or the next night."

Nodding, his smile strained, Barry turned away.
His shoulders were slumped and his steps were
heavy as he walked toward the trading post.

Mercy had dinner almost ready, and she finished
it and put the bowls and dishes on the table. They
ate while the sun set and flooded the cabin's front
room with soft, golden light. Mercy washed the
dishes as the sounds of activity in the fort were
dying away into the evening calm. It was a homey,
comfortable sort of evening for a while. Maria went
into her room, got one of the pistols she had bought
from the trading post and began cleaning the heavy,
preservative grease from its lock and barrel with a
washstand cloth. Later, Ludlow came over, his face
clean shaven, his hair slicked down, warily and defensively friendly toward Maria and ebulliently

cheerful toward Mercy. He chopped wood and carried it in and took all the buckets to the creek and filled them.

Mercy went outside and sat on the bench in front of the cabin with Ludlow. The light in Maria's room became dim. She lit a Betty lamp and put it on the table, refilled her coffee cup and sat back down to continue cleaning the pistol. She heard Harnett's voice outside as he approached, speaking to Mercy and Ludlow. Then he stepped inside, smiling at her.

"Hello, Seth. Get yourself a cup of coffee and sit down."

Harnett nodded. He got the coffee from the fireplace and came over to sit with her, putting his hat on the table. "Getting her all shined up, are you? Durned if you ain't going to be like a walking armory, Maria."

Maria kept scrubbing at a spot of grease behind the pistol's hammer. "I keep thinking about that day we rode out of Pierre's Hole, Seth," she said quietly. "There was a minute when only one of them had me. If I'd had a pistol or another knife or anything I could get my hands on, things might have turned out differently."

Seth's smile faded. He took a sip of coffee, brooding. "I was just funning you, Maria. It would suit me fine for you to have a cannon if there was some way you could drag it around with you." He was silent for a moment, watching her. Then he took another sip of coffee and tasted it reflectively, smiling again. "You don't think you could get your ma to learn you how to make coffee before we leave, do you?"

"I'll get her to show you, you damned old goat," Maria laughed. "I know I can't cook."

"No, it ain't that you can't cook," he said teasingly. "It's just how you do cook that I'm talking about. What with making bread that would do for a rock to weight a trap and making coffee that would float a nail, a body can get plumb scared to look in a kettle you're stirring." He chuckled. "Did you get your buckskins finished?"

"Mmm, I finished the shirt today."

"Here, let me take the hammer and the pan lid off for you, and you can get at it better." He reached for the pistol, taking out his pocketknife, and began removing the screws with the tip of the blade. "Do you think you'd like to go west of here again, or would you like to try somewhere else, then?"

Maria hesitated, leaning on her elbows on the table and musing. Then she shrugged. "We can think about it."

Harnett, returning the separated parts of the pistol to her, said, "Every time I bring up where we're going, you ain't got nothing to say, Maria. Now, we're going to have to make up our minds before we leave, or else we won't know what direction to head in, will we? What are you being so skittish about?"

Maria started scrubbing the parts. "I've been thinking about doing something, but I don't know whether or not I have any right to ask you to do it."

He looked puzzled. "Why don't you just ask me and let me do the deciding, if it has to do with me. What the hell could you have in mind that you'd be afraid to ask me about, Maria?"

Maria looked at him, thinking, then glanced at the door and leaned toward him, talking quietly.

"To begin with, if someone had a lot of furs here to get to St. Louis, how would they do it?"

"What do you mean, how would they do it? Like anybody else does it. They'd pissant them on horses with a brigade of—"

"Shh! I don't want anyone to know about this. No, I mean, would they have to go all the way back to St. Louis to recruit bush lopers? I've heard that a lot of Bridger's and Fitzpatrick's want to go back."

His expression became more perplexed. He glanced at the door, leaned toward her and replied quietly. "That's right, a bunch of them have got scared about the trouble with the Blackfeet, and they want to go back. And Jim and Tom are ready to see them go, if they can get shot of them. I also heard that Kruger has a big bunch that came in with a supply train that needs to get back, so a body could get two or three brigades together around here. But what's that got to do with anything?"

Maria bit her lip. "All right, I'll tell you. When Stephen Kruger had me in the trading post at Fort Merrill, a man named Rees came from Montreal to see him."

"Rees? Oh, I've heard of him. He's a big man in the Hudson's Bay Company. It must have been something mighty important for him to come out from Montreal."

"It was. They were talking in the room next to the one I was locked up in, and I heard everything they said. There was a big load of furs that Stephen was supposed to have sent to Montreal during the winter. The Blackfeet were supposed to either take them or help take them. They got held up because

of all the trouble Stephen stirred up to set the Blackfeet against the Pawnees. Rees was glad about the
trouble, but he was mad as hell about the furs. On
top of that, they talked about furs that had been
sent in from the Columbia, Upper Missouri, Teton,
the Marias, and other places. And Rees told Stephen that if they weren't sent to Montreal this winter, he was going to lose his scalp. But for some
reason, he didn't want them before this winter."

"It's easier to travel in Canada during the winter," Harnett said, nodding. "In crossing a lot of it
during the summer, a body don't do nothing but
fight water and mud up to their eyeballs. And the
mosquitoes drive horses crazy. Also, the way companies move furs has something to do with the
price of them. They want them at just a certain
time, and they don't. . . ." His voice faded, comprehension dawning on his face. "The furs are cached
somewhere, ain't they?"

Maria nodded, pushing the pistol and loose parts
to one side and wiping her hands with the cloth.
"Only a very few people know about the caches.
From what they said, the Hudson's Bay Company
has been using them for a long time. They're caves
along a creek they called Limestone Creek."

Harnett frowned and scratched his beard. "I've
never heard of it."

"It's south of the Musselshell."

He started to shake his head, then hesitated.
"Cave Creek," he said, snapping his fingers. "I'll
bet that's it. It's south of the Musselshell and not
that far from Fort Merrill, or where Fort Merrill
used to be. There's a lot of caves along it that are
good and dry and where furs could be stored without them spoiling." He looked at her with a musing

smile, then shook his head. "Maria, you're the durnedest that ever lived. Who else would even think of that, even if they had found out about the caches? Going right up into the middle of Blackfoot and Hudson's Bay Company territory, stealing Hudson's Bay Company furs. . . ."

"What do you think about it?"

He sighed and looked away, pondering, then looked back at her. "Maria, you're talking about over a season's catch for a good portion of the Hudson's Bay Company territory. You have any idea of how many furs you're talking about?"

Maria leaned toward him excitedly. "No. How many?"

"Hell, I don't know. But it would be a mountain of them, I can tell you that. And it would probably take a herd of horses to carry them. We couldn't go into Blackfoot country with a great big bunch of horses, or we'd get caught for sure."

"We wouldn't have to. All we have to do is get them out of the caches and move them somewhere else, and we could do it a few at a time."

He mused again, slowly nodding. "Yes, that would be the way to do it, I expect. We could get a couple of extra horses apiece and pissant them down to north of the Bighorn, cache them, then form a brigade and move them out of there. But nobody on earth needs that much money, Maria. What would you do with it?"

"Things I want to do, and things that need to be done. I'd run the Krugers out of the mountains. I'd teach the Hudson's Bay Company to stay north of their border. If anyone ever did something to me again like Stephen Kruger did, I'd hire an army, track him down and kill the son of a bitch. And there are other things I'd like to do. I don't know how many furs are there or what they're worth, but I need it, Seth. Or half of it, anyway."

He chuckled and shook his head. "If I did anything like this, it would be all yours. I've told you before that I don't need money, and I don't. I own everything I need, and since I met you I have everything I want. Besides that, I'm a fur trapper, not a fur trader." He smiled. "Or a fur thief. If I had a bunch of furs like that, all I'd know to do with them is bring them here. I wouldn't even know who to talk to in St. Louis. Do you?"

Maria shook her head. "No, but I can find out."

Harnett said, "I don't doubt that, Maria. I'll bet you can find out if anybody can, so I don't doubt that for a minute."

Maria looked at him in silence for a moment. "What do you think about it, then?"

He took a drink of his coffee, looking back at her, then put the cup down and motioned toward the pistol. "Pass that back over here and let me put it back together. Where we're going, you might need the durned thing."

Maria smothered her glee and smiled at him radiantly as she pushed the pistol and loose parts across the table.

18

The rushing noise of the creek smothered other sounds, making it impossible to hear if anyone or anything approached her. There seemed to be constant movements on the edge of her vision. Maria stood against the tree, turning her head nervously from side to side and scanning around her as she held her rifle ready to shoulder. A jay screeched nearby, a penetrating shriek that cut through the blurring noise of the creek, but she couldn't pinpoint the direction from which it had come. There was a movement through the underbrush to her right, and she stiffened, lifting the rifle. Then she relaxed as she saw Harnett. She walked toward him.

He shook his head in disgust. "I didn't find a thing," he said loudly over the noise of the creek. "Nothing but caves."

"I didn't either. Do we have time to look at another stretch before sunset?"

Harnett glanced up at the sky, then nodded as he turned and walked back into the underbrush. Maria followed him, glancing around herself and watching behind. The creek was a few yards to their left, concealed by a dense growth of white birch and underbrush. Its roar echoed from the high limestone walls of the valley, making it even louder. Boulders had rolled down from the valley walls and littered the ground, some so large that trees taking root under them had curved around them, and the underbrush there was thick and matted. The noise coupled with the limited visibility gave Maria a feeling of being hemmed in.

They walked a hundred yards farther along the creek. Harnett walked from that point toward the valley wall, craning his neck and looking along it through the trees. "Start up there where that big rock is on the edge," he said, pointing. "Come on down as far as where that tree's hanging over. I'll start at the tree and go on down a piece, then I'll come back up and meet you down below the tree."

Maria nodded, and Harnett turned and walked away through the trees. She walked back along the valley wall a few yards, looking for a way to climb up. She found a large boulder at the bottom of a pile of limestone that had slid down. As she started to climb on up the slide, she quickly shifted her weight and stepped back. A rattlesnake was coiled loosely on one of the rocks, sunning itself. She hopped off the boulder, gathered up a handful of gravel from around the bottom of it, then climbed back up on the boulder and began tossing the pebbles at the snake. It coiled tighter, lifting its head and looking around angrily as it rattled, then it uncoiled and crawled away. Maria began climbing the slide, hopping from stone to stone and balancing herself with her rifle.

The two pistols stuck under the front of her belt were heavy and a hindrance to her movements, but their solid weight and feel was comforting, giving sure knowledge of a powerful lethal ability. The noise of the creek diminished as did the feeling of being closed in as she climbed higher, but when she was above the top of the trees, a feeling of being exposed to view over a long distance grew. The opposite valley wall was a hundred yards away across the top of the trees. It was an expanse of limestone spotted with patches of brush, caves and rock slides, and all the dark shadows seemed to be hiding places for hostile eyes. The sense of imminent danger had been with her for days, since leaving Fort Henry. Harnett had casually commented that the attack on Fort Merrill had probably stirred up the Blackfeet, and it had been an understatement. North of the headwaters of the Snake River, the mountains had been alive with parties of them, and she and Harnett had traveled only at night, slowly feeling their way along and making wide detours at any indication of Indians. Even out here, there had still been times of wrenching fear, knowing that Blackfeet were nearby. Once they had passed a campfire that was still hot, and another time they had been within earshot of the Indians' horses.

Maria stood and looked back and forth along the opposite wall of the valley for a moment, searching the shadows with her eyes. Then she looked up at the wall above her. It was criss-crossed with ledges, crumbling in spots, and had several caves between the large rock at the top and the fallen tree Harnett had pointed out. Three of the caves were so high on the wall that they seemed unlikely places to cache furs because of the difficulty in getting the furs up to them, but Harnett had pointed out that the Hudson's Bay Company people could have picked caves for that very reason, using ropes and pulleys to get the furs up.

She worked her way along a narrow ledge that went up the wall at an angle, climbed onto a wider ledge that ran along in front of the three caves, and approached the first one. There was no animal hair on the ledge in front of it, the sides of the entrance weren't worn by an animal passing in and out, and there was no characteristic odor of a bear or cougar around it. She stooped and walked cautiously into it. It was several feet high inside, a few yards deep, and had a gravel floor. The air inside it was dry, cool and fresh. It was a perfect place to store furs for safekeeping, but there weren't any furs in it. The cave was a more or less spherical bubble in the limestone, with no tunnels or chambers walled up with rocks and plastered with mud, the way Harnett had speculated the furs would be stored to protect them from animals. Maria paused in the entrance of the cave and looked back and forth along the opposite wall of the valley again, then went into the next cave. There were smudges of ancient soot on the walls from fires of countless years before, flint nodules and bits of flint flaked off in the process of making tools or weapons, and the bones of some large animal that turned into dust at a touch. But there were no furs.

Harnett moved around on the limestone wall on

the other side of the large tree drooping over the
edge, taking stiff, cautious steps and testing rocks
and ledges to make sure they were safe before he
put his weight on them. Maria had the confidence
and agility of youth. Her moccasins clung to the
rough limestone, and she leaped from one ledge to
the next and climbed rapidly up and down the wall.
There were several caves farther down and farther
along the wall, most of them too small for her to
get into, and the others had nothing in them. The
last one she looked in was a tight squeeze for her,
and the darkness inside was total. Immediately inside the cave, there was a feeling of a vast open-
ness in front of her, damp air brushing her face,
and a distant sound of dripping water. She felt
around and found that she was standing on a ledge
above a chasm, and she climbed back out.

The debris of a small rock slide bulged out from
the foot of the wall almost directly under the tree
drooping over the edge. The slide seemed unusual
for some reason, and she glanced at it again. There
were no splintered remains of crumpled brush or
other vegetation as there usually was in a slide. She
dismissed it from her mind, looking around. The
noise of the creek blanketed other sounds around
her again, stirring an instinctive fear of someone
creeping up behind her, and she moved to a tree
and stood against it, watching around her as she
waited for Harnett.

Harnett came through the trees, and she walked
toward him, shaking her head. He nodded morosely,
glancing up at the sky, then turned toward the
creek. They walked through the trees and underbrush to the edge of the creek, and Maria waited
on the bank as he lifted his rifle and powder horn

and waded out into it. He looked up and down the creek, then motioned to her as he waded toward the other side. Maria lifted her rifle and powder horn over her head, stepping into the water and feeling for a firm footing on the bottom, and waded after him. The rocks were slippery under her moccasins, the current was strong, and the water was icy, fresh from mountain springs. It came up to her knees, then to the middle of her thighs, and she leaned into the current and moved her feet slowly along the bottom, balancing herself against the current.

The water became shallow again, and she took longer steps. Harnett stood in the shallow water with the water rushing around his calves and pulling at his leggings, and he pointed to a rock in the water as Maria approached. "Look at that!" he shouted over the noise. "That's a mark made by a horseshoe if I ever saw one! It's old, but it was made by a horseshoe! And they're all over the place here!"

It was a dim line of lighter color almost fading into the mottled grey of the rock. Maria nodded. Harnett shook his head in exasperation, glancing along the bank, then stepped to a cluster of large rocks at the edge of the water and climbed out onto them to avoid leaving a footprint in the soft soil on the bank. Maria followed him. He turned down the creek and walked toward a large slide, his attitude and expression reflecting dissatisfaction. They had been searching in the valley for two full days, finding abundant evidence of where horses had been up and down the creek, but finding no sign of fur caches.

They climbed the slide to the top of the valley

wall, went along the edge of the valley to where it curved to a line parallel with the slope of the mountain, then turned up the mountain. The noise of the creek faded behind, and the soft, reassuring sounds of the forest were around Maria again, the whisper of the breeze in the trees, the rustle of the leaves underfoot, the singing and chirping of the birds, the scurrying of small animals. The slope leveled off, and they circled around it, picking their way through piles of boulders that had rolled down from the peaks above. The horses were hobbled in a small, grassy meadow strewn with boulders, and they were grazing contentedly. Maria and Harnett checked their hobbles, then went on up through the clearing and into the dense thickets of spruce above it, where they had stored their belongings, and made camp in a windfall.

The sun had set and the light was fading rapidly as they sat under the thick tangle of dead limbs and ate. Harnett chewed glumly. "I had my doubts at first, but now I know that they're in that valley, Maria. There's been horses all up and down that valley several times, and that's the only reason anybody would have horses in there."

"Well, it's just a matter of time, Seth. We'll find them sooner or later."

"I should have found them a hell of a lot sooner than this, and we shouldn't have to look from cave to cave. But I haven't been able to find a track anywhere but in the creek."

"It looks like that valley is flooded just about every spring. That would take care of any tracks in the dirt. In any event, we still have a lot of caves to check. We'll find them."

"Yes, but we shouldn't have to do that. I should be able to figure out where they are without looking at every cave and rock in that valley."

"Well, if they cached furs where they would be easy to find, they probably wouldn't be there for us to find, would they? At first it didn't seem like a very safe way of handling furs, but it's looking safer all the time to me."

Harnett nodded, taking a drink from the water bottle and crunching a bite of raw turnip. "Considering what happened, it wouldn't have been very smart to have them at Fort Merrill, would it? And even the friendliest Indians get to feeling greedy when they see a lot of furs laying around."

"I noticed they kept those at the fort out of sight. No one down our way ever caches furs, do they?"

"Sometimes, but it's different there. We have half a dozen big companies, a bunch of little ones and a passel of tree trappers and traders, with most of them trying to outdo each other and beat each other to St. Louis with furs. The Canadians just have one big company, and they have a different way of doing things. And some of the things they do make the prices go up, for some reason or other. There's also plenty of finagling over prices in St. Louis amongst the big traders like Astor, Robideaux and such, but I don't know nothing about how they go about it or anything." He took another drink of water from the bottle and belched, unrolling his blanket. "And I don't want to know. I'm a trapper, and that's all I want to be."

Maria chuckled and nodded, chewing on a bite of jerky. Harnett took his tomahawk and long knife out of the back of his belt, put them and his rifle by him, and rolled up in his blanket, grunting and sighing as he settled himself.

Darkness fell, and Maria finished eating the unappetizing, unsatisfying meal of jerky, parched corn and raw turnip, visions of hot stewed meat and beans, fried potatoes and onions, steaming coffee and fresh bread passing through her mind. The moon rose, beams penetrating the tangled mass of the windfall and making dappled spots of white on the jumble of bags, packsaddles and other things piled in the small enclosure. Maria took a drink from the bottle, arranged her weapons beside her, then rolled in her blanket. It was cold and cheerless without a fire, the sparse, frugal meals during the past days had become drearily monotonous, and the constant peril from being deep in Blackfoot territory had frayed her nerves to the extent that it took her a long time to relax enough to go to sleep. But she went to sleep thinking about the fur caches.

The screeching of a jay woke her, and she felt for her weapons and listened closely, looking up at the grey light of dawn coming through the windfall overhead. Then she heard a bear shuffling through the underbrush as the jay called again, and she relaxed. She took out a piece of jerky and chewed it with distaste, gathering up her weapons, and crawled out of the windfall. Harnett yawned, coughed and groaned, and crawled out after her. They walked down to the horses and checked their hobbles, then circled around the mountain and walked on down to the creek.

The sun rose above the peaks, warming the damp, cold air in the valley, and Maria climbed up and down the ledges once again, looking for the caves and checking them. By midday they had searched along another long stretch of the valley wall. Maria sat down on a boulder at the base of a slide and took a handful of parched corn from the hunting bag, glancing around and munching the corn as she waited for Harnett. She was not discouraged. She still felt it was a matter of time mostly, and she could afford plenty of that for the riches it would bring her at the end. Harnett came through the trees and underbrush, sighing heavily and shaking his head. He sat down by her and took a piece of jerky from his hunting bag.

"I found what looks like a horseshoe mark on a rock down there, but it was made a long time ago, if that's what it is. Other than that, I ain't seen a thing."

Maria nodded, chewing. "We should finish this side within the next couple of days, shouldn't we?"

"About two days, more or less. Then we'll start on the other side. And then we'll come back over here and start over. I ain't going to leave here until I find them, even if I have to wait until they come after them and have to fight the bastards for them."

Maria smiled. She felt about the same way. There was a movement on the edge of her vision, and she turned her head and looked. Another rattlesnake, this one large, was crawling across a stone several feet away, coming toward them. She stood up, looking around the bottom of the slide for gravel. There was none, but there were several small rocks on a ledge a few feet away. She stepped to the ledge, gathered up the rocks, and sat back down, tossing them at the snake. The snake coiled up, its rattle a blur of motion but the sound almost inaudible over the noise of the creek. Then it turned and crawled away as Maria kept tossing the rocks at it. Maria dropped the rest of the rocks and put more corn into her mouth as she looked absently down at the ground.

Her eyes focussed on the ground. There was no gravel around the base of the slide. She stood up, looking at the slide again. It was made up of several large boulders in a jumbled pile at the base of the limestone wall, with progressively smaller stones toward its top. The slide was made up entirely of stones, with no dirt, gravel or other debris in it. But the valley wall wasn't solid limestone. It was interspersed with places where scrubby vegetation and weeds were growing in thin soil, and there were pockets of soil and vegetation even on the limestone faces. Typically, a slide was made up of a mixture of dirt, gravel, rocks and crumbled vegetation that had poured down from the top of the wall. As she looked at this one, it began to appear more and more artificial.

"There isn't any gravel or dirt!"

Harnett looked at her, tearing another bite from the piece of jerky, then looked at the slide behind him and back at her. "What?"

"There isn't any gravel or dirt!"

He started to shrug. Then he stopped chewing, his head snapped around and he looked at the slide again. He stood up to look at it. He muttered something under his breath, his eyes moving over the slide, and he laughed as he crammed the rest of the jerky into his mouth and slapped her shoulder. "I'll be durned if these rocks ain't been piled up here, Maria! I was sitting on it all the time and didn't even see it! You've got some eyes in your head, girl!"

"I'll go get some poles to roll these rocks out of the way," Maria said excitedly, turning away.

"No, wait your hurry," Harnett said, taking her arm and pointing. "You see that line along there? That's where it's flooded up to in the spring at one time or another, and they sure wouldn't put them below that. Let's just roll the little ones down from the top and see what we find."

Maria nodded, scrambling up the slide, and began pulling at the rocks. Harnett climbed up the other side and began rolling the rocks down, and rocks clattered down the pile and bounced through the trees and underbrush. The top edge of a heavy mat of interwoven limbs became visible, and Maria tore at the rocks and jerked at the dessicated sticks.

Harnett chortled at Maria's excitement. He too began pulling the limbs out of the way. The mat covered a cave entrance, keeping the stones from falling into it, and the yawning hole was gradually uncovered as they tumbled the rocks down and pulled the limbs out. The musky scent of beaver furs came from the cave entrance. Maria could see the ends of large canvas bundles in the dim light inside. She pulled at the rocks harder, not feeling the nicks and bruises on her hands from their rough limestone edges.

She wriggled down into the opening, and Harnett pushed a few more rocks out of the way and climbed down in beside her. Sixteen large, oblong, canvas-covered bundles were stacked against the walls of the cave, each with HBC painted on its side in large letters. Before, finding the furs had been a goal in Maria's mind, an objective that hadn't been defined in concrete terms. Her mind reeled as she tried to imagine the value of the immense quantity of furs around her.

"A dozen to fifteen packs of furs in each one of them, I'd say," Harnett mused quietly. "There's a bunch of furs here, Maria."

Maria nodded, wiping her trembling hands on her buckskins and thinking. "Seth, I saw another slide just like this one yesterday. Let's go check it and see if it isn't another cache."

"Oh, I'm sure it is. There'll be more of them, and you found out the secret, all right. We'll be able to find all of them now."

"Let's go check and make sure. It won't take but a few minutes to pull down enough of the rocks to see the cave."

"No." He chuckled, shaking his head. "No, we don't want to do that, Maria. How does a body go about swallowing a buffalo?"

"What do you mean? A person can't swallow a buffalo."

"Oh, yes, they just take it a bite at a time. And we've got us one hell of a bite to gnaw up right now. There's a lot more here than what our horses can pack, and we've got to cover it up like it was to keep the varmints out of it while we're taking what we can carry down toward the Bighorn. If we start right now, we can just about be on our way by nightfall, I expect. So let's get this bite gnawed up and swallowed before we start looking around for another one."

Maria hesitated, then nodded, and Harnett patted her shoulder as he turned toward the entrance. He climbed back out. Maria glanced around at the bundles again as she too walked toward the entrance, her initial excitement over finding the furs beginning to fade. Finding them had been an important step, but only a step. The next step was transporting them through Blackfoot territory to the south.

19

The rocks bruised Maria's feet through her moccasins as she clambered up and down, dragging the heavy packs of furs out of the cave. Her arms became leaden from helping lift them onto the pack-saddles, and she began slipping and falling on the rocks and skinning herself painfully as she became more fatigued. The sun set and the light began fading as they gathered and carried the rocks back to the pile and replaced them. Her hands became blistered and sore from handling them. When the last were in place, Harnett rummaged in a supply bag for jerky, corn and a turnip each for their dinner, and Maria put hers in her hunting bag. They rode out of the valley as the moon was rising, Maria slumped in her saddle, almost totally exhausted and tormented by the pain of her bruises, cuts, and blisters. Then her shared responsibility to watch for danger asserted itself in her mind, and she wearily gathered herself and sat up in the saddle, looking around and listening as she felt for kernels of corn in her hunting bag.

The hours of the night slowly dragged by, the horses trudging up and down slopes and through winding valleys under their heavy loads and Harnett frequently stopping to look and listen. At first light they stopped and camped at the head of a small grassy valley, where the horses could graze. Maria was stiff and sore. Her hands were so swollen that she had difficulty in helping Harnett untie and lift the packs of furs off the horses. She ate a few bites, then rolled in her blanket and fell into a deep sleep.

Harnett woke her during the afternoon, motioning for her to be quiet and pointing down the valley. A strong odor of woodsmoke hung in the air. Maria pushed her blanket aside and reached for her weapons as Harnett crept away into the underbrush. He returned a few minutes later and gathered up the halters to catch the horses as he whispered quietly. A party of twelve to fifteen Blackfeet had stopped along the creek to cook. Maria hastily rolled up her blanket, gathered up her weapons and went to help Harnett collect the horses.

There was another close brush with a small party of Blackfeet the next day, and when they camped they found evidence of where a large party had recently passed by. Then the signs of Blackfeet diminished as they crossed the rugged mountains dividing the water shed of the Musselshell from that of the Upper Yellowstone. They continued traveling at night, descending into the deep gorge of the Yellowstone and winding their way back out of it. Maria made herself a pair of crude mittens from pieces of buckskin to use in loading and unloading the furs. The swelling in her hands diminished and some of the painful soreness in her bruises and cuts began to fade.

They crossed over into the high valleys above the Bighorn, spent part of a day in finding a dry, sandy cave and carrying stones to seal the entrance, then stored the furs in the cave and hobbled the horses in a meadow to rest and graze for a day. The area was relatively safe, and after dark they built a small fire and cooked. They ate, and Maria sat looking into the dying coals of the fire, basking in the comfort of the full, hot meal and in the satisfaction of having the first load of furs in a safe place.

She counted in her mind the days it had taken to bring the furs this far, then pondered about the distance between the Bighorn and Fort Henry. "Do you think we'll be able to get the furs to St. Louis before winter?"

Harnett stirred and yawned wearily on the other side of the fire. "It depends on how long it takes to get them collected together here, Maria, which depends on how many we find back at the caches. And it depends on how early winter comes. It looks like it's going to be a late one this year. It don't come in really hard on the prairie until November sometimes, but it ain't very smart to be out that late in the year."

Maria mused. "They'll sit up and look when we bring all these furs into Fort Henry, won't they?"

"No, they won't, because we ain't going to."

"Why?"

Harnett yawned again, then sighed. "Maria, from now on you're going to have to keep your cards covered and not let nobody know what you're up to.

Now take these furs, for instance. Them bags is marked and every fur in every bag is marked that they belong to the Hudson's Bay Company. Everybody will more or less figure out the whole story sooner or later, but you don't want to go spreading it all over God's creation. You never can tell how much misery just the right person can cause you if they found out."

"Yes, that's true. They are stolen, and there could be a lot of trouble."

"I imagine so. Like I said, I don't know nothing about trading and I don't know who could cause trouble or what kind they could cause, but there's no sense in taking chances when you don't have to. When I go to Fort Henry to get extra horses, I ain't going to say we lost our horses, but I ain't going to say that we didn't, neither. Nor am I going to say why we want so many. I'm going to be quiet about collecting up the bush lopers too. Don't look for people to help you when you're going into business against them."

"But the people at Fort Henry are my friends."

"You said you was going to run Kruger off, right? I guess by raising the price on furs was what you had in mind. What do you think you'll be doing to the bunch at Fort Henry while you're doing that? And what about after that? Every fur you trade for is a fur they'll wish they had, and you'd better bear that in mind."

Maria nodded as Harnett looked at her, pulling his blanket around himself and lying down on the other side of the fire. She looked into the bed of glowing coals, thinking. The paramount difficulties of finding the furs, getting them out of the valley and transporting them to St. Louis had been foremost in her mind. She hadn't thought beyond them. But there would be many problems. Disposing of the furs and obtaining a fair price for them in St. Louis wouldn't be easy, because neither she nor Harnett had the slightest knowledge of how to go about selling them. She remembered names her father had mentioned of men in the fur trade, but they might be skeptical about discussing business with a young woman. And once the furs were sold and she returned to the mountains with trade goods, she would be competing with experienced traders and she knew nothing about trading. She sighed, pulling her blanket around herself and settling herself to go to sleep.

Speculation and worry about the future became of less concern to her again as they went back through Blackfoot territory and returned to Cave Creek. They had to work their way slowly along at night and keep constantly alert. When they reached the valley, they found two more caches in the vicinity of the first one, and the second one they opened had twenty of the bundles in it. They took the remainder of the furs out of the first cache and part of the furs out of the second, and set out again for the Bighorn, Maria bruised, battered and sagging in the saddle from exhaustion.

On the third trip, Maria began to seriously consider at what point taking advantage of a windfall became an all-consuming greed, illogical to the point of subjecting herself and Harnett to unreasonable danger simply to have more and more of the furs. She broached the subject with Harnett. He was casually noncommittal and even remotely amused by her train of thought. He exercised caution when in a dangerous situation, but he had lived in more or less constant peril for much of his life, accepted it as a condition of life and had the fatalistic viewpoint that his end would come when it was due. He was convinced that that had happened to the many mountain men he had known who had been killed.

Harnett left it up to her to decide, seemingly indifferent about whether the continued toil, hardship and danger outweighed the value of the rest of the furs to her, and the philosophical issue of where unreasonable greed began remained unaddressed. But the question as to what Maria wanted to do was resolved by her reaction when the ties on a pack on one of her horses near the rear of the train came loose and spilled part of the furs during a night's trek. Her immediate, unthinking response was to take a horse and lead it back along the trail to collect the furs, sacrificing part of her day's rest and risking the danger of moving about during daylight. Having been presented an opportunity, she wanted to wring the most from it and that was all there was to it; her goals meant more to her than any amount of discomfort, labor or danger. As she started back, she found that Harnett had been following her in event she met with trouble, and he chuckled wearily and shook his head with admiration over her determination as they walked back.

The question arose again on what they thought would be the fifth and last trip. There were only four bundles of furs left in the third cache, and they anticipated having only light loads for the horses and making an easier and faster return. Then they found another cache up the creek, containing eight bundles. The horses were gaunt and weary from the lack of adequate time to graze during the repeated trips back and forth across the mountains. The twelve bundles were more than they could carry. Harnett and Maria looked carefully along the creek to make sure they had found the last of the caches, then loaded the horses with what they could carry and set out again. When they reached the Bighorn, they delayed an extra day for Maria to decide what she wanted to do and give the horses a rest. On the second day, they prepared to return to Cave Creek once more.

Harnett had varied the route to an extent on each trip so as to lessen their chances of finding Blackfeet waiting in ambush somewhere along the trail. But there were only a limited number of routes over the peaks and through the gorges between the watersheds of the rivers. So on the last trip, the horses carrying lighter loads, Harnett decided it would be safer to go higher into the mountains south of the Musselshell and farther to the east, crossing the Yellowstone somewhat farther downstream and circling through to the Bighorn along a high-mountain route he remembered from several years before. On the first night, they climbed high into the mountains above Cave Creek and camped in a high valley, and on the second night they turned to the east and traveled across the southern slopes of the mountains, crossing rolling swales of dense spruce thickets and outcroppings of shale and limestone.

The horses were unsure of their footing on the shale, and the high bluffs were nerve-wracking in the darkness. Twice they got out on ledges that became too narrow for the wider loads, and they had to dismount, turn the horses around one at a time, and lead them back off. Dawn began breaking as they were crossing a wide expanse of shale dotted by stunted, wind-gnarled spruces. They hurried across it and onto the next wooded slope. The thickets there were broken by grassy clearings, too open for good concealment, but they found a small bowl-shaped valley that had a rivulet running through it and ample graze for the horses.

They unloaded the horses, ate, then rolled in their blankets to sleep and wait for sunset. Maria was unnerved by what had happened on the ledges the night before. Harnett's amused unconcern indicated that it would probably happen again, so she shivered from more than the thin, cold, early morning air in the high mountains as she tried to relax. Then the sun rose higher and warmed the air, the leaden fatigue made her racing thoughts slow and become muddled, and she slept.

She woke, lifted her head and glanced around, then relaxed and rested her head on the saddle again. It was afternoon, and everything appeared normal, Harnett snoring softly and the horses stamping and cropping the grass. She stretched and yawned, then sat up and reached for the water bottle. The memory of the terrifying experiences on the ledges the night before returned as she drank, and she looked toward the east and tried to see what lay ahead of them as she pushed the cork back into the bottle. Trees blocked her view from where she was sitting, but the outer edge of the small valley was open and free of trees and the mountain sloped away on both sides of it. She took a piece of jerky from the supply bag and chewed on it as she rose and walked to the edge of the valley, looking to the east again. There seemed to be an abundance of rock faces ahead, many of them high ones.

An eagle floated above, its wings motionless as it circled and scanned the grassy clearings on the mountain slope. Maria watched it absently, chewing the jerky, then looked to the east again. A small spot of a different color in an opening in the trees that way caught her eye, and she looked closer. It moved. Another one came into sight behind it. Then another one. It was a line of men on horses. She leaped up, ran back to Harnett and leaned over him, shaking his shoulder.

"I see some riders."

His eyes opened wider, and he scrambled up, snatching up his rifle. Maria trotted back to the edge of the valley, crouching as she approached it so she wouldn't be silhouetted against the skyline. She pointed. The riders were disappearing into the trees on the other side of the distant clearing. Harnett rubbed his eyes and looked, then sat down. Maria sat down, watching for them to come into sight again. Long minutes passed. Then there was movement and Maria pointed.

Harnett grunted. "They're a good way away, and I can't tell whether or not they're Indians. But it's likely they are, and Blackfeet, no doubt."

"The first two are wearing trapper's hats, and the other four are Indians. And they have two pack horses."

"And you've got good eyes. They're probably Hudson's Bay Company men then, because I don't think anyone else would be riding around in the open in Blackfoot country."

"Do you think they might be heading for Cave Creek? If they are, we got out just in time."

Harnett shook his head. "It depends on where they're coming from, but I doubt it. The way they're going, they're more likely headed for Fort Merrill." He chuckled softly. "Or where it used to be. If it's been a while since they've been there and they ain't heard the news, they're going to get a surprise."

Maria looked at the riders again. They disappeared into trees and several minutes passed. Then she glimpsed movement again. "If they keep on coming in the same direction, they'll pass by us down the slope there. I'd better check the horses' hobbles."

"They shouldn't come very close to us, but it wouldn't hurt. Keep well down, Maria."

Maria nodded, crouching down and creeping back from the valley's edge. Then she went down into the valley and walked around the horses. Most of them had finished grazing and were dozing, a few were still nibbling half-heartedly at the grass, and all of the hobbles were secure. She climbed back up the bank, got a couple of pieces of jerky from the supply bag, then crawled back and handed one to Harnett. He nodded, taking it, and Maria lay down on her stomach and chewed the other piece.

The riders were out of sight again and she watched for them to reappear. There was a movement of contrasting color through trees in the distance. They were much closer, but the trees obstructed her view and she couldn't see them clearly. She waited, pushing the last of the piece of jerky in her mouth and chewing it. They came into sight again in clear view, riding across a clearing. Her eyes passed back and forth across them, then became fixed on the first one. There was something familiar about him. Then she stopped chewing and stiffened convulsively, an icy, sinking feeling gripping her.

"It's Stephen Kruger."

Harnett looked at her quickly, his eyes narrowed as he looked back at the riders, and he pursed his lips, musing. Then he looked back at Maria, studied her face and nodded. "See to your priming."

Maria slid back through the grass on her stomach, then climbed to her feet and ran to where she had left her weapons by her blanket. She pushed her tomahawk and fighting knife into the back of her belt, opened her powder horn and freshened the priming in her rifle and pistols, then trotted back toward Harnett, tucking her rifle under her arm and pushing the pistols into her belt.

The rivulet in the valley disappeared into the ground and surfaced again a few yards below it, making a long, shallow gully down the side of the mountain. They splashed through the gully, passing by thickets and openings, Harnett occasionally lifting his head and craning his neck to look over the gully's edge and locate himself. He motioned to Maria and slowed as they approached one thicket. They climbed out of the gully and walked through it, slowing as the trees began to open out. They stopped near the edge of a clearing, and Harnett pointed.

"They should pass right along here. You've got some trees in the way, so take your time and get a good shot, Maria. When you get a good bead on him, just go ahead and shoot. I'll be waiting for you to shoot first."

"There'll be four of them left."

"I figure we could take on ten without working

up a sweat. Make your first shot count, Maria. He's a slick one. He got away from us once."

Maria nodded. Harnett turned and walked off a few yards through the trees. A clump of underbrush was growing at one end of a log. Maria lay down and crawled under it, sliding her rifle across the log. Harnett's soft footsteps faded. Then the only sounds were the sighing of the soft breeze in the trees and the distant croaking of a crow, a harsh, lonely sound.

Her hands were damp and trembling, and her mouth was dry. At Fort Merrill, the sound of Stephen's voice outside had incited terror in her, a wrenching fear that he was coming into her locked room in the trading post again, and the sound of his footsteps approaching had filled her with a desperate hopelessness. Even knowing he was near and riding toward her now made the fear swell again. From the first time she had seen him, he had cast a pall over her life, some blight that had always remained in the back of her mind and haunted her. In some ways he seemed an invincible, inimical force that would always be threatening her, something that was impervious to weapons. She checked the priming in the rifle and pistols again, pulled the hammers back and put the pistols on the log in front of her.

The clearing in front of her was narrow, little more than a wide path through the woods. Spruces of various sizes were scattered about in it, so that there was no clear line of fire in any direction. Maria wriggled from side to side, settling herself comfortably. Her thoughts kept returning to him, his vicious, sneering laughter as he casually tortured her, the times he had brought a lamp into the room and beat her until she agreed to walk around naked in front of him, his repeated threats to turn her over to the other men unless she did his bidding. Could they have been worse? She wondered. She wiped her damp right hand on her shirt and shouldered the rifle. The rifle didn't feel like hers; it didn't have the solid, reassuring weight of other times.

The distant sound of a horse's hoof striking a stone made her jerk convulsively. The hoofbeats became louder, moving toward her at a walking pace. Then there was a movement on the left side of the clearing. Maria leaned into the rifle, sighting down the barrel and swinging it to the left. Stephen came into sight through an opening between trees. He was looking back and saying something to the man behind him. The distant sound of his voice carried to Maria's ears. Her hands began trembling violently. She steeled herself and tracked him with the rifle barrel. When he disappeared behind trees, she tracked his direction at the walking speed of his horse. The bead was on his head as he came into sight again. On the right edge of her vision, she saw an opening between trees several yards ahead of him, a good place to shoot. Her hand was damp again. She wiped it quickly on her sleeve and slid it around the trigger again. He disappeared behind trees again, laughing at something the man behind him had said and turning back to the front. Maria tracked the rifle barrel across those trees, her hands trembling as fear and hatred churned within her from the sound of his laughter. He came back into view, crossing the wide opening. Maria drew in a deep breath, released half of it, then put the bead on his head, easing the trigger back. The hammer snapped, the pan flared, and she continued tracking. The rifle boomed, belching smoke, and Stephen flew off his horse, his arms flailing.

Harnett's rifle cracked, and the other white man behind Stephen was slapped off his horse. The frightened horses stamped, reared and neighed shrilly. The four Indians reacted instantly, attacking while rifles were unloaded. A rifle cracked, a ball slammed into the log by Maria, and two of them were charging toward her and shrieking wildly as the other two charged toward Harnett. Maria pushed herself up to her knees, picking up a pistol and pointing it at the nearest Indian. She pulled the trigger back. It misfired. She picked up the other pistol and pointed it, groping for her powder horn. The Indian was close, wheeling his horse around with one hand as he lifted his tomahawk to throw it. Maria's pistol cracked, and the ball hit him in the stomach, doubling him over as it knocked him off his horse. The other Indian hesitated, swerving his horse and glancing in Harnett's direction. Harnett's rifle cracked again and one of the other two Indians went down.

Maria picked up the pistol that had misfired, thumbed the hammer back and dumped powder into the pan. The second Indian swerved his horse toward her again, leveling his rifle. Maria pointed the pistol at him and snapped the trigger back. Its overcharged pan flared, burning her hand as it went off. His horse went down with a shrill scream. The Indian sprawled on the ground, his rifle firing. Maria dropped the pistol and snatched up her unloaded rifle.

Tomahawks clattered and war whoops in Harnett's and an Indian's voice rang out farther along the clearing. Maria fumbled with the ball, patch and ramrod. The wounded horse screamed again, thrashing its legs. The fallen Indian gathered himself, climbing to his feet and shaking his head, then jerked out his tomahawk and lifted it as he raced toward Maria, shrieking. Maria was still reloading, the rifle butt against her stomach as she dumped powder into the pan. The Indian's painted face was contorted with savage triumph as he lifted his tomahawk higher, scant yards away. Maria dropped the powder horn, jerked the hammer back and released it. Triggered, the rifle thundered and kicked against her stomach, a huge cloud of smoke billowing from it.

The Indian staggered backwards, smudges of burned gunpowder on his face and naked chest. The splintered shards of the ramrod stuck out of his neck. He clutched at his neck as the blood spurted, and a dry, gasping sound came from his open mouth. His knees trembled, and his eyes bulged with effort as he held himself erect and lifted the tomahawk higher to throw it. Maria dropped the rifle, plucking her tomahawk smoothly out of the back of her belt. The handle fell into her hand as she balanced herself, her left foot forward and her weight on her right foot. She aimed with her left hand, bending backwards, then snapped forward, putting her shoulder behind her throw. The tomahawk flipped once as it shot through the air. Then the sharp blade slammed into the Indian's chest with a heavy thud. The impact knocked him sprawling onto his back and his tomahawk fell from his lifeless hand.

Maria became aware that the clattering sound in her ears was her teeth rattling together. She clamped her jaws closed, wiping her sweaty hands on her shirt and her face with her sleeve. She began gathering up her pistols. Harnett walked toward her, whooping with gleeful laughter.

"By God! Two on six, and we done them right, didn't we? By God!"

Maria smiled weakly and nodded. She noticed the blood on his sleeve. "Did one of them get you?"

"It ain't nothing but a scratch. Shot this one with your ramrod, didn't you? And then tomahawked him. If that son of a bitch ain't dead, then cooking him won't kill him. That sort of put paid to your ramrod, but you can use one from one of their rifles. It'll be a little long, but we can trim it down when we get time. Do you want these scalps?"

"No."

"Well, I think I'll pull them just for the hell of it. Here's your tomahawk."

Maria took the tomahawk, wiped it on the grass and slid it back under her belt, then reloaded her pistols. While Harnett scalped his Indian and the one she had killed, she walked over to the horse she had shot. It was dead, its eyes glazed. She turned and got a rifle one of the Indians had dropped. Harnett pulled the ramrod out of it and handed it to her, his hand bloody from his own wound and from scalping the Indians. Maria took the ramrod and reloaded her rifle. Then she walked toward Stephen.

Fear rose within her again as she looked at Stephen lying on the ground. He looked so much like Curtis; it was almost as if she had killed Curtis. But it was not Curtis she had killed, despite the blondness, despite the now relaxed lines on his face. Even sprawled limp and lifeless on the ground,

Stephen seemed to emanate some malevolent power that found its way into the inner recesses of her being. Then an all-consuming rage rose within her, a choking, smothering anger for what he had done. He had aroused the Blackfeet, and many had been killed, including her father. When she had been in his power, he had treated her as less than a human being, as an object only for his sexual and sadistic enjoyment. And it was he who had killed Curtis, gleefully and triumphantly.

And in return for all he had done, she had only killed him. It was far too little, an inadequate and puny retaliation.

Harnett was walking back to their pack horses while she was fingering the handle of her skinning knife, looking at Stephen's thick blond hair. She had a nagging, instinctive anxiety that somehow he would continue to stalk her, even though dead. She knew she was being irrational, but she felt that having his scalp as physical evidence of his death would bring reassurance to her in dark moments. And it would be a token of reducing him to the level of an animal, as he had her. It would be something more than just killing him. She bent over his head with her knife.

The movement of his chest seemed like an illusion at first. Maria bent lower, looking closer. The thick smear of blood on his temple and cheek was from a deep crease the rifle ball had scored, not from a hole. He had moved his head as she fired. Or her hands had trembled too hard. Maria pushed the knife back into the sheath, looking down at him and musing exultantly now. She glanced around. With Harnett, the pack horses Stephen had been leading were standing a few yards away, their halter ropes caught and tangled in brush. Maria walked toward them.

"Well, we've got us some good rifles," Harnett said cheerfully. "Every one of them is about new. And we can use these horses too."

Maria nodded, untying the rope holding the bags on the packsaddle on one of the horses. She dropped the bags to the ground as she pulled the rope from around them.

"What are you doing that for? We'll probably be able to use that stuff too."

"I need the rope. He isn't dead."

"He's not? Well, slit his throat, then."

"That's not enough."

Harnett nodded uncertainly, looking at her as she returned to Stephen and knelt by him, knotting the end of the rope around one of his wrists. Then he turned and walked away. She pulled the rope around a small tree near Stephen, jerked it tight and knotted it, then cut it off and stepped back to him to tie his other wrist to another tree close by. Harnett collected up all the weapons and put them in a pile on the ground. He caught one of the saddle horses and rode it around, catching the other ones. Maria tautened the ropes, pulling Stephen's arms wide apart. Then she stepped back to him, pulled off his boots and tied his ankles to other trees, tautening them as well. Off some distance, Harnett found some rawhide thongs in the bags Maria had left on the ground and began retying the bags onto the packsaddle.

When Maria had Stephen in a spreadeagled position, she picked up his hat and carried it to the gully. She stepped down into it, dipped the hat into the water, then carried it back to Stephen and threw it on his face. He stirred, making a sound in his throat and tugging weakly at the ropes holding him. Maria returned to the gully, knelt, opened her powder horn and poured gunpowder into her palm. She dipped her hand into the water. The gunpowder turned into thick, black liquid. She poured part of it into her other hand and spread it over her face, covering her forehead and cheeks, pressing her lips together as she wiped it across her mouth.

Harnett looked at her with an inscrutable expression as she walked back. He was silent for a long moment, then he sighed and nodded as he turned away. "I guess the mountains was more a part of your blood than I thought, Maria. You took to them faster than anybody I ever saw, and I think you're passing me up in a lot of ways and still going strong. We've made a lot of fuss here, so I'll go load our horses and get everything ready to leave while you're doing what you have to do."

Maria nodded, folding her arms and looking down at Stephen. Harnett tucked his rifle under his arm and walked away. Stephen moved, his head turning and his limbs twitching. The fear had subsided within Maria, overcome by her raging anger as she looked at him and thought about what he had done. His eyes opened, and he blinked and glanced quickly around. He looked at her blankly, then in recognition. The sardonic smile began forming on his face, but it was weak and faltering. He lifted his head and looked at the ropes, pulling at them, then looked at her again. The fear in his eyes made hers diminish still more.

"What are you doing? What are you going to do?" His voice quavered. He lifted his head again and watched her as she stepped to the pile of weapons, picked up a rifle and began collecting twigs and sticks. She piled the twigs near Stephen, poured gunpowder onto them and snapped the lock of the rifle over them. The gunpowder flared up. The twigs smoldered, then burst into flame. Maria piled sticks on them and stood up, pouring gunpowder into the barrel of the rifle.

"What are you going to do? Listen, I know where a lot of furs are, and you can. . . ."

His voice broke, then faded. Maria put a patch on the muzzle of the rifle, pushed it in with the ramrod to hold the powder in place, then lifted the rifle and primed the pan. Stephen's face became transfixed with fright as she stepped toward him, closing the pan and pulling the hammer back. He shook his head rapidly, his mouth opening and closing as he tried to say something. Maria pointed the rifle at his genitals and pulled the trigger. The powder in the rifle ignited with a soft thud. Flame shot from the end of the barrel and licked across the front of Stephen's trousers. A huge cloud of smoke billowed up. His body arched off the ground, and a shrill, gagging scream tore from his throat as the grains of nitrate blasted into his skin, still burning as they penetrated. Maria lowered the rifle and put the butt on the ground, pouring powder into the barrel. He began thrashing convulsively against the ground and twisting from side to side, his screams battering at Maria's ears. She pushed a patch down the barrel of the rifle, lifted the rifle and primed the pan, then pointed it at his genitals and snapped the trigger again. Flame shot from the barrel and smoke boiled up. His body thudded against the ground heavily as he undulated, jerking at the ropes. Maria put the rifle butt on the ground and poured more powder into the barrel.

The front of his trousers burned away, the ragged edges smoldering. His skin was blackened by burned gunpowder and his genitals blistered as the flames seared them. Maria put the rifle on the ground and took out her skinning knife. He jerked his head away as he felt the touch of the knife on his hairline, uttering hoarse, ragged screams. Maria slashed and dragged the blade around the top of his head as he struggled to pull away, throwing his head from side to side. Blood spurted, matting his hair and dripping on the ground. Maria wiped the knife on the ground and put it back in her sheath. She put her feet on his shoulders, gripped the front of his hair and threw her weight back. His scalp began peeling off, and his screams became shrill, infant-like shrieks.

His head was grotesque. There was thick blond hair around the sides and a red, gleaming skull at the top. His mouth gaped wide open and his tongue thrust out as he kept sceraming. Maria stepped back around him, tossing the scalp down. The end of the rifle barrel was dull red. She picked it up. His mouth closed and his eyes opened wide in stark horror as he saw the smoking end of the rifle barrel approaching his face. Maria put her foot on his neck to hold his head still and put the tip of the rifle barrel first on his right eye, then on his left.

Stephen's screams rose to a crescendo, and his body kept thudding against the ground convulsively.

Maria stepped back, folded her arms and waited, looking at him.

His screams died away into loud, sobbing moans, and his body rolled from side to side on the ground as he clawed at the air sightlessly and aimlessly. After a while, though his moans shortened into quick, high-pitched whimpers, he lay relatively still.

Unblinking, Maria walked to the gully. A burning, nauseated feeling in the pit of her stomach swept over her as she knelt by it to wash the gunpowder from her face. She began vomiting. Dry spasms then wracked her for long minutes. When they finally stopped, her body was damp with cold sweat and she felt weak and lifeless. She finished washing her face and tied her hair back.

Harnett was standing and looking down at Stephen's body when she returned. Stephen's shallow breathing showed that he was still alive.

"You ain't going to finish him off?" Harnett said.

Maria silently shook her head, fumbling with her knife. She cut Stephen's ropes, letting him sag free to the ground. Then she wiped the knife on the ground and put it back in the sheath. She picked up her rifle and walked slowly toward her horse with faltering steps.

Harnett followed her, taking her arm to help her on the horse. "We probably drawed some Blackfeet with our shooting. They might find him and take care of him. He might not die."

Maria dragged her leg across the saddle and slumped in it, resting her rifle across the horn of the saddle and taking the reins as Harnett handed them to her. She turned her head and looked at Stephen. He was trying to get to his hands and knees, his arms and legs folding weakly under him and a wailing, mewling sound coming from his throat. Maria looked back to the front. "Good."

Harnett said quietly, "Did you do as much to him as you did to yourself, Maria?"

"I hope so, Seth."

Harnett nodded, walked to his horse and mounted. He clucked to his horse, turning it toward the edge of the clearing. The pack horses and the extra horses began walking along behind his. Maria shook her reins, and her horse began walking slowly after the last horse following Harnett. She turned and looked back. Stephen had got to his feet and was swaying from side to side as he felt blindly in front of himself. He fell heavily to the ground and began painfully gathering himself, trying to get back to his feet. Maria turned back around, looking ahead.

20

The woman's face was thin and pale, her grey hair pulled back in a small, tight bun. Her clothes were a little shabby, her dress faded and worn and the heavy shawl around her shoulders threadbare around the edges. Her smile was vaguely anxious as she bobbed her head and opened the door wider. "Yes, come right on in, Miss DeVises. I'm Martha Meekin, and I'm mighty pleased to meet you."

"I'm pleased to meet you, Mrs. Meekin. This is Mr. Seth Harnett."

"I'm pleased to meet you, Mr. Harnett."

"How do, ma'm."

"Well, just come on in and sit down, and I'll fetch Mr. Meekin. Would you like to take off your coats?"

"No, we won't be staying long. I hope we haven't inconvenienced you and Mr. Meekin."

343

"Oh, no, this is his day off, and he's expecting you. A body can use a coat inside or out in this weather, can't they? Just go ahead and sit down, and I'll fetch him."

Maria put her umbrella down inside the door and walked to the settle, and the woman disappeared through a doorway, pulling her shawl tighter. Harnett sat down on a chair, folding his arms and stretching his feet out in front of him. Maria took off her gloves. The parlor was drab and cold, the feeble heat from the small fire in the fireplace lost in the damp drafts stirring the thin, greyish curtains. The rain made a hollow sound as it beat against the window panes. The settle, chairs and a table under the window were blocky, heavy, homemade furniture, the wood floor was bare except for a small hook rug in front of the hearth, and the cushions on the settle were hand-stitched. A pump organ near the door and a walnut whatnot shelf in the corner looked out of place in the room, remnants of more prosperous times.

Harnett yawned, and Maria shifted on the settle, adjusting her hat. Her shoes pinched, her pantaloons and petticoat felt bundlesome, the fashionably tight bodice and sleeves on her dress made it bind under her arms, the voluminous, full-gathered skirt gave her the precarious feeling of perching, the large hat with its clusters of veils and ribbons felt awkward, and the heavy coat compounded everything. Harnett was amused by her discomfort in the new clothes. She looked at him from the corners of her eyes and stuck out her tongue, and he chuckled again.

A door closed in the rear of the house, and there was a muffled sound of a man's voice, telling the woman to get his tie and collar. Footsteps came through the house a moment later, and he came into the room, buttoning his suit coat. He was a small, intense, earnest looking man and like the woman, he was a little seedy. His boots were worn and his tweed suit, shiny with age, had been repaired around the cuffs and buttonholes.

"Mr. Harnett? I'm Clarence Meekin."

"How do, Mr. Meekin. This is Miss Maria DeVises."

"I'm pleased to meet you, Miss DeVises, and I'd like to extend my condolences over what befell your father. I was shocked when I heard about it."

"Thank you, Mr. Meekin. My father mentioned you many times, and in very cordial terms."

"I was pleased to call him my friend, as well as occasional business associate. Well, let's sit down, then. Are you in the city on business or between trips, Mr. Harnett?"

"I'm just with Maria. It's her business we're dealing with."

"I returned to St. Louis to see to some family matters, Mr. Meekin," Maria said. "And while I was here, I thought I would inquire into the fur markets. My father mentioned you many times as one of the most knowledgeable traders in St. Louis, so I immediately thought of you and had the note brought around to see if we could call."

Meekin nodded cautiously, unsure and puzzled by the situation and adjusting his frame of reference to discussing business with a young woman. He glanced between Harnett and Maria, then sat back in his chair and looked at Maria. "Yes, well . . . well, I'm not a trader any more, Miss DeVises, as a matter of fact. The large houses in the city have taken over the market, for all practical purposes, and I've been out of it for some months now. Just now I'm working as a clerk. Do you have to do with the Rocky Mountain Fur Company, then, Miss De-Vises? I understand your father was with them. . . ."

During the past days, Maria and Harnett had talked with other small traders her father had mentioned, and one of the first things that had become clear to her was that everyone in the fur trade expected a certain amount of secrecy from everyone else. Maria hesitated and chose her words carefully as she answered, giving the impression that she was avoiding a direct reply. "Not in the sense you mean, I believe, but all the partners are friends of mine, of course. So I take it you're quite out of touch with the market just now, Mr. Meekin?"

Meekin pondered her reply, stroking his chin and looking at her thoughtfully, then shook his head. "Oh, well, I still hear what goes on, and I follow what's happening. The market has gone flat for the past few months, because Astor has a monopoly on it. But that gets very complicated, and it probably wouldn't interest you beyond the fact that it's a very good time for someone who has furs to sell. Of course, few small companies do at this time of year. . . ."

"I'm very interested, Mr. Meekin. Does that mean that Astor's the only one who has any furs?"

Meekin mused again, studying her, then folded his arms and shook his head again. "Not just in so many words, no. But he controls the New York market completely and has done for some time. For the past few months he's been buying all the furs on the St. Louis market and paying whatever price it takes to get them. . . ."

He talked on, confirming what she had gleaned elsewhere and making it clearer and more meaningful to her at the same time, because his explanation was more thorough than that of others had been. A few smaller companies on the Missouri, Mississippi and Ohio had contracts with certain fur dealers in St. Louis. Through them a trickle of furs were going to the European markets. More were being shipped from Canada. But a large part of the normal supply to Europe had been cut off when Astor had begun buying up all furs on the open market and stockpiling them with the furs from his own companies. As a result, the prices on the European markets were rising to astronomical levels.

". . . and so while he is investing large amounts just now, the potential profit is quite high. Once control of the market is gained, it isn't all that difficult to manipulate it. All he will need to do is sell furs in moderate amounts and the price will remain high. And he acquired the Rocky Mountain Fur Company furs as well this year. They went on auction, and no other company could match his bid. But I'm sure you're aware of that, aren't you?"

"Yes. It would appear that Mr. Astor risks losing a lot of money if someone put a large number of furs on the market in Europe."

"It would take a very large number of furs indeed. No one else has furs in that quantity, to my knowledge. Nor will they have, as long as he keeps buying them all up." He hesitated, looking at her thoughtfully again, then smiled slightly. "If I were looking into this matter from the standpoint of seeing if the situation could be worked to the advantage of the Rocky Mountain Fur Company, I would have to conclude that it couldn't be. The only possibility would lie in shipping the furs directly to Europe, and I should think that would be out of the question. Obtaining authority to export from this country and import into Europe is difficult and involved, and I believe certain . . . ah, interests with influence in Washington would see that it was made even more so."

Maria smiled knowingly and sighed. "Yes, it seems that everyone will have to be contented with things as they stand. Still, the Rocky Mountain Fur Company got a very good price for furs this year. . . ."

"Indeed it did. Miss DeVises, would you know if the company ever has a requirement for traders? Leaving the city has never appealed to me before, but with the state in which things are now, I've been thinking of contacting some of the companies."

Harnett's eyelids were drooping with boredom, and Meekin had stopped glancing at him and including him in the conversation. And his perplexity over why Maria had come to see him had disappeared. He was convinced now she was in some way associated with the Rocky Mountain Fur Company, mostly because he wanted to be convinced. Maria had looked into Meekin's background and present circumstances before visiting him. He wanted to be hired as a trader, and he was being as ingratiating as a self-respecting man approaching middle age could be to a young woman.

"Do you mean as a trader at a post in the mountains, Mr. Meekin?"

"Yes, that would suit me far better than what I'm doing, Miss DeVises. And I'm experienced in dealing with Indians, free trappers, and so forth, because

I was all up and down the Missouri as a young chap."

Maria bit her lip, thinking, then gathered up her gloves and rose. "I wouldn't want to give you false hopes, Mr. Meekin, but it could be that I will hear of something of that sort. If I do, I'll contact you. For now I've taken up enough of your time, and I'm most grateful for your courtesy."

"The pleasure was all mine, Miss DeVises," Meekin replied, rising. "And I'll be more than happy to talk with you again or to look into anything concerning the markets for you."

"That's very kind of you, Mr. Meekin. I'll be in the city for some weeks, and I'll keep in contact with you."

"I'd appreciate that very much, Miss DeVises. It was nice to have met you, Mr. Harnett."

"Glad to have met you, Mr. Meekin."

Meekin opened the door, shaking hands with Harnett again and smiling and nodding to Maria. She opened her umbrella and gathered the hem of her coat and skirt in her hand as she crossed the porch and went down the steps. The rain drummed against the umbrella and pocked the water standing on the muddy path as she and Harnett walked along it.

"He seemed a very pleasant man, didn't he?"

Harnett grunted. "Trader," he said tersely. "I've never seen a trader I'd trust with a spoonful of spit."

Maria gave him a playful push, and Harnett smiled. The carriage driver, humped up on his seat in his shapeless greatcoat and tall hat, climbed down and opened the door. Maria closed her umbrella and climbed into the carriage, ducking her head to

keep from knocking her hat. Harnett climbed onto
the driver's seat, where he always rode, and the
driver climbed back up and shook the traces. The
horses turned, and the wheels jolted through a deep
rut as the carriage swung around on the street.

A curtain moved in the front window of Meekin's
house. Maria could barely make out his outline in
the window through the driving rain. He was watching the carriage leave. She sat back in the seat,
smiling to herself as she thought about her conversation with Meekin. All along the Platte, she
had worried about her lack of experience as a trader.
She didn't even know such basics as what kinds and
what quantities of trade goods she would need. Then
it had occurred to her that her inexperience could
be offset by hiring an experienced trader, if she entered trading on a large enough scale to be able to
afford it. And it was becoming increasingly evident
that she would be able to afford it if the furs could
be sold at a reasonable price.

The street was muddy and pitted. A couple of
drays and a cart were moving along it, the animals
black with rain and their heads hanging, the heavy
wheels splashing up muddy water from the ruts. The
houses were small and dingy, with peeling paint,
rusty corrugated iron roofs and sagging picket
fences. The rain pelted down on winter-dried weeds
in tiny front yards. The carriage turned a corner
into a street where the houses were somewhat larger
and in better repair and were set back from boardwalks, the heavy timbers sagging, broken and sinking into the mud in places. The traffic increased.
Aside from more bustling, rain-soaked people and
noisy carts, there were businesses with porches extending out over the boardwalks and wares dis-

played in inset doorways and in windows. Men stood under the porches in twos and threes, chatted, lifted their hats to and ogled women carrying umbrellas and shopping baskets. Linen shops, hardware stores, banks. Then the carriage entered the congested business district. The streets crowded with vehicles and pedestrians and the buildings rose five and six stories high. In Maria's heart, the surroundings of St. Louis felt very different from the bright ones she had known. But in her mind she knew the city was the same. It was she who had changed.

The carriage stopped in front of their hotel, not one of the best but far from the docks and docklike atmosphere in which they had lodged when they first arrived in St. Louis. Its prices made Harnett wince. Maria hopped from the carriage step to the boardwalk, and Harnett closed the door and splashed through the gutter, following her. Some people on the boardwalk glanced curiously at his buckskins. Maria closed her umbrella and entered the hotel lobby. Harnett followed her in, his wet moccasins making damp sounds on the floor. He had found his clothing tolerated rather than welcome in the hotel dining room, and Maria's presence in the lobby was frowningly discouraged by the management unless she was passing rapidly through it. The lobby was quiet and dim, reeking of drummers' and other tradesmen's cigar smoke as they sat, read newspapers and talked drowsily. The desk clerk looked at Maria musingly, his expression indicating he was once again pondering the smutty implications of a young woman and an old, bearded man in buckskins occupying adjacent rooms.

The man Maria had been seeing in the lobby with increasing frequency during the past couple of days was there again, sitting in a chair between the door and stairway and reading a magazine. He was in his late twenties and, as always, nattily but not fussily dressed, a tall, smoothly handsome man with a quick, engaging smile and shining blue eyes. And he apparently had ample leisure to sit about in the lobby. Other lobby-sitters usually tipped their hats to Maria as a matter of custom, and a few stared speculatively, but this man was always so demonstrative that he gave the impression that he had been waiting to see her. He glanced up from his magazine, then rose hastily, smiling and nodding to Maria and Harnett as they passed. Maria nodded, and Harnett grunted.

They started up the stairs, and Harnett made an amused sound in his throat. "That fellow reminds me of a wolverine eyeing a mountain lion, wondering if he's going to eat or get eat."

Maria chuckled, taking her room key from her reticule as they reached the top of the stairs. "It is curious, isn't it? I wonder who he is."

"I don't know, but I'd bet a dollar that you're going to find out sooner or later. What do you want to do now, Maria?"

She bit her lip and thought. "I believe it's time to contact one of the trading houses."

"Whatever you think, Maria. We've got all winter, though. We can go see some more people your pa knew and give you more time to think about it."

Maria shook her head, unlocking and opening her door. "I know all I'm ever going to know, Seth, and we have a lot to do this winter. Come on it."

Harnett went into her room with her. Maria got a valise from her closet, opened it and took out a small canvas bag containing two beaver pelts. She glanced at them before pulling the drawstring closed and handing the bag to Harnett.

"Which one?"

"Robideaux. Talk to the head clerk in private and show him these. Then bring him here, and we'll go down to the warehouse together to show him how many we have."

Harnett nodded, tucking the bag under his arm, and went back out. Maria hung up her coat, pulled the hatpins out of her hat and put it on the dresser, then sat down in the chair by the window with a deep sigh. Getting possession of the furs had been dangerous, laborious and nerve-wracking, but disposing of them had turned out to be much more complicated than she had anticipated. During her first conversations with men in the trade, it had become clear that she couldn't turn them over to the auction warehouse, because there would be widespread and public interest over how she had come into possession of a large number of furs, each of which was stamped as the property of the Hudson's Bay Company.

It was conceivable that the furs could have been obtained from Indians, notorious looters of caches from what she had heard, but that couldn't be used as an explanation because Indian traders were licensed by the government and she wasn't. And while there had been ample hints that dealers weren't concerned with the fine points on how furs were obtained, it was a certainty that they wouldn't want the purchase of a large number of stolen furs broadcast to the world at large. She had had to proceed slowly and carefully with traders, keeping the fact that she had the furs a secret and leading them to believe that she was associated with the Rocky

Mountain Fur Company and "looking into something" for them.

Newspapers she had read during the past days were stacked on the table. She had the wilderness habit now of conserving everything. She picked up the top one and began looking through it again. The front page was devoted to President Jackson's belligerent reaction to South Carolina's attempts to nullify federal tariffs, arguments supporting South Carolina's actions by a states' rights advocate, and Congressional action on a compromise tariff bill to defuse the situation. Inside, there was news of tensions in Europe and, in an article of more interest to her, news of a steamboat that had been up the Missouri River as far as Fort Tecumseh.

Articles about the West were scattered through all the newspapers, most of them based on interviews with someone who had recently been there and who had a substantial talent for fanciful and exaggerated description. Two days before, one article that had drawn her intense interest. It reported from Montreal, that an American employee of the Hudson's Bay Company, Stephen Kruger, had been brought in from a remote outpost, mutilated and more dead than alive. Maria pulled the article out and read it once again. No coherent story had been obtained from Kruger, it said, because of the difficulty in communicating with him, but from the condition in which he was found it was speculated that Indians had tortured him. His survival was called "a miracle." Maria put the newspaper on the table, stood by the window and looked down at the street through the rain streaming down the pane. The knowledge that Stephen had lived and still suffered was satisfying, but not healing. Neither what she had done to him nor the passage of months had helped ease her agonizing sense of loss at Curtis' death. She sighed, sat back down and began turning the pages of the newspapers again.

Heavy footsteps came along the hallway outside, followed by a knock. Maria opened the door. It was the moccasined Harnett, along with a tall, burly, expensively dressed man of about fifty. The man wore a beard and mustache neatly trimmed, his expression was cordially businesslike, but his dark eyes were sharp and unsmiling. A large diamond gleamed on his hand as he took off his hat, bowing slightly at Maria.

"Miss DeVises? I am George Massie, an associate of the Robideaux Company."

"I'm pleased to meet you, Mr. Massie. Are you interested in the furs, then?"

He nodded, studying her reflectively, then smiled slightly. "Indeed we are, Miss DeVises, indeed we are. May I ask if you are a relation of the late Pierre DeVises?"

"He was my father."

"Then please let me express my condolences, Miss DeVises. While I wasn't personally acquainted with your father, I know he was well respected and admired by all who knew him."

"Thank you, Mr. Massie."

His bland expression revealing only a hint of curiosity and puzzlement, he said, "So you have also entered the fur trade, Miss DeVises? More common for a son than for a daughter to follow in the father's footsteps, but still . . . may I ask if you are associated with the Hudson's Bay Company, Miss DeVises?"

"The Hudson's Bay Company would hardly be

trading through St. Louis, would it, Mr. Massie? Is it necessary that I be associated with them?"

He seemed both amused and impressed. "They hardly would, would they? And it isn't at all necessary, Miss DeVises, not at all. My carriage is waiting in the street if you'd like to go now and show me the furs."

Maria nodded. She put on her coat, went to the dresser and pinned on her hat, and gathered up her reticule, umbrella and gloves. Harnett opened the door. Massie bowed and motioned Maria ahead of him, and Harnett's lips twitched and he winked as she passed him.

The man was gone from the lobby. The magazine he had been reading was open on a table by the chair where he had been sitting.

In his gleaming black carriage, into which he had helped Maria, Massie radiated curiosity but remained silent as it rumbled along the streets. Maria, nervous and tense as the climax to what had occupied her every waking thought for months approached, clenched her reticule on her lap, keeping her features neutral and looking out the isinglass window in the door. The carriage went downhill toward the river, where the traffic thinned out. Among the taverns and dingy lodging houses near the waterfront, the dray teams of mules and oxen, were several warehouses. The carriage turned onto a side street and stopped at one of them. Massie stepped out, opening the umbrella and holding it over Maria's head, and he took her arm as they climbed the steps to the office. The clerk in the tiny, cluttered room turned on his stool as they entered. Maria opened her reticule and took out her bills of lading, unfolding them and handing them over. The clerk looked at them nearsightedly, then nodded.

"You want to take them out now?"

"No, I only want to look at them with this gentleman here."

"And we'll need a lantern," Harnett said.

The clerk rose from his stool and handed the bills back to Maria. "Be careful with it back there. We don't want no fire." Harnett grunted and nodded. The clerk took a lantern from a shelf and lit it. He handed it to Harnett, and they went through the inside door into the warehouse.

It was dark and damp, and the air was musty and stale between the walls of large boxes and barrels stacked to the low ceiling on each side of the narrow aisle. Water dripped and hit the floor with a smacking sound, and there were squeaks and scurrying noises ahead of the pool of yellow light from the lantern. It shone on Harnett's bearded face as he held it up, mumbling to himself. He hesitated at one point, lifted the lantern higher and peered, then nodded and walked on. The canvas bundles were stacked in tight rows to the ceiling near the end of the aisle. There were blotches of dark paint on their sides where the initials of the Hudson's Bay Company had been painted over and Maria's last name had been hastily printed.

Massie stiffened and looked at Harnett in disbelief as he shone the light on the bundles and indicated them with a wave of his arm. He took the lantern and stepped closer, moving along them. "All of these?"

Harnett said, "All of them. Tons, ain't they?"

"Yes, but where . . . ?" His voice faded and his composure abruptly returned. He came out from the bundles and, in the dim light of the lantern as he stepped back toward them, said quietly, "How many people know about this, Mr. Harnett?"

"Us three. We left the bush lopers in Westport and some of them are probably back down here by now, but you know bush lopers—they don't pay any attention to what goes on around them, and nobody pays any attention to them. From Westport we brought them by keelboats going on down river, and had them put straight in here. And they're listed as buffalo skin rugs on the papers there. Of course, everybody will know at least part of the story sooner or later. . . ."

"Yes, we can assume that, I'm sure. But for the moment, it's exceedingly fortunate that a limited number of people know. That's very important in an . . . ah, transaction of this sort."

"Most important," Maria said quietly. "If no one knows about it, it might be possible to get them down to New Orleans and ship them to Europe without anyone finding out about it until they're placed on the market there, mightn't it?"

Massie looked at her, his lips pursed and his eyes narrowed, then slowly nodded. "Yes, that might be possible, Miss DeVises. It might indeed. Well, at this point, we would normally begin a lengthy bargaining, but. . . ."

"Talk to Maria," Harnett said, folding his arms and leaning back against the bundles.

Massie looked at Maria again, his eyes wary. "I am in a position to offer six dollars a pound, Miss DeVises, weighed in on our dock. And that will take two or three days, because I want to use only certain employees and move them . . . well, it will take two or three days."

"The price aside for the moment, Mr. Massie, I would like to be able to buy from your stores of trade goods."

"Certainly, Miss DeVises, and at cost. That is a courtesy we extend to our associates, and I trust you will be that."

"And I need a license to trade with the Indians."

He hesitated, then nodded. "I'm sure that can be arranged easily enough. We have good relations with the Superintendent of Indian Affairs in Washington."

"Very well. As to the price, one of the reasons I chose to deal with Robideaux is that it is a large house and has an export license. In other words, you are in a position to ship the furs directly to Europe and take advantage of the enormously high prices on furs at present. And you will also count coup on Mr. Astor, which I am sure is a consideration. That being the case, six dollars a pound is far too low. Eight dollars."

"No, I'm afraid I can't exceed six dollars, Miss—"

"Would you be so good as to make arrangements for me to speak with one of the partners, Mr. Massie? I will be free all day tomorrow."

"Well, perhaps we could say six fifty, because this is—"

"Seven seventy-five."

"No, I'm afraid . . . well, six seventy-five, Miss DeVises, but—"

"Seven fifty."

"No, I absolutely can't go any higher, Miss DeVises. It would be worth my position in the company if . . . well, seven dollars, and that is the absolute limit. And more than any of the partners would offer, I'm sure. I've split the difference with you, and that's a very high price, you know, even the way the market is now."

It was the final offer, because his tone and expression were firm and unyielding. Maria opened her reticule and took out the bills, holding them up. "Seven two and a half."

Massie hesitated, frowning, then laughed and nodded as he took the bills. "Very well, Miss De-Vises, seven two and a half." He looked at Harnett as he put the bills in his coat pocket. "I believe we could find a place for Miss DeVises in our company."

Harnett, reaching for the lantern, said wryly, "She'd just run everybody else off and take it over."

Massie laughed again, touching Maria's arm and guiding her ahead of him as they followed Harnett back along the aisle. They returned to the office, Harnett gave the lantern back to the clerk, and Massie opened Maria's umbrella and held it over her head as they walked down the steps to the carriage. They got in, Harnett and the driver climbed up to the seat, and the carriage wheeled around and started back toward the hotel.

The light was beginning to fade into the early twilight of winter. Massie looked at Maria in the dim light in silence for several minutes, unconcealed curiosity on his face. Then he sighed, shaking his head and looking out the window. "In my profession, one learns not to be unduly inquisitive, Miss DeVises, but I find this matter very intriguing. It is most remarkable to find a young lady such as yourself engaged in a matter of this nature, but somehow the more I know you, the less remarkable it seems. And most curious of all, I don't find it at all strange that you want a license to trade with the

Indians. Shall I call on you in . . . oh, let's say three days hence during the afternoon? We can finalize everything then, with the exception of your license. That should take some two weeks or so."

"That will be very satisfactory, Mr. Massie."

"And I'm sure we'll be hearing from you again, won't we?"

"I'm sure you will, Mr. Massie."

He nodded, then looked at her again and laughed. "I'm sure many people will, Miss DeVises."

Maria smiled, looking out the window. The carriage pulled up in front of the hotel, and Massie got out, opened her umbrella and walked her to the door. He bowed over her hand, shook hands with Harnett and trotted back across the boardwalk to the carriage. Maria pulled the door open, and Harnett grinned at her widely in satisfaction as they went in. They walked toward the stairs, and Maria glanced at the chair where the man had been sitting. The chair was empty, and the magazine was gone.

21

"They could sure use somebody to put an edge on the knives they've got here," Harnett grumbled, pushing his plate away. "They look like pretty good steel, but they won't cut butter."

Maria smiled, pushing her plate away and sipping her coffee. Harnett used only a knife and spoon to eat and blandly disregarded all the other silverware, to the distress of the waiter. "Perhaps you should bring your skinning knife."

"I'd ruin it cutting meat on a plate, and they'd probably get mad if I put the meat on this sheet thing to cut it, wouldn't they? Well, you and Massie got everything straightened out, did you?"

"Yes, except for my license. That'll take another ten days or so."

"How does it feel to be a rich woman?"

"The same as before, except that I have more to

worry about. And I owe it all to you, Seth. You've done so much for me, even giving up a whole trapping season."

"I told you that don't make any difference. It'll do me good to spend a winter in town. I spent a winter in town ten or twelve years ago, when I was getting over being shot, and I—"

"Excuse me, please. You wouldn't happen to be Mr. Jim Bridger, would you?"

They looked up. Two or three days had passed since Maria had seen him, but it was the man she had seen numerous times in the lobby, and he was looking at Harnett with a politely interrogative smile. He gave Maria only a courteous, passing nod. Harnett took a noisy drink of his coffee and shook his head as he belched and sucked his teeth.

"I've got Bridger by ten years, and he's got me by two hands and twenty pounds. My name's Seth Harnett."

"I beg your pardon for disturbing you, then. I've been noticing your buckskins, and I thought you might possibly be—"

"I've been noticing you too, young fellow," Harnett chuckled, pointing to a chair on the other side of the table. "Her name's Maria DeVises, so just sit down and tell her what your name is."

The man looked discomfited by Harnett's blunt, amused manner. He blinked and cleared his throat as he looked at Maria, touching the back of the chair. "My name is Charles Turner, and I'm very pleased to meet you, Miss DeVises. Do you mind if I sit down?"

"No, if you wish. And I'm pleased to meet you, Mr. Turner."

He smiled widely, pulling the chair away from

the table and sitting down. "Please call me Charles."

"Very well, and you may call me Maria."

"Thank you very much." He hesitated, then looked back at Harnett. "You are a trapper or a trader, aren't you, Mr. Harnett?"

"Trapper," Harnett said, taking another drink of his coffee. "What do you do besides sit around in the hotel?"

He glanced at Maria, looking a little uncomfortable again, then looked back at Harnett. "I work with my father in property investments. We're in Chicago, and I'm down here seeing about several properties."

Harnett's smile abruptly disappeared as he put his coffee cup down. "Property investments?" he said suspiciously. "You mean you're a land speculator?"

"Land speculator? You mean like a . . . oh, no, what we do is entirely different. To begin with, we deal in business properties."

"Is that right? Tell me this, then—if'n somebody wants some of these business properties as you call them, why don't they just buy them theirself instead of paying you to get it for them?"

"Well . . . we base our business on knowing what's available, and it would take a lot of time and effort on the part of someone else to find that out. But sales are only a part of it. We buy many properties and rent them out, and we. . . ."

Maria sipped her coffee as Charles explained, trying to convince Harnett that he wasn't a land speculator. His left hand lay on the table as he gestured with his right. It was a large, strong hand, the nails short and clean, and there were tiny scars on it that had come from something more active than dealing in property investments. She looked at his hand again from the corners of her eyes, suddenly realizing that it was tense. His manner was frank and straightforward enough, but rather than bold, there was a slight self-effacement about him that was pleasant. It had been clear enough for several days that he wanted to meet her, and he had chosen the right way. If he had walked up to her to introduce himself, it would have repelled her. Curtis had been quiet, a little reserved, slightly shy. Stephen had been bold.

His tension indicated that he wanted things to go right in meeting her. It was flattering, because he was handsome and personable. The waiter came to the table and began gathering up the dishes, and Maria gestured to him to bring coffee for Charles. Charles glanced up when it came, then sat down, nodding.

"Thank you very much. So you see, Mr. Harnett, it isn't the same thing at all."

"So say you," Harnett grumbled. "But I'd hate to try to lay a hair on the difference between——"

"Oh, leave him alone, Seth." Maria waved him off, smiling. "He said he isn't a land speculator, didn't he?"

Harnett blinked at her and shrugged. "I'm not sure what he said now." He looked up at the waiter. "You could pour some of that in here, if you wanted to. And tell the fellow who dulls the knives that he done a real good job on mine."

Harnett was hopeless. Maria kept shaking her head at him, then said to Charles, "Have you been here long?"

"Just over two weeks now, but I still have quite a bit to do. Are you from . . . no, you wouldn't be staying in a hotel if you were from here, would you? Could I ask where you're from?"

"Yes, I'm from Fort Henry on the Snake River."

He looked at her blankly, then smiled apologetically as he shook his head. "I'm afraid I don't . . ." His voice faded, and his eyes widened with surprise as he sat forward. "You don't live in the unorganized territory, do you?"

"Yes, that's where the Snake River is, Charles."

"Good Lord! I had no idea that . . . but I didn't even know there were any white women there."

"Oh, yes. My mother's there now, as a matter of fact."

"She is? Well, that must be . . . well, it's dangerous, isn't it? And aren't a lot of the Indians hostile?"

"If one gets feisty with Maria, she just shoots him or flings a tomahawk at him," Harnett chortled in a teasing tone.

Charles looked at him, laughing heartily, then suddenly sobered and shook his head. "But it really isn't very funny, is it? And there are a lot of Indians there, aren't there? But if it's a fort, I suppose there are plenty of men about all the time, aren't there?"

Maria glared at Harnett from the corners of her eyes. He was about to explode into gleeful, boisterous laughter. The glare succeeded in silencing him, though he then thrust his lower lip out at her. Maria sighed and turned to Charles. It would take a lot of explaining. "Yes, there are a lot of men about the fort, Charles," she said.

"Durned tooting there is," Harnett said, standing and taking his final shot. "And they take turns looking after her. . . . Well, I'm going to mosey down the street. If you see any Indians on the way to your room, Maria, just give me a holler and I'll come running."

Maria looked at him resentfully, and he walked away from the table. Charles watched him go, smiling as best he could. "That really isn't funny, though," he said when they were alone. "I've heard and read enough about the unorganized territory to know that it can be very dangerous there."

"I can shoot a rifle, Charles."

"Why, I'm sure you can, Maria. Good Lord, it's a matter of necessity, isn't it? I must say, it doesn't seem right that a person like you should have to . . . well, never mind. Doesn't it get boring there?"

Maria hesitated, thinking, then shook her head. "Seth is a great one for joking, Charles. You see, I trap, and do things like that."

"And hunt as well, don't you? Yes, I'm sure there are things to while away the time. But don't you miss parties, friends and all the other things young ladies enjoy?"

His smile was very sincere and solicitous, and the impression that Harnett had created had obviously taken deep root in his mind. Maria gave up, shrugging and nodding. "I did at first, as a matter of fact, but I found things to occupy me. Do you like to hunt and trap, and things like that?"

"Oh, no, not really. But I do like to be outside. I do a lot of boating when I have time. And I like sports. I boxed when I was in college. . . ."

He was anxious to tell her about himself. It came out almost hurriedly, his childhood in Chicago, school and college, working with his father. He made no mention of girls reasonably enough, but the omission was glaring because there had obviously been many. He had all the necessary qualities, and in addition, made passing references that indicated his family was very well situated, if not wealthy. In terms of the standards her mother had instilled in her, he had highly desirable characteristics. Once Maria would have found herself trying to respond avidly to these characteristics and becoming confused and guilty over her failure to do so. Now she did not. She liked Charles well enough. He was handsome, charming, pleasant to be around.

He turned the conversation to her, tactfully probing for information, and she told him about her father's death. He had assumed that Harnett was a relative and was mildly surprised that he wasn't. He also assumed that her mother had a measure of authority over her that she didn't have. "Well, I'm sure that Mr. Harnett must be a very trustworthy friend for your mother to allow you to come all this distance with him. That's a very difficult journey, isn't it?"

"Oh, it's that, if nothing else. Well, it was enjoyable meeting you and talking with you, Charles."

His face fell. "Do you have to go right now? It isn't very late, but if you have something to do. . . ."

"I've become too accustomed to retiring at dark, I suppose. That probably shows the extent of my social life, doesn't it? But I do have several things to do tomorrow."

"There's a very good play on at the Fairmont," he said as he rose and pulled her chair back for her. "I have two tickets for tomorrow night. Would you go with me?"

They walked toward the doorway to the lobby. Maria felt a bit flattered. She had the distinct impression that Charles had thought out everything in advance, finding out what time she and Harnett ate dinner so he could approach them, buying the tickets so he would have them if he was successful in becoming acquainted. And she wanted to go. The sale of the furs and the dread that something would go wrong had been totally involving. But now the furs were sold, and while there were other things and probably other problems that would have to be dealt with, she had little to occupy herself with and the hotel room was already becoming confining. Her hope of renewing old friendships in St. Louis had suffered a telling disappointment a few days before when she had met a girl she had known on the street. She'd remembered the girl as warm and cheerful. Now a married woman with two small children, she was wan, shrewish, complaining, jealous of Maria's clothes. The thought of searching out others was unappealing.

Maria accepted the invitation. "I'd be happy to go with you, Charles. Thank you."

It seemed to surprise him a little, because he blinked. Then a beaming smile spread across his face. "I'll meet you here in the lobby, then. After dinner?"

"Very well, Charles. Good night."

"Good night, Maria."

She felt him looking at her as she went up the stairs.

When in her room she examined her reaction to meeting and talking with Charles, she realized that while it bore no comparison with the wild, throbbing exhilaration of her meeting on the prairie with Curtis, she had been suffused with warmth and satisfaction nevertheless. She'd had the feeling of a budding friendship, and it was good. In bed and waiting for sleep, her thoughts moved to other things, the appointment to meet Meekin again the next day, the meeting in the bank that afternoon with Massie and the substantial, tangible form the transaction with the furs had taken in the subdued, masculine atmosphere of the bank president's office. She dozed off. Then noises woke her again. Harnett was in his room. His footsteps were unsteady, and he was mumbling to himself. Maria smiled to herself, going back to sleep.

The evidence of Harnett's visit to a tavern the night before was obvious at breakfast the next morning. His eyes were red and bleary, and there was a tremor in his hand as he chopped at his eggs with his spoon. He grunted and nodded as Maria sat down at the table.

"And how are you this morning, Seth?"

"I'd be a lot better if somebody in this hotel knew how to fry eggs until all the snot was gone."

Maria laughed and shook her head. "You'd be better off if you'd mend your ways. You know, I've been thinking about what you said once about going into Blackfoot country with someone whose wife was a Blackfoot. Who was that?"

"Rufus Hany. She was a prisoner of the Crows when he got her, and we took her along in case we run into any Blackfeet. But I just went with him once, to get the lay of the land. As you know, it ain't that hard to stay away from Blackfeet or any other kind of Indians as long as nothing really bad goes wrong and as long as a body keeps their mind on what they're doing."

Maria ordered breakfast and began musing. "Is trapping all that Hany has ever done?"

"He's trapped, traded, and done a little bit of everything, I guess. Why?"

"I wondered if he might like to go into Black-foot country and set up a post."

Harnett's eyes narrowed in thought as he sipped his coffee. "That's a good idea, Maria. Your head's working all the time, ain't it? And Hany would be a good man for it, because he knows Indians, he's not afraid of work and he's honest enough. But trying anything with Blackfeet is chancy. The Hudson's Bay Company is in there strong, and you might be biting off too big a chunk, setting up on the Snake and trying to set up in Blackfoot country at the same time."

"When I set up on the Snake, I'm going to raise the prices to run Kruger off. If I had someone deal-ing with the Blackfeet at a profit, that would make my bite easier to chew, to my way of thinking."

Harnett thought again, then nodded, sucking his teeth. "You're right, Maria. Hany's up at Fort Osage, or was the last time I heard of him. I'll just mosey down to the docks directly and see if any-thing's going up that way so I can send him a mes-sage to come and see us."

"Do you think he'll want to do it?"

Harnett pushed his plate away and sipped his cof-fee, shrugging. "If he thinks he can, he'll probably want to. But like I said, Maria, dealing with Black-feet is chancy. Just getting in with them is a real problem, and nobody knows that better than Hany. Hell, you know yourself what they're like." He glanced up at the waiter as he brought Maria's breakfast to the table, and he put his cup down and pushed his chair back. "Well, I'll walk on down to the docks. Are you going to go see Meekin this morning?"

"Yes, and I'm going to a play with Charles Turner tonight."

"Is that right? Well, maybe I'd better see how that turns out before I go sending messages to Hany and doing things like that. You might decide you want to settle down here."

Maria snorted. "Don't hold your breath until I do."

Harnett rose from his chair, chuckling, and he patted her shoulder before walking toward the door.

Maria began eating, thinking about the conversation. It would be an inroad into the Hudson's Bay Company trading area as well as a potentially lucrative operation if a trading post could be established among the Blackfeet. But her own memories of the Blackfeet made the possibility seem less than promising, and while Hany might have an advantage because his wife was a Blackfoot, Harnett hadn't in general been too hopeful. It would be a delicate operation, at best. She'd have to provide a lot of good-will presents for chiefs, and it still might fail.

She finished eating breakfast and stopped at the desk in the lobby to order a carriage. The desk clerk's sly smile was explained when she got up to her room to get ready for her talk with Meekin. There was a large box of candies and a card with Charles' name on it in her room. She smiled as she looked at the card and the box, started to turn away to get her coat, then looked at the box again.

It was made of tin, had an embossed pattern on top and was gaily decorated with bright enamel.

The pattern was like a cameo with wreaths of ribbons around it. Or like a medal to be hung around the neck. It gave her an idea. Historically, Indians had always coveted medals presented as a special mark of favor by governments. And the Indian love of ornamentation was something she could understand because she shared it. The Blackfeet chiefs might be swayed by some sort of medal. They were in United States territory, she was an American, and the Hudson's Bay Company was British. She ran her fingers over the pattern on the box, thinking about it, then walked toward the closet to get her coat.

Meekin was less surprised by her offer of a job as a trader than she had anticipated. He was frank with her, telling her that there had been quiet rumors of a large fur transaction in the city and that he had deduced the rumors might have been connected with her first visit to his house. Maria was also straightforward with him about her lack of knowledge of trading. She had expected at least some reservations on his part because she was a woman, but his only one was a disinclination to become involved in a small operation. That was resolved when Maria said she was prepared to invest thirty thousand dollars in trade goods, aside from her investment in horses, supplies, equipment and a cash reserve. They agreed on terms. Meekin would continue in his present job until the beginning of January. Then he would begin working for her, selecting the trade goods and making other arrangements.

The rain turned to snow during the late afternoon. There was a soft, white blanket on the ground that muffled the sound of the carriage wheels as

Charles took Maria to the theater. And the play was incomprehensible to her, with virtually everyone in the theater in spasms of roaring laughter and Maria wondering blankly what they were finding so amusing in the lines and in the acting. Toward its end it finally became clear that it was a political satire ridiculing the marriage of John H. Eaton, the Secretary of War and an aging widower, to Peggy O'Neale, the spirited daughter of an Irish tavernkeeper. But the play still seemed too caustic and silly to her to be amusing. And she was vaguely annoyed by the vapid fluttering of many of the women and the pompously domineering attitudes of the men who came to see it and to dine afterwards. It seemed a long time since she had accepted such behavior as normal and expected by both men and women.

Her disdain for it seemed to make an impression on Charles as they sat in the restaurant. He moved his coffee cup around on his saucer absently, glancing at the other tables, then looked at her. "Did I tell you when it was that I first saw you? You were getting out of a carriage and going into the hotel, so then I started sitting around in the lobby to see if I could see you again. I was trying to think of some way to go about meeting you. I wasn't sure precisely how to go about it, because you're . . . well, different. One of the first things I noticed was that you act older than you are. I can tell that you're about nineteen or so, but you act older. It makes you more attractive, but it made me unsure of how to go about meeting you."

Maria smiled and shrugged. "You managed, didn't you?"

"Yes, but I don't mind admitting that I was a

little frightened that I might do something wrong. I haven't been that way for . . . well, a long time. And I also noticed that you don't appear to be overly concerned with what people think of you."

Maria silently smiled and shrugged again.

"And you don't talk unless you have something to say. That's very refreshing, because a lot of people go ahead and say nothing when they have nothing to say. May I pry and ask you why you came to St. Louis?"

"To get a license to trade with the Indians, and to buy some trade goods."

"Well, I'm sure you'll be very successful in trading with Indians, Maria. Ah . . . people can't travel to the mountains in the winter, can they?"

"It's difficult, because there are blizzards on the prairie this time of year, and very little graze for horses. We'll leave here when the river thaws in the spring, then leave Westport when the grass begins to sprout."

He frowned slightly, looking down at his cup and moving it on the saucer again. There was a long moment of silence. Then he looked back up at her with a cheerful smile. "Are you ready to leave?"

Maria nodded, reaching for her coat as she started to rise. Charles stood, pulling her chair back and picking up her coat. He helped her on with it. They walked toward the door, and he took her arm, looking down at her.

"That's a nice dining room at the hotel, but I'm sure it becomes tiresome after a while. Would you let me take you to another restaurant for dinner tomorrow?"

He looked at her with the same hopeful smile of

the night before. Maria nodded, and he beamed at her happily.

The snow was thick on the ground and still coming down heavily, and the streets were deserted and quiet. The carriage was cold. Charles hesitantly put his arm around her, then slid it on around as she moved toward him. The hotel lobby was silent, deserted and dim, the night clerk dozing behind the desk, and Charles walked her up to her room.

The kiss was a lot like him. It was gently insistent, carefully restrained. It was a light, tentative pressure that communicated feeling without force. It left a warm glow that remained after she went into her room, and she thought about him as she went to bed.

22

A box of pastilles and a card from Charles were in her room the next day. He moved into the hotel during the day, bringing his belongings from the hotel where he had been staying and taking a room on the floor above Maria's. Maria didn't see him and didn't find out that he had moved until he met her to take her to dinner. He was behind on the things he had come to St. Louis to do and was busy during the day. She didn't see him in the hotel dining room or lobby during the following days, because he continued to be busy each day, but he asked her out every night, to other theaters and to restaurants, and there were small presents in her room every day, candy, handkerchiefs, perfume, and other things.

Maria searched through the city for engravers. The first ones she found didn't work in bronze.

Then she found one who did. He had an ample stock of discs somewhat larger than a saucer, about the size Maria wanted, but he had reservations about doing the work because Maria refused to tell him why she wanted it and he feared there might be something illegal involved. But it was a substantial job and the engraver wanted the money, so after Maria made several visits to his shop to discuss it, they agreed on a compromise. He would copy the eagle insignia from the reverse of a United States coin on one side of ten discs, engrave President Jackson's bust on the other side and solder on hooks that Maria wanted around the rim of the discs. But he wouldn't put President Jackson's name on them.

Maria's license came, an impressive-looking document with a government seal and the signature of the Superintendent of Indian Affairs on it. She mentioned it to Charles, but his ideas about the unorganized territory were based on highly-fictionalized newspaper accounts, and he still had more or less the same impression of her activities that had been left by Harnett's joking the first time they had met. Changing his mind was as difficult as her grasping the full implications of the lines in some of the plays they saw. Neither fazed Maria; she simply avoided the subjects in conversation. The engraver completed the discs, sent a message to the hotel, and Maria picked them up, shopped through sundries stores for the things to finish them and worked on them in her room.

There had been no word from Hany since Harnett had sent the message to Fort Osage. Harnett occasionally met an acquaintance in a tavern who came back to his room to talk to him, so Maria absently noted then disregarded the voices she heard through the wall one night after Charles brought her back to the hotel. She put her coat away and took off her hat, then began undressing to go to bed. The voices in Harnett's room stopped. She heard a quiet footstep in the hall, and Harnett knocked. Maria buttoned her dress back up, walking to the door, and opened it.

Harnett smiled widely. "Rufus Hany is here. He got in just a little while ago."

"Hany?" Maria said excitedly, fastening the buttons and tugging at her dress. "Just a minute . . . all right."

Harnett walked back toward his room as she pulled her door closed and followed him. He pushed his door open. "Rufe, this is Maria DeVises. Maria, this is Rufus Hany."

Hany was a small, leathery man in his forties, wearing greasy buckskins, wolverine boots over his moccasins and leggings, and a long, odorous buffalo skin coat. "I'm mighty proud to meet you, Maria. I've heard a lot about you, and it's good to finally meet up with you."

"And I'm very pleased to meet you, Rufus."

They shook hands, and Hany glanced up and down her musingly as he stepped back to his chair. He said to Harnett, as he chuckled, "I'll take your word that it's her, but she don't look like the one I've heard so much about."

"That's her, all right," Harnett said. "Don't get her riled if she's where she can put her hand on a tomahawk. Maria, just sit down right there, and I'll sit here. Now me and Rufe have been talking about what you want, and he's willing to try it. But on the other hand, he says too, it's going to be mighty chancy."

"That's right," Hany said. "Now I might be able to do some business in my wife's tribe, but they ain't going to want every other tribe in the Blackfoot nation mad at them, so it just depends on how it strikes them. I could go in with a bunch of presents for the chief and subchiefs of her tribe. The worst that's going to happen to me is I'm going to get robbed and run off. But then you'd be out the presents. . . ."

Maria sat down on the chair, looking him over and thinking. Then she nodded. "I can easily afford that risk, if you're risking your life. Where is your wife's tribe located?"

"West of Three Forks. Did you have a special place in mind where you wanted to put a post?"

"Yes, at Fort Merrill."

Hany coughed wryly. "Well, I want to do what you want, but that's smack dab in the middle of another tribe's territory. I expect they're still pretty mad about that fort getting burned down, too. It could be that I could get in really good with my wife's tribe and then get them to take me over there so I could take some presents, but I wouldn't look for it to happen any time soon."

Maria rose and walked toward the door. "I have something I want to show you—I'll be back in a moment."

The two men nodded and began talking as she went out. She returned to her room, opened the closet and reached into the corner where she had stacked the finished bronze discs in flat boxes. She took one box back to Harnett's room. They became silent with curiosity. She opened the box on the dresser and held up the disc for them to see. It was a magnificent medal, with a wide necklace of red, white and blue ribbons, the embossed bronze features of the president in the center, strings of red, white and blue beads hanging from the sides, and three small mirrors twinkling at the bottom.

"By God!" Hany gasped in admiration. "If that ain't about the prettiest durned thing. . . ."

"What is it, Maria?" Harnett asked. "And where in the hell did you get it?"

"It's a medal. And I had it made."

"Durned right it's a medal," Hany said. "See the picture of Andy Jackson here? And the same thing that's on a dollar on this side? Maria, if this is a present for the chiefs, I'm having a lot better thoughts about what I'm fixing to do. I seen a couple of medals the Government give to the Crow chiefs, and they ain't nothing compared to this one."

"That's what it is, and I have ten of them. I want you to tell them that the great white father in Washington wants them to trade with his people instead of the Canadians, and every chief who does will get one of these."

"Are you supposed to do things like that, Maria?" Harnett said worriedly. "I ain't so sure about this. . . ."

"Oh, hell, it'll be all right," Hany said, looking at the medal eagerly. "And I want one of them myself, Maria. They'd figure that I'd get one for coming to talk to them, wouldn't they?"

Maria nodded, turning back to the dresser and putting the disc back into the box, tucking the ribbons, beads, and mirrors into place. "You may have one, and I'll probably have a few more made in event we need them. But I don't want anyone around here seeing them, because Seth's right, it might be something we're not supposed to do. In Washington, they're still talking about unicorns on the prairie and mermaids in the Columbia, and they think Three Forks is something three people eat with, so I'm not worried about them finding out about the Blackfeet having them. But they do know what happens in St. Louis. You meet us at Westport, Rufus, and I'll give you a couple of these, some horses, and some trade goods for presents."

"All right," Hany said, nodding confidently. "I think we'll be in business, Maria. If I had to bet, I'd bet I'll be trading out of Fort Merrill by next snowfall, if I can get it rebuilt by then."

"With an American flag over it."

"You get me the flag, and I'll fly her."

"I'll be taking plenty of them along. Clarence Meekin will be the head trader at the main post. For terms for other traders, he suggested two hundred dollars a year, three percent of the net pofits and all hoses, equipment, and supplies furnished."

Hany said amiably, "That sounds fine to me, Maria. Anyway, Seth said you'd treat me right, so I ain't worried about it. Now when I get done with the chiefs, and figuring that everything goes all right, where do I come to get the medals and my goods for trading?"

"We'll be set up somewhere on the Snake. There's a man named Kruger there. The first thing I want to do is run him out of the mountains."

"That one with the American Fur Company? It's past time somebody was doing that. Well, if you're going to set up on the Snake, you might be able to move into Fort Henry. I've heard the Rocky Mountain Fur Company is moving out of there and down onto the Laramie."

"Where'd you hear that?" Harnett said. "That's the first I've heard of it."

"Jacob McCallister was through Fort Osage about a month ago. He told me," Hany replied. "He said three or four of the partners had talked it over, and they were going to build a fort on the Laramie at the Platte and call it Fort William."

"Well, ain't that something," Harnett said. "What do you think about that, Maria?"

Maria said thoughtfully, "It sounds interesting, Seth. Very interesting indeed."

There was a momentary silence. Hany glanced from Harnett to Maria, yawning and stretching. "Well, I don't know about you folks, but if we're finished with our business, I'm ready to coil up on the floor here. I had a hard ride today, and I'm looking at another one tomorrow."

"You don't have to get back so soon, do you?" Harnett said.

"Well, my wife's having another baby and I want to be there, Seth."

"We certainly appreciate your riding down to see us," Maria said, rising and tucking the box under her arm as she walked toward the door. "And we'll have breakfast in the dining room before you leave in the morning."

"I'm mighty obliged, Maria. It was nice meeting you. I think we'll be able to do some good business together."

"I'm sure we will, and it was nice meeting you, Rufus. Good night."

Maria went back into her room. She put the box in the closet, undressed and went to bed, then lay and looked up at the ceiling in the darkness, thinking.

Gossip and rumors were rife in the mountains. They were frequently misleading, for stories pondered over lonely campfires were frequently improved upon for the next telling. The Rocky Mountain Fur Company could be branching out by building another fort, or what Hany had reported might be totally erroneous. But it was fascinating to contemplate. Fort Henry had been built by Andrew Henry, one of the pioneer explorers and fur traders in the Rocky Mountains. He had built it in 1810, years before she had been born. Events that had happened there were already legend, and there was a solid, substantial atmosphere about its old buildings. Its roots went deep. She wanted it. She went to sleep thinking about it and was still thinking about it the next morning when Hany left, riding a thin, shaggy horse back to the mountains.

Charles became dejected while Maria was having dinner with him that evening. His father wanted him to return to Chicago for the holidays, they had exchanged several letters in which the subject had been mentioned and in which Charles had tried to make excuses, and that day he had received a letter demanding that he come home to spend the holidays with his family. He wanted Maria to go with him, and this invitation she did not accept.

Maria was firm in her decision. She had tried to keep what she regarded as a friendship from developing into a courtship. She had responded to hints about marriage with candid comments on her intention never to marry. Charles hadn't quite believed her. He'd also made remarks that seemed to contain an implicit assumption that she would be happy to remain in St. Louis if she could. In both instances, he had shown the same lack of acceptance of her values that Barry Fitzpatrick and her mother had when she had told them she didn't intend to marry. She didn't want to go to Chicago with him. Beyond the fact that there were many things she needed to do in St. Louis, she didn't like the tacit implication in the invitation that once she met his family and fell under their sway of wealth and social grace she would be eager to marry him. No matter how delicately he tried to put this, he presented it almost as a foregone conclusion and this as much as anything resolved her not to go.

The last few days before Charles left were depressing, because his cheerful attitude was patently a facade and she didn't want to be repeating her reasons for not going. She still felt a strong affection for him. It was lonely for a few days after he left. Then the time drew near for Meekin to begin working for her and she threw herself into the business at hand. Meekin had drawn up long lists of goods that they pored over and discussed. The amount they would be taking would require many bush lopers. A man would be needed to oversee them, and Harnett located an acquaintance for the job, Isaac Gillman. The number of horses in the pack trains and the operation at the post in the mountains made it advisable to have a farrier along, and Harnett found another man, Israel Barton. Letters came from Charles, and Maria tried to make her replies interesting.

Meekin was undecided about taking his wife along. Maria talked to both of them and explained what was involved. The couple had no children at home, and they both agreed that she should go. Christmas and New Year's passed almost unnoticed for Maria, except for the decorations in the hotel dining room. Meekin began making up the final lists of trade goods and supplies, and Barton began looking around for the extra horses that would be needed. There was a consensus of opinion that spring would be early. The first traffic up the river promised to be heavy, and Harnett contracted for and reserved keelboats to make sure they would be available.

A letter from Charles was apologetic, explaining that he had been detained in Chicago by business affairs, and Maria felt guilty because the date he was supposed to have been back had passed and she hadn't noticed. It was three days before she had time to answer his letter. There was a cost tradeoff between the anticipated spring rise in the prices of trade goods from Robideaux and warehouses expenses that she and Meekin worked night and day for three days to compute. It turned out that it would be more economical to buy the goods and warehouse them now, so Meekin began picking them out, having them drayed to the waterfront. There was also a price tradeoff on the spring rise in the prices of horses and the cost of feeding them. Barton couldn't read and write and he counted over ten by tying knots in a string, but he knew the precise day on which the tradeoff occurred and he began picking out horses.

It was almost like stepping back weeks in time when Maria entered the hotel lobby one afternoon and Charles rose from a chair, smiling radiantly at her and dropping his magazine. Maria felt a rush of affection for him when she saw him, and her smile became brilliant. She was tired, but she pushed it out of her mind when he asked her to go to dinner with him.

His boyish enthusiasm and pleasure over seeing her again was almost pathetic, however. Maria wanted to make the evening pleasant for him, but she was weary from her long day of many different feelings. She'd been distracted by small problems that had come up but had also burned with eager anticipation of returning to the mountains. Fort Henry was so vivid in her mind that she could almost taste it, whereas the city around her with its crowded streets seemed a fantasy of noisy confusion. She longed for the gigantic spaces of the prairie. Charles had either forgotten everything she had said to him or during his absence had idealized what was between them into something of a totally different character. He had talked to his mother and father about her, he said, and they were anxious to meet her. His mother had sent a box of handkerchiefs. His father would be coming to St. Louis in a few months and wanted to meet her then. Charles had bought a large house in Chicago that had come on the market while he was there, even though he and his father dealt only in business properties, and he talked about it.

Maria restrained her annoyance. She patiently tried to disillusion him, going over all the things they had gone over before, which caused only hurt perplexity in him. Much of the time there was no communication. She talked about the preparations, the trade goods, horses and other things, and Charles smiled and nodded, looking at her, listening to her but not hearing her. It continued on through dinner. He didn't understand. His chimerical concept of the unorganized territory, his views on the roles and functions of women, the lingering impression created by Harnett's joking—all these things were a barrier to his comprehension. But he didn't want to understand. He didn't want to be refused.

She searched her mind for ways to help him see better as they returned to the hotel through the dark, quiet streets, the wheels of the carriage grinding through the crust of the dirty snow. She waited on the boardwalk while Charles paid the driver. Then they went in, crossed the dim lobby and walked up the stairs. Outside her room, Charles smiled down at her in the dark hallway and stepped closer to take her in his arms and kiss her. Maria turned away, taking her key out of her reticule. She unlocked the door and opened it.

"Come in, Charles. I want to show you something."

He hesitated in the doorway, then stepped in and closed it. Maria turned up the lamp, shrugged out of her coat and dropped it on a chair, tossed her gloves and reticule on it, then stopped in front of the dresser, unpinning her hat. Charles stood in front of the door, glancing around.

"Sit down, or take off your coat if you wish, Charles. You know that Seth is a trapper, don't you? Did you know that I've done the same things that he does?"

He looked at her, unbuttoning his coat, and smiled tolerantly as he took it off. "Yes, I remember your telling me that, Maria. But it's hardly the same thing as what a man who—"

"The same thing, Charles, and I told you that as well, but you didn't listen," Maria said, crossing the room to the closet. She took out her buffalo skin coat and dropped it, took out her buckskins and draped them over a chair, then took out her hat and tossed it onto the buckskins. "This is what I wear, Charles. A little cleaner and fancier than what Seth wears, but they're about the same thing, aren't they? I told you I had come to St. Louis to get a license and goods to trade with the Indians, Charles, and I won't be trading bags of beads for vegetables or something. I'm an Indian trader, Charles. I have trade goods that will fill three keelboats."

He walked over to the chair, looking down at the buckskins with a dazed expression, then looked at her and motioned toward her dress, shaking his head. "But. . . ."

"I can't wear a dress in the forest, Charles. And I can't wear buckskins here, because I don't want everyone in the city stopping and staring at me. Believe me, if I could, I would. Buckskins are far more comfortable." She turned back to the closet, took her rifle out of the corner and gathered up her knives and tomahawk. She leaned the rifle against the wall and dropped the knives and tomahawk on the buckskins. "There aren't many men who can beat me in shooting a rifle if they use a rifle with a barrel that short, Charles. I can't use a long barrel, because I'm not strong enough to hold it steady, but I can put a hole in the bottom of a cup at two hundred feet."

He blinked, his eyes moving over the weapons, then smiled wryly and nodded. "Yes, I see that I didn't quite grasp what you were telling me. And I'm sure that you're very good with a rifle. . . ."

There was still a reservation in his tone and expression. Maria picked up the tomahawk, balanced it in her hand and threw it. It tumbled in the air as it flew across the room. Then it slammed heavily into the side of the window frame, rattling the panes. "Seth is a great one for joking, Charles. If an Indian or anyone else bothers me, I don't call for help."

He looked at the tomahawk, stunned, then lifted his hands and dropped them in a helpless gesture. "Yes, I see, Maria. I really didn't grasp what you . . . but all this isn't necessary, Maria, don't you understand that? You don't have to do all this. . . ." He motioned toward the buckskins and weapons, stepping closer to her. "Maria, you don't have to trap animals, trade with Indians, or—"

"But I want to, Charles. It's what I want to do."

"Want to? How could you, Maria? The danger and the things you must endure are more than any woman should have to—"

"All that means nothing to me, Charles, because it's what I want to do. I get cold, I get scared, and there are a lot of other things, but it's what I want to do. Charles, when I said I was from Fort Henry, I was telling the truth. That's what I'm from, and that's where I want to be. In the mountains."

He sighed heavily, looking at the rifle leaning against the wall and biting his lips as he pondered. A long moment passed. He sighed again and nodded. "Very well, Maria. Then I'll come with you. If that's what you want, then—"

"No!" Maria shook her head emphatically. "That would be utter foolishness, Charles. Dear, you'd never make it to the Laramie."

"What do you mean?" he said resentfully, flushing. "I can do what anyone else can, whether you believe it or—"

"It's not a part of you, Charles," she said, stepping closer to him and putting her hands on his shoulders. "I don't mean that you're any less a man or anything like that, because it isn't true. But like Seth Harnett would be lost trying to do what you do every day, you'd be lost in the mountains. Believe me, Charles, the mountains aren't for you. You wouldn't belong."

"But you could belong here, Maria. I know you could."

"No, not really, Charles. I can make do for a while, like you could there, but I don't belong. And I really don't want to, you know."

"But I love you, Maria."

Maria looked up at him and smiled sadly, touching his face with the tips of her fingers. "You mustn't, Charles."

"I can't help it, Maria. I do."

"No, you mustn't. There are mountains between us, dear. There really are."

His anguished eyes moved over her face. He put his arms around her, pulling her closer, and she leaned against him as she slid her arms around his neck. He started to say something, and Maria breathed a negative, looking up at him and pushing his hair back from his face. Then he bent down, and his arms closed around her tightly as he kissed her. The kiss was demanding, his lips covering hers hungrily, and she released herself to it, feeling pangs of conscience and wondering if she had done or omitted to do things that might have made it easier for him or might have prevented the situation. His strong arms clasped her firmly and the taste of his lips and mouth filled hers as she opened her lips. A warm, blissful glow began throbbing within her.

He pulled her tighter against him, and she pressed herself to him as the warmth became a tingling fire racing through her. There was an instant when volition remained, a choice between paths and the option to choose. Then the caress had a life of its own, seizing her and carrying her along with it. The heady throbbing enveloped her. He hesitated for an instant, unsure or willing to commit himself, and she drove him on, pulling him to her and demanding.

The wrenching ecstasy she'd had with Curtis was missing, but what life she'd had while Curtis lived was missing. There was a gratification at fundamental levels, a hunger that became a craving and fulfillment that became satiation, and there was a triumphant joy in matching his strength with her own strength of its different nature. And there was a deep pleasure in lying in his arms and feeling his body against hers, all remorse for what she might have done to him gone, because she knew she had done all she could.

His lips moved over her face as his hands moved over her, touching and caressing. "This isn't the way I wanted us to be, Maria. I wanted for us to be married and—"

"This is all we have, Charles. Now kiss me and go to your own room. I don't want to be thrown out of the hotel, you know."

He sighed heavily, pulling her closer, and his hands moved gently up and down her back as his lips covered hers again. The kiss became a caress, then an impassioned embrace. It began again, the golden glow enveloping her and instinctive impulses arising and guiding her. She coaxed him, then pulled him to her. The wild, headlong drive for fulfillment began again, peaking again and again in stabbing pangs, then satiation came once again. He clung to her, unwilling to be separated, and she whispered and pleaded. Then he left.

In some ways Maria and Charles were worse off than before, their friendship complicated with longing desire on his part that had been stimulated rather than satisfied. But Charles understood. They were together each night, going to dinner or to a theater and then to her room, and the moments were rich with a bittersweet poignancy that came from knowing there was an end that the inexorable flow of time was steadily bringing closer. It saddened him for her to talk about the things she was doing during the day, the arrangements and preparations to leave, so she avoided the subject. But the arrangements and preparations proceeded, and they took on a quickening pace as the days passed.

Meekin had finished all the purchases and was making out instructions by which the goods and supplies would be bagged and loaded on pack horses in Westport. He'd sold his house and his wife had already sold most of their things. Barton left for Westport with all the extra horses and two bush lopers to assist him; they were to add the horses to those Maria and Harnett had left on pasturage there. Gillman had a son who wanted to go along. He, his son and Harnett began recruiting more bush lopers in the taverns and lodgings near the docks. They were needed because of the size of the undertaking, in horses and goods alone. Maria herself didn't have a full grasp of the expedition's scope until she saw all these bush lopers at once, long lines of thin, tattered, drunk, and bedraggled men of every possible combination of French, Spanish, and Indian, the dregs of the docks and the foot soldiers of the fur trade. Spring came in a rush, the snow disappearing rapidly as warm days followed one another, and the river ice softened and began breaking up.

On the last night, Maria went to Charles' room. It was a torture that had to be endured. Yet it became a pleasure in some twisted way. He was desperately eager, frantically striving to overcome human boundaries, and she comforted him. She remained until the icy feel of the still, early hours of the morning hung in the darkness. Then she left and went to her room. As she started to pull the covers back on the bed to lie down, she heard Harnett moving around in his room. There was no time for sleep. She turned the lamp back up and began dressing.

The lobby was silent, the dim glow of the guttering lamp on the desk shining on the gleaming surface. The desk clerk woke with a snort and looked at Maria with a startled expression. He turned up the lamp, his eyes moving over the rifle under her arm, her hat and buffalo skin coat, her buckskins. He leafed through papers for the bill, and Maria took her purse from her hunting bag, removed a handful of gold eagles from it and counted out the money. The clerk was still shaking his head when she went back upstairs.

Harnett carried her trunk down. A wagon stopped outside, and Meekin came in, breezily bright. He and Harnett carried out the trunk and valises and Maria followed them. The wagon and team were darker shadows on the other side of the boardwalk in the dark street. The valises thumped and the trunk clattered against the bedboards, and they climbed in. Maria climbed over the sideboard and sat on the trunk. The driver clucked and shook the reins, and the wagon began moving. Martha Meekin's face was a pale oval in the feeble light of the canopy of stars.

"Well, we're on our way, Maria," she said, her voice falsely hearty and cheerful.

"Yes, we're on our way."

"The sky's good and clear," Harnett said. "It looks like we're going to have a good day."

"Yes, it's good and clear," Meekin said. "It's going to be a good day."

One of the wheels squeaked and rasped as the wagon rumbled along the street. Whispering echoes of the bedboards squeaking and the harness chains rattling bounced off the buildings. The wagon turned a corner, and a dim halo of yellow torches lay like a nimbus near one of the warehouses by the dark river. The wagon started downhill. The hulks of buildings along the street blocked the yellow glow from Maria's excited view for a time, but then it came up brighter and closer, along with the damp, muddy smell of the river.

The bush lopers were moving boxes, bales and barrels from the warehouse to the gangplanks of the keelboats. The flames of their torches guttered and danced in the breeze sweeping off the river. In the bustle they frequently stumbled and ran into each other, something which made Maria smile in recognition even as Gillman's tall, overgrown and overseeing son cursed and stormed at them to get it right. Harnett, jumping from the wagon, pitched in to help with the loading, while Meekin waited for a break in the boisterous activity to lead his wife down a gangplank.

Maria's eyes danced as she stood and watched, shivering in the damp, frigid dawn air. Gillman rushed up, his eyes bleary and his face pouchy with sleep. He barked his somewhat overbearing son away from the put-upon bush lopers and, waving his arms, began leading them in "Old Jean Jacques with the Wart on his Nose," in a hoarse, croaking voice. The bush lopers started chanting the song, picking up its rhythm as they worked, their lines straightened out. There was room between them and none of them ran into each other now as they found the beat and sang, bent almost double under their heavy loads. They were enjoying themselves. The mounds of cargo in the boats rapidly grew larger.

Grey showed in the east. The roiling surface of the river became dimly visible and the breeze off it was colder. The bush lopers chanted the faster rhythm of "Three Little Ducks," and the stacking of cargo speeded up. Gillman and Meekin moved around inside the warehouse with the clerk, checking with lanterns to see if all of Maria's goods had been removed. There were quiet footsteps on the dock near Maria, approaching her, and she turned and looked. It was Charles.

"You shouldn't have come down here, Charles."

"I had to."

"It just makes it worse."

"I know, but I had to."

He kissed her, then stood with his arm around her shoulders as she leaned on her rifle. The light of the torches paled as the sky brightened. Most all the bush lopers were on the keelboats now, stacking; a few were sorting out the long sweeps and arranging them along the sides of the boats. The river was a slate grey, broken by ripples and floats of ice. There was a last-moment flurry of activity as bush lopers carrying out the final few things and Gillman shouting orders dividing them among the boats.

"Goodbye, Charles."

"Goodbye, Maria."

He kissed her again, and his hand lingered on her shoulder, trying to prolong the contact. Maria moved off at a lope down the gangplank into the first boat, and four bush lopers lifted the gangplank and heaved it onto the dock. She smelled the planks and the river close now, and they were everything to her. She climbed across the cargo toward the bow and sat down on a keg, tugging at her hat as the breeze freshened. Gillman shouted orders from the third boat as it moved away from the dock, its sweeps rattling and thumping against the gunwales. Harnett bellowed orders from the second boat and it too moved away from the dock. A bush loper trotted past Maria, jerked the knot out of the rope at the bow, and her boat, piloted by Gillman's son, swung lazily around into the current.

Maria couldn't see Charles. The sweeps thumped and rattled as the boat swung sidewards, then began floating lazily downriver. She cringed and laughed as Gillman's son screamed at the bush lopers and they stormed and cursed at each other, struggling with the sweeps to turn the boat around against the current. An uproar of bellowing came from the other two boats. Then Gillman's voice rose above the others as he began croaking "The Black-Eyed Josette Whose Skirts Fly Up." The bush lopers in all three boats took up the chantey. The sweeps began moving in unison as its echoes rolled back and forth across the river. The boats slowly turned upriver and forged into the current.

The sun rose. Charles was a small figure silhouetted against the brilliant sunrise as he stood on the edge of the dock. He lifted his arm and waved. Maria waved.

23

The river was a sparkling, silvery ribbon in the light of the setting sun, and the rocky mounds on the other side were black, mottled shapes against the blinding light. On her horse, Maria narrowed her eyes and shaded them with her hand, trying to make out the features of the mounds. "I can't tell if anyone is building anything over there or not."

"I can't see nothing either," Harnett said. "If there is anybody over there, I hope they've got a boat or a raft."

Maria nodded, turning in the saddle and looking back. The long line of pack trains was still filing over the top of the last hill, puffs of dust rising from the horses' hoofs in the dry, sandy soil and forming into a thin haze that eddied in the light breeze and swept away across the brown, sun-baked grass. She turned back around, lifting her reins as the ground underfoot became softer and her horse's hoofs began sinking into it. They rode on a ways. She looked at the river again. In the distance, she could see now a thin, straight line stretching across it.

"Whoever it is has a rope across the river."

"I think I see some people over there, too."

The opposite side of the river was in thick, dark shadow against the sun, but the rope was moving, bobbing and splashing in the water. Then the square shape of a raft became visible as it inched out into the river.

"Yes, there's someone over there. They're sending a raft over. Guess they saw us before we saw them."

Harnett nodded. "I see it now."

The sun sank lower. With the light less brilliant, Maria made out several men on the other side. The rope, she saw, was doubled and stretched between two crude windlasses, and the men were heaving at it, moving the raft jerkily through the water. High on the far bank were small blocky buildings with smudges of smoke from campfires rising among them, the mottled shapes she had seen before. Maria breathed a deep sigh of relief. Hany had been at least partly right. The men, whoever they were, were building a fort. Harnett whooped and waved his rifle. Puffs of smoke welled on the other side as some of the men fired rifles in welcome, and the muffled reports carried across the river.

They drew up to the raft as it reached their side of the river. Maria dismounted, as did Meekin and his wife, who'd reined up behind her, as well as other leaders in their party. The raft was a large square of rough, heavy timbers, bobbing as it rested against the bank. Maria, the Meekers, Harnett and Barton got on it, along with some bush lopers who helped pull them across while the others were unloading the pack horses to make camp.

The water splashed and gurgled around them, the angle of the sun lowered, and soon the men on the far bank became clearly visible. They were Rocky Mountain Fur Company men, thirty or more bush lopers along with William Sublette, Jim Bridger, Barry Fitzpatrick, Jed Smith and Amos Porter. Sublette, Bridger and others nudged each other, pointing at the approaching party and commenting. Barry Fitzpatrick stood to one side, looking at Maria.

The raft bumped against the bank and Maria hopped off. The men crowded around, shaking hands and laughing and talking boisterously.

"By God, somebody said that might be Maria coming there, but I didn't believe it," Sublette said. "Did you leave any horses or goods in St. Louis for anybody else, Maria?"

"There might be some I missed. This is Clarence Meekin and his wife Martha, and this is Israel Barton. This is Bill Sublette, Jim Bridger, Jed Smith, Amos Porter and Barry Fitzpatrick. Hello, Barry."

He came forward from the back of the group, still looking at her. Then he smiled and shook hands. "It's good to see you again, Maria."

"Old Barry thought it might be you and got hisself a shave," Porter laughed. "He had him a right nice piece of a beard growing."

Others laughed, but Maria stood looking at Barry. At one time he would have flushed with confusion, but now he smiled good-naturedly and nodded in agreement. Maria glanced around. "Who's seen my ma lately?"

"We saw her about a month ago," Barry said. "She was doing fine, Maria."

"Real fine," Bridger said. "We couldn't get Jake Ludlow to come over here and help with this fort. It seems as how he just had to stay at Fort Henry."

They laughed again, and Sublette moved away, motioning. "Well, you folks come on up and sit down. We've got coffee on, and we've got meat and beans cooking. I expect you could use a bite."

"I ain't so sure," Harnett said. "Knowing better, I let Maria make the bread last night, and I've felt like I've swallowed a cannonball ever since."

Maria grinned, tucking her rifle under her arm, and turned to pick up her saddle. Barry stepped aound her and picked it up for her, and they walked together quietly, following the others up the slope to the new fort. The smell of the fire and of the things cooking on it reached them. Barry, taking a deep breath, shifted the saddle to his other shoulder with a practiced hand.

Maria glanced at him. "Did you and Jim find the way through the mountains that you were looking for?"

He smiled and shook his head. "No, but I enjoyed looking for it, and we brought back a good amount of furs. We'll be heading back over that way after the rendezvous. Maybe we'll find it this time. You have a good-sized outfit there, Maria."

Maria looked over her shoulder at the other bank. There were long picket lines of horses, dozens of bush lopers still unloading some, and huge mounds of canvas bags. She had a deep sense of satisfaction. She almost always did when she stood off at a distance and looked at what she'd accomplished. She nodded, turning back. "It'll do."

His quiet smile reflected his understanding of how she felt. The others were gathered around a large fire in the center of an open area between a half dozen small rock-and-timber buildings. A larger, cornerstone building was still under construction, its foundations stretching between the lines of the smaller ones and forming the fort's conventional open-ended rectangle. Barry put Maria's saddle down, and she nodded and smiled in thanks. They joined the others and sat, Maria taking her hand weapons out of her belt and putting them by her side.

Sublette tossed wood on the fire and moved the coffeepot closer to it. "Maria, I heard something I couldn't hardly credit," he said teasingly. "Somebody said that a big cache of Hudson's Bay Company furs just sort of disappeared about the time you found the money to set up that big outfit. Now you wouldn't make off with a Hudson's Bay Company cache, would you?"

The others had been talking among themselves. They became silent, looking at Maria. She laughed and shook her head. "No, I wouldn't do that, Bill. No more than General Ashley would use a cache of Hudson's Bay Company furs to set up the Rocky Mountain Fur Company."

The men roared, and Amos Porter looked at her as the laughter died down. "Maria, old Rufus Hany was through here three weeks ago, and he said he was working for you. Is that right?"

"That's right, Amos."

"What have you got him doing?"

"He's doing some scouting for me."

"What for?"

"Whatever he finds, Amos. I won't know that until I see him again, will I?"

The others chuckled, and Porter grimaced and shook his head. "You ain't saying much, are you?"

"I'm not the only one who doesn't say much. How did building this fort here get started all of a sudden?"

"We've been thinking about it for a while," Sublette confided, shaking the coffeepot and glancing in it. "We didn't say much about it, I guess, but we wasn't sure we wanted to build here until this spring. Where are you going to set up, Maria?"

"The Snake. The first thing I want to do is run Kruger off."

Sublette glanced at Bridger and Smith, then looked back at Maria. "Well, if you want to set up on the Snake, you might be able to use Fort Henry. We was thinking of moving out of there sooner or later. . . ."

From his tone, they had been discussing it. Maria laughed. "Shucks, Bill, if I like that creek, I can build on the other side of it."

"We wouldn't want much for it, Maria," Smith cautioned.

"Trees are free, Jed," Maria said nonchalantly. "I have plenty of bush lopers and axes."

Sublette cleared his throat. "Well, you know what all we have there, Maria, and maybe you ought to think about it. We have a blacksmith shop all set up, a lot of tools, furniture in the cabins, and all such as that. We have about two thousands dollars worth of goods there, and maybe we could just let you have it just for that. What do you think about that, Jim, Jed? We could let her have it for that, couldn't we? I think Tom and the rest of them would go along with that."

The two men murmured and nodded, looking at Maria. She kept her expression carefully neutral, taking off her hat and pushing her hair back from her forehead, then shrugged as she pulled her hat back on. "Oh, I don't know, Bill. You see what I have myself in trade goods . . . is that two thousand trade or cost?"

"That's cost, Maria. You know we wouldn't sell to you at trade."

"Well, you said about two thousand, and a dollar's a dollar to me, Bill. What if we said about twelve hundred?"

Bridger and Smith snorted. Sublette glanced at them and looked back at Maria, shaking his head. "No, we couldn't do that, Maria. We might be able to come down a little just to keep from packing them out, but we couldn't do that. Could we go to eighteen hundred, Jim, Jed? Maybe between friends, we could go down to eighteen hundred. . . ."

"Well, it's the time of year when everyone needs money more than goods, Bill," Maria said. "I'm that way, and I'm sure you are, but I'll give you fifteen hundred in gold. I need the money more than I need the goods, but I'll take them off your hands. And that's the best I can do. I'll pay you in cash before I leave in the morning."

There was a long silence. Smith frowned down at the ground, then shrugged and looked away. Bridger looked at Maria with a wry half smile, then glanced at Sublette and nodded. Sublette sighed heavily, moving back to the fire. He began pouring coffee into the cups. "All right, Maria. Jake and Sam

Innes are up there now. We'll give you a note to them to turn it over to you."

Maria nodded and yawned, lifting her hat again and wiping away the beads of perspiration that had formed on her temples. She owned Fort Henry. Her eyes met Harnett's as he sat on the other side of the fire. His pale blue eyes twinkled at her.

Across the river, Maria's bush lopers were preparing to swim some saddle horses over, hers and Harnett's and some for the others who had come with them. That way, they'd be free to work the packs over on the rafts at dawn. They'd be on their way then, further west. Meanwhile, campfires were blazing up on the far bank, here, there, perhaps for a quarter mile's worth of hungry riders.

Darkness fell. Sublette took the kettle off the fire and passed out paltes. Maria filled hers and sat down by her saddle again, silently eating with Barry, listening and smiling at the men's noisy banter. Then Stephen Kruger's name was mentioned, and most of the conversation died, the people around the fire looking at Maria.

"Does anyone know where he is, or if he's still alive?" Maria asked.

"Frank Harkness said he was talking to Jacques Rees over in the Mandans early this spring," Smith said. "Frank said that Rees told him that Kruger's still alive. The Hudson's Bay Company is sort of looking after him. I guess they're doing it because they figure they ought to. He's just sort of wandering around from place to place. But he's still alive, and likely to stay that way for a while, from what Rees said."

Maria took a drink of coffee and swallowed, then nodded as she took another bite of food. "Good."

The silence stretched out. Then the conversation began again. Bridger talked about his trip to Alta California, and the men laughed as he told about Barry's problems with a balky horse. Others talked. The fire burned down, and Porter built it back up and brought out a bottle. Maria shook her head as the bottle was passed around to her, and she refilled her coffee cup. Meekin and his wife went into one of the small buildings for the night. It was getting late.

All this time Barry hadn't said much, nor had Maria. She was thinking about how Hany was probably far into Blackfoot territory by now, as he'd reported being very optimistic about his chances of success when he had left Westport. It could be that one of the large American flags in his bags would be flying above Fort Merrill within a short time. Barry had been looking at her campfires across the river.

"You'll probably have a hold on a lot of the fur trade within the next year or two, Maria," he said quietly. "You have enough goods to get off to a really good start."

Maria said, "It depends on how things go, Barry. You say my ma is all right?"

"She's doing fine and looking forward to seeing you again." He took a sip from his cup, looking into the fire, then looked back at her. "I'm not doing much here right now. We got the foundation laid and our bush lopers are doing the rest. So, since it'll be a while before Jim has his brigade ready to start out for Alta California again, I'd just as soon go over to Fort Henry with you and help you get set up. I thought maybe I could tell you a little more about Curtis, I mean the way I knew him, in battle. And, you know me, I kind of like to help out when new things get done."

Maria looked at him, thinking. He had matured a lot during the past year, losing much of his boyishness but still retaining enough to stir fondness. In many ways he would be like his uncle, authoritative yet giving of himself in friendship, in compassion, in common enterprise. He was far more handsome than his uncle, even now.

She took a sip of coffee and looked up at the naked, lonely stars. "If you're asking, I'd like you to come along, Barry," she said. "I'd like it fine."

Dell Bestsellers

☐	EVERGREEN by Belva Plain	$2.75	(13294-0)
☐	WHISTLE by James Jones	$2.75	(19262-5)
☐	A STRANGER IS WATCHING by Mary Higgins Clark	$2.50	(18125-9)
☐	MORTAL FRIENDS by James Carroll	$2.75	(15789-7)
☐	GREEN ICE by Gerald A. Browne	$2.50	(13224-X)
☐	THE TRITON ULTIMATUM by Laurence Delaney	$2.25	(18744-3)
☐	AIR FORCE ONE by Edwin Corley	$2.25	(10063-1)
☐	BEYOND THE POSEIDON ADVENTURE by Paul Gallico	$2.50	(10497-1)
☐	THE TAMING by Aleen Malcolm	$2.50	(18510-6)
☐	AFTER THE WIND by Eileen Lottman	$2.50	(18138-0)
☐	THE ROUNDTREE WOMEN: BOOK 1 by Margaret Lewerth	$2.50	(17594-1)
☐	TRIPLE PLATINUM by Stephen Holden	$2.50	(18650-1)
☐	THE MEMORY OF EVA RYKER by Donald A. Stanwood	$2.50	(15550-9)
☐	BLIZZARD by George Stone	$2.25	(11080-7)
☐	THE BLACK MARBLE by Joseph Wambaugh	$2.50	(10647-8)
☐	MY MOTHER/MY SELF by Nancy Friday	$2.50	(15663-7)
☐	SEASON OF PASSION by Danielle Steel	$2.25	(17703-0)
☐	THE DARK HORSEMAN by Marianne Harvey	$2.50	(11758-5)
☐	BONFIRE by Charles Dennis	$2.25	(10659-1)
☐	THE IMMIGRANTS by Howard Fast	$2.75	(14175-3)
☐	THE ENDS OF POWER by H.R. Haldeman with Joseph DiMona	$2.75	(12239-2)

At your local bookstore or use this handy coupon for ordering:

DELL BOOKS
P.O. BOX 1000, PINEBROOK, N.J. 07058

Please send me the books I have checked above. I am enclosing $ _____
(please add 75¢ per copy to cover postage and handling). Send check or money
order—no cash or C.O.D.'s. Please allow up to 8 weeks for shipment.

Mr/Mrs/Miss _____

Address _____

City _____ State/Zip _____